PRAISE FOR
Only Love Can Hurt Like This

"A tightly paced blend of angst and joy and hope. Perfect from start to finish. I absolutely adored his book!"
—Christina Lauren, author of *Love and Other Words*

"*Only Love Can Hurt Like This* is the story of small towns, big secrets, and even bigger love. Paige Toon's writing is emotional and riveting. Even while her novel was breaking my heart into tiny pieces, I couldn't put it down."
—Jill Santopolo, author of *The Light We Lost*

"A gorgeous story that reminded me why Paige Toon is the queen of this genre. I adored Wren's story, and the beautiful, rural American setting. This is a book that will have you swooning, crying, and turning the pages late into the night. I'm a huge fan of romance novels with questions or dilemmas at their heart, and *Only Love Can Hurt Like This* delivers a truly heartrending conundrum. The family dynamics are so well developed, and the relationships so real, that I had a hard time saying goodbye to these characters when I closed the last page."
—Sophie Cousens, author of *Just Haven't Met You Yet*

ONLY
LOVE
CAN
HURT
LIKE THIS

Paige Toon

G. P. PUTNAM'S SONS
New York

PUTNAM
— EST. 1838 —

G. P. PUTNAM'S SONS
Publishers Since 1838
An imprint of Penguin Random House LLC
penguinrandomhouse.com

Library of Congress Cataloging-in-Publication Data

Names: Toon, Paige, author.
Title: Only love can hurt like this / Paige Toon.
Description: New York : G. P. Putnam's Sons, 2023.
Identifiers: LCCN 2022052216 | ISBN 9780593544334 (trade paperback) | ISBN 9780593544341 (ebook)
Subjects: LCGFT: Romance fiction. | Novels.
Classification: LCC PR6120.O58 O55 2023 |
DDC 823/.92—dc23/eng/20221117
LC record available at https://lccn.loc.gov/2022052216
p.   cm.

Printed in the United States of America
1st Printing

Book design by Ashley Tucker

"Compulsively page-turning, wildly romantic, and beautifully heartbreaking. I stayed up all night and inhaled it in one big gulp. A totally brilliant read—I could not love it more."
—Emily Stone, author of *Always, in December*

"Emotional."
—*Publishers Weekly*

"Oh my GOD. This book! Only Paige Toon can make me believe in the power of love this way. Wren and Anders took me on a sweeping journey through America's Midwest that left me giddy and breathless. This is going to be totally massive, because it has everything: family, love, secrets, sexy descriptions of brooding, hot men . . . just sublime."
—Laura Jane Williams, author of *Our Stop* and *The Love Square*

"Heartbreaking, gorgeous, and unforgettable. *Only Love Can Hurt Like This* is Paige Toon at her best, with characters you care about so much it's a genuine wrench to say goodbye at the end of the book. Filled with torn loyalties, family conflicts, and a sizzling love affair under Indiana skies, this is the perfect story to get lost in. Only Paige can write like this."
—Dani Atkins, author of *Then and Always* and *The Story of Us*

"A beautiful love story that simmers in such a heartwarming and heartbreaking way, I sobbed!"
—Giovanna Fletcher, coauthor of *Eve of Man*

ONLY
LOVE
CAN
HURT
LIKE THIS

For Greg,
my best friend
and the love of my life

PROLOGUE

ON DAYS LIKE THIS, I LOVE LIVING IN BURY ST. Edmunds, when the spires of the cream stone cathedral seem illuminated against the vivid blue sky and even the black flintstones on the ruined abbey walls gleam under the sunshine as though they've been polished.

It's only early April, but it's the warmest day of the year so far by a *mile*, and I'm already feeling so much better after getting out of the office. I've just come off a phone call with a nightmare client—she and her home renovations are enough to put me off architecture for life: I *need* this coffee break.

I'm wandering among the abbey ruins, looking for a wall low enough to perch on and drink my coffee, when I see my fiancé, Scott, sitting on a bench in the shade of a giant fir tree. Before I can call out a delighted hello and go join him, I register that he's with Nadine.

Scott set up his own landscape gardening business when we moved here from London a year ago, and Nadine started working for him soon after that, days before he asked me to marry him in the rose gardens of a local manor house. She's twenty-nine and is tall and strong with golden skin and an infectious laugh. I liked her the moment I met her and on every occasion since then, so I'm not sure why my intended greeting has lodged in my throat.

My partner and his co-worker are almost two feet apart, but there's something about their body language that strikes me as odd. Scott is leaning forward, his white T-shirt stretched taut across his broad back and his forearms planted on his thighs. Nadine has her arms and legs crossed, her face tilted toward Scott's and her typically bouncy, high blond ponytail seems preternaturally still. The angled position of Scott's face mirrors Nadine's, but neither of them is looking at the other. Nor are they speaking. They seem frozen. Tense.

A squirrel runs along the jagged wall to my left. Birds are singing in the surrounding trees. Children laugh in the distant playground. But I stand and stare, unease creeping over me.

They're sitting apart. They're not doing anything wrong. And yet . . .

Something does not feel right.

Then, suddenly, Scott turns and stares straight at Nadine. There's a strange look on his handsome face, an expression I can't decipher. My heart is in my throat as she slowly lifts her chin and meets his eyes, two perfect side profiles: his thick, dark eyebrows to her flawless arches; his straight nose to her small, upturned one; two sets of full lips, serious and unsmiling.

Seconds tick past and darkness washes over me. To go from feeling light and warm to sick and cold is completely hideous.

They are still staring at each other. And not a word has passed between them.

I jolt as Scott launches himself to his feet and strides off in the direction of town. Nadine watches him until he's out of sight, then visibly exhales, hunching forward and placing her head in her hands. She stays like that for a minute or so before getting up and slowly following Scott.

I realize I'm shaking.

What *was* that?

Is my fiancé having an affair? And if not, is he thinking about having one?

Hang on. They only *looked* at each other. They didn't do anything wrong. I like Nadine. I trust Scott.

But something does appear to be going on between them.

My mother has always told me to trust my instincts. But it's hard to trust your instincts when they're breaking your heart.

1

Three months later

NEW YORK WAS SHROUDED BY CLOUD COVER. I'VE only ever flown to Indianapolis via Chicago, so I was hoping to see the infamous green void of Central Park bordered by skyscrapers, but by the time the sky finally clears, all it reveals is a patchwork landscape of fields and farms far below.

I've been traveling all day and it will be after 5 p.m. by the time I touch down, which is ten o'clock at night back in the UK. I'm shattered, but thankfully Dad is coming to collect me from the airport. I know that my exhaustion is not entirely due to lack of sleep. The last three months have taken their toll on me.

SCOTT WAS SITTING at the kitchen table when I arrived home from work that day back in April, after a horrible afternoon of seesawing between emotions. One minute I'd felt wildly unsettled and the next I'd convinced myself that the look he and Nadine shared meant nothing. But as soon as I saw Scott's face, I knew that my intuition had served me correctly. There *was* something going on between them, but it was an emotional connection, rather than a physical affair.

He wanted to talk to me as soon as I walked through the front door, which threw me as I was expecting to have to demand answers, not have them dished up to me on a plate. And when he started to confess his feelings, I still thought he planned to ask for my forgiveness—which I know I would have granted. We were getting married in December and were hoping to try for a baby in the new year. No way was I throwing away our beautiful future just because he'd developed a silly crush.

Maybe I was being naive, but it took me a while to realize that he was leaving me.

I remember the details of our conversation so clearly. I even remember that his fingernails still had an arc of dirt buried deep, close to his skin, and that he smelled earthy, of fresh air and garden soil. He was so familiar to me and yet so like a stranger. I'd never seen him looking so torn and tormented.

"I do love you, Wren," he claimed, tears clumping his brown lashes together in spikes. "In some ways, I wish I'd never met her because I think you and I could have been happy. But lately I've started to wonder if we're really right for each other."

It had taken him meeting Nadine, working with her almost every day, to recognize how well suited they were, how they clicked on another level.

At that point, they hadn't even spoken to each other about how they felt. Nadine had taken some time off to go and stay with her parents and Scott had sensed it was because she wanted to get some distance from him to clear her head. But when she came in to work that day in April and handed in her resignation, he realized he couldn't let her go.

I asked him, tearfully, if he thought she was his soul mate, and when he met my eyes, his expression said it all.

I'd read about it in books, seen it in films: the protagonist who is in a relationship with someone who doesn't understand them. Finding love with someone who well and truly does. Nothing can stand in their way. The entire audience is rooting for them.

I never in a million years thought this would happen to me, that I'd be the one standing in the way of true love.

Agony and complete and utter helplessness engulfed me as the seriousness of our situation finally dawned on me. There was nothing I could do. There was no fight to be won. The love of my life was already lost to me.

Scott and Nadine are together now. I've seen them around town a few times and I'm always on my guard in case I bump into them, but the last straw came the week before last, when I was sitting in my favorite café opposite the Abbey Gate.

Suddenly they were spewed out of the Gate's mouth, hand in hand and smiling, the sun glinting off Nadine's blond hair as Scott guided her across the busy road. When they walked into the café and saw me sitting with my mum, Scott apologized and quickly backtracked, but catching his eye as he passed by my window, seeing his face, grim and drawn, made me feel physically sick.

"This town is far too small for the both of you, darling," Mum said with sympathy as I blinked back tears.

"Why should I be the one to leave?" I asked in a small voice.

"His landscape gardening business is here. He's not going anywhere anytime soon. Get away, Wren, even if only for a couple of weeks," she implored. "Put some distance between you, give your heart time to recover."

She was right. I did need a break from home, from work, from Scott, from walking the same streets that we used to walk together, back when he'd hold *my* hand and step in front of traffic for *me*.

So I called my dad that night and asked if I could visit.

DAD IS HOVERING behind the rope when I walk out into Arrivals, his navy-and-red-checked shirt tucked into jeans.

At the sight of me, his face breaks into a wide grin, his heavily bristled cheeks seeming even rounder than they did when I last saw him at Christmas. He and his wife, Sheryl, went to Paris on holiday, so Scott and I caught the train over and spent some time with them there. This is my first trip back to America in two years.

"Hey, you!" he chirps.

"Hello, Dad."

I experience a flood of warmth as his arms close around me. I breathe in his familiar scent—soap and laundry detergent—and know that this will be the last time we hug until we're standing in this very airport in two weeks' time, saying goodbye. The realization gives me a pang as I withdraw.

His notoriously scruffy hair, once the same mid-brown shade as mine, is now riddled with gray. Although we both have hazel eyes, that's probably where our resemblance ends.

I don't have much in common with my mother, Robin, either, apart from the fact that we're both named after small birds. Mum likes flowing clothes and bright patterns; I like structured skirts and shirts in dark colors. Her features are warm and open while my face is narrower and, well, I once described it as "pinched," but she hotly refuted that, telling me I had fine bone structure, like an aristocrat, which made me laugh.

"How was your flight?" Dad asks buoyantly as he relieves me of my suitcase.

"Pretty good," I reply.

"Tired?"

"A bit."

"You can nap in the car. Our new home is a couple of hours away."

My half sister, Bailey, who's six years my junior, got married earlier this year and settled in her husband's hometown in Southern Indiana. Dad and Sheryl recently relocated to this same small town to be close to them.

There's a lot about this scenario that stings.

My dad is a devoted husband and father. But *I* don't have a whole lot of experience of him being like that. I do know that he loves me, but he's never really been there for me. He doesn't really know me. How could he when we live almost four thousand miles apart and spend no more than a couple of weeks a year in each other's company?

The July air when we step out of the airport terminal feels like a warm blanket being draped around my shoulders. Before long, we're on a three-lane highway heading away from Indianapolis. We're too far from the city to see its skyscrapers, but I remember them from previous shopping trips. Out here the landscape is mostly flat and far-reaching, peppered with big red barns and grain silos.

"How's Bailey settling into married life?" I ask, trying to ignore a small spike of jealousy.

I've never considered my beautiful half sister to be particularly competitive, so I'm sure she *wasn't* racing me down the aisle when she decided to tie the knot in Las Vegas, but now that my wedding has been called off, the ring on her finger does seem a little galling.

"She's happy," Dad replies with a shrug, turning down the air-con now that the car has cooled.

"Do you get on with Casey?"

I haven't even met Bailey's new husband yet. Scott and I were invited to the wedding, but with only a week's notice, we didn't feel it was expected of us to go. Bailey has always been impulsive.

"Everyone gets along with Casey," Dad replies. "He's a good guy."

"That's cool."

I don't mean for my voice to sound thin, but Dad shoots me a pained look.

"I was sorry to hear about Scott," he says. "I thought he was a good guy too."

"He was," I reply quietly. "I guess he still is." I swallow down the lump in my throat and add with forced flippancy, "Can't help who you fall in love with, right?"

Dad clears his throat. "Right."

We let that sit between us for a while.

My parents met when they were in their early twenties and traveling around Europe. They fell hopelessly in love, and when Dad's visa ran out, Mum moved to Phoenix, Arizona, to be with him. They were married and expecting me within a year.

It was a straightforward case of too young, too soon. At least, that's how Dad described it to me when, as a resentful teenager, I tried to get to the bottom of why his head was so easily turned by another woman, a professor at the University of Arizona where Dad was working as a groundskeeper.

It's always been a mystery to me how someone like Sheryl could fall for a man like Dad—she's nine years older and a whole lot wiser. I get the attraction part—objectively speaking, my dad was kind of hot: Sheryl used to take her coffee breaks outside in the gardens so she could chat with him.

Harder to understand is how an affair between an academic and a groundskeeper turned into something serious enough that they were willing to devastate his wife and child.

Because when Sheryl fell pregnant with Bailey, Dad chose them over us. Sheryl convinced Dad to move to Indiana to be closer to her family and found a position at the university in Bloomington. My heartbroken mother took me home to the UK, and Bailey got to grow up with my dad as her own.

This trip is not without its emotional complications.

I MUST NOD off because it doesn't feel like we've been traveling for two hours when Dad rouses me.

"We're coming into town," he says. "I thought you might like to see it."

I force my stinging, tired eyes to focus on the view outside my window. We're on a long, straight road, whizzing past fast food restaurant chains: Taco Bell, KFC, Hardee's, Wendy's. We pass a car wash and a garage and then the road morphs into a residential street with regular intersections. Some of the homes are two-story with gabled dormers, red-tiled roofs, and basement windows peeking out above neatly mowed lawns. Others are bungalows of white weatherboard with brightly painted shutters in lime green or cornflower blue. We crest a small hill and continue over the other side, where there's more of the same before we reach what Dad says is the "historical downtown."

Ahead is a large square around a central courthouse with a tall clock tower. The building gleams white in the fading sunshine, and as Dad drives around it, multiple Doric columns come into view.

"That's the Hoosier National Forest off in the distance," Dad says as we leave the town center and head through another residential sector where many of the homes have red, white, and blue banners hanging from their front porches. I've missed the Fourth of July celebrations by only a week.

"And Bailey and Casey live along there," Dad adds, nodding out the window.

There's a sign at the edge of the road that reads: WETHERILL FARM—PICK YOUR OWN, with an arrow pointing in the direction we're heading.

"Yours?" I ask.

"Yep." He nods proudly.

Beneath the cursive black-with-white-infill lettering are painted illustrations of fruit and vegetables. I make out peach, pear, apple, pumpkin, and watermelon before we drive past.

"You do watermelons too?"

"Not this year," Dad replies as we cross over a tumbling river on an old iron bridge that's painted rust red. "Only pumpkins for Halloween. The previous owners grew melons, but we figured we'd better give ourselves time to get to grips with the orchards first. Hopefully we won't get into trouble for false advertising," he jokes.

Mum bristled when I told her that Dad and Sheryl had bought a pick-your-own produce farm. She was a fruit picker at a citrus farm when we lived in Phoenix and she works at a garden center now. She's always loved being out in the open and tending to nature, even if the work itself isn't particularly challenging.

She once confided that she felt Dad had rubbed salt into her wounds when he left her not just for another woman, but for a professor. Now Sheryl has swapped academia for what is basically Mum's dream job. It's no surprise she feels sore.

Laid out before us on the other side of the bridge is farmland, vast and sprawling for miles. We drive alongside a field of something green and leafy for a short while before Dad takes a left onto a dirt track.

"Here's home," he says, turning right almost immediately into a long, tree-lined driveway.

There's an identical WETHERILL FARM—PICK YOUR OWN sign on the grassy verge and the drive splits, leading to a black wooden barn on the left, beyond which are fields of fruit trees. At the end of the right-hand fork is a two-story farmhouse fashioned out of light gray weatherboard. The left-hand third of it has a gabled front with three big windows. On the right, three smaller, matching gabled dormers protrude from the gray slate roof, beneath which runs a long veranda. The rose beds at the front of the house are bursting with pinky-orange blooms and there are three stone steps leading up to a door painted midnight blue.

This door opens as Dad cuts the engine. I reach for my handle and climb out of the car to greet Sheryl.

"Wren! Welcome!" she calls, coming down the steps.

I once saw Sheryl wide-eyed with horror at finding a rogue gray strand among her lustrous dark-chocolate locks, and she never used to leave the house without a full face of makeup. But in the last few years, Sheryl has gone au naturel. In place of long, shiny hair is a short gray bob, and her face is cosmetic-free—even her trademark plum-pink lipstick is missing.

Her personality, I'm sure, remains unchanged. She'll still be as bold and opinionated as ever and I could see from the way she came down the steps that she still carries herself with an air of importance. But despite this less-than-favorable-sounding description, I don't dislike her. In many ways, I respect her, and I even refer to her as "dynamic" to friends, a label that always makes me feel disloyal to Mum. We get on okay, but it's taken us years to reach this point, and our relationship is far from perfect.

"Hello, Sheryl." I give her a hug, making it quick because she doesn't like people invading her personal space.

At five foot nine, she's taller than me by four inches, and she's always been enviably curvier and bustier, even more so now. Dad told me she's been baking a lot since retiring from her university position, which made me smile because he always did the lion's share of the cooking. I could never have pictured Sheryl as a country girl, but the image is less blurred now that she's in front of me.

"What a beautiful house," I say.

Sheryl beams and places her hands on her hips, looking up at the first floor. "We love it. Come and have a look inside. Or shall I give you a tour of the orchards first? No, come inside," she decides before Dad or I can get a word in edgeways. "You must be exhausted."

The interior of the house is very traditional, with walls painted in muted shades of green, gray, and blue and white-accented details on the window frames, cornices, and banister. The furniture I recognize mostly from their previous home: antiques that Sheryl inherited from her parents when they passed away. The floor is polished dark wood, broken up by worn rugs, except in the kitchen where it's tiled terra-cotta. It smells of cinnamon in here.

"Cinnamon peach cake," Sheryl says proudly when I spy the baked goods on the counter. "I made it especially for you."

"Aw, thanks," I reply, touched.

The farm opens to peach-picking customers next weekend. Apples and pears will follow later in the season.

"Do you want some now or would you like to have a look upstairs?" she asks. "Let's put your bag upstairs first. See your bedroom."

She's off down the corridor before I can answer. Dad and I smile at each other and follow in her footsteps.

I can just about cope with Sheryl's bossiness these days, but there was a time when I wasn't as relaxed. When I was younger, I'd tug against Sheryl's ropes and try to mark territory that had long been marked by her. That wasn't much fun for anyone.

I've since learned that it's better not to go into battle with her, and I'll certainly be trying to abide by her rules over the next two weeks.

God knows, I don't need any more stress in my life right now.

2

I WAKE UP EARLY THE NEXT MORNING, AFTER A MIRACU-
lous full night's sleep. I managed to hang on until about
10 p.m. before crashing out in the same marshmallowy double bed that Sheryl and Dad had in the guest room of their
former home.

They used to live in Bloomington, a pretty, vibrant university city, where they moved just before Bailey was born. It's an
hour north, the midway point between here and Indianapolis,
and they had a cream brick house on a tidy corner plot in a
leafy green suburb.

I once visited in autumn and the colors of the trees lining
practically every street were breathtaking.

That's the thing about Indiana: it gets very cold and very
hot and the extreme temperatures mean that autumn is the
star of the seasonal show. I'd like to return again at that time
of year, but right now it's the height of summer.

Pale yellow light oozes beneath the white blinds of the two
dormer windows and, when I check the clock on the bedside
table, I see that it's not quite 7 a.m.

It smells of cinnamon in here too, albeit a synthetic version, courtesy of the potpourri on one of the windowsills. I like

the scent—it reminds me of America's shopping malls and home stores: warm and welcoming.

Mum always said that Phoenix smelled of orange blossom. She claimed the desert air was infused with it.

I was only six when we left, so my memories of Phoenix are vague. I remember the three tall, fat cacti in our backyard, the man-made city beach that had sprinklers on the sand because it was too hot to walk on, and the local swimming pool that was so highly chlorinated it turned my hair green. I remember the desert sands sweeping down the roads and Camelback Mountain fading into the skyline beyond distant bungalows. I remember the vast, multicolored layers of the Grand Canyon and the clear green water and smooth rock edges of Lake Powell. I remember tiny hummingbirds that fluttered like butterflies and prairie dogs that I tried but never managed to feed by hand. And I remember my dad tucking me in at night, calling me his "Little Bird," the nickname he came up with when I was small and has long since stopped using.

I also remember the arguments. The screaming. The tears that were shed. I remember the tracks on my dad's cheeks as he kissed me goodbye and left through our front door for the last time.

I shut off my mind to these images because there are some things I'd rather forget.

BAILEY ARRIVES AS we're sitting down for breakfast, without forewarning or an invitation. She lets herself in through the front door and is in the hallway before we even realize she's there.

"Heeeyyy!" she shouts like the Fonz, only a taller, curvier, prettier version. She's Sheryl's mini-me and everything I'm not.

I get up from the table and she's upon me in seconds, dressed for work in a smart black skirt and white cap-sleeve blouse and smelling of ylang-ylang perfume.

"It's so good to see you!" she cries, squeezing the breath from my lungs with the force of her brief embrace.

"You too," I reply.

Our father's smile beams back at me, though his two dimples are currently hidden behind stubble. Her eyes are so big, brown, and gorgeously expressive that she earned the nickname "Boo" when she was younger.

"How was your flight? How are *you*?" Bailey asks, sweeping her glossy chestnut-brown locks over one shoulder.

As a teenager, her hair came almost to her waist in wavy curls, but the last time I saw her, she was wearing it at just below jaw-length.

I've had the same dead-straight mousy-brown hair all my life. I can't even call it chestnut or chocolate: it's pure vermin.

"Good and good," I reply. "How about you? How's Casey?" The knot in my stomach is a reminder that I won't be following her up the aisle anytime soon.

"Great. Hey, I wondered if you're free for dinner later?"

I glance at Dad and Sheryl.

"Not you," Bailey says to Dad with a frown, and he freezes, mid-nod. She laughs at his put-out expression. "I want my big sis all to myself. It's Friday night. I thought we'd go to Dirk's."

"I'm guessing Dirk's is a bar, not a person?" I flash Dad a look to check he's all right with being excluded, but he's good-naturedly shrugging at Sheryl.

"Both. Dirk is the owner of Dirk's the bar. It's a bit like that bar we went out to last time in Bloomington? Remember that night?"

I do remember. It was five years ago: she was twenty-two and I was twenty-eight and we both got smashed. It was the best night we'd ever had together, the first time I could see possibilities for us not only as siblings, but as friends.

It's not that we didn't get on before that, but it was harder when I was a teenager and she was a pesky brat running rings around our dad.

Unfortunately, our last night out together was also the last time we saw each other in person. She moved to the West Coast soon after that.

"I'll come get you at seven."

"Is that okay?" I check with Dad, wondering if it will be possible for Bailey and me to pick up where we left off.

I feel a small surge of optimism at the thought, but it's quickly chased away by doubt. So much has happened in the last five years. So much has happened in the last five *months*. The simple truth is, I barely know my half sister and she barely knows me.

"Fine by us," Dad replies. "We've got plenty of time to catch up."

"Don't know how long I'll last," I warn Bailey. "I'll be jet-lagged."

If she's expecting me to be the life and soul of the party, she'll be sorely disappointed.

"Yeah, yeah," she brushes me off before checking her watch. "Gotta go! I'm late for work! See ya later."

"See you."

With kisses on Dad and Sheryl's cheeks, Bailey the whirl-wind is off.

MY HALF SISTER returns to collect me bang on seven.

"You look great!" she exclaims.

I'm wearing a fitted, knee-length, sleeveless black dress with white beading around a V-cut neckline. It's the sort of thing I'd opt for at home on a night out, but looking at Bailey, who has changed out of her work clothes into a denim skirt and white T-shirt, I feel overdressed.

"You too. But are you sure I'm all right in this?" I ask uncertainly.

"Absolutely," she reassures me firmly. "Come on, it gets busy on Friday nights. Let's go."

Dirk's is on the west side of the town square we drove around yesterday, in the basement of a three-story, flat-roofed, utilitarian-looking building. Large rectangular windows with black frames break up the plain redbrick face. The riff from "Fever" by the Black Keys is playing as we enter the building, and the music grows louder as we walk down the stairs and open the door to the venue. The walls are exposed red brickwork hung with framed posters of rock bands—everyone from the Rolling Stones to Kings of Leon.

It's a bit low-rent and kind of dirty, but I like it, and as "Fever" morphs into "R U Mine?" by the Arctic Monkeys, I like it even more.

I may not look it, but I'm a bit of a rock chick at heart. Scott wasn't really into music—if he had a choice, he'd rather have the TV on than the radio. I wonder what Nadine prefers.

No. I don't want to think about Scott and Nadine tonight. I very much doubt that they're thinking about me.

"What are we drinking?" Bailey asks as we reach the bar, squinting at the lineup of spirits against the wall.

I pick up a menu lying discarded on the counter, suddenly determined to throw myself into having a good time. It's sticky to the touch and lists a selection of burgers, hot dogs, loaded fries, and nachos. I flip it over, searching for a cocktail menu, but the other side is blank.

Silly me. This is so not a cocktail kind of place.

The barman materializes in front of us. He has gauges in his ears and blond hair so wispy you can see his scalp through it. He doesn't smile or speak, merely slaps two cardboard coasters on the bar in front of us and nods at Bailey.

"Hey, Dirk!" she exclaims brightly. His expression remains unchanged. She glances at me. "Rum and Coke?"

"Sure."

Dirk gets to work, and Bailey laughingly says in my ear: "He's an asshole, but that's part of his charm. I'll get him to smile at me if it's the last thing I do."

I believe her.

"Want to grab that table? I'll bring the drinks."

Several pairs of eyes follow me as I wind my way across the room, making me really regret my outfit choice. I wish Bailey had told me to change. She's so much more outgoing than I am—being overdressed wouldn't bother her. It's one of the many, many ways in which we are different.

I sit down between a table hosting four grizzled old biker dudes, and another seating three middle-aged men in primary-colored T-shirts and baseball caps. Bailey and I appear to be the youngest people in this joint, and we're also the only women, but if this bothers her, she doesn't show it.

"Cheers!" she says as she joins me.

"Cheers! And hey, congratulations on your marriage!"

In overcompensating for my insecurities, I sound overenthusiastic, but she seems oblivious to my tone.

She laughs. "Mom's still pissed that I denied her of her one big chance to prance around as mother of the bride. At least I gave notice, even if it was only one week."

"Was there any reason for the rush?" I ask hesitantly.

"Nah," she replies, guessing where my thoughts were heading with that question. "We wanted to tie the knot without any hassle. I deal with enough of that crap for work."

Bailey is an events manager.

"How is work? You're at the same place as Casey, right?"

"Yeah, at the golf club." She jabs her thumb over her shoulder. "It's on the outskirts of town, about a ten-minute drive that way."

Casey is a golf pro. He and Bailey met in California when he was competing at a tournament she'd helped to organize. He never made it to the big time and now he's an instructor. He was offered a position back here and, as his parents and brother still live in this town, he was keen to return to put down roots.

"And you like your job?" I ask.

She shrugs. "It's all right. I've done three weddings and two retirement parties so far, but the work's not very varied. I'm worried I'll be bored out of my brain by Christmas and then I don't know what I'll do. If Casey and his parents get their way, I'll have a bun in the oven by then."

"Is that what you want?"

"Hell no, I'm *way* too young for that!"

Her eyes go into full-on baby "Boo" mode and I can't help but laugh.

"How old is Casey?" Bailey is twenty-seven, but I'd heard he's a fair bit older.

"Thirty-four. Completely over the hill," she teases, knowing full well that her husband is only a year older than I am.

"Oi!" I exclaim, dipping the tip of my finger into my drink and flicking it at her.

She squeals with laughter and a surprising bubble of joy bursts inside my chest. Maybe we *can* pick up where we left off . . .

Indeed, the longer we sit there chatting and drinking, the happier and more relaxed I feel. I did need a break from everything that was going on at home, but I'm also glad of this chance to bond with my half sister. This wouldn't be as easy if Scott were here.

We grab a couple of burgers and more drinks to wash them down with and then Bailey heads off to use the restroom while I return to the bar for round three.

Or is it round four? I've lost count.

"Ain't No Rest for the Wicked" by Cage the Elephant is blaring out of the speakers and I almost sing along because I love this song, then Stevie Nicks's "Edge of Seventeen" kicks in and there's no way I can keep still.

Dirk hands over our drinks and I swear his eyebrow lifts when I beam at him. Out of the corner of my eye, I see that two tall, broad men have come through the door, but then all my attention is directed at trying not to spill our drinks as I weave my way back to the table. By the time I sit down and look over at the bar, they have their backs to me.

The guy on the right with shaggy brown hair, wearing faded blue jeans and a gray T-shirt, is fractionally bigger than the guy on the left, in height and breadth. His friend has carelessly messy dark blond hair and he's wearing black jeans and desert boots with a checked shirt, the sleeves rolled up to his elbows. He places one hand on his friend's shoulder.

"Wren?"

I look up to see that another man has arrived at our table.

"Casey!" I belatedly realize, jumping to my feet.

I've seen him in photos, of course, but his pin-straight black hair used to be longer and he had a mustache.

"It's so good to finally meet you!" Casey exclaims into my ear, giving me a fierce hug.

"You too!"

"Case!" Bailey cries as she reappears, throwing her arms around him.

He's only an inch or so taller than her.

He laughs and pats her back, his cheeks pink as she lets him go and flops into her seat. He pulls out a chair with far more control.

"Do you want a drink, Casey? Can I get you a drink?" I'm trying to sound sober and failing.

"No, no, I'll go to the bar." He scoots his chair back out from the table and pauses. "Are you good?"

"So good," Bailey says, lifting up her full glass and knocking it against mine as he gets to his feet.

"I'm making a terrible first impression on your new husband," I whisper, not as quietly as I meant to.

"Not at all! He'll love you! He already does. You're related to me. And he loves me. Very, very much."

"I can tell."

"And I love him." She enunciates her words slowly and deliberately.

"He seems very lovable," I agree.

"You've only just met him!" She slaps her hand on the table and stares at me accusingly. Her features relax a moment later and she nods wisely. "But you're right. He is very, very lovable."

"I'm glad to hear it," Casey says as he sits back down.

Bailey and I gawp at him with astonishment.

"How did you get served so quickly?" she asks as he swigs from his bottle of beer.

"Dirk had it ready on the bar for me," he replies, smacking his lips.

"But Dirk is an asshole," Bailey says with genuine confusion.

Casey chuckles and shakes his head. "Nah, he's okay. I've known him forever. This is the first place I got legally wasted. Dirk drove me home to save me ending up in a ditch."

"How have I never heard that story?" she asks with a frown.

"I don't know," Casey replies with a shrug.

"I thought you hated it here."

"I don't hate it, but I don't want to come here every other weekend."

"Anywhere is better than the golf club," Bailey says in a monotone voice.

My eyes have been darting back and forth while they've had this conversation, but then my half sister seems to remember I'm there and smiles at me brightly.

"Anyway!" she exclaims. "Wren likes it here, don't you, Wren?"

"I do. The music's cool."

The two guys from the bar have made their way over to the pool table. Bailey sees where my attention is headed and glances over her shoulder, clocking them. She turns back to me and gives me a cheeky grin, raising one eyebrow.

"What?" I ask.

"What do you mean, *what*?"

"What do you mean, what do I mean, *what*?"

She bursts out laughing. "How can you say that without tripping over your words?"

"I've had six more years to perfect speaking drunk."

"'To perfect speaking drunk,'" she repeats, putting on a plummy English accent. I'm not sure if the added lisp is intentional, but it sounds hilarious.

Casey looks bemused as we both drunkenly crack up.

"Sorry, Casey," I say when we've more or less calmed down. "You are way behind. I think you need to get a tequila shot or something."

"I thought I'd drive you guys home. You left your car in the parking lot, right?" he asks Bailey.

"Case, *NO*," Bailey shouts. "We can walk!"

"Come on, Casey," I say cajolingly. "Join us for a few drinks. This is the best night out I've had in months."

"Aah!" Bailey seems tickled by my statement.

"It's true."

She grins into her drink, oblivious to the pain I feel at *why* I haven't enjoyed going out lately.

She hasn't asked me about Scott. We've talked about work and our parents and lighthearted subjects like music and movies, but she hasn't gone near the subject of my ex-fiancé.

That's probably a good thing. I don't want to talk about

Scott tonight anyway, and I'm not sure I want to talk about him at all to my half sister. Things are obviously going well between Bailey and Casey and I have no desire to bring down the mood.

There are a few more women and younger people in here now, including some preppy-looking guys in pastel polo shirts, but the men over at the pool table still stand out. The taller of the two is facing this way and he's ruggedly handsome, a description I don't think I have ever used about another human being, but which feels uncannily fitting. He's deeply tanned with a broad forehead and a jawline that you can tell is strong, even though it's graced with heavy dark stubble. He's like a male model crossed with a caveman.

His friend with the dirty-blond hair and yellow-and-black-checked shirt still has his back to us.

Bailey's head pops into my line of vision, waggling from side to side in an impressive execution of the dance move from "Walk Like an Egyptian."

"Earth to Wren." She glances over her shoulder before returning her gaze to me with a grin.

"Sorry," I apologize, reaching for my drink.

"Someone keeps getting distracted," she sings. "Or perhaps someone is *looking* for a distraction?"

I almost choke on my mouthful.

"That's Jonas, right?" Bailey glances significantly at the model-caveman, then at Casey, who nods. "If you're looking for a distraction, I hear he's a good one," she adds.

"Bailey." Casey's tone is mildly chastising.

"Oh, come on," she replies, slapping his arm. "Last time we saw him here, you told me he'd slept with half the women in this town."

"That's an exaggeration," Casey replies. "But I don't imagine your sister wants to be another notch on his belt." He looks at me for confirmation.

"I don't want to be another notch on *anyone's* belt right now, thanks."

I'm not sure I even fancy him.

If I were sober, I'd be able to tell.

"Who's his pal?" Bailey asks Casey.

"Can you stop staring at them, please?" he asks her reasonably.

Bailey smirks at me but does as she's asked. She's partially blocking my view, so at least I can look past her without it being too obvious.

"That's Anders," Casey answers her question. "And they're not friends, they're brothers."

"Case knows everyone in this town," Bailey tells me as an aside.

"I know *of* people," Casey corrects her. "I don't know them well enough to talk to. Anders was in the year above me when we were in school. Jonas is a couple of years older than that."

That makes them about thirty-five and thirty-seven.

"Are they from around here?" I ask. "Their names sound Scandinavian."

"The whole family has Swedish names, going back generations. They take their heritage very seriously. The Fredrickson farm has been passed down for something like two hundred years." There's a touch of reverence in his tone.

"They're farmers?" I ask.

"Jonas is," Casey replies. "Their parents too. Anders lives in Indy, though." That's the nickname for Indianapolis. "Last

I heard, he was working for an IndyCar team, which is pretty cool."

That *is* pretty cool. Dad and Sheryl once took Bailey and me to the Indy 500, a five-hundred-mile-long car race around an oval racetrack. It's billed as "the Greatest Spectacle in Racing" and is part of the Triple Crown of Motorsport, along with the Monaco Grand Prix and the 24 Hours of Le Mans, but I thought it sounded boring when Dad told me he'd bought tickets. Once I was there, though, I got swept up in the high-octane excitement of it all.

"Haven't seen Anders in ages," Casey continues. "Although I heard he lost his wife a few years ago."

"What happened to her?" Bailey asks.

"Car accident, I think," Casey replies.

At that moment, Anders walks round the back of the table and comes to a stop, in full, clear view.

My breath hitches.

Unlike his brother, there isn't a hint of caveman about him. He's clean-shaven, his skin kissed with a golden tan, and he has eyebrows that are bordering on sharp. He's wearing his black-and-mustard-checked shirt open over a faded black T-shirt, and the phrase "effortlessly cool" comes to mind as he leans over, lining up a shot. A few strands of his dark blond hair fall across his eyeline, but he doesn't push them away before striking the ball. I hear a clunk from the ball shooting straight into a pocket, and a split second later, his eyes lift to meet mine.

The air holds in my lungs as he slowly straightens up, our gazes locked across the crowded room. My heart flutters. And as seconds tick past, the flutter becomes a thump that ricochets off my rib cage. I watch, fixated, as his eyes seem to darken.

Then his brow furrows and he breaks the contact, raking his hand through his hair.

Blood rushes to my face and I reach for my drink, feeling as though my pulse has been hijacked. Luckily, Bailey is preoccupied speaking to Casey and doesn't notice how choppy my breathing has become.

Anders doesn't look my way again, at least not to my knowledge. I keep feeling my attention being pulled toward him, an inexplicable draw that's impossible to ignore.

In the end, the only way I can distract myself is to shift in my seat so that Bailey is entirely blocking my view.

3

Y OU'RE BEING RIDICULOUS NOW. DAD AND SHER-
yl's house is right there!" I exclaim, pointing across the
river. "Go home!"

Bailey and her hilariously inebriated husband have walked
me as far as the bridge, but they should have turned off a couple of minutes ago.

"Okay, fine," Bailey concedes, launching herself forward
and throwing her arms around me so forcefully that I stumble
backward and almost fall over. "I'll come and see you tomorrow," she promises. "We can nurse our hangovers together."

"You're at work tomorrow," Casey reminds her, wobbling.

"Not until noon," Bailey replies. "I'll see you in the morning," she adds to me.

"It's a plan." I grin at her, already looking forward to it.

It's 11 p.m., which means it's four o'clock in the morning
back in the UK, but I feel oddly awake and exhilarated. The
only sounds I can hear are the rushing water beneath the
bridge, my ankle boots scuffing the asphalt, and the odd car
humming away in the distance.

As much as I enjoyed my half sister and her new husband's

company tonight, I find I'm kind of glad to be walking this final stretch alone. It's nice to have the mental space to be with my own thoughts for a while.

As I leave the last streetlight behind, the night sky becomes illuminated over my head. The full moon is shining like a torch high above and not a single cloud mars the brightness of the stars. The air smells of freshly cut grass and as I lower my gaze from the sky to look at the field spread out before me, I gasp with wonder. Tiny lights are hovering above the knee-high crop, twinkling and flashing like fairy dust.

Fireflies. Or lightning bugs, as Sheryl calls them.

I've seen the odd one on previous trips to Indiana, but I've never seen so many together in one place. The sight is nothing short of magical.

I have a sudden urge to be among them. There are two narrow tracks straight ahead, carved out by tractor wheels, which are more than wide enough for a person to walk along.

A breeze lifts my sweat-damp hair away from my neck. A split second later, I hear the crop whispering as the wind blows through it.

On impulse, I start forward, straight onto one of the tracks. The earth is dry and crumbly beneath my ankle boots and the incline slopes gently downward. I don't know how long I walk for—ten, twenty minutes—but I'm not sure the smile ever leaves my face. I'm hypnotized by the fireflies, the open air and darkness, the starlight and the moonlight. The sense of freedom.

I really *am* "free" now. Free and single. For the first time since our breakup, the thought of being alone doesn't frighten me. I feel content, almost like my old self again. A surge of euphoria rushes through me.

I come out of the field onto a long strip of freshly mowed

grass, but here the fragrance mingles with something even sweeter. Ahead is a field of maize and punctuating the moonlit sky are fronds—or flowers—protruding from the top of each ten-foot-tall stalk. I walk forward, away from the knee-high crop and its glittering fireflies, and soon find myself inside a forest of maize. After a couple of minutes, I come to a stop.

What the hell am I doing? I could get lost in here. Feeling a small spike of panic, I turn around and walk back the way I think I came, but I'm not certain I'm heading in exactly the same direction.

The sound of a very loud mosquito causes me to tense up, until I register that what I'm actually hearing is a motorbike. I'm sure town is up the hill, but this noise is coming from the other way and it's growing louder.

I run toward the sound and emerge from the maize at the same moment a burst of light streaks across the strip of grass to my left. I hastily jump back and press myself against the stalks, but too late. The light scorches my face and a man shouts with alarm as the engine lets out a desperate scream before falling silent.

I open my eyes to see a dark mass in front of me. The headlamp blinded me so I can't make out much more than that.

"What the hell?" the man exclaims in an American accent, as he wrestles his bike off him and scrambles to his feet.

"Are you okay?" I ask.

I probably should have taken that opportunity to run. He could be a psychopath, but I'm too shit-faced to feel scared.

"What are you doing out here?" he demands to know. "Are you lost?"

"No!" I reply defensively. "What are *you* doing out here?" Who rides a motorbike around fields at this hour?

"That's none of your business."

"It's none of your business what *I'm* doing here, then," I retort, feeling oddly on edge at the sound of his voice.

It's low and deep, but not too deep. There's a richness to it that makes me think of honey.

"You're trespassing, so, actually, it is."

Oh. My scattered thoughts come crashing back together.

"Well, I'm on my way home now, so never you mind."

"Where are you going?" he asks with exasperation as I determinedly set off along the track I think I walked here on.

My eyes have yet to readjust to the darkness—I'm still seeing spots.

"You need to go up to the road and turn left if you're heading back to town," he calls after me.

I spin around, stumbling a little. "Up where?" I'm not heading back to town, but I do need to find the road I was on.

"Up there."

He's a tall, dark silhouette against the moonlit sky, but I can make out his long, lean arm, pointing toward the stretch of grass.

"It'll be much quicker to go straight through," I argue, noticing the impressive breadth of his shoulders when his arm drops to his side.

I wish I could see his face—who *is* this guy?

"If you *want* to go trampling through soybeans like a frickin' elephant . . ."

Soybeans? Is that what was growing in the firefly field? Hang on, how rude!

"I'm hardly damaging them, there's a track!"

"It's not a track for people, it's for tractors."

"Oh whatever. Get off your high horse. Or motorbike. Or

whatever it is. Actually, you're already off your motorbike, aren't you?" A drunken giggle escapes at the thought of him crashing. It's probably not funny, but . . .

Christ, it's funny.

"You're wasted."

"I'm not that drunk."

"It wasn't a question."

"Getting sobererer by the minute. Sobererer?" I ask aloud, not expecting an answer because I'm talking to myself. "Is that a word?"

"Oh man," he mutters. "Where are you heading?" He picks up his fallen bike as I walk past him.

"Up and left," I reply. "Just like the satnav man told me."

"No, I mean, where are you staying? You sound as though you're a long way from home."

"My dad lives over there." I point across the field as his motorbike light comes back on, illuminating the stretch of grass.

"That's where *my* dad lives, so I doubt that."

"There, then." I adjust my arm direction.

"You're Ralph's daughter? Of course you are. My mom said his daughter was coming from England. That's you?"

"That's me."

"In that case, it would be quicker to go downhill and turn right along the farm track."

I sigh dramatically, turn around, and shout out with annoyance as I'm blinded by his headlight again.

"You don't have to follow me," I say when I realize he's planning on doing exactly that. "Go back to whatever it was you were up to out here in the dark."

"Last thing I need is you breaking an ankle. My mom would kill me."

"You sound a bit too old to be worried about what your momma thinks," I say dryly.

"Nobody is too old to worry about what their momma thinks."

"So, this is your land, is it? What are you, a farmer?"

"Nope, that's my brother."

I stop dead in my tracks.

"Watch it!" he yells, almost running me over.

I spin around and am blinded again. "For goodness' sake!" I shout, shielding my eyes. "I could see better in the moonlight!"

He barks out a laugh and I avert my face, my heart jumping at the awareness of who it is I'm likely talking to.

"You're Anders, aren't you?" Before he can answer, I add, "And your brother is Jonas?"

"Yes," he replies after a slight hesitation, probably wondering how I know that.

I have a flashback to our extended moment of eye contact and feel incredibly skittish, despite the units of alcohol that are supposed to be dampening my senses.

"Are you going to tell me your name?"

"Wren."

I remember, then, that he averted his gaze first and I'm pretty sure he didn't glance my way again, not even on his way out through the bar. I'm embarrassed to admit I was watching when he left to see if he would, finally giving in to the inexplicable ache I'd felt since that moment he'd first caught me in a stare.

I steel myself against him, his snub.

"You really can stop trailing after me."

"I don't want you getting lost, now, do I?"

I scoff. "I won't get lost. I'm an architect. I've got an excellent sense of direction."

He lets out a low chuckle that tucks itself beneath my rib cage. "Is that right?" There's a beat and then he exhales with what sounds like resignation. "Let me give you a lift home."

I jolt to my senses and let out a single loud laugh. "You must be joking. No thanks. I've seen how you ride that thing."

No way am I going to be some random man's damsel in distress.

"I only crashed because you jumped out of the corn like an apparition," he snaps.

"Still not risking it."

"Don't be an idiot: get on."

"Not a chance. I'd rather walk, and I promise I won't go trampling through your precious soybeans like a great big fricking elephant."

Dickhead.

"Turn right here," he directs me as we come out onto the farm track, his motorbike light sweeping across a big red structure.

"I know," I reply.

"Of course you do. You're an architect with an excellent sense of direction."

I give him a look.

It kills me that I can't make out any of his facial features.

"So how long are you in town for?" he asks casually as he wheels his bike along beside me.

"What, we're doing small talk now?" I reply with disbelief.

"We're not animals," he bats back.

"No, but you don't strike me as a small-talk kind of guy."

"That's an interesting conclusion to jump to about some-one you've only just met."

"So you *do* like small talk?"

"No, I hate it, but I only asked you how long you're here for, not what your favorite color is or whether you have any pets. Jeez, you're hard work."

I smirk to myself. "Two weeks, black, and not anymore, but I used to have a cat named Zaha."

"After Zaha Hadid?"

"Yes."

She's one of my favorite architects.

"I'm more of a dog man myself."

"You are no friend of mine," I whisper solemnly.

I'm joking. I love dogs.

"We haven't been friends since the moment you made me crash my bike. And black is not a color."

"Oh, we're going to argue about that, now, are we?"

"No argument. It's a fact."

"Has anyone ever told you you're a pain in the arse? Don't answer that," I add at the same moment that he replies, "Yes."

His ensuing laugh makes me feel giddy.

"If you want to get rid of me, all you have to do is climb on the back of my bike and I'll have you home in no time." His voice is laced with amusement.

"Absolutely no effing way."

We're back at Wetherill Farm before I know it.

"Well, that was a very refreshing walk, thank you," I say sweetly as I stand at the end of the drive, shielding my eyes be-cause his damn light is directed right at my face again.

"You're very welcome, Wren," he replies in a low, teasing voice. "I'm so glad I ran into you."

"Ha! You almost did. Next time."

"Sadly, I'm unlikely to have the pleasure."

"Don't be such a pessimist. I'm here for a couple of weeks, remember?"

"And I'll be gone by Sunday so I doubt we'll meet again."

I hear his words curling around a smile as he says them, but I have the strangest feeling that his lips have straightened now.

Silence falls around us. His light is still directed at my face and it suddenly strikes me as grossly unfair that he can see my expression and I can't see his.

And then the light veers away and I blink into the darkness as I hear him turning his bike around.

I open my mouth and close it again as he sets off in the direction we came. After talking nonstop the whole way here, I'm confused as to why neither of us found the words to say goodbye.

4

"OOD MORNING!" SHERYL SHOUTS FROM THE kitchen.

I can't raise the strength to reply at a volume that would reach her. The highly polished wood of the banister is sticking to my slightly sweaty palms as I gingerly make my way down the creaking steps, cringing at the assault on my ears. I make it to the bottom and have to take a moment, seriously wondering if I'm going to throw up.

"You girls have fun last night?" Sheryl asks with a knowing look from the kitchen.

I nod slowly and continue on my way toward her. "Where's Dad?" My voice sounds croaky.

"He's out in the orchard, picking peaches."

"Already?"

"Storm's coming. Thought he'd better get some of the ripe ones off the trees."

"I'll go say hi."

"Want to take a tea or coffee with you?"

I shake my head as gently as possible.

"Well, take one for your dad." She pulls out a chair for me at the table.

I sit down, my stomach churning, as she gets out a tray and fills it with a mug of steaming black coffee, a glass of water, a plate of cookies and crackers, plus a whole banana.

I thank her for what I can see is, in part, a hangover cure, and pick up the tray.

Last night feels surreal. There were moments when I actually felt *happy* without Scott. And then there was that walk through the firefly fields and my run-in with Anders.

As I balance the tray on one hand and open the front door with the other, I wonder what on earth came over me, waltzing off through dark fields in the middle of the night. No wonder Anders fell off his motorbike at the sight of me: a white-faced woman dressed all in black, appearing from the corn with a full moon overhead. I snigger with amusement at the mental image as I step out onto the veranda.

The clear blue skies of yesterday have been invaded by towering, ominous-looking clouds, and as I make my way over to the orchards, other snippets from our encounter drift back to me. The memory of Anders's laugh makes me feel as though someone has dropped an effervescent vitamin into my bloodstream. But then I remember that I've probably seen the last of him and my fizzy feelings are washed away by a wave of loneliness.

It's a sensation I'm all too familiar with. Last night was a distraction, a welcome respite from missing Scott, but I'll be thinking about him again now, I'm sure of it.

I find Dad in the nearest orchard, up a ladder. The leafy branches of the peach trees are drooping with the weight of the fat orange globes attached to them. They look like thousands of miniature setting suns.

"Hi, Dad. Coffee for you," I call.

"Great!"

There's a wooden crate nearby so I use my foot to gently toe it over into an upside-down position before placing the tray on this makeshift table.

Dad, meanwhile, eases himself down the ladder, one hand gripping the rungs, the other clutching a wicker basket. He has a twig lodged in his unkempt hair.

"You be careful up on that thing," I caution.

Although Dad used to be a groundskeeper, he was promoted to student services coordinator during his time at Indiana University Bloomington, and in recent years has spent more time sitting behind a desk than toiling outside in the elements.

"Always," he replies with a smile, setting the basket down on the ground and groaning slightly as he straightens up, the buttons on his blue-and-black-checked shirt straining as he leans into a backward stretch.

The checks recall Anders in his large-checked black-and-mustard shirt, sleeves rolled up to the elbows, worn open over a faded black T-shirt with black jeans and desert boots, though that outfit was a world away from anything my dad would wear.

"So, a storm is coming, hey?" I ask, trying to tug my thoughts away from Anders as I unpeel my banana.

"Looks like it," Dad replies, scrutinizing the sky, his coffee cup now wedged in his hand. "Thunder and lightning, all things frightening."

"That's what Mum used to say."

"I know she did," he replies, not meeting my eyes as he takes a sip of his coffee. He places his mug on the tray and turns over another couple of crates, gesturing for me to take a seat. "How was your night with Bailey?"

"Good. Feeling a bit rough today, though."

"You two drink much?" Dad asks, assuming my flat mood is entirely to do with my hangover.

"Quite a bit."

Dad tuts and shakes his head, his crate creaking. "So who's the bad influence?"

I don't know if he genuinely wants an answer or if he's teasing me, but I think on it anyway.

"We're probably both as bad as each other," I decide, trying to remember if Bailey and I have only ever really clicked when we've been under the influence of alcohol.

She's naturally outgoing and super sociable, and I come out of my shell more when I've had a few, so it wouldn't surprise me.

Dad picks up a cookie, munching away contentedly. He still has that twig in his hair.

"I met your neighboring farmers," I tell him. "One of them, anyway. They were out at Dirk's."

"Patrick and Peggy were at Dirk's?" Dad asks with surprise.

"No, Anders and Jonas."

"Oh. Well, Anders doesn't farm." He tells me what I already know. "Jonas does, though. He's been taking over things from his parents."

"Patrick and Peggy?"

"Yes."

"I thought they all had Swedish names."

"Yes, well, Peggy married into the family and it's Patrik without a c."

"Ah." I abstractly pluck that letter out of the spelling of his name.

"We haven't seen much of Patrik and Jonas since we moved here, but Peggy's a real friendly lady," Dad says. "She's tried to get us to come to church a couple of times, but you know Sheryl."

I do. She's defiantly atheist.

"Peggy didn't mention Anders was coming home," Dad muses. "He works for an IndyCar team, you know."

"Yes, Casey mentioned it."

"I've been hoping to meet him."

"You haven't yet?"

"No. Peggy said that he never comes home during racing season, but obviously that's not entirely true if he's here now. He'll be heading to Toronto the week after next, so he must be very busy at work."

Dad has been a motorsports fan for as long as I can remember. I'm not surprised he knows Anders's racing schedule.

"He's only here for the weekend," I say.

"Maybe we could invite them over for a drink later?"

"Fine by me," I reply, wondering if he can hear the waver in my voice that's caused by a kaleidoscope of butterflies taking flight in my stomach.

WHEN WE GET back inside, Sheryl reports that the radio warned of tornado weather. It certainly looks dark out there.

Hailstones arrive before rain and I stand at the living room window and watch, awestruck, as round white ice cubes pelt down from above, turning the lawn almost as white as snow. The sound of them hitting the roof is like a hundred thousand hammers banging away at once. It's ear-shattering, and the rain that follows soon after is almost as deafening. The sky flashes with distant lightning, followed by thunder that reverberates through the walls. I keep an eye out for lightning forks and wonder if the main body of the storm is yet to reach us.

"I hope Bailey made it into work okay," Dad says with concern from beside me.

I check my watch. It's twelve thirty. So much for her coming here this morning to nurse our hangovers together.

It's not the first time Bailey has made a decision on the spur of the moment and a promise she won't keep. But she did cheer me up last night and I'm grateful for that. Maybe it's enough that we have fun together occasionally without any great expectations of sisterly bonding. It's unlikely we're going to grow much closer in the next two weeks, anyway, despite my earlier optimism that we might without Scott around.

"I'll call her," Dad decides, digging his phone out of his pocket as he leaves the room.

Jealousy needles me. He hardly ever calls *me*.

Bailey lives nearby, I reason with myself. *She's in the same time zone. It's easy, convenient, to call her.*

But there's no denying that Dad and Bailey have a much closer relationship than he and I do. She would never hesitate to pluck a twig out of his hair.

Dad returns a couple of minutes later when the rain has died down.

"She and Casey are at work," he says with relief. "The golf club has a cellar."

I turn to look at him properly. "Are you genuinely worried about a tornado?"

"It's the right weather for 'em," he murmurs, scratching his peppery stubble.

Suddenly, he tenses, his eyes widening.

"What?"

He holds up his hand to silence me.

And then I hear it, a high-pitched whine coming from out-side.

"That's the tornado siren. Sheryl!" Dad shouts up the stairs.

"I heard it! I'm coming!" she shouts back.

"What are we going to do?" I ask with a flutter of panic as the town's warning siren continues to wail.

"Basement," Sheryl replies. "Call Bailey, let her know."

Dad whips out his phone again and ushers me toward the door under the stairs.

Why do we have to let Bailey know our every move? I wonder as Dad hastily fills her in.

The answer, I realize, is probably so the emergency services know where to find us if our house is flattened.

Terror momentarily locks my feet in place. I've seen *Twister*. This is happening.

I've never experienced a tornado warning. Sheryl had some close run-ins when she was growing up in Oklahoma, a state that's right in Tornado Alley. Her father moved her family to Indianapolis for work when she was a teenager and she had a couple of near misses there too, and also with Dad in Bloom-ington. But somehow, the thought of a tornado siren in a pop-ulated city seems less scary than hearing one out here in the middle of nowhere. I feel very vulnerable.

Someone pounds on the door. Dad hurries over and wrenches it open to reveal a senior woman in a bright pink raincoat standing there with water running off her hood.

"Quick," she urges. "Come use our shelter!"

"Thank you, Peggy!" Dad gushes with relief. "Grab your coat, Wren. Let's go!"

As soon as I pull the hood of my gray coat over my head,

the wind rips it off again. Leaves are being torn from the trees and my mid-length brown hair is whipping round my face like I'm Medusa with a headful of snakes.

Peggy is sliding behind the wheel of her Gator—a small green utility vehicle—and there's enough room for two more people to squeeze onto the front bench seat beside her, but before I can get my head round the idea of climbing into the sodden, open loading bay, I hear a sound that is all too familiar.

A mud-splattered white-and-yellow motorbike roars into our drive, sending a cascade of rainwater hurtling outward as it skids into a one-eighty and jolts to a stop. I leap backward, but too late: I'm soaked from the knees downward. I'm wearing a skirt, but the socks beneath my ankle boots are drenched.

"Get on," the rider commands, his face half hidden by the dark green hood of his raincoat.

Sheryl and Dad are already clambering onto the front bench of the Gator.

My heart is rabbiting against my rib cage as I hesitate, eyeing the cargo space behind them. The siren is still sounding in the distance.

Peggy sets off and I catch sight of Dad's pale face, wrought with anxiety as he looks back, shouting words that are snatched away by the wind.

"Wren!" Anders yells, because, obscured though his face might be, of *course* it's him.

"Bloody hell," I mutter, my butterflies spiraling into a frenzy as I hoick my leg up and over the back of his bike.

It's not a beast of a machine, not like the ones you see out on the road, but the navy seat is higher than it looks and the rain coating it seeps straight through the fabric of my skirt.

I've barely placed my hands on Anders's waist before the motorbike lurches forward, almost sending me flying straight off the back.

There's nowhere to put my feet, so I grip him hard, too shocked and breathless to cry out as he tears down the dirt road, water and mud splattering in our wake. The sky is dark and there's an eerie, greenish tinge to the clouds.

Up ahead looms the big red barn I saw last night, but Anders turns right well before it, down a tiny dirt track between the farmhouse and a field of maize.

The house mirrors the barn in style and color, but that's all I have time to notice.

"Go," Anders orders, nodding toward Dad as we pull to a stop at the back of the house.

Dad and Sheryl are out of the Gator, the latter running across the sodden lawn after Peggy while Dad frantically beckons to me. Peggy and Sheryl reach a mound about twenty feet away, which has a metal door built into its side at a forty-five-degree angle. It opens to reveal a dark tunnel and the glowering face of a man I don't recognize. He holds out his hand to help Sheryl inside.

I scramble off the bike. Peggy is looking over at us anxiously, but Anders is not getting off his bike.

"Are you coming?" My pulse is racing.

He shakes his head. "Not yet."

"Why not?" I ask with alarm.

"I've got to find my brother."

"ANDERS!" Peggy gives a startled cry as he revs up his engine and tears away.

A feeling of dread comes over me as I watch him go.

Where *is* his brother?

5

"P ATRIK, PEGGY, THIS IS MY DAUGHTER WREN." DAD introduces us when we're safely in the belly of the storm shelter, the door closed behind us.

The air is dense and stifling and it sounds as though a freight train is whooshing past over our heads. You wouldn't want to be claustrophobic.

"Thank you for having us," I say breathlessly as Patrik slides the latches across the door. He does this slowly, with one hand, because his other is secured in a cast and held in a sling. He nods at me stoically as he limps down the steps. Sheryl mentioned that he'd had a fall last week, broke an arm and two ribs. Apparently farming has one of the highest rates of death and serious accidents of any profession. I learned this only after Dad and Sheryl had signed the deed to their place.

Patrik is tall and thin, with Jonas's coloring and broad facial features. I bet he was once a giant of a man, but his stature has waned with age. He must be upward of eighty, and Peggy seems only a few years younger than that. Do they still work? Surely not. But Dad had said that Jonas was taking over the farm from them, not that he *had* taken it over.

"Of course, dear," Peggy replies to my thanks, removing her

pink coat and revealing shoulder-length white hair. She offers me a shaky smile but is obviously worried sick about her boys.

I am too, and I barely know Anders, let alone Jonas. I try to distract myself from what's going on by taking in our surroundings.

We're in an underground bunker that's about ten feet by twelve feet wide. The walls, floor, and ceiling are bare concrete. There's a well-worn, faded purple two-seater sofa against one wall and a few storage boxes lined up against another. A chest of drawers sits to the right of the door.

Peggy flicks on a light and a smaller second room at the back becomes illuminated.

"This is some storm shelter," Sheryl says with amazement.

She once told me about her family's tiny, dark shelter in Oklahoma. It had no electricity and it leaked, and when her dad and older sister siphoned out the floodwater one time, they found a snake in there.

"Our family's been here a long time," Peggy replies wryly, getting a radio out of one of the storage containers and turning it on. "We've seen our fair share of bad weather, and we've had time to make this more comfortable over the years. The boys used to play in here." She blanches, as though remembering that they're still outside. "Would you like a water?" she asks us weakly, getting a few bottles out and handing one each to Sheryl and me. She nods toward the second room. There are four wooden chairs and a small table, on top of which is a stack of tatty-looking board games, the images faded and scratched and the cardboard fraying at the edges.

Dad remains with Patrik by the door. Patrik is muttering a reply to something Dad has said, but I gather he's not much of a talker.

"Has a tornado ever come right through the farm?" I ask nervously as I open my bottle.

This shelter seems sturdy and safe enough, and it's clearly been built away from other structures to avoid being buried beneath rubble. That'll be why the door is at an angle too: any debris that hits it will be more likely to just slide off.

But what if the door is ripped clean away? What if we're all sucked out into the eye of the storm?

I can't believe Anders and Jonas are still out there.

"One tore its way through a couple of fields once," Peggy replies to my question, pulling out a couple of chairs at the table.

Sheryl acknowledges the gesture by taking a seat. I remain standing, too fidgety to sit still.

"That wasn't a good year for us," Peggy continues. "But the house stood. Here's hoping the Fredrickson luck holds."

Sudden thumping on the metal door sends my attention shooting in that direction. Patrik climbs the stairs surprisingly agilely and hastily unlocks the latches, pulling open the door to reveal a dirty-looking sky littered with flying debris. Jonas's face appears.

"Come *on*, son!" Patrik shouts, dragging him inside.

I look beyond him to see Anders, a rush of relief surging through me as he follows his brother inside and closes the door, sealing out the hissing wind.

Jonas seems even taller and broader in this small space. He's soaked through and his wet T-shirt clings to his skin, emphasizing all his grooves and contours.

"What the hell were you thinking?" Patrik yells suddenly, making me jump.

Anders is still at the top of the stairs, sliding the latches into place.

"Where *were* you?" Patrik continues his tirade at his elder son. "I can't have you disappearing all the time, boy!"

Boy? He's, like, thirty-seven! And so much for my assumption that Patrik is not much of a talker. He may be an old guy, but he appears to still be very much the patriarch of his family.

Dad makes a speedy exit into the next room. I linger apprehensively off to the side of the door arch.

"We're here now, Pa," Jonas replies, a bite to his tone.

If it's a warning, Patrik hears it and heeds it because he lays off, stalking past me to grumpily take a seat at the table. Anders comes down the stairs and turns toward the chest of drawers, pushing back his hood and unzipping his wet coat. He throws it toward a hook on the wall, where it catches and hangs.

"Oh," Jonas says, noticing me. "Hello." He sounds mildly surprised.

"Hi," I reply. "I'm Wren."

"Hello, Wren."

Anders looks over his shoulder and pins me with a hard stare, and in that moment, I stop breathing. His face has been frustratingly shrouded in darkness since I saw him at the bar, but now I realize that my memory has not served me well. He's even more heartrendingly gorgeous than I remembered him, tall and broad with dark blond hair shoved haphazardly away from his face. But now his sharp eyebrows are drawn into a dark scowl and his strong jaw is rigid with tension.

I feel as though all the air has been sucked out of the room by the storm as he yanks open a drawer and gets out a towel before turning at the waist and hurling it at his brother. Then he braces himself against the chest of drawers, his shoulders rising and falling with heaving breaths.

This is not the same man I met last night. This man is stone-cold sober and utterly furious.

Jonas, who caught the towel with one hand, seems unaffected by his brother's mood as he dries off his dark shaggy hair and collapses on the sofa, a cloud of dust flying up around him.

Anders turns and stalks past him to the corner of the room near where I'm standing. He doesn't acknowledge my presence or give any indication that he's pleased to see me again; if anything, it's the opposite. He slides his back down the wall until he's sitting with his legs drawn up, his wrists resting on his knees. His head falls back against the concrete wall and his eyes stare straight ahead. Even from this angle, I can see the shadowing of his jaw as it clenches and unclenches. And that's when I realize that I might have got it wrong: I don't think he's angry, he's upset.

Dad and the others at the table begin to talk, quietly and hesitantly at first, then gradually at a more normal volume. Sheryl is studying the board games, reminiscing about some she hasn't seen since she was a child. She's opening boxes and pulling out tokens and passing them to Dad. Peggy makes the odd comment and Patrik speaks once or twice, but their voices sound strained.

Jonas, on the sofa, has shifted so his head is leaning against the back cushion. He's folded his arms over his eyes, an action that has made his biceps bulge and his chest fill out his wet T-shirt. I can see why women would be drawn to him, and plenty are, if what Bailey and Casey said is anything to go by, but I don't fancy him myself.

I knew that, once I was sober, I'd be able to tell. There's something a little too raw and masculine about him for my tastes.

It belatedly occurs to me that I'm the only one still standing.

Dad doesn't ask if I'm okay. If Mum were here, I'm not sure she would either. Scott once speculated that their lack of care—which is what it sometimes feels like—is not actually because they *don't* care, but because they feel secure in the knowledge that I'm fine. They see me as capable and competent, the sort of person who gets on with things. They don't feel the need to check on me at every turn.

Dad is different with Bailey. He always has been. But it's not because she's *less* capable and competent, because she very much *is* those things.

Maybe it's because she welcomes his help more. She welcomes his care and attention. And maybe this makes her easier to love.

I'm more closed off than Bailey is. I had to be that way in order to protect myself.

I feel a sudden pang of longing for Scott. If he were here, he'd be breaking the ice right now—he's good at talking to strangers, better than I am, in any case.

I eye the space on the sofa next to Jonas, getting quite keen to sit down. It looks comfortable, if a little dusty, but I'm filthy now anyway. I stick out a leg and turn it this way and that, scrutinizing the mud streaking my skin.

Anders's head tilts in my direction, or at least, in the direction of my legs. His attention makes me feel edgy. He lets out a quiet sigh and looks away again, rubbing his hand over his jaw. The tension in his shoulders seems to have eased a little when he returns his hand to his knee.

On impulse, I walk past him and take a seat on the storage container closest to him.

I quietly say in a dry voice, "The lengths you will go to, to get me on the back of your motorbike."

He huffs out a laugh on a breath and slides me a sideways look, his lips tilting up at the corner into a crooked smile. The edginess in my stomach spreads, prickling all over my skin. His eyes are green, I realize: the cool, clear green of a mountain lake. But there's a hint of something else in there, something alien and out of place. Before I can get a proper look at him, that flash of color has gone.

He's wearing another checked shirt, which is hanging open over a white T-shirt. It's similar in style to the one he had on yesterday, with black and charcoal as the dominant colors, but with patches of light gray instead of dark yellow.

"Do I have something on my shirt?" he asks me, lifting his arm and inspecting his elbow.

My blush at being caught staring is instant. "No. I like it." The heat on my face intensifies at the admission. "I like the detail," I add stupidly, managing to stop myself from explaining further, but detail is everything in my line of work.

Opposite, Jonas lifts his arms and peeks out at us from beneath the shadow.

"I like your shirt too," he drawls at Anders. "It looks lovely and warm and dry."

Anders gives him an unimpressed look and stands, stripping off his shirt down to his T-shirt. He throws it at his brother's chest, but with a lot less aggression than earlier.

"There you go, you big baby." He reaches past me to grab a bottle of water and I freeze at his close proximity. His arms are golden brown and leanly muscled.

"Why, thank you," Jonas replies with a smirk, lazily getting to his feet as Anders sits back down. He drags his sodden red T-shirt up and over his chest, his hands hitting the ceiling above his head as he pulls it off.

I'm not particularly drawn to overly sculpted bodies, but no one is going to believe it if they catch me staring at his, so I stop doing that *right* away.

There's a damp patch on the sofa cushion from where he's been sitting in his wet jeans. Peggy notices as she comes into the room.

"Why didn't you put a towel down?" she asks Jonas tersely.

"You've never given a crap about the state of the couch before," Jonas says as he finishes buttoning his shirt.

"Language!" Peggy chides. "We have guests," she adds pointedly, glancing at me.

"Yes, welcome to our humble abode," Jonas drawls, sitting down on the towel his mother has now laid out on the sofa. His brother's shirt pulls tight across his chest. "You like what we've done to the place?"

Most people would hate it in here. But as someone who thinks the Southbank Centre is an architectural masterpiece, I'm not at all opposed to a bit of raw concrete.

"It has a certain appeal," I reply coolly as I run my hand down the smooth surface of the wall. "I'm a big fan of the brutalist movement."

I'm not being entirely serious—I mean, I do like brutalist architecture, but I wouldn't go about claiming it in this context— so it gives me a buzz when Anders laughs.

I dart my eyes toward him, trying to catch his smile and succeeding. His teeth are attractively imperfect, clean and white, but not dead straight.

Scott had very little interest in art or architecture. I still remember suggesting we visit Tate Modern the morning after our first night together and he pulled a face and booked us tickets to the London Eye instead.

Anders opens his bottle of water, a smile hovering at the edges of his lips as he drinks. It's an effort to tug my attention away.

Peggy takes a seat next to Jonas. "Everything okay in here?" she asks guardedly, and I have a funny feeling she was waiting for the air to clear before venturing into the room.

"All good, Ma," Jonas replies.

She reaches across and pats his knee and there's something reassuring about the gesture.

I know that she was worried about him earlier, but is she worried about him still? But of course she would be worried. They must *all* be worried. This farm is their livelihood—if a tornado is out there tearing it to shreds, where will that leave them?

"Wren is an architect," Peggy enlightens her sons, nodding at me, and I sense she's trying to take their minds off what's happening aboveground.

"Is that so?" Anders sounds innocent as he flashes me a sly sideways look, raising an eyebrow and going along with his mother's attempts to lighten the mood.

"Have you two already met?" Jonas asks suspiciously.

"I gave her a ride here," Anders replies, stretching his long legs out in front of him and crossing them at the ankles.

"And you had time to talk?" Jonas presses, not buying the explanation.

He clearly knows his brother well enough to recognize when he's being hoodwinked.

"We bumped into each other last night when I was walking home," I reveal, coming clean. "I cut across one of your fields."

"Scared the shit out of me," Anders grumbles. "It was like something from *Children of the Corn*."

Laughter bursts out of me.

"What were you doing, cutting through the fields?" Jonas asks with a smile, mystified.

"I wasn't really aware that I was trespassing. Sorry."

He waves away my apology. "It's just that the people who go walking around the fields in these parts either own them or are escaping from penitentiaries."

We *all* crack up at this.

"I won't do it again," I promise.

"You can walk wherever you like," Peggy says firmly. "Can't she?" She's asking Jonas, not Anders.

"Fine by me," Jonas replies.

Anders gets to his feet and picks up the radio from beside me, turning down the volume and cocking his ear to the door.

"How are things looking up there?" Peggy wonders.

"I think the siren's stopped." He replaces the radio and heads up the stairs. "Wind's died down too." He unbolts the door and cracks it open while I sit up straighter. "I think we're good." He opens the door fully and climbs out.

Jonas hunches over and clasps his hands between his knees, his earlier smile nowhere to be seen. Peggy quietly says something to him, her expression fretful as the others around the table get to their feet. Peggy and Jonas make no move to stand, so I'm the next to head upstairs after Anders.

"House is still there," I note with relief.

Anders nods seriously, turning to survey the barn's roof. It looks intact from this angle. There's tree debris scattered around the place, but that's the only sign of high winds. If a tornado touched down, it doesn't appear to have come through here.

Patrik emerges from the shelter next, his expression dark.

"I'm going to check for damage," Anders tells him.

Patrik responds with an abrupt nod.

"You want a ride home first?" Anders asks, looking at me directly.

My heart skips a beat as I realize that the strange flash of color I caught a glimpse of earlier is a defect in his right eye: a tiny splodge of orangey-brown, just to the bottom left of his iris.

"Or you could walk," he adds, scratching his eyebrow.

I jolt to my senses, realizing I've taken too long to accept.

"Yeah, you won't be getting me on that thing again anytime soon."

His lip curls upward into a smirk. "All right, then, Wren. Guess I'll be seeing you."

I'm distracted by Dad and Sheryl emerging from the shelter, loudly expressing their relief at being back out in the open. When I return my gaze to Anders, he's already walking away. The sight has an uncanny knack of stilling my butterflies.

6

THE NEXT DAY, DAD, SHERYL, AND I PUT ON OUR RAIN-
coats and venture out into the orchards to see how much
of the fallen fruit can be salvaged. Sheryl wants to puree
the peaches for Bellinis, a drink she first tasted at Harry's Bar
in Venice ten years ago. The owner of the bar invented the tip-
ple and Sheryl is keen to see if she can re-create it.

I'm over my hangover now, so I'm completely down with
this idea.

"I wonder if Anders is on his way back to Indy already,"
Dad says, turning a peach around in his hand and surveying it
for bruises.

I've been wondering this too. I've been finding it hard to put
the intriguing Fredrickson family out of my mind, especially
Anders, with his freaky green eyes. It bothers me that our last
encounter ended so abruptly.

"You'll get a chance to chat with him next time he's in
town," Sheryl replies impatiently as she swoops down to pick
up two peaches from the grass.

This is not the first time Dad has expressed his disappointment that the storm scuppered his plans to invite the family over for drinks. He asked Peggy as we were leaving, but she

regretfully declined, saying they'd be too busy on a clear-up mission. We offered to help, but she turned us down. I think she was quite keen for us to leave them to their own devices.

As it transpired, the tornado touched down a few miles south of here, ripping its way through a forest and some fields. Thankfully, no lives were lost, nor were any homes or farms destroyed, but the storm did cause some minor damage to properties, and we saw a lot of debris lying around on our way back to Dad and Sheryl's.

Sheryl told me that there are around twenty tornadoes a year in Indiana, mostly in the spring and summer months.

I'm thinking next time I might visit in the dead of winter.

"There sure was a lot of tension in that shelter," Dad continues. "Didn't really feel right, striking up a conversation with Anders about motor racing, although I was tempted."

"Do you think he came home because of Patrik's accident?" I ask, remembering Dad saying that Anders normally never visits during the racing season.

"Maybe," Dad replies. "I can't stop thinking about Patrik laying into Jonas like that. Didn't realize he had it in him to get so angry."

"Oh, I did," Sheryl replies flippantly. "Don't let his age fool you. That man is someone to be reckoned with."

What was it that Patrik shouted? *I can't have you disappearing all the time, boy!*

There was something about Jonas that seemed kind of . . . *off.* Why *did* Anders feel the need to go looking for him? And why was Anders so upset when he arrived at the shelter?

Jonas sat on that sofa for ages with his face buried under his arms and he barely said two words when he eventually emerged from the shelter and stalked away across the farmyard.

Spying a particularly fat peach on a branch above my head, I reach up to pluck it off. But I have to tug harder than I was expecting and my effort brings down a cascade of raindrops, making me flinch as water runs down the inside of my coat.

"Not ripe yet, Wren. Stick with the ones on the ground," Sheryl commands.

I surreptitiously roll my eyes at her bossiness as she lets out an "oof" and straightens up, stretching her back.

"Maybe you should let Dad and me do this if your back is hurting," I say, aware that this will probably annoy her, yet failing to hold my tongue.

"Don't be ridiculous, I'm fine." Sheryl brushes me off with a predictable scowl, bending down to scoop up another peach.

I'm at the edge of the peach orchard, close to the barn, when I notice a grubby-looking tarp covering something bulky. When the wind catches it, a corner lifts to reveal a flash of pale silver.

"What's that?" I ask Dad.

"Caravan," he replies. "Came with the farm."

"It's not an Airstream, is it?"

It's the right color for aluminum and seems to be the right shape.

"I think so," Dad replies. "Haven't had a lot of time to investigate."

A surge of excitement rushes through me.

"Can I?"

"Sure." He nods encouragingly. "You know much about them?"

"A bit. They're a design classic. I've always wanted one."

"I don't know what shape it's in, but you're welcome to it."

I laugh. "If only I could take it back to the UK."

"You could use it when you come to visit," Dad offers. "Go on a trip across America or something. Didn't you always say you'd like to do that?"

"I *would* like to do that one day," I reply. It was actually something Scott and I talked about doing together.

Dad and Sheryl retire inside while I go take a closer look.

The air is laden with moisture and the trees are still shaking off the earlier rainfall, so I avoid walking under any branches as I make my way toward the tarp-covered caravan. It's smaller than I'd initially thought, and hemmed in on all sides by what looks like a load of old junk: wooden crates and pallets and a bunch of rusty old farm machinery. It's easiest to access the corner where the tarp lifted in the wind, so I move some crates out of the way before lifting up the cover.

Wow. It is definitely an Airstream: it says it right here on a long rectangular silver badge, printed in faded capitals. I wonder how old it is. It looks vintage, but I can't be sure until I get a proper look.

I continue moving crates and pallets and other bits of junk until I can see where the tarp has been attached to the caravan. The rope is slippery with grime and my fingernails are coated with green-and-black goo by the time I manage to release it. I repeat the process at the other end of the caravan before plucking a tissue out of a pocket in my shirtdress and cleaning off the tips of my fingers. There are more pallets leaning against the side of the van, so I move them, one by one, and then peek under the tarp, hoping I'm at the right end for the door. I am. It's there in front of me and on a badge to the right, written in silver cursive, is the model name: *Bambi*.

My heart jumps with excitement. I've heard of this model. I think Airstream does a modern version, but what I have in front of me is definitely old. Getting my phone out of my other pocket, I do a quick Google search and discover that Airstream launched the Bambi model in 1961. At sixteen feet, it's one of the smallest they ever made, but that size must refer to its over-all length including the hitch, because the actual body is tiny.

I pocket my phone again and tug on the tarp, feeling it give a little. Checking that there's nothing else resting against it, I return to the side and tug even harder. Slowly, the tarp comes off toward me, bringing a shower of grimy water down with it. I'm splattered, but I'm far too full of anticipation to be put off at this stage. This dress is going in the wash later anyway.

The Bambi is small and perfectly formed, although its silver aluminum color has been muted by dust and age. It is single-axle, so it rests at one end on a stand fixed to the hitch. Two rusted propane tanks sit atop the hitch, in front of an old spare tire. There's a large rectangular window at this end, and when I step on my tiptoes and peer inside, I can make out two more large rectangular windows on the side that backs into the black barn wall.

I stand and stare, drinking it all in. It has tear-shaped indi-cator lights and domed silver hubcaps. The door is arched and curves inward to follow the rounded line of the body, and it has a tiny matching arched overhang above the door to stop rain from running down the sides and falling straight inside. The metalwork all over is a bit dinged-up and dented, but the beauty of the overall object is undeniable. The Bambi is a work of art.

I walk forward and try the door. It doesn't budge. Damn.

I head inside to ask Dad if he knows where the key might be and find him flat out on the sofa, watching TV.

"Check the desk drawer in the office," he tells me absent-mindedly.

The office is a small room adjoining the kitchen and the desk has six drawers in total—three on either side. I start with the top left, moving past stationery and various bits and bobs before coming to the deeper bottom drawer. There are no keys visible, but an old and familiar smell wafts out and I pause for a moment, staring at the photo album.

It's brown with a decorative gold trim. Mum and I have one identical to this at home that contains my baby and childhood photos up until I was about the age of three. It even smells the same. I've always wondered if it's what our home in Phoenix smelled like.

I gently lift out the album and open it up. There's a flimsy sheet of soft paper at the front, and then next, in my mum's handwriting, are the words: *Elmont Family*.

The same words appear in the album we have at home, although that one has a three-year date span. Here, there's only one year listed, the year I turned four. There's a dash beside it, as though the album was never finished, and when I flip to the back, I see that the last six sleeves are empty.

Returning to the front, I study the first two photos, secured behind yellowing film. The top shot shows me wearing a lime-green swimsuit and standing on the lawn of our old house back in Phoenix. The sprinkler is on and I'm laughing, my arms spread wide and my chin dripping with water as I'm caught in the spray.

Behind me are the three fat cacti I remember so vividly, and, in the distance, Camelback Mountain rises up beyond the brown rooftops of the bungalows across the street. The sky is pale blue and my shadow is cast long across the muted green grass.

Below this photograph is one of our house, squat and cream, with a red-tiled roof and matching red awnings above the windows. It has an archway leading to a porch and front door. The lawn spans the width of the house and is bordered by a gravel pit housing the cacti and various other shrubs. The white stones in the gravel pit were too sharp to stand on, but all the other plots in the neighborhood had them in place of lawn.

Mum once told me that we were the only family in the local area who had grass—she wanted it to remind her of England—and every evening the sprinklers would go on to keep it alive. I made the most of the regular outdoor showers.

I remember the feeling of that grass beneath my feet, coarse and prickly, unlike the soft, lush lawns back home or the one planted in front of this place.

I turn the page and find a photo of Dad and me at the man-made city beach in Phoenix. He's standing beside me in bright orange swimming trunks, his body tanned nut-brown and wet strands of his longish hair sticking to his cheeks. There's a row of fake rocks protruding from the cloudy pale blue water behind us, looking like the spiny back of a stegosaurus, and beyond them is a large lagoon dotted with people. Farther still is a white sand beach and a row of tall, skinny palm trees. The whole scene feels achingly familiar.

Another photograph shows me perched on a stone wall in a red dress with the striped creamy-orange-and-yellow layers of the Grand Canyon laid out behind me. In another, I'm sitting on Dad's shoulders beside a wiggly-limbed Joshua tree, and in another, I'm standing in front of a giant cactus outside a restaurant in Rawhide. I remember the restaurant's brightly colored candleholders on the outdoor wooden tables.

At least, I think I do. I'm not entirely sure whether I'm reliving memories or have simply seen these photos before.

We *did* have *some* good times as a family, didn't we? How did it all go wrong? What was it about Sheryl that Dad couldn't live without? She's so different from my mum. Mum isn't ambitious or particularly well educated, but she's warm and unguarded. Loving. Why wasn't she enough for Dad?

These photographs show so many of our happy times. Were there lots of bad times that I don't remember?

Maybe my parents simply weren't a good match. But on paper, surely they—a groundskeeper and a fruit picker—made more sense than a groundskeeper and a professor.

For some reason I think of Scott and Nadine.

"Any luck?" Dad asks from the doorway, making me jump.

Reflexively, I snap the album shut.

He smiles and nods at it, either ignoring or not noticing my guilty expression at being caught snooping. "I found that in a box when we were packing up the house in Bloomington."

"Mum has one that's identical, only it contains photos from earlier years."

"She wanted to keep that one too, but I put my foot down."

"Why?" He's just told me he found it in a box, so he can't have cared about it that much.

"Your mum had the negatives. She was going to get copies, but I guess she never did?"

"Not that I know of," I reply quietly.

"Never got around to it."

Maybe it was too painful a task, to be reminded of the time lead-ing up to you abandoning us.

I don't voice my thoughts out loud. I don't think I'll ever be able to make sense of my dad's rejection and we don't have the sort of relationship where we talk openly to each other.

I was much more vocal as a teenager, much more willing to speak up if I felt that something was unfair. I'd bounce back from the myriad little rejections that I faced whenever I came to visit, from Sheryl snapping at me over something small to Dad failing to chastise Bailey for being a brat to me.

But I've long since given up fighting for my dad's time and attention. These days, I prefer to accept the situation for what it is, which is that Sheryl and Bailey are his priorities and I'm farther down his list.

I'm tougher than I used to be, not because I fight, but be-cause I don't. That's the way I cope, the way I ensure that things don't hurt me as much as they used to.

That's not to say that they don't still hurt to some degree, though.

"Can I take it upstairs with me?" I ask Dad about the photo album.

"Sure you can. Did you find the caravan key?"

"Not yet."

"Check the middle drawer on the right," he instructs.

I open the drawer in question and find a whole bunch of keys. I wouldn't know where to start, but luckily, Dad comes over. He rattles around, discarding this set and that before fi-nally pulling out a flimsy-looking key ring with two small sil-ver keys attached.

"I reckon this is them." He hands them over.

"Thanks."

I take the photo album upstairs first and lay it carefully on my bedside table, resting my hand on it as though it's a precious, living thing.

I have to blink to clear my vision before returning downstairs.

7

"WREN!"

Sheryl is calling me.

I climb down from Bambi, gratefully breathing in the fresh air.

It's what I'm calling the Airstream now. A name as cute as that doesn't need an article.

"Would you run this down to the Fredricksons?" Sheryl asks when I appear round the side of the barn. She's holding up a bottle of what looks like fizz and a jar of the peach puree she made earlier.

"Thank-you gift?" I ask as I approach.

"Yep."

"Shall I change first?" I glance down at my grime-splattered charcoal-gray shirtdress.

She shakes her head dismissively. "They're farmers. They won't think twice about what you look like."

"That's a bit judgmental."

"I only mean that they're used to getting their hands dirty. It's a good thing," she snaps.

Whatever you say . . .

I take the bottle and jar from her, realizing that Anders is probably already on his way back to Indianapolis.

Not that I care what he thinks of my appearance, I lie to myself.

I WAS FULL of hope when I unlocked the Airstream, but swiftly came down to earth with a bump. It *reeks* of mold and damp. Its former owners laid down a carpet that's now rimmed with black mold and curling at the edges. When I lifted up a corner, I found rotting floor tiles underneath. The original fixtures and fittings remain, but they're in bad shape. Moths have been at the curtains, mice have shredded the faded yellow bench-seat cushions, and something else has been eating away at the woodwork.

I'm gutted. It's far too big a restoration job for me to tackle in the short time I'm here, but I can't quite bring myself to replace the tarp yet.

One of the cool things about the caravan is its door within a door—there's a solid metal outer door and an inner mesh one that keeps out creepy-crawlies. I leave the outer one open so it can air out.

THE FREDRICKSON FARM is about half a mile away, separated from Dad and Sheryl's property by their pumpkin patch and a field. The big red barn comes into view in the distance first, even though the farmhouse is closer, but the house is obscured behind the tall stalks of maize that I'm walking beside.

The barn is a stunning piece of historic architecture, painted a deep red and built almost entirely out of wood with a mansard roof. I think they call mansard roofs Dutch or gambrel roofs here—they're symmetrical in shape, with two slopes on each side of the roof to give added height and storage space.

At the end of the maize field is the narrow track Anders rode along yesterday to get to the storm shelter. It butts up to a white picket fence that also runs adjacent to the main track. Behind this fence is a lawn and the farmhouse.

Yesterday, I noted that the house mirrors the design of the barn, but only now can I take time to appreciate it. It's red, like the barn, but much smaller and more decorative, with white window surrounds breaking up the weatherboard facade and a central gabled dormer built into the terra-cotta-tiled roof. The windows are rectangular and symmetrical, but below the roofline at the sides and at the top of the dormer are small triangular-shaped windows.

As I unlatch the gate and begin walking up the garden path, I notice that there's a dark gray BMW with its boot open parked on the drive to the left of the house. Climbing up the three steps to the central front door, I reach for the doorbell and pause at the sound of raised voices coming from around the side of the house.

"You're being stupid!" Patrik exclaims, and a side door to the house opens and closes, making a rattling noise. "There are a million and one ways to kill yourself on a farm!"

"Yeah, well, this is the easiest," Anders replies as he appears in my line of vision.

"Do what you want, then," I hear Patrik snap before the side door bangs shut again, causing Anders to flinch.

He shakes his head resignedly and places three long rifles

or shotguns—I wouldn't know, but they are *guns*—in the boot and closes it. Then he sees me on the porch and freezes.

"I brought these for your parents." I dazedly lift up the bottle and jar.

"Ma!" he shouts. "Wren's here!"

Footsteps approach from behind the front door and Peggy opens it up with a slightly frantic smile on her face.

"Hello, Wren!" Her tone is imbued with warmth, but she's visibly on edge.

"Hi! I wanted to give you these from Sheryl and my dad. And me!" I pass her the peach puree. "I'm not sure if you like Bellinis, but if you add peach puree to this sparkling wine, they make a good cocktail. You're supposed to use prosecco, but I don't know if they sell that in town? This was the only bottle we had in the cupboard. Just a little thank-you gift for saving us yesterday."

I've come over all wordy.

"Well, you didn't need saving, as it turned out. Tornado didn't come close."

I laugh nervously. "We might not have been so lucky."

Glancing to my left, I see that Anders is still standing there, watching us.

"Anyway, thank you again!" I say overly cheerfully. "I'd better get home for dinner!"

I hurry down the steps and along the garden path.

"Anders could give you a lift?" Peggy calls after me. "He's just leaving."

"No, no, it's okay!" I reply hastily. "I'm happy walking."

I glance over my shoulder in time to see him shoving his hand through his hair and staring after me, a look of disconcertion on his face.

I turn away and go through the gate.

I don't know why I reacted like that. Was it seeing him with all those guns? Or was it seeing him, *period*?

Every time we say goodbye—or more accurately, *don't* say goodbye—I figure it'll be the last time, but then there he is again, making me feel all edgy and off-kilter.

I haven't gone more than a couple hundred feet or so when I hear a car crawling up behind me. It begins to go past, then slows.

"You okay?" Anders asks.

I nearly jump out of my skin at the unexpectedly close proximity of his voice. It slipped my mind that the driver's side is on the left in America—I was anticipating him calling across from the other side of the car.

"You are *tense*," he says from literally right beside me.

"You think?" I reply sarcastically, glancing at him and immediately pulling my gaze away again. I should watch where I'm going.

"You know, you're starting to give me a complex." He lifts up his left arm and sniffs his armpit, then rests his elbow on the window ledge.

Narrowing my eyes, I ask him outright, "Why do you have all those guns?"

He scratches his chin and stares at the road. "Farmers have guns." He sounds resigned. "*People* have guns."

"I know they do, but why do *you* have so many in the boot of your car?"

"I'm taking them home with me."

"To Indianapolis?"

"Yep."

"Why?"

"Because I'm—" he starts as though he's going to tell me, but his sentence breaks off. "It's complicated," he says at last.

"Are you worried about Jonas?"

The car comes to a stop, but it takes my brain a moment to catch up, so I have to backtrack a couple of paces.

"Why do you say that?" He seems hyperalert as he stares at me through the open window, and I feel jittery as I return his gaze, noticing once more that strange fleck of orangey-brown in his eye. No, *amber*.

"It's only a feeling I had," I say hastily. "But your mum seemed concerned about him during the storm and your dad was pretty upset when he went missing. Obviously, that's all understandable, considering what was going on, but I couldn't help but wonder if everything was all right with him."

He sighs. "My brother hasn't been . . . Well, he hasn't been himself lately," he admits heavily. "My mom called me because she was worried."

So *that's* why he came home during racing season: Jonas.

I ask, very tentatively, "Are you scared he might hurt himself?"

Is that why he's removing the guns?

"I hope not. But it's not a risk I'm willing to take." He swallows and stares out the windscreen, suddenly looking vulnerable. "It feels wrong leaving."

"You can't stay?" I ask gently, my heart going out to him.

"Not if I want to keep my job."

"I'm so sorry, Anders." I instinctively press my hand to his elbow.

"I should get going." He withdraws his arm inside the car

and then glances at me, his gaze drifting downward over my charcoal-gray dress. His brows bunch together as I belatedly remember what state I'm in.

"You look as though Jackson Pollock's been at you with a can of green paint," he muses.

I laugh and his ensuing smile makes me feel as though the sun has come out after a long, cold winter.

Would Scott know who Jackson Pollock is?

"Take care," he says.

"You too."

And, just like that, it's winter again.

8

RETURN HOME TO DAD AND SHERYL'S TO FIND BAILEY'S
car on the driveway. She's only a day and a half late.

I'm not in the mood for her lively chatter tonight. I wish
I could say that I'm only grumpy because I'm hungry and the
dinner smells wafting through the cracks in the doorway
aren't helping, but I've been feeling flat ever since Anders drove
away. I determinedly shove him out of my mind and press the
doorbell, irritated that I left my key behind.

Bailey answers. "Hi!" she exclaims, her smile wide and bright.

"Hi." I can't control my less-than-enthusiastic-sounding
reply.

"Heard Mom was doing a roast and I couldn't resist," she
says as I step over the threshold, shutting the door behind me.

"Is Casey here?"

"Still at work," she tells me over her shoulder as she leads
the way back into the kitchen.

"Really? That's late."

"Private instruction. Has to fit in with clients."

"Wren! You took your time," Sheryl says annoyingly.

"I'm not sure I could have gone much faster," I mutter.

"Can you carry those to the table?" She nods at the serving dishes containing roast potatoes, carrots, and peas.

Dad and Bailey are discussing which bottle of wine to open. I feel as though I've walked in on a family dinner. Someone *else's* family dinner.

I try to ignore this feeling as I take the dishes into the adjoining dining room.

There are four place settings at the table. Although there's a leaf that can be added to seat eight—I remember this from past dinner parties—right now it's in a six configuration and two of the spare chairs have been removed from the table and pushed up against a wall.

Since I arrived, I've sat to Dad's left and Sheryl has sat opposite me, with Dad in between us at the head of the table, but now there's a fourth setting at the other end, opposite him.

I place the vegetables on the heatproof mats that have already been laid out and hesitate, my old insecurities rearing up.

"Take a seat, Wren," Sheryl commands, appearing with a roast chicken.

Dad and Bailey come through, Bailey still chattering away as she opens a bottle of red wine and begins to pour some into Dad's and Sheryl's wineglasses.

I hover at the end of the table.

"Wren?" Bailey asks, proffering the bottle.

"Sure," I reply, pulling out the chair opposite Dad.

She decants wine into my empty glass and goes to sit down on Dad's left.

Although the chairs have been spaced out along the table, the gap between me and Sheryl and Bailey is much wider than the gap between them and Dad.

A feeling comes over me of being out on my own, separate from this part of my family, as if I'm not really a part of this family at all.

I can't help withdrawing into myself after that. I'm not sure anyone notices—Bailey and Sheryl keep the conversation flowing, as they always do.

SHERYL AND DAD are having their Opening Day on Saturday, so I spend the next few days helping to get the farm ready for its first customers.

The previous owners had a shop inside the black barn. Everything came included with the sale, from the cash register to the scales for weighing the fruit and even the large stack of wicker baskets that customers use to carry their produce from tree to barn.

I set about giving the interior of the barn a good clean. I sweep the floor, de-cobweb the wooden walls, and dust and wash the shelves and countertops. I wipe down the baskets and I also attack the cash register with a sponge and disinfectant.

It's Thursday and I've been here a week. It's not panning out to be the most relaxing holiday of all time, but I've liked keeping busy and going to bed with aching muscles and tired eyes. I keep hoping that all the hard work will help me switch off at night, because ever since Sunday, I've taken to lying awake in bed, thinking about Scott.

After our roast dinner, I asked Bailey if she was planning on taking any leftovers home to Casey and she remarked that I'd make a better married woman than she does.

Sheryl noticed me wincing and chided Bailey for being

insensitive, but it took my half sister a moment to realize how she'd offended me. Once the penny dropped, she apologized, but that night, the pain of losing Scott felt fresh and raw.

The last time I visited America, he came with me and I'd never felt less alone. He was on my side, in my corner, squeezing my knee or surreptitiously raising an eyebrow whenever Sheryl drove me round the bend. It was during that holiday that I realized he was someone I could spend my life with, someone I could depend on. It's still sinking in that he'll never be with me again when I come to visit this side of my family.

And then, yesterday, I got a call from our florist, chasing me for the deposit for our wedding flowers. Scott promised he'd take care of canceling everything and I took him up on the offer, figuring it would hurt him less than it would hurt me. I handed over my wedding planning folder and left him to it, but forgot to add the florist's details. Having to endure her pity when she learned the nuptials had fallen through was like suffering a physical blow.

I've walked past that florist in Bury St. Edmunds countless times. Before I came away, it had a big bucket of sunflowers sitting on the ground outside. The memory of them prompts a flashback to our camper van holiday through France, Spain, and Portugal last summer.

Scott and I were in France, driving alongside a field of sunflowers. All the blooms in the field were facing away from us except one, and I noticed this at the same moment as Scott, who turned to me, letting go of the wheel for a couple of seconds to do jazz hands at me.

I cracked up laughing at his impression of that flower.

I'm smiling now too, but then I remember that Nadine gets to laugh at his jokes these days, not me.

9

THE NEXT MORNING, I HAVE AN IDEA TO PUT UP BUNTING and festoon lights inside the barn. Dad and Sheryl love the suggestion, but they're busy preparing party food for the Opening Day event tomorrow, so, with Dad's car and credit card at my disposal, I head into town.

East of the square, in an area of town I haven't ventured into yet, I'm pleasantly surprised to find a couple of independent stores and a cozy-looking café, as well as a party store. When I reach for my door handle to get out of the car, I'm taken aback to find Jonas sitting in the dusty black truck that's parked right beside me. I've been keeping my eyes peeled for him ever since Anders admitted he was worried, but this is the first time I've seen him all week.

I pause for a moment. He's staring at the grocery store next to the party shop and when I peer closer, I realize that there's a woman at the checkout counter in his line of vision. She's around his age—mid-to-late thirties—and is attractive, with dark hair tied up in a high, messy bun. She's holding the hand of a small, curly-haired boy.

I return my attention to Jonas. He looks miserable. I'm wondering whether I should go and ask if he's all right when he starts up his engine and reverses out onto the road, driving back toward the farm.

Well, *that* was curious.

Curious, but none of my business.

The party store comes up trumps and I return to Wetherill with plenty of festoon lights and bunting. The design is a bit "country kitchen" for my personal taste: a variety of prints, from florals to polka dots, and all in pastel colors. But it will suit the inside of the barn, so, with a long ladder and a staple gun, I set about fixing it to the walls.

"That's looking good!" Dad exclaims when he comes into the barn later.

"Thanks. I'm almost done," I tell him, securing the last string. "I don't think this will be strong enough for the festoon lights," I say as I climb back down the ladder and hand him the staple gun.

He peers up at the high ceiling. "You planning to crisscross them from the rafters?"

"That's what I thought, but what you do you think?"

"That would work well. Let me go get some nails and a hammer."

I hop up onto the counter and wait for him, watching the bunting flutter in the breeze that's coming in through the barn's large double doors. It's cooler than it was yesterday.

My phone begins to vibrate in my pocket. I'm perplexed by the sight of my boss Graham's name in the caller ID. I hope he's not calling me about the Beale job.

I used to work at a cool young practice in Clerkenwell and the projects I ran were interesting and varied: an interior fit-out of a riverside apartment, for example, or a conversion of an old warehouse into a bar and restaurant.

My practice in Bury St. Edmunds is comparatively prosaic.

After spending ten months working on boring school-roof details and hospital-door schedules, I begged my boss for a residential job. Earlier this year, he gave me the Beale house, a renovation and extension. But Lucinda Beale is a client on a total power trip and with no imagination. She shuts down my design suggestions at every turn and treats me like a lackey who's at her beck and call. I hate working with her.

Planning permission has now been granted for her house and the work is due to begin on-site the week after I get back. I'm absolutely dreading it. She'll be making changes left, right, and center, causing no end of contractual disputes. It's going to be a total nightmare and I have no one to blame but myself because I asked for a residential job.

I love being an architect, getting paid to design pieces of art that people live and work in. But architecture has its downsides, just like any other profession.

I answer Graham's call. "Hello?"

"Wren, hi!" he replies. "How are you?"

"Good, thanks. How are you?"

"I'm very well. Listen, I'm ever so sorry to bother you on holiday, but something's come up and I thought I should run it by you."

"Okay."

"Freddie has had to deal with a couple of things on Mrs. Beale's job while you've been away and she's taken a bit of a liking to him."

I bet she has. It'd be just like Lucinda Beale to fawn over a hot, young, not-yet-fully-qualified male architect rather than defer to me, a more experienced female.

"There's no easy way to say this," Graham continues. "She's

asked if he can be the site architect and take over running the job."

"Oh!" *What the hell?*

"Obviously, I can tell her that Freddie isn't available, but I got the impression you weren't that happy."

I prickle with embarrassment. He's not wrong, but I hadn't realized I was being transparent.

"I do find her a bit difficult to work with," I admit.

"So you wouldn't mind if Freddie took over?" he asks hopefully, seeking an easy solution.

I *would* mind, but more because of the principle.

"What would I do instead?" I ask, trying to convince myself that this is a positive outcome—she would have been a proper devil once the work started on her home.

"Well, now that Raj has gone, you could do the tender drawings for the Heathfield Primary School extension," Graham suggests. "And then we'd need the construction drawing package after that."

My heart sinks. This is exactly the sort of thing I was trying to move away from. There's absolutely no design involved, just a whole bunch of tedious technical drawings showing everything from roof and window details to sewer pipes and every single socket and light switch that an electrician will need to put in. The tender drawings will go out to five contractors who will cost them up and submit their quotes, and then I'll need to go into more detail still for the winning contractor. This will keep me busy for two to three months, possibly longer.

Dad comes back into the barn with the tools we need. "Sheryl's almost done in the kitchen so I'll help you fix these."

I waggle my phone at him to show that I'm on a call and he mouths an apology.

"Have a think about it," Graham says. "You can let me know on Monday."

"Okay, thanks," I reply.

"Everything all right?" Dad asks as I sigh and put my phone away.

"Yep, fine." I hop down from the counter. "Are you sure you've got time to help?"

"Absolutely. This was a great idea of yours," Dad says with a smile as we fix the first row of lights. "I can tell you're a designer."

His praise embarrasses me. Anyone can string up lights and bunting.

"How's work going?" he asks.

I'm about to brush him off and say that it's fine, which is my usual response to him asking me anything personal, but this time I stop myself. I'm halfway into my holiday and we haven't talked about anything meaningful. We rarely do. I knew he would be busy with the farm when I chose these dates and that didn't concern me, but I'm going home in a week and who knows when we'll see each other again. Am I really destined to only ever have a surface relationship with my dad? Is that what I want?

I think of Bailey and how she's more open and welcoming of his care and attention. Maybe I *could* be a bit more like that.

On impulse, I find myself opening up about my job, telling him about how much I miss my old practice and how trapped and uninspired I've been feeling lately.

"It's not surprising you've been feeling uninspired," he says, hammering in a nail. "You've been through a lot."

"I was feeling uninspired before that," I confess, passing him the festoon lights to hang.

"You're not thinking about a change of career, are you? There seems to be a lot of that going on these days."

"Not after seven years of training." Not to mention my student loans that I'll probably be paying off until I'm seventy. "I'm not about to throw that away anytime soon."

"I remember when you used to draw all the time," Dad says with a smile, handing me the hammer before climbing back down the ladder. "You were always doodling away in your sketch pad. While other kids were drawing ponies, you were drawing houses." He reaches the bottom of the ladder and turns around to look at me. "Remember when our neighbors in Bloomington brought over that bagful of LEGOs? You sat there for hours every day, building houses and shops and even a three-story hotel," he says with amazement. "You were only about eight. I always knew you'd grow up to do something creative."

I smile at him as I grab a couple of nails from the box and climb the ladder. We've been taking turns.

"I'll tell you what, if that boss of yours doesn't realize how lucky he is, you should stick it to him and get another job."

I snort and hold the nail steady as I tap it with the hammer, lightly at first, then with more purpose. "Architectural jobs at cool practices aren't exactly falling out of the sky at the moment. Not where I live, anyway."

"Could you move to another area? Have a change of scenery?"

"I *am* having a change of scenery. I needed to get away because I kept bumping into Scott and his new girlfriend. But despite him living in the same town as me, I like where we settled. I'm not ready to pack up and move yet. I'd feel too bitter, as though I'd been forced to leave when *he's* the one who left *me*."

Dad makes a noise of compassion as he passes up the lights. I hook the cable over the nail, adjusting it so it hangs at around the same height as the last couple of lengths we've strung up.

"These drawings you've been asked to do . . . Would you have to visit the site much?" Dad asks.

"No, not at all. We have all the surveys and loads of pictures."

"Could you do this work from anywhere?" Dad asks as I come down the ladder.

I turn to face him, tucking my hair behind my ears. "Theoretically, yes."

"Why don't you ask your boss if you can stay here for the summer? Two weeks isn't nearly long enough for a real break."

I stare into his hazel eyes, the same shade as mine, and realize that Graham would probably agree to it if I made this suggestion. I could easily do the drawings remotely and it would soften the blow of having Lucinda Beale bump me off her job.

But does Dad mean it? Would he like me to stay? The idea of spending the summer here in Indiana is extremely tempting, but then reality kicks in.

"I wouldn't want to encroach on your space," I say awkwardly, picking up the ladder.

Not just his space, but Sheryl's. *Especially* Sheryl's.

"You wouldn't be encroaching," he claims as he follows me to the far corner of the barn, a kind of nervous energy radiating from him. "You're my daughter! Maybe some more time away would have you feeling inspired again. You could get a new pad, do some sketching. At the very least, you could tackle these drawings in a nice setting." He carries on talking as I climb the ladder. "We could put a desk upstairs in front of one of your dormer windows so you'd have a view out over the farmland."

Would I see Anders again? I chide myself for wondering. I don't need another man to be taking up any more of my mental headspace.

But I *would* have time to renovate the Airstream. *That* thought fills me with joy. I forgot to close it up when I got back from the Fredrickson farm on Sunday, but even with the extra airing out, it still stank the following morning. What I wouldn't give to be able to rip out all that rotten stuff and start again . . .

Mum would be okay. She has a new boyfriend, Keith, and things seem to be going well with them. I'm sure she'd encourage me to take the extra time.

"I think you'd better speak to Sheryl before you make any promises," I say as I come back down the ladder.

His mood deflates slightly and I feel guilty for not being a bit more enthusiastic. A bit more impulsive. A bit more like Bailey.

But I don't want to get my hopes up unless I know that Sheryl is one hundred percent on board with the idea, and there's every chance she won't be. I once stayed for a month when I was younger and the tension in the house felt unbearable after only two weeks, so after that I shortened the length of my visits.

"You do the honors." I point at the plug socket.

"No way. You," Dad replies.

I walk over to the wall and pause for a moment, my hand on the switch.

"Can you imagine if they didn't turn on?" I ask with a smile.

"Don't keep us in suspense."

I flick the switch and the barn is illuminated with the warm glow of two hundred bulbs zigzagging above our heads. The effect is beautiful.

I glance at Dad to see him staring up in wonder, the lights reflected in his eyes, and I'm overcome with a sudden urge to go and give him a hug.

Would he really like me to stay with him for the summer?

"Sheryl is going to love this," he says. "Let me go get her."

I stay where I am as he hurries out of the barn.

10

OPENING DAY TAKES US ALL BY SURPRISE. WAY more townsfolk come than expected and the event has a gorgeous summer-party feel about it, with music playing in the barn and children tearing around.

Bailey and Casey join us, as well as Casey's parents and his brother, who are all as genial as Casey. Peggy and Patrik also drop in, but there's no sign of Jonas. I overhear Peggy telling someone that Anders is at a race in Toronto today, but she doesn't enlighten them as to her elder son's whereabouts. When we speak, she asks if I've been on any more walks around their property. I tell her I haven't dared in case I get told off by one of her boys. She laughs and assures me that I can wander wherever I please. I promise to take her up on the offer.

LATER THAT EVENING, I do exactly that, after the heat from the sun has died down to a more bearable temperature. I walk down the track, keeping my eyes averted as I pass the Fredrickson farmhouse in case anyone is by a window. I don't want to invade their privacy, but I worry less about taking in my surroundings once I reach the Fredricksons' barn.

Behind it are two giant steel sheds and the door of the first one is open, revealing a large green tractor near the entrance. To the right are two big silver grain silos with conical-shaped hats that remind me of the head of the Tin Man from *The Wizard of Oz*, minus his facial features.

There's some kind of junkyard farther along, but my attention is diverted by a line of trees at the bottom of the hill and a silvery snake of water. As the dirt track is swallowed up by grass, I continue walking, keen to take a closer look.

I soon find that what I thought might be a large stream is in fact a small river that runs parallel to the main road at the top of the track. The water is running freely.

It's rocky by the bank and I climb up on a boulder, trying to get a closer look at the water. Is it deep enough to go swimming? I smile at the discovery of a rope, old and frayed at the edges, dangling from a thick branch. I bet Anders and Jonas used to swing from that when they were younger.

The thought of taking a dip here on a hot day is appealing. I quite fancy taking my shoes off now and having a paddle and am seriously contemplating doing this when a twig cracks behind me. Startled, I look over my shoulder and find a great big hulk of a man standing in the shadows.

My heart leaps into my throat at the same moment he says, "Don't slip."

But I'm so terrified, I do exactly that, my scream ringing out through the treetops as I slide off the rock and into the river.

JONAS IS LAUGHING at me.

"Aargh, it's cold!" I gasp, flailing toward the bank. The water is only waist-deep, but my top half was drenched by the splash from my fall.

"Are you okay?" Jonas asks, his eyes wide as he clambers over the rocks to the water's edge.

"You frightened me!" I yell at him.

I must look like a drowned rat—my brown hair is hanging limply past my jaw in wet strands.

"I'm sorry." He holds out his hand and seems contrite, but I can tell he's struggling to keep a straight face. "I thought it would be worse if I didn't say anything and then you saw me and freaked out."

"I don't actually think there was a clever way to handle that," I mutter, taking his hand.

He hauls me straight from the water, as if I weigh next to nothing. I jump up and down on a rock, trying to warm myself, and my no-longer-quite-white trainers squelch and squeak with the movement.

Jonas looks down at them and chuckles.

"I'm glad I amuse you," I say darkly.

I'm teasing, because the situation is obviously very funny, but instead of laughing more as I expect him to, my comment seems to sober him.

The sound of a ringtone breaks our awkward moment. He sighs and digs his phone out of his back pocket. The screen is lit up with a picture of Anders pulling a goofy face. Jonas stares at it and I do too—he looks younger in the picture, maybe in his mid-twenties.

"You're not going to answer that?" I prompt.

He shakes his head and shoves the phone back into his pocket. "What are you doing down here?"

"I went for a walk. Your mum said I could, remember? She ran it by you when we were in the shelter. I hope that's okay."

"Yeah, I don't care," he replies glibly as his phone starts to ring again. He sighs and answers this time with what sounds like "Yello."

"I've called you like a million times, bro!" I hear Anders berate him.

"What's up?"

"Where have you been?"

"I thought you were at a race today."

"I am! Why didn't you answer?"

"I've been out."

"Where?"

"I went for a walk. Bumped into Wren, actually." Jonas casts me a look, raising one eyebrow.

There's silence at the other end of the line.

"Wren?" Anders asks at last.

"Yeah. She's right here."

"Put her on."

My insides squirm as Jonas offers up his phone. "He wants to talk to you," he prompts.

I tentatively put the device to my ear. "Hello?"

"What are you doing with my brother?" Anders demands to know.

Is he angry? Why?

"Nothing. I bumped into him down by the river." I sound defensive.

Jonas is walking out from under the trees, but I stay where I am, shivering in my wet clothes on the rocky bank.

"What was he doing there?"

"I don't know."

"Did he have anything with him? Is he okay?"

I realize then that he's not angry—I've got it wrong again. He's worried.

"He's fine, I think." I watch as Jonas comes to a stop at the edge of a field. It's muddy, greenery barely breaking through the soil.

"What's your number?" Anders jolts my attention back to him. "Can we talk later, when you're alone?"

"Um, yeah, I guess so." I relay my contact details, my heart picking up the pace.

"I'm calling you now so you have mine. Call me back when you get a chance."

He ends the call and a few seconds later I feel my phone buzzing in my pocket. It stops again almost immediately. Thankfully, it's waterproof.

I squelch my way over to where Jonas is standing.

"You all right?" I peer up at him. He's so tall, it's crazy.

He nods, staring at the field. He's wearing a faded yellow T-shirt that's ripped at the shoulder and grubby jeans that look as though they haven't seen the inside of a washing machine in months. His brown hair has separated into distinct waves, the way hair does when it hasn't been subjected to shampoo in a while. Definitely more caveman, less model.

"Your brother worries about you," I say as I hand back his phone.

"I wish he wouldn't."

He has such a deep voice. It's several keys lower than his brother's on the octave scale, and his Midwestern accent is stronger.

"Shouldn't he?"

He doesn't answer, pocketing the device. It's not a very reassuring response.

I sigh and look down at my appearance. "Guess I'll be getting home, then."

"Do you want my T-shirt?"

"No, thanks, I'll be fine."

I appreciate the offer, but it's warmer out here, away from the shade of the trees. Anyway, it would feel superweird if he stripped off his top and walked home half naked.

"I'll give you a lift when we reach the farm," he says.

"That would be great. Not on a motorbike, though, I hope."

He snorts. "I forgot my brother got you on the back of his."

"It was that or a tornado."

As memories of Anders come back to me, my stomach is hit by a flurry of nerves. He wants me to call him. I assumed I'd seen and heard the last of him.

"Was there any damage to the farm after the storm?" I ask as we set off.

"Nothing bad, at least not to the property, but it looks like we've lost a cornfield." He nods at my squeaking trainers. "You should take those off. You'll get a blister."

He's right. He waits while I wobble around, yanking off my wet shoes and socks, one after the other.

"Which field of corn was it?" I ask as we set off again.

"The one along the track between our farm and yours."

"How can you tell there's anything wrong with it?" I hadn't noticed any stalks lying down when I'd walked past earlier.

"Hail damage to the tassels."

"What are *tassels*? Sorry, I know nothing about farming, but I'm interested."

"They're the flowers that sprout from the top of the stalks." He points at the field of maize in the distance. "The pollen falls onto the ears of corn and pollinates the silks. Without tassels there'd be no corn kernels. Luckily, hail's highly localized, so it skipped the other fields."

"So what will you do? Will you take it out and plant something else?"

He shakes his head. "It's too late in the season for that now. We'll leave it and harvest it with the rest of the fields."

"You could create a maize maze!" I exclaim.

He glances down at me, his heavy brow furrowing. His eyes are a very dark blue. "A what? Amaze amaze?"

"A *maize* maze," I repeat with a grin, swinging my trainers in my hands and hoping they'll dry out a bit.

I'm enjoying the feel of the ground beneath my feet. It's been so long since I've walked anywhere without shoes and socks on.

"Oh, *maize*." He gets what I'm saying. "That's what you call corn in the UK."

"That's right."

"Yeah, I can just see my dad going for that."

His tone is as arid as the desert sands in Phoenix, but I'm undeterred.

"Think about it. People could come to Wetherill to pick our pumpkins and then visit your maize maze afterward. Or corn maze—whatever you want to call it."

He humphs. A moment later he says, "I'm going to run ahead and grab the Gator."

I guess he didn't like that idea very much.

PULLING ON A fluffy white robe after showering, I return to the bedroom with my phone and perch on the end of the bed. I'm all fidgety and nervous.

Anders answers on the second ring. "Hi, Wren."

At the sound of his quiet, deep voice, my nerves seem to settle.

"Hi."

"Are you home?"

"Yes."

"Did Jonas walk you?"

"He drove me in the Gator. Why?"

"Just wondering." His tone is softer than earlier and suddenly I can see him, clear as day, inside my mind, raking his hand through his hair and staring after me as I walked away through his parents' gate. "Thanks for calling," he says. "I was worried."

I hug my free arm around my waist. "He seemed okay."

"What was he doing down by the river?" he wonders aloud. "Did he have anything with him?"

"Not that I saw." He's already asked that. "What sort of thing were you thinking?"

"I don't know, a rope . . ."

The jittery, light feeling that's been building inside my chest is slammed out by a block of ice.

"Are you serious?" I ask.

"I'm sorry, I didn't mean to freak you out."

"No, I mean, you really think he could do something like that?"

I picture the rope swing fixed to the branch and switch it out with a noose, the mental image filling me with horror.

"I hope not, but you never truly know what's going on inside another person's head."

"He really did seem okay just now," I try to reassure him as well as myself. "We were talking about farming."

"He puts on a good act for strangers."

"Is he depressed?"

"Undoubtedly."

"Do you know why?"

"Loads of reasons. He feels isolated, trapped, overwhelmed, out of control . . . If that tornado had torn through the farm . . . I don't even want to think about the consequences of something like that. Just the debris alone caused a lot of extra work. If it's not cleared from the fields, it can damage farm equipment during harvest."

"He was telling me he'd lost a cornfield to hail and that the river flooded last month and ruined some of the soybeans." He mentioned this last part on the drive home.

"Yeah. Can you imagine how soul-destroying it was for him to work all hours harvesting wheat, drilling and fertilizing the fields, washing the combine harvester and headers and putting them all away, thinking that the hard work was done for the summer, and then having to get everything out again to replant forty acres? It's so much work, and that's not even taking into account the financial loss."

He sounds so sorry for his brother.

"No wonder he feels overwhelmed right now," I murmur.

Anders must feel overwhelmed too—*and* helpless and out of control, especially if he can't get time off work to come home and support his family.

"Yeah, it's no surprise depression is so common among farmers. But most are too stubborn to get help, my brother included."

"Did he always want to be a farmer?" I shuffle back on the bed until I'm propped up against the pillows.

"He was happy about it when we were growing up, always wanting to get stuck in, do stuff around the farm. Even when he lost a chunk of his finger, he was back at work within a couple of days."

"How did he do that?" I ask with alarm.

"Sliced into it with an auger."

"What's that?"

"It's a spiral-shaped tool that's used to drill into the ground. We were putting a fence in."

"We?"

"I was helping him."

"How old were *you*?"

"Ten. He was twelve."

"Ten and twelve?"

"Yeah. He got his sleeve caught. Luckily, I was there to turn the damn thing off or he probably would have lost his whole hand."

"Where were your parents?" My tone has been growing more shocked with every question.

"They didn't know what we were up to," he replies airily. "Jonas had got it into his head that he wanted ducks, so we decided to put in a pen first and ask our parents later."

My smile is sudden, my heart expanding at the thought of them as boys, setting their sights on a goal. "I hope they agreed to the ducks after all that."

"No, they said we could get a dog instead."

"Aw."

I like him. There's no denying it. I like Jonas too, but there's something about Anders that draws me to him on a different level. He's much more my type, a bit more cultivated and less ruggedly masculine than his brother. Every time we speak, I feel a little bit more awake, a little bit more alive.

It's just as well we're unlikely to cross paths again while I'm here. My heart couldn't cope with another upheaval right now, and an unrequited crush—or even a holiday fling—wouldn't do me any good at all.

The line has gone quiet. I hear Anders draw a long, slow breath.

A thought comes to me, something I feel I should mention.

"Anders," I say carefully. "There's a length of rope hanging from a branch down by the river."

"It's a swing. We used to play on it as kids."

"Do you want me to . . . I don't know . . . climb up there somehow and cut it down?"

"How do you think you're going to do that?" He sounds amused. "Hop out along the branch like a little bird?"

I let out a huff.

"I'm kidding. I'm sorry. If he wanted to take that way out, he wouldn't bother with that old rope, he'd use a new one."

My stomach turns over at the visual that claws its way into my head.

"Fuck," Anders mutters, joking over.

"My dad used to call me Little Bird." I latch on to the first change of subject I can think of.

"What?" He's still distracted by his dark thoughts.

"You teased me about hopping out on the branch like a little bird. It's what my dad used to call me when I was younger: Little Bird."

"He doesn't anymore?"

"Not since my parents split up."

"When was that?"

"I was about five or six. He left when Sheryl fell pregnant with my half sister."

"Was she with you at the bar that night?"

"Yes, that was Bailey."

"I recognized the guy you both were with."

I thought he barely looked at us.

"Her husband, Casey."

"I think we went to the same school."

"You did," I confirm.

"You know that for sure?"

Walked right into that one.

"He mentioned you and Jonas." I try to explain how I have any knowledge of him without making it sound as though I had asked. "He told us your family owned the farm next to Dad."

"Ah. So that's how you knew who we were."

I hear knocking in the background, along with a muffled shout.

"Hang on. I'm coming!" Anders calls back, covering the receiver.

"You've got to go?"

I don't want the conversation to end.

"Yeah, I told the guys I'd go for a beer."

"Your teammates? Are you celebrating or commiserating?"

"Celebrating," he replies. "We won."

"Congratulations."

"Thanks. Hey, and thanks . . . Thanks for calling me back. I appreciate it."

"Anytime."

"When are you going home?"

"Thursday."

There's been no more talk of me staying. Either Dad hasn't raised the subject with Sheryl or she's already dismissed the idea.

"Well, have a safe trip," he says. "Maybe I'll see you next time you're in town."

"Maybe."

But knowing what I do about his busy racing schedule and how rare it is for me to be able to visit, there's every chance we won't see each other ever again.

11

A S SOON AS I HANG UP, THE DOOR BANGS OPEN.

"Don't you knock?" I squawk at Bailey.

It's a stupid question. Bailey never knocks.

"What are you doing here?" I ask.

"Casey's hanging out with his brother. I was bored. Who were you talking to?" She comes in wearing a cheeky smile.

I glare up at her. "Were you listening at the door?"

"Not for long. I didn't want to interrupt. I thought you might be on the phone with Scott."

Finally, he gets a mention.

"Not likely," I mutter, tugging my robe more tightly around my chest.

"So, who was it?"

"Stop being such a busybody!" I berate her, edging off the bed. I should probably get dressed.

"Wren!" she snaps, giving my shoulder a shove and causing me to fall backward onto the mattress. "Why are you no fun?"

"Excuse me?" I reply indignantly, half laughing as I sit back up again.

This is the Bailey I know from my teenage years.

She pushes me backward again.

"Stop that!"

"Just tell me!"

"No! Bugger off!"

"Damn, you're annoying," she erupts, flopping onto the mattress beside me.

"*I'm* annoying?" I ask with disbelief, sitting up again. I feel as though we've jumped back in time.

"Yeah, yeah, I know you've always thought I'm a pain in the ass."

She casts her eyes to the ceiling as I stand up and go to the dresser. I don't deny it, because it's true. Or at least, it certainly used to be.

I get some clean clothes out, intending to go to the bathroom to change, but when I turn around, Bailey is looking wounded. She spies the photo album on my bedside table and perks up.

"I remember this!" she exclaims, pulling it onto her lap and opening it up. "I used to look through it all the time."

"You did?" I ask with surprise, pausing at the door.

"Yeah! I loved these photos of you."

"Really?"

"Yes!" she repeats insistently, turning the page. "Mom used to get this look on her face whenever she saw me with it, all pursed lips and tight eyes." She grins at the description and continues perusing. "I hid it under my bed for a while until she found it and put it away somewhere."

"Dad told me he uncovered it in a box."

"That sounds about right. Mom was so jealous."

I'm outraged. "How could *she* be jealous? He left *us* for *her*!" *And you* . . . I add silently inside my head.

Bailey shrugs. "Jealousy isn't always rational. I'm sure she had a whole lot of guilt too, that she wouldn't have known how to channel."

"I can't believe she hid it away," I grumble, dumping my clothes on the bed and taking the album from Bailey's grasp. "I don't know if I've ever even seen these pictures before."

Bailey's brow furrows. "That sucks. Do you remember much about your parents' divorce?"

"Yeah, a fair bit."

"What was it like?"

"Hell."

She stares up at me, her big brown eyes serious. "Do you resent us for it?"

It's the most direct, most personal question she's ever asked me. And I don't know why she's asking it now. It feels as though it's coming out of the blue, yet at the same time, I can't believe we've got to this age without talking about it.

Are we doing this? She's still staring at me, her gaze open and unflinching.

"Yes," I reply.

Her shoulders slump. She studies her nails, turning them this way and that. They're short, filed into a gentle arc and painted coral pink. The color contrasts prettily with her tanned skin.

"I thought so."

"I know that's unreasonable, though." I shove my clothes aside and sit down on the bed, drawing up my knees so I'm facing her. "It's hardly your fault, is it?"

She sighs. "I can't imagine what it must have been like for you, getting on a plane, all on your own, flying all the way over here to see your dad. I always used to think of you as my brave supersister. I wanted you to like me, so much. But you could barely stand the sight of me."

"That's not true," I reply with a frown, grappling with her heart-on-her-sleeve admission. Her honesty has a domino effect and I find myself wanting to open up in turn. "You were cute, a lot of the time. I was just . . . Well, *I* was jealous. You had Dad and your mum. I had Mum and hardly anything of Dad. I felt like an outsider. I still do."

She recoils. "You don't, do you?"

"I do." My voice comes out sounding small. "Even things like you sitting next to Dad at the table last week make me feel left out."

I can't believe I've confessed this, and as soon as her eyes widen, I regret it.

"But *you* sat down there, Wren! I placed that setting for *me*!"

"Did you?"

"Yes!"

Okay, now I'm surprised.

I cast my mind back, trying to work out how I came to be sitting at the end of the table instead of next to Dad as I had been in the days previously. I was so sure that the place at the end of the table, out on its own, was meant for me.

Am I at fault here? Am I so used to telling myself I'll always come second that I'm fulfilling my own prophecy?

"Dad loves it when you come to visit," Bailey is saying. "*I* love it when you come. My *mom* loves it!"

"Come on, no, she doesn't," I can't help but interrupt. "She tolerates it, but *likes* it, let alone *loves* it, is a stretch."

"Oh my God, you are *so* wrong!" Bailey exclaims. "You have no idea how stressed she used to get, worrying what you'd think of her. She was *desperate* for you to like her! You should have seen her, cleaning the house like a maniac, dusting down every single inch of it, *and* putting fresh flowers in your room. *I* never got fresh flowers."

On cue, we both look at the small vase of roses sitting on the dresser. I'd taken them for granted, barely even acknowledged their existence. But now it dawns on me: Sheryl put those there. Sheryl went out into her garden, chose five perfect rosebuds, cut them, and put them in a vase. For *me*.

"But I always feel like a visitor," I say with bewilderment, my head not quite able to process what Bailey is saying.

"You *are* a visitor," she replies. "You're never, *ever* here long enough. I'd give anything for you to be able to spend more time with us."

"I wish I *could* stay longer. I'd love to hang here for a few more weeks, but you know, *work*." I hold back from telling her about Dad's suggestion.

"You don't even *like* your job at the moment."

We talked about this at Dirk's.

"Yeah, but I can't just quit. I have rent to pay. And I can't move out until our lease expires. I don't even *want* to move out, but I can't face getting a flatmate, yet."

"Fucking Scott," she mutters.

"Yeah. Fucking Scott," I agree.

"I'm sorry he was such a dick to you," Bailey murmurs.

I smile at her, even as my eyes prick with tears. "At least he's still helping to pay the rent for a while."

"So he should. It's the least he can do."

I nod. "He's probably still feeling guilty."

"Will you tell me what happened?" she asks seriously.

"You really want to know?"

"I do. I wanted to ask you about him that first night we went out, but I didn't want to upset you."

"Don't worry, I didn't want to talk about him then anyway."

She listens with compassion and empathy as I tell her about that day at the park and the conversation Scott and I had afterward.

"He said he felt I sometimes looked down on him." I screw up my nose, because I'm embarrassed to admit this part.

"Did you?"

"No! Of course not! But I get the feeling Nadine looked *up* to him, and maybe he needed more of that. I never hung off his every word or constantly sought his opinion. Perhaps I never looked at him completely adoringly either. We were equals. I thought that was a good thing."

"*Were* you equals, though?" Bailey asks astutely, narrowing her eyes.

"Salary-wise, we were pretty much on a par." Architecture really doesn't pay that well considering the seven years of training it takes to become fully qualified. "But he *was* intimidated by the fact that I was an architect." As professions go, mine can seem a little daunting. "I don't know. Maybe I *did* get a bit snappy when I felt that he didn't understand the pressures I was under. And maybe I did come across as a little patronizing when I accused him of not getting it."

"Nah. He's just an insecure jerk," Bailey replies loyally.

I can't help but laugh.

"Anyway, enough about Scott," I decide abruptly.

"Fine, we'll talk about something else," she agrees. "Who were you on the phone with?"

I grab a pillow and whack her with it.

She bats it away, undeterred. "Oh, *please* let me live vicariously through you!" she begs. "I've been with Casey for four years. I'm bored!"

"No, you're not."

"Yes, I am."

I turn on my side and prop myself up on one elbow, my head resting on my hand. "Are things not okay between you?"

"They're fine," she replies, chewing one of her nails.

"Don't do that, you'll ruin your manicure," I chide.

She obeys, pulling her finger out of her mouth and then lying down beside me so we're facing each other.

A tiny bottle of something carbonated opens up inside me. It has felt so good to talk like this, on a deeper level. As with my dad, I've only ever had a surface-level relationship with my sister, but I realize that I'd like to change that.

"Wren! Bailey!" Sheryl calls up the stairs.

"Yes?" we shout back in unison, shooting our heads toward the door like a couple of meerkats in sync.

"Anyone for a drink?" Sheryl asks.

Bailey and I look at each other and grin.

"Yes!" we shout back simultaneously, giggling as we scramble off the bed.

"This conversation is to be continued," I warn, gathering up my clothes because I *still* need to get dressed.

She nods. "Whatever you say, sis, whatever you say."

12

ON MONDAY MORNING, BEFORE I EVEN GET OUT of bed, I ring my boss and tell him that I'm happy for my colleague Freddie to take over the Beale house. I'll tackle the tender drawings for the primary school. Graham is thrilled to hear it. Throwing caution to the wind, I ask if he might let me work remotely.

"I don't see why not," he replies. "Why, are you thinking of staying over there longer?"

"I'm not sure yet, but I'd love to have the option."

"It's a great idea. I can email you everything you'll need."

"Thank you so much."

"I'm glad it's all worked out."

I don't mention the call at breakfast, but after Saturday night's conversation with Bailey and the cozy evening that followed with all four of us staying up and chatting until late, I feel a bit more inclined to ask Sheryl if she'd mind me extending my stay. I decide to bring it up tonight if Dad doesn't broach the subject in the meantime.

I'M IN BAMBI that afternoon when Sheryl hunts me out.

"Did I miss a customer?" I ask.

I've been taking turns with Dad and Sheryl to serve people. I'm not expected to help, but I quite enjoy playing shop. We can hear when cars come down the track, and failing that, customers can ring a bell that sounds in the house, so no one needs to spend hours in the barn alone.

"No, no." She shakes her head.

She's wearing blue denim overalls over a red T-shirt. It's an outfit I hadn't seen before this summer, but one she's worn every other day since I arrived. There's a dusting of flour on the fabric and flecks of batter in her short gray bob. She was making a cake earlier.

"I was wondering what you were up to." She places her hands on her hips and surveys all the junk I've pulled away from the Airstream.

"Sorry about the mess. It's a work in progress. I want to move some of this stuff to the back of the barn, out of sight, but a lot of it is too heavy."

"I can give you a hand if you like?"

"Really?"

"Of course. We can get your dad out here too. In fact, maybe Jonas could bring over his tractor for those pieces." She nods at the rusty farm equipment. "He might have a use for some of it."

I wouldn't want to burden him with it right now, knowing what I do.

"You really must love Airstreams if you're willing to put in all this effort," Sheryl muses.

"I do. It feels like such a travesty to see this one hidden away under a tarp. I doubt I'll get much done in the next few days, though." *Hint, hint.* "Everything okay with you?" I ask. "Is there anything I can help you with?"

She looks momentarily uncomfortable and I get the feeling she has something to say.

Oh no, what have I done wrong?

"Ralph mentioned you might like to stay a bit longer."

Here we go . . .

I shrug indifferently, but my heart squeezes at the pained look on her face.

"I don't have to."

"No, I'd *like* you to. *We'd* like you to."

I glance at her with surprise.

"You're always welcome here."

Even after everything Bailey said, I have my doubts about this, and they're not helped by the way her eyes dart away from me.

"My boss did say I could work remotely," I admit hesitantly. "But I wouldn't want to impose. I mean, I'd only stay another week or two if I did change my flight," I add quickly.

"You are welcome to stay for as long as you like," she tells me firmly. "I mean it, Wren."

I must not look convinced, but then her expression is not at all convincing, and if it's this hard for her . . .

"I noticed you found your old photo album," she says unexpectedly. "Bailey reminded me that I took it away. That I put it in a storage box. That you hadn't seen it in all these years."

My stomach contracts.

"I'm sorry, honey," Sheryl murmurs.

I belatedly realize that, while the emotion I'm seeing on her face is undoubtedly discomfort, it's not discomfort due to the idea of me staying. She's *ashamed*.

"That was the wrong thing for me to do," she continues. "I'd forgotten all about it, but that's no excuse. I'm sorry."

I'm so taken aback by her apology that I feel dizzy.

"That's okay," I mumble.

"No. It's not. It's going to take more than a simple sorry to make up for that and all the other mistakes I made when you were younger. But I hope I can make up for some of them now."

She meets my eyes and, this time, holds my gaze.

Suddenly, I'm blinking back tears.

"Come here," she says huskily, and then I'm in her arms and *Sheryl* is hugging me, comforting me, just like my mother would. It's the first time she's ever instigated real, substantial physical contact with me.

"Please stay," she murmurs into my ear. "I would *like* you to."

I nod against her shoulder and my voice is muffled when I reply, "I'd really like that too. Thank you."

13

THE LIGHT IS PALE AND GRAY AND IT MUST BE VERY early in the morning, but I feel wide awake. It's Friday and I should be back in Bury St. Edmunds by now, but I'm not. I'm still here in Southern Indiana, smiling at the ceiling.

Bailey wants to go to Dirk's again later—she was so happy when I told her I was staying. It will probably be another late one, but there's no chance at all of me falling back asleep now. What *is* the time?

As I reach for my phone to check, I catch sight of flashing red and blue lights bouncing off the white wall at the edge of the blinds. My heart lurches and I leap out of bed, shoving the blinds aside in time to see an ambulance heading in the direction of the Fredrickson farm. All my joy is swallowed up by dread as I remember the guns that Anders removed and the rope he was worried his brother might have taken down to the river. Peggy called Anders home for a reason—they all had cause for concern.

Please, please, please don't let that ambulance be for Jonas.

The lights were flashing, but there was no siren. Is that because the roads are quiet? Or is there no need for urgency?

What sort of living hell might Anders and his parents be in right now if that ambulance *is* for Jonas and it's already too late?

I fight the urge to pull on clothes and walk down to the farm. Whatever has happened to that family is none of my business.

Eventually the ambulance comes past again, its lights flashing and its siren still silent.

NEWS COMES AT ten thirty that morning after the most sickening wait. The ambulance was for Patrik: he had a nonfatal heart attack in the early hours of the morning, but will likely make a full recovery. Sheryl flagged down Jonas as he was taking a bag to the hospital.

Despite being concerned about Patrik, I'm light-headed with relief for the rest of the day.

IN THE EVENING, I wander down to the Fredrickson farm with a basket of peaches and a "Get Well Soon" card from us all. Sheryl asked me to leave them on the doorstep if no one answers.

I'm at the gate before I see him—Anders—sitting on the front steps, with his elbows on his knees and his head in his hands.

My stomach does cartwheels.

It did occur to me that he might make the two-hour journey back from Indy, but I didn't want to think on it too much. I'd convinced myself that I probably wouldn't see him again this summer, even though I'm now staying.

He looks up slowly at the sound of my footsteps, his expression bleak as he watches me approach.

"Hi," I say as I reach him.

His eyes have widened slightly, but other than that, his features remain unchanged.

"You're still here," he notes in a low voice, staring up at me with his flawed green eyes.

I nod, feeling as though his look has somehow entered my bloodstream, warming me up, *waking* me up. It's an effort to find my voice.

"I'm so sorry about your dad." I offer up the peaches. "These are for him."

He stares at the basket for a couple of seconds before reaching out and taking it from me. He does this unhurriedly, as though his brain is taking a while to instruct his limbs.

"Thank you," he replies in a gruff voice, placing it on the doorstep behind him.

There's an open bottle of beer at his side.

"Where's Jonas?" I ask.

His temple twitches as he swipes the bottle. "I have no idea," he mutters. "Somewhere out there." He nods past me at the vast green fields and glugs down a few mouthfuls of his beer.

"And your mum?"

"Bed. She was up half the night."

I hesitate before asking, "Do you want some company?" I'm reluctant to leave him like this.

He doesn't answer, doesn't nod or shake his head, but then his broad shoulders lift in a half shrug and he edges over a few inches.

I sit on the step beside him, feeling strangely wound up.

The sky is mottled in shades of gray and white. It's only seven o'clock—sunset is still about two hours away—but the thick cloud cover makes it seem later.

"Weren't you supposed to fly home yesterday?" he asks.

"My boss said I could stay longer and work remotely."

"You don't have anything else to get back to?"

"My mum is in the UK, but she's glad I'm staying."

He glances at me, baffled by the admission.

"She's not glad to see the back of me," I clarify. "She wants me to take some more time for myself. I've just come out of a relationship." I wasn't planning on going into detail, but the more I say, the more I feel I have to explain.

Anders nods and lifts up his bottle to inspect the level of beer inside. "You want a beer?" he asks, getting to his feet and picking up the basket.

He's wearing a petrol-blue T-shirt and his black jeans are dusty from where he's been sitting on the step. My black dress will suffer the same fate.

"Sure."

He exhales heavily as he opens the mesh screen door and lets it fall shut behind him with a clatter. I sit there nervously until he returns, passing me a beer and sitting back down. I resist the urge to knock my bottle against his out of habit. It's not really the occasion for "cheers."

"This is going to stress Jonas out even more, isn't it?" I murmur empathetically.

He nods and swigs from his beer.

"Would your family ever think about selling?"

He pulls the bottle away from his lips on a laugh and looks at me, and it's not happy humor I see on his face.

"I'm sorry if that's a stupid question."

He shakes his head and picks a fleck of mud off his jeans. "No, it's not stupid. Not in any normal sense. But this farm has been passed down from oldest son to oldest son ever since our ancestors moved here from Sweden in 1851. Jonas and I were raised knowing we had to protect the family legacy. We have a *duty* to protect it."

"Is it true that all your names are Swedish?"

"Yep. The whole family's: Dad's sister Agata, my grandfather Erik, his father, Aan. I could go on."

I turn around and look up at the red-and-white farmhouse. "Did your ancestors build this house?"

"And the barn," he confirms, jerking his chin toward it. "They're replicas of the farmstead back in Sweden."

"Did *you* ever want to farm?"

"It's not what I'm passionate about, but I'd step up if I had to."

"Really? You'd quit your job?"

He nods.

"You're a mechanic for an IndyCar team, right?"

"No, a race engineer."

"Oh! What does that involve?"

"I'm like the interpreter between the driver and the mechanics." He glances at me to gauge my interest before continuing. "The driver will give me feedback about how the car feels and I analyze all the technical data and work out what we need to do to make sure the car is set up for maximum performance. I relay this to the mechanics and they instigate the changes."

"Wow, that sounds like a really important job. Do you enjoy it?"

"I love it."

"Yet you'd give it up?" I press, struggling to understand.

"If something happened to Jonas, yes." He sighs. "I feel like I should be home right now anyway."

"You can't quit your dream job," I say gently.

He turns to look at me and his expression is so stark, it tears at my heart. "My family is falling apart, Wren. My dad shouldn't be working at his age, Ma's blood pressure is sky-high. Already was—God knows what this is doing to her—and my brother is . . ." He shakes his head desolately and I'm *that close* to reaching out and putting my arm around his shoulders to console him when my phone begins to buzz in my pocket.

I pull it out and curse under my breath at the sight of Bailey's name in the caller ID.

"I'm so sorry," I say to Anders before answering. "I'm coming, I'm sorry!" I tell Bailey before she can demand to know where I am. "I'll be there in five!"

"Meet you at Wetherill."

"Okay. Sorry!" I apologize again, ending the call and looking at Anders. "I really hate to go, but I'm late for my sister. I was supposed to be meeting her on the bridge."

He nods, tilting his bottle to his lips.

"Want to come to Dirk's with us?" I ask on a whim, slightly mesmerized by the sight of his Adam's apple bobbing up and down as he drains his beer. I blink up to his face. "Get out of the house for a bit?"

"I think I'd better hunt down my brother."

"Not on your motorbike, I hope." I stare pointedly at his empty bottle as he sets it aside.

"I've only had two."

"Still, what would your momma say?"

"She knows I know these fields like the back of my hand," he replies, his eyes dancing at my gently mocking tone.

As I stand up and dust myself off, a thought occurs to me. "Is that what you were doing that night? When we met? Were you looking for Jonas?"

"Yep."

I can't believe it's taken me this long to put two and two together.

"And there I was, thinking you were simply the village idiot," I tease.

His lip tugs up at the corner and I feel as though there's an invisible line attaching the gesture to a hook lodged just behind my rib cage.

"Who says I'm not?"

brother and his mom and dad. He couldn't believe his luck when a position came up at the golf club."

"But if you don't want to be here . . ."

"I'll suck it up. Don't look so serious!"

The conversation is still playing inside my head when we arrive at Dirk's.

"All My Favorite Songs" by Weezer is blaring from the speakers. That's the first thing I notice. The second is that Jonas is at the bar.

I tug on Bailey's sleeve. "Hang on."

"What is it?" she asks as I drag her back into the stairwell and get out my phone. "What are you doing?"

"Texting Anders."

"Wait, what? Why do you have Anders's number? Why are you texting him? I have so many questions!"

"I saw him earlier. He was worried about Jonas," I reply absently, tapping out: Jonas is at Dirk's.

I hope he sees the message. Who knows how far he's already roamed, looking for his brother.

I glance up from my phone to find Bailey staring at me demandingly.

"How did you get his number and how is it any of your business? And how do you know Anders? And why do you care about what Jonas is doing? And was that who you were speaking to the other night?" Her eyes are practically bulging out of her head. "*Was* it?"

"Calm down. We went into their storm shelter, remember? And I dropped some peaches around for Patrik earlier. Anders was there. We got talking."

"Is that why you were late?"

14

Y OU'RE STILL IN AMERICA!" BAILEY SQUEALS, HAVING
forgiven me for being late. She hooks her arm through
mine and squeezes me as we walk.

We didn't bother to drive this time and we're almost there:
the town square is at the end of this road.

"You're my bar buddy. My new drinking partner," she says
with a giggle.

"Don't you have any friends your own age?" I ask, my insides radiating at her joy.

"There's one girl at work who's okay. We went out a few
times when Case and I first moved here, but now she's pregnant and no fun at all."

"How are you finding work at the moment?"

"Dull."

"What are you going to do about it?"

She gives me a funny look. "Nothing. This is my life now,"
she adds melodramatically.

I frown at her. "That doesn't sound very good. Have you
talked to Casey about it? Is he happy?"

"Deliriously. He loves being back home, living near his

"Yes, I'm sorry," I repeat. "But I was worried about him and his family. I'm kind of like their neighbor now, remember?"

Her face bursts into a grin. "I can't believe you stayed!"

"I know!" I smile at her, hoping, but also doubting, that that's the end of the Fredrickson-brothers inquisition. "Come on, let's get a drink."

Jonas is still at the bar when we walk through the door. He's hunched over, his elbows resting on the sticky wooden bar top and his hips jutting out to the side as if he's either very relaxed or very drunk. I have a strong feeling it's the latter.

"Hey," I say, touching his arm.

He lifts his head from where he's been staring into his glass and looks at me, his navy eyes glazed. I think it takes him a moment to place me, but eventually his face breaks into a sleepy, lopsided smile.

"Hey, Wren!" he slurs.

"You okay?"

"Yeah, I'm fine. I'm good." He wobbles and puts his hand on the bar to steady himself. It looks as though he's drinking neat whiskey. "I didn't recognize you without wet clothes on. And you have your hair up."

He waggles his finger around in a circle, his eyes roaming around my face.

I never wear my hair up, but I discovered earlier that it's long enough to scoop into a bun.

Most people get their hair cut when they go through a breakup. I decided to grow mine instead. It still falls shy of my shoulders, but the length is a novelty.

"What's this about wet clothes?" Bailey interrupts, her sparkling eyes darting between us.

"Wren fell in the river," Jonas replies, propping up his face with his hand and squishing his cheek into his grin.

"Did you?" Bailey turns to me, eyes in "Boo" mode.

"I'll tell you about it later," I reply, directing my next sentence at Jonas. "Anders was looking for you earlier."

He chuckles and lifts his head. "Anders is always looking for me."

"He worries about you," I remind him gently. "He cares."

Jonas reaches for his drink and looks at Bailey. "You're Ralph and Sheryl's daughter, aren't you?"

"Hi, yes, I'm Bailey." She grins and offers him her hand.

It takes him a second to respond and when he does, his hand dwarfs hers.

I'm surprised they haven't already met, but then, it doesn't sound like he's been particularly sociable lately.

"What can I get you?" Dirk asks, materializing in front of us.

Jonas is still shaking Bailey's hand. She doesn't seem to mind.

"The usual," Bailey replies as Jonas finally releases his grip.

"Which is?"

She rolls her eyes, then rallies herself. "Two rum and Cokes, please, Dirk! And whatever *he's* having!"

She could not sound more enthusiastic.

Jonas laughs into his glass, then knocks back the dregs of his whiskey.

At that moment, Anders comes through the door and my stomach does cartwheels for the second time tonight. His gaze alights on us and he doesn't look surprised, so I gather he got my message.

"Hey, bro," he says quietly as he reaches us, giving me a single nod of acknowledgment, a thank-you for the heads-up.

"Heeeyyy, bro!" Jonas replies overenthusiastically.

"Come on, let's go home." Anders squeezes his brother's shoulder.

"I'm not going home," he says. "Bailey has bought me a drink."

Anders glances at Bailey.

"Hiiii." Her smile is coquettish.

"Hi, I'm Anders," he replies shortly.

Dirk places our drinks on the bar.

"Stay for one," I urge Anders softly enough that our siblings can't hear us. Bailey is paying for the round and Jonas is facing the bar. It's clear Anders is not going to be able to get his brother to leave anytime soon.

He sighs and lifts his chin at Dirk.

"Beer?" Dirk asks him.

Anders nods in response.

I turn to Jonas. "Hey, sorry to hear about your dad."

His smile slips a fraction. "Too drunk to care about that right now."

"You do seem to be quite a happy drunk," Bailey muses as Anders digs his hand into his pocket for his wallet.

"I *am* a happy drunk," he agrees. "Unlike our father. He was *not* a happy drunk, was he, *bro*?"

Anders stiffens and glares at him as he taps his credit card to the card reader.

My insides clench. What does *that* mean?

"Anyone up for a game of pool?" Bailey asks.

"Sure," Jonas replies, surprisingly perkily.

"I'm sorry about this," Anders mutters, picking up his beer and walking beside me as we follow Jonas and Bailey over to the pool table.

"It's cool. I invited you to join us earlier, remember? As long as Bailey's happy, I'm happy."

And Bailey does seem happy. She looks absolutely gorgeous tonight in red cotton shorts and a white tank top. It's a simple outfit, but she's so stunning she could wear a potato sack and still look a knockout.

I'm wearing a black shirtdress, its long sleeves rolled up to the elbows, with my now-scrubbed-clean white trainers. It's a more casual outfit than the one I wore the last time I came to Dirk's, but it's still smarter than what most of the people in here are wearing.

I need to go shopping. I only brought my best stuff with me, as you tend to do when you go on holiday, but my wardrobe is not exactly primed for a long, hot summer. Especially not a long, hot summer in grungy bars, which seems to be the destiny Bailey has in mind for me.

Jonas finishes racking up the balls while Bailey stands by, chalking a cue.

"Us against them?" Jonas asks her.

She's tall, at five foot eight, but he towers over her, his milk-chocolate hair falling forward around his temples in messy waves. Despite his inebriation, he looks more put together than the last time I saw him, down by the river.

"Sounds good," Bailey replies.

Anders chalks up a second cue, seemingly resigned to his fate.

Jonas pulls a coin out of his pocket. "Heads or tails?" His eyes move between Anders and me.

"You can break," Anders replies, unsmiling.

"Cheer up, bro." Jonas pockets his coin and walks round to the end of the table. "You wanna break?" he checks with Bailey first.

"No, go ahead."

"I'm crap at pool, sorry," I say to Anders as Jonas sends the balls scattering all around the table. One goes in.

It feels slightly surreal that, two weeks after I first saw him playing in this bar, I'm his partner.

"We're just killing time," Anders mutters.

If I *was* enjoying this turn of events, I'm not so much anymore. He is *so* unhappy to be here.

"You're up," Jonas prompts us.

Anders waves toward me deferentially. I walk up to the table and try to hit a green striped ball, missing the pocket by about half a foot.

I pull a face at him. He raises his eyebrows at me.

Bailey goes next, grinning as her blue spot goes straight in, then yelling with annoyance when the white follows it.

Anders has two shots. He pots a yellow stripe on his first and nothing on his next two.

"You lost your mojo?" Jonas asks him.

Anders shrugs and grabs his beer from where he's placed it on the sill of the high-level window.

Every time Jonas or Bailey pot a ball, Anders evens things out on his next turn. I just do my best to hit one of ours each time.

"You really do suck at pool," Anders muses toward the end of the game.

"Yep, so please can you hurry up and get these last couple in, because I need to go to the bathroom."

We've been trying to pocket these last two balls for a while. I have a feeling Anders could clean up if he wanted to, but he's trying to string this game out for as long as possible.

He walks round to the other side of the table, lines up his shot, and lifts his eyes. My blood zings as the green of his gaze locks with mine. I couldn't look away even if I wanted to. He breaks the contact and shoots the ball straight into a pocket, just as he did the first time he caught me in a stare at this bar, and suddenly I'm remembering another detail from that night: Casey said that Anders was married, that he lost his wife in a car accident.

"Dammit!" Jonas complains when Anders pots the black ball. "Let's go again."

How could I have forgotten?

Anders sighs. "Guess I'll go to the bar, then. What are you drinking?" he asks me.

"Rum and Coke, please," I reply distractedly.

"Bailey?" Anders asks.

"Same, thanks!"

I belatedly realize that he's stopped trying to convince his brother to leave.

"I'll have a whiskey!" Jonas calls after him.

Dirk is finishing up serving Anders when I'm on my way back from the bathroom, so I help him carry the drinks to the others.

"I said *whiskey*," Jonas complains when Anders hands him a beer.

"You're too heavy to carry home," Anders replies.

Jonas tuts with disgust and raises his bottle, preparing to drink. "You guys can go first."

I offer Anders the cue. He shakes his head.

"You want to see me make a fool of myself?"

"Why stop now?" He smirks and folds his arms across his chest, his biceps filling out the sleeves of his T-shirt.

I narrow my eyes at him.

"But I bet you don't make a fool of yourself often," he concedes.

My insides sparkle because he's right. I'm almost always quite composed. Unless I'm drunk. And then I really can't account for my behavior.

I jab my cue at the white ball as hard as I can, but it barely makes a dent in the triangle of colored balls. As I bury my head in my hand in shame, those bloody brothers *and my own sister* laugh at me.

"How did you get to be so good?" I demand to know when Bailey strikes the balls and sends them bouncing off cushions and all over the place.

"Dad taught me," she replies, taking another shot because one went in.

The happy bubbles in my stomach all pop at once. She said it so nonchalantly.

I catch Anders's eye, but he's no longer smiling. I blink and look away, retrieving my drink from a nearby table.

"*I* need to pee now," Bailey declares to the table after Anders and Jonas have taken their turns.

"Me too," Jonas says, leaning his pool cue against the table. "Don't cheat!" he yells back at us, following Bailey as she practically runs off through the bar.

I force a laugh that I'm not really feeling and go to take my shot.

"Do you want some help?" Anders asks me.

I've already given him a mock dirty look before I realize

that he's not being sarcastic. He's standing between two framed tour posters, one for Wolf Alice and the other for Radiohead. Lana Del Rey's "Blue Jeans" is spilling from the speakers, its beat slow and sultry.

"Doesn't really matter if I can play, does it?" I reply shakily. "You do well enough for both of us."

He shrugs and leans against the exposed brick wall, crossing his feet at his ankles. It's a casual gesture, but his eyes remain trained on me, his gaze calm and knowing.

I have a sudden change of heart.

"Go on, then, show me what I'm doing wrong."

He lazily pushes off from the wall and I swear the temperature of the room rises as he approaches me.

"Put your left hand on the table and hold the cue at your waist with your right hand," he quietly instructs. "Relax. You're too tense. Now spread your fingers." He nods at my left hand. "Thumb out. No, your bridge isn't strong enough, you won't be able to shoot straight like that. Look."

I move aside and he puts his left hand on the table, showing me how to create a better rest for the cue.

"Let me try."

He passes the cue back. "Your elbow is like a hinge, it needs to stay more or less in this position."

I jolt as he squeezes my elbow to demonstrate before letting go.

I can still feel the ghost of his touch as I practice moving the cue back and forth. This time, it more or less stays pointed in the same direction.

"If you can hit it here," Anders says, leaning over the table and indicating a point on the left-hand side of a yellow spot, "it'll go straight into that corner pocket."

"I do understand the angles," I tell him.

"Of course you do. You're an architect," he replies with a teasing grin.

My toes curl as I laugh. I try to focus and this time, when I take a shot, the ball goes in.

"Yay!" I cry with elation.

"There you go!" he replies warmly.

I'm about to offer up my hand for a high five when our attention is diverted toward the bar area. Bailey and Jonas are standing there laughing, as Dirk pours what appears to be tequila into two shot glasses. Jonas glances over at us and hastily averts his gaze, saying something in Bailey's ear. She shoots us a guilty look and hunches forward over the bar top, and then the pair of them giggle conspiratorially as they pick up their shot glasses and not-so-surreptitiously clink them.

"Those bastards are doing sneaky shots without us," I murmur.

Bailey downs her shot and starts coughing and Jonas puts his hand on her shoulder, almost pulling her over with the drunken weight of it. This only makes them laugh more.

Beside me, Anders sighs. "I think we're in for a long night."

We meet each other's eyes and he presses his lips together, suppressing a smile.

I can't say I'm upset about it. It seems these brothers could do with blowing off some steam.

15

WE STAY UNTIL CLOSING TIME, WHEN DIRK KICKS us out.

"I've got to get my bike from the parking lot," Anders says to me, calling after Jonas to tell him to wait.

"You're not planning on riding it home, are you?" I ask with alarm, as I follow him around the corner of the building.

He doesn't seem that drunk to me, but I'm pretty sure I can't be trusted to make that judgment call.

"No, I'll walk it back. It's not street-legal so it's bad enough that I rode it here in the first place."

The sound of Jonas heaving his guts up causes us to come to a sudden stop, and at the same time, the back door of the bar flies open.

"Oh, you did not just puke on my hood," Dirk says darkly, standing there with a bulging black garbage bag in his hand and glaring at the elder Fredrickson brother.

"Shit," Anders mutters, because yes, it does indeed appear that Jonas has vomited all over the bonnet of a big red pickup, and from how shiny and clean it looks under the light of the streetlamps, I'm guessing that Dirk's truck is his pride and joy.

"I'm gonna bust open a can of whoop-ass on you!" he hollers, his expression furious as he hurls the garbage into a nearby dumpster.

"We'll clean it up," Anders calls placatingly.

"You goddamn better!" Dirk shouts at him, brandishing his finger at us all. "Or you guys will be banned for the rest of the month!"

As soon as the door bangs shut behind him, Bailey and Jonas glance at each other and crack up laughing.

There's only another week left of July, so they're not taking the threat of punishment very seriously.

Anders stares at me long-sufferingly.

"What's 'a can of whoop-ass'?" I ask him solemnly.

His face breaks out into a grin and a moment later, we both lose it.

I haven't laughed that hard in a long time.

There's a hose by the back door so it's not too difficult for Anders to wash off his brother's vomit. I offer to help, but he waves me away, and the perpetrator of the crime is nowhere to be seen. We can hear him around the corner, in hysterics, with my sister. The sound of their laughter is bouncing off the walls of the surrounding buildings and echoing back at us.

"Has it always been like this?" I ask with amusement as Anders winds the hose back in. "*You* taking care of *him*?"

He shakes his head. "It used to be the other way around. What about you and Bailey? She's a bit younger than you, right?"

"Yes, by six years. But I haven't had much of a chance to be a protective big sister."

He stares at me and nods, an intensity in the depths of his green eyes. When he gets all serious like this it makes my insides go a little funny, but I don't feel a whole lot of relief when he looks away, either.

He goes to grab his motorbike and we set off in the direction of home, Anders wheeling his bike on the road beside me. Bailey and Jonas are up ahead. They're getting on well. Too well? Should I be worried? Should *Casey*?

"How long has Bailey been married?" Anders asks me, as though reading my mind.

"About five months," I reply, my unease growing. "Your brother wouldn't make a move on a married woman, though, would he?"

Casey did say that Jonas had a reputation for sleeping around.

"It hasn't stopped him in the past."

Oh shit. I really hope Bailey wouldn't be cruel or stupid enough to cheat on her husband, but she hasn't exactly been raving about how fulfilled she feels. If she's looking to inject some excitement into her life . . .

Anders shrugs. "I don't know, maybe it's only a line he crosses with his ex."

"His ex is married?"

He nods. "She was his girlfriend when we were in school. Jonas was madly in love with her, thought they'd get married themselves one day, but she left him for another guy when she went to college. She went on to marry this same guy and have kids with him and Jonas has never got over it."

"So they had an affair?" I ask with a frown.

"They were on and off for a while, but she ended it, supposedly for good, a few years ago. Jonas hasn't had a serious relationship since. He's still hung up on her."

"Does she live around here?" For some reason I'm thinking of the woman at the grocery store.

"She actually moved back to town recently," he replies. "I think it's partly why he's been messed up, but he hasn't said anything to me about her. He wouldn't, not since the hell I gave him the last time I suspected they were fooling around. I hear everything Heather-related from Ma these days."

"That's her name? Heather?"

He nods.

"What does she look like?"

"Long dark hair, blue eyes . . ." He glances at me. "Why?"

"I saw Jonas in town about a week ago," I reveal. "He was parked outside a grocery store. There was a dark-haired woman inside, paying. She had a small boy with her."

"How old was the boy?"

"About two."

"She has three kids, but that could be her youngest."

Instead of turning left toward the bridge, Jonas and Bailey head right. I wonder if Jonas has even realized that he's walking her home.

Bailey and Casey's neighborhood is a little run-down, but their house looks shiny and new, with fresh white paint and a bright purple door.

Scott and I were planning to buy a house together, but we couldn't get a mortgage until he could provide two years' worth of company accounts from his relatively new business.

Now he'll probably buy one with Nadine.

That thought doesn't hurt me as much as it would have only a couple of weeks ago. I guess I'm finally feeling better for getting some distance from him and Bury St. Edmunds.

Then again, the present company could have something to do with it.

Bailey spins around and faces us, grinning. "I'd invite you in, but . . . Yeah, no, I can't invite you in."

"Where *is* Casey tonight?" I ask, and I confess, it's a tactical question.

"With Brett. They probably spent the whole night shooting up kids on the PlayStation."

"Who are Casey and Brett?" Jonas interrupts.

"Bailey's husband and his brother," I reply.

Jonas pulls a face at her. "You're *married*?" Job done.

"I know, it's incredibly boring of me," Bailey replies with a shrug.

"Well, see you tomorrow after work, maybe?" I step forward to give her a hug.

"Not tomorrow, we're going to Casey's parents' place, but soon." She looks past me at the brothers. "See you around?"

"Yep," Jonas replies, saluting her before turning away.

Bailey heads up the path to her front door, flashing me a small smile over her shoulder as she goes inside and shuts the door.

I don't know why I feel sorry for her, but I do.

ON SATURDAY AFTERNOON, I head out to the barn to take over for Dad. It's a perfect day, in the mid-twenties with a cool breeze, and being the weekend, it's busy.

I've just finished weighing one family's haul when another family comes in, a man and a woman in their mid-to-late thirties with three young children. The mother seems familiar and suddenly I realize she's the woman Jonas was staring at. Is this Heather?

She's quite beautiful up close, with piercing blue eyes and long dark lashes that may or may not be natural. She's carrying the small boy she had with her at the grocery store on her hip. He has a gorgeous head of light brown curls and is nestled into her shoulder, sucking his thumb.

I say thank you and goodbye to the other customers and smile at the family. "Hi there! Are you here to pick peaches today?"

To my surprise, the woman sniggers.

Her husband, if that's who he is, smiles amiably. "Yes, please."

I guess it *was* a stupid question—why else would they have come?—but it's the welcome Dad and Sheryl have been using and I've adopted it because I thought it seemed like the sort of thing a nice, friendly American peach farmer *would* say.

My smile wavers. "How many baskets would you like?"

"There are five of us, so five," the woman responds, as though I'm dumb for asking.

Okaaay . . . I lift five baskets onto the counter. "Here you go."

"Put that down, please, Jacob," the dad says to their eldest child, a boy of about seven or eight, who's picked up one of the glass jars of Bellini mix. His sister, who's aged somewhere between her brothers, copies him.

"Evie, can you put that down, please?" her dad asks, equally patiently.

"They're fine," the woman snaps. "Come and take the baskets."

"Do we really need five?" he asks her, and obviously I think it's a reasonable question because I was wondering the same thing.

"Just bring them." She stalks out through the open barn door.

"Evie! Jacob!" he calls.

They're still messing around with the jars of peach puree and either haven't heard him or are choosing to ignore him.

"Evie! Jacob!" he calls in that same merry voice. "Come take a basket!"

Evie looks over her shoulder and lets go of the jar she's holding. I gasp as it falls to the floor, but luckily it bounces.

Then, Jacob, noticing what his sister has done, throws his own jar forcefully at his feet.

How it doesn't smash into a million pieces, I do not know, but as he stares at it, still whole, I get the feeling he's disappointed.

"Gently!" the dad says cheerfully as his children run over and each snatch a basket from his waiting hands.

I stare at him, agog.

Isn't he going to tell his children off for dropping the glass jars, or, in his son's case, for *hurling* one at the floor? Isn't he going to check that the jars aren't cracked and offer to pay for them if they are? Isn't he going to, at the very least, put them back on the shelves? *Or say sorry?*

"So we just pick what we want?" he asks as his daughter tries to tug him out the door.

"That's right. Pick only what you plan to pay for," I explain through gritted teeth.

"Gotcha. Come on, then," he says as his son drops his basket on the floor and runs out of the barn. He swoops down to pick it up, adding it to the ridiculous number he's already carrying.

On impulse, I get out my phone and text Anders: The woman who may or may not be Heather is here. I press send, then feel rude for not adding any pleasantries, so I quickly type out another: How's your dad? I hope Jonas isn't feeling too rough today.

Once I've restored the thankfully intact jars to the shelves, I head out to the back of the barn.

With Dad and Sheryl's help this week, we've cleared almost all the junk around Bambi. There are still a few larger pieces of farm machinery to go, but they don't inhibit access, so I've been removing the soft furnishings and ripping out the damp and rotten floor tiles. I think the whole caravan will need to be stripped bare before I'll be able to determine exactly what can be salvaged. Mice are getting in somehow, and, with the mold and damp, I'm assuming there's a leak.

I'm desperate to give the outside a proper wash. It's going to take a hell of a lot of scrubbing to rid it of several decades' worth of grime, but I can't wait to see if the aluminum gleams once it's clean. I still haven't worked out how I'm going to climb up on top to wash the roof. *Fly up there, like a little bird*, I imagine Anders teasing me.

Thinking of Anders, I pull out my phone to see if he's replied. He has.

Text me a pic.

No! I'll look like a freaky stalker! I tap back, smiling.

He hasn't told me how his dad or Jonas are, but no news is good news, I hope.

I return my attention to Bambi.

I'm still buzzing with excitement that I'm getting to do

this, that I'm renovating a vintage Airstream. Scott would have killed to own an Airstream—he'd be beside himself if he was here.

The twinge of pain I usually feel when he comes to mind is muted.

I probably should tell him that I'm staying in Indiana. Mum has agreed to go into the house to water the plants and check up on things, but we still need to sort out the possessions we bought jointly. I don't feel entitled to them simply because *he* left *me*. I gave him his engagement ring back too, within days of him telling me that he'd fallen for Nadine. My ring finger missed it for weeks, felt its absence almost constantly.

It was beautiful—a traditional diamond solitaire—but it wasn't really what I would have chosen for myself, if he'd asked, which he didn't.

Maybe one day I'll be given a ring that I'll love with all my heart. And maybe the man who bestows it on me will be just as perfect a fit for me as I am for him. I hope so.

The important thing is, I have *hope*.

AFTER A WHILE, the family finishes picking peaches, so I head back to the barn.

"Where are the other three baskets?" I ask as the woman places two on the countertop.

"I don't know." She shrugs. "Out in the orchard somewhere."

"Could you bring them back, please?"

"I'll go get them," the man offers.

The woman gives me a dirty look as he jogs out of the barn. I'd like to give her the benefit of the doubt and assume she's having a bad day—it can't be easy with three small children—but I can't help but think that if this is Heather, I don't care much for Jonas's taste. Surely he can do better than this.

The thought of him drunk and merry, as he was last night, lifts my spirits. I wonder if that's what he's normally like, when depression isn't dragging him down.

"Are you from around here?" I ask "Heather" as I set about weighing what they've brought in.

"I grew up here. We've just moved back."

"Oh, right."

Their eldest starts messing around with the Bellini jars again, so she's distracted, and then *I'm* distracted by the sound of a motorbike skidding to a stop in the car park . . .

16

ANDERS COMES INTO THE BARN AFTER THE FAMILY has left. I heard him exchanging a few words with them outside.

He looks surprised to see me standing behind the checkout counter.

"You're *working*? Aren't you supposed to be on vacation?"

"I'm a farmer's daughter now," I reply with my tongue firmly in my cheek, trying to contain my delight at seeing him again so soon.

"I hear you," he says with amusement, placing an empty basket on the counter. "Pa said to say thank you for the peaches."

He's wearing a white T-shirt and navy shorts that come to a couple of inches above his knees. His legs are long and tanned and I really should stop looking at them, but it's the first time I've seen him out of jeans and it's hard.

"How is he?" I ask, managing to drag my eyes northward.

"Good. The doctors are saying he might be out on Monday."

"That's great!"

"Anyway, I thought I'd better bring the basket back."

"And do a little detective work while you're at it? Is it Heather?"

"Afraid so. About as happy to see me as I was her."

"You're not friendly?"

"Did you get the impression she's a friendly type of girl?"

"Can't say I did," I reply with a wry smile, folding down the handles of the wicker basket so I can add it to the stack, along with the other two Heather's husband eventually brought in. The fifth and final one is still out there somewhere. "They left one of their baskets out in the orchard, actually, as well as a few half-eaten peaches." I saw the kids tucking in when I looked over. "I should probably clean up and find the lost basket."

An orchard littered with peaches with bite marks is not a good look. Unsurprisingly, all the ones Heather brought back into the shop were pristine.

"How's Jonas?" I ask as I come out from behind the counter.

"Hungover."

"I bet. Is he okay though?"

"Yeah, not bad," he replies with a shrug, wandering around the side of the barn with me. He stops short at the sight of Bambi. "No way." He glances at me with amazement. "This is Bill and Eileen's old Airstream."

"Were they the last owners of this place?"

"No, the owners before that. I always wondered what happened to it." He runs his fingers over the badge. "It's original, right? Must be, what, early sixties?"

"Yes, Airstream made this model between '61 and '63. They do a modern version now."

"I can't believe it's been here all this time," he says with awe, absentmindedly rubbing his thumb and fingers together to dislodge the dirt. "What a waste."

"It was under a cover. It's not in great shape, but I'm keen to renovate it."

"And then what? Sell it?" He shoots me a look.

"No. Keep it! I've always wanted an Airstream."

"Me too." He walks round to the back, his eyes roving over every inch of the bodywork.

The amber flaw in his eye is even more startling in the sunlight. He rarely meets my eyes long enough for me to get a proper look at it.

"I was thinking of you earlier," I admit. "I want to give this a good clean and was imagining you laughing at me trying to climb up onto the roof."

"Like a little bird," he says with a chuckle, knowing where I'm going with that thought. "We should take it down to our place. We have a pressure washer. I could help you tomorrow, if you like?"

"Really? That would be amazing. The only thing is, the tires are flat," I point out.

"Jonas will be able to order new ones, if they don't already have them at the garage."

"Garage?"

"He works at a garage in town."

"As well as being a farmer?"

"Yeah, there's not really enough work to keep him going full-time, not on a farm our size. Except at harvest, then it's all hands on deck." He nods at Bambi. "This thing is so small, I bet we could take it to our place on a tractor."

"Would Jonas mind helping?"

"No, but I can bring the tractor up myself. It's no trouble."

"That would be awesome, thank you! Actually, Dad and Sheryl wondered if you might have a use for any of this old farm equipment?"

He walks around the caravan, surveying it dubiously. "Not

really, but if you want to get rid of it, I can probably stick it behind the shed."

"Oh yeah, I noticed when I went for a walk that you have a bit of a junkyard down there."

"*Junkyard*? It's a motocross trail!"

I laugh at his mock indignant tone. "A *what*?"

"A dirt-bike trail, you know, a track to ride motorbikes around on, do jumps and tricks."

"That sounds dangerous."

"Well, it's not *safe*," he replies with a smirk. "Jonas and I used to ride a lot when we were younger, but it's been a while. I thought about getting him back out there, see if it cheers him up."

"Is it fun?"

"*So* much fun." Now he's grinning. "You get such a strong sense of freedom with it, which is something Jonas could really use right now."

"Have you always liked bikes and cars and stuff?" I ask, touched by how protective he is of his brother.

"Ever since I can remember."

"Did you always know what you wanted to do?"

"I mean, I always loved watching motor racing—I grew up fixated on IndyCar, NASCAR, and Formula 1—but I don't think I ever imagined I'd be lucky enough to get into racing as a career." He shrugs. "I was pretty good at school, though. Math and physics were my strongest subjects. And I had a good physics teacher who encouraged me to think big. Mr. Ryland," he says fondly. "He was a total race-car fanatic. What about you?" he asks. "How did you get into architecture?"

We're interrupted by Dad appearing from around the corner of the barn. "Hey there!" He's thrilled at the sight of Anders.

"Hi," Anders replies, going over to shake Dad's hand.

"Have we got a customer?" I ask.

"No, I was just wondering if you wanted a coffee. Anders?" Dad asks hopefully. "Can we tempt you?"

Anders glances at me before nodding at Dad. "Sure."

It's just as well I've warmed him up with a few questions. The poor guy has no idea what he's letting himself in for.

17

CAN'T BELIEVE YOU WERE AT THE SAME RACE," ANDERS
says to me.

We've just discovered that we were both at the Indy 500
during the weekend that Luis Castro scored the first of his
three 500 wins. I was only about sixteen or seventeen at the
time, and this was well before the Brazilian racing driver went
on to become a four-time Formula 1 world champion.

Some of Dad's enthusiasm about racing has rubbed off on
me over the years, so it's actually been kind of riveting, hearing
Anders talk. In the last half hour, Dad has bombarded him
with questions.

I now know that there are two drivers in each team and Anders is the head race engineer for one of them; his driver, Ernie
Williams, is currently leading the championship by only a few
points; Anders never normally takes any time off during the
season and every May feels particularly long and brutal because
the Indy 500 is squeezed into an already jam-packed calendar;
he's one of the last to leave the track at night, and double-
header race weekends are the worst, often with him working
all night long to sort through the computer data and decide
how the car's set-up should be tweaked for consecutive race

days. He should be eight hours away in Iowa right now, at one of these double-header weekends, and he feels guilty because the assistant race engineer has to cover for him, but he'll be back in Indianapolis for a speedway race next weekend, and in Nashville the weekend after that.

I've also learned that he did a motorsports engineering degree at IUPUI and that he started out as an intern in Indy Lights, the feeder series to IndyCar, but was quickly promoted and later headhunted by one of the better IndyCar teams.

And I get the feeling that he's climbed the ranks faster than most, that he's probably, *likely*, really quite brilliant.

My dad seems to have come to this same conclusion, judging by the way he's hanging off his every word. I myself am feeling a teensy bit starstruck, which is probably why I'm now standing up and taking the empty coffee cups to the kitchen and telling myself to get a grip.

I hear Sheryl ask Anders something, then turn to see that Dad has followed me into the kitchen.

"Jeez," he says, shaking his head with amazement. "What an interesting guy."

"Yes." I make the mistake of looking at him and it's abundantly clear where his head is at. "Don't even think about it," I say, quietly enough that Anders won't be able to hear from his position on the sofa.

He laughs under his breath and holds up his palms. "I don't want to interfere, but you could do worse if you were looking for a summer romance."

"Urgh, Dad, stop!" I clatter the cups into the sink. "I am definitely not interested—"

I freeze at the sound of a throat being cleared and turn with horror to see that Anders is standing in the doorway. Blood rushes to my face, and judging by his slightly bashful smile, it's clear he's overheard our conversation.

"I should get back," he says. "But thank you for having me."

"Please! The pleasure was all ours," Dad gushes, guiding Anders down the corridor to the front door. "You're welcome anytime. I'm sorry I asked so many questions, but I find what you do fascinating."

"No problem at all," Anders replies affably.

I'm right behind them, cringing.

"I'll walk you to your bike," I tell Anders, then give Dad a pointed look and close the door in his face.

Anders laughs under his breath as we set off across the drive to the car park outside the barn.

"I did *not* mean that to sound as rude as it did." I'm mortified, but desperate to explain. "The last thing I need is my dad playing matchmaker. He *knows* that my head is in no place for a relationship right now, not after my fiancé ditched me for someone else, and, oh God, I'm not saying that I thought you were interested in me!" I say hastily, my cheeks flaming. "I'm sure you're not."

This is going from bad to worse, but the fact that he's showing absolutely no sign of being offended is telling. He *doesn't* fancy me, I realize. That's why he doesn't care whether or not I fancy *him*.

"No, I'm not," he confirms, giving me a sideways smile as we approach his bike.

I didn't think he *was* interested in me, but my stomach still lurches at his admission, at the fact that he felt he had to make it clear.

We come to a stop on either side of his bike and I can barely look at him, I feel so humiliated.

"My mother and I had that exact same conversation after the storm," he confesses, and my eyes lift at his tone. He's no longer laughing. "I'm also in no place for a relationship."

I hesitate before confiding, "Casey said you lost your wife a few years ago. In a car accident."

He releases a long breath. "It was four years and four months ago, and it was a go-karting accident."

My heart squeezes. "I'm so sorry."

"I'll be honest with you. I am nowhere close to letting her go. And it sounds as though you're still struggling to come to terms with what your fiancé did to you." He pauses, waiting for my confirmation, which I give to him by nodding. "But if you want a friend . . ."

"Even after I made you crash your bike?" I ask weakly, somehow finding it in me to joke with him.

"I forgive you," he whispers.

We smile at each other, but I feel oddly hollow as he climbs onto his bike.

"I'll come by with the tractor tomorrow. Help get your little Airstream cleaned up."

"I'd love that. Thank you."

"And I still need to know how you got into architecture."

"I'll bore you with it another time."

He laughs and kick-starts his engine, lifting his hand at me as he turns onto the dirt track.

However much I try, for the rest of the day, I can't stop replaying his words inside my head: *I am nowhere close to letting her go.*

18

ANDERS CHECKS I'M FREE BEFORE TURNING UP AT four o'clock the next afternoon with Jonas in his dusty black truck.

"Jonas had them at the garage," Anders explains when my face lights up at the sight of the tires in the cargo bay. "I think these are the right size. Thought we'd tick off a job and then it'll be supereasy to tow her down to our place."

"This is amazing. Thank you," I say to them both as they lift the tires out, arm muscles bulging.

I'm not quite over my embarrassment of yesterday, or the disconcertingly strong sense of disappointment about Anders's rejection, but he isn't acting awkward, so that helps. I need to move on.

"No problem," Jonas replies, slugging a big black bag over his shoulder and wheeling one of the tires round the back of the barn. Anders bounces the other across the gravel.

As the caravan is single-axle, it only requires two tires, although I'll also have to replace the spare at some point.

"Have you been to the hospital today?" I ask.

"We went earlier," Anders replies. "Pa's doing well, but he's sleeping now. Ma wanted to stay with him."

"I'm glad to hear he's on the mend. What can I do?" I ask as Jonas gets a jack out of the bag.

"Stand there and look pretty," he chirps.

I narrow my eyes at him. "Don't you make me bust open a can of whoop-ass on you."

He throws back his head and laughs, low and deep, the sound traveling all the way up from his belly.

When Anders laughs, the sound is lighter—I feel it in my chest, wrapping its way around my heart.

I *really* need to stop thinking things like this.

"It's the way she says it with her English accent," Jonas says to Anders once they've recovered.

"Priceless," Anders agrees, his green eyes sparkling.

I wonder how I didn't immediately peg them as brothers. Yes, Jonas is a bit bigger and more muscly, and Anders's features are more refined, but there's something about their expressions that yells family resemblance.

"You two look so alike when you're smiling."

"Whereas *you* look nothing like *your* sister at all," Jonas remarks.

"Well, we *are* only half sisters," I remind him, but it stings to hear him say it.

Bailey and I *do* look different. She's so pretty and shiny and I'm just . . . *lesser*.

"Seriously, how can I help?" I persist.

"It's a one-person job," Anders assures me, smiling.

"Yet you've both graced me with your presence," I reply sweetly. "And I'm very grateful," I add quickly, trying to sound serious.

Scott and I shared his truck and he did everything when it came to the maintenance of it. I know I should've been more

Down with the patriarchy! and learned about these things myself, but the truth is, I find it sexy when a guy knows his way around a car.

As Anders tackles a particularly stiff wheel nut, the sleek muscles on his arms tightening and flexing, I remind myself that he just wants to be friends.

But he's a very *hot* friend. And it's okay if I appreciate *all* of his assets, right?

IT'S SEVEN O'CLOCK by the time Jonas and Anders have changed the tires, towed the Airstream down to their farm, and helped me scrub and pressure-wash it clean. They've both got stuck in and it's been a laugh, with lots of banter being batted back and forth. My clothes are damp and dirty and my arms are aching, but my insides feel as effervescent as the soapsuds bubbling away on the dusty ground.

I read something recently about the importance of doing things in life that bring you joy. Anders had the right idea when he said he wanted to get Jonas back out on their old motocross trail. I haven't personally had a whole lot of happiness in my life lately, but standing here now and staring at Bambi, I can't wipe the smile from my face.

It's not as shiny as most of the Airstreams I've seen online—the metal has definitely dulled with age—but I like this matte-look finish.

Peggy arrived back from the hospital soon after I got here, looking weary but pleasantly surprised to see the three of us together. She invited me to stay for supper. Insisted, actually. I didn't want to impose, not with everything she's going through, but Anders gave me a look that implied I should accept. When she left us to it, he commented that it would help take her mind off things.

I feel too grubby to be sitting down at her table, but the sun still has real heat in it, so at least my dress will probably be dry by the time we reach the house.

"When are you going back to Indy?" I ask Anders as we wait for Jonas to put away the pressure washer.

"Tuesday."

"Do you think you'll come here again this summer?"

"I wouldn't usually, but Jonas has been bugging me to take some time off."

"I thought it was difficult to take a break during racing season?"

"It is, but I'll see what I can do."

I get the feeling he'd move mountains for his brother. Will Bailey and I ever be that close? Six years is a big age gap, but it's less noticeable now that we're older. I never thought we had enough in common to be sisters who are also friends, but I'm not as daunted by her outgoing personality these days. I used to retreat into my shell around her, but I'm more confident now. There's definitely hope for us.

Jonas reappears. "I think we deserve a beer. Want me to tow this back to your place first?" He nods at Bambi.

"Or you could leave it in the shop overnight?" Anders suggests, nodding toward the first of the two big sheds from which Jonas just exited. "I could bring it back in the morning."

"That would be great. There's no rush. I'm working tomorrow anyway."

"What are you working on?" he asks as we walk toward the farmhouse.

"A primary school extension," I reply.

"Cool."

"It's really not very exciting."

"Why not?"

"There's no design involved—I'm just doing a series of technical drawings—but at least I can do the work remotely."

There's a small wood off to our left and between the tree trunks a large pool of water is visible, glinting in the evening sunlight.

"I didn't know you had a lake," I say. "Do you ever swim in it?"

"Sometimes," Jonas replies. "Why, you thinking about taking another accidental dip anytime soon?"

I stick out my tongue at him. "Next time, I'll bring a swimming costume."

"You should."

I was joking, but I think he's serious.

"I'm gonna take a shower. Tell Ma I'll be over in a minute," he says, trailing off toward the lake.

"Where's he going?" I ask Anders with confusion.

"To his place." He points at a log cabin by the water.

"Oh, I thought he lived in the farmhouse."

"With Ma and Pa?" Anders snorts. "No."

"How long has the cabin been there?" From its size, I'm guessing it's only a one-bedroom.

"About fifteen years. Jonas and Dad built it using trees from the woods."

"You didn't help?"

He shakes his head. "I was away at college."

"Did Jonas go to college?"

"Yep, agricultural college. He lived at home, though. Went in for classes."

Anders leads me to the side of the house, opening up a mesh screen door and holding it back for me. I walk into a laundry room. There's a gray dog bed lying on its side on the floor, covered with sandy-colored hairs.

"You have a dog?" I ask as he pulls the door closed with a clatter.

"Actually, she died a few weeks ago."

"Oh, I'm sorry."

"She was fourteen, but yeah, it hit Jonas hard. She used to go everywhere with him."

He really has had a terrible time of it lately—it's no wonder he's felt down. He seemed happy enough today, though, and on Friday night, albeit when he'd had a few. I wonder if it helps having Anders at home.

"I've always wanted a dog," I say, pausing a moment.

"I thought you were a cat lady?"

"Nah, I was only teasing you about that. I like cats and dogs equally."

He smiles. "What would you call your dog?"

I think he's remembered that I named my cat after Zaha Hadid.

"Eames, I reckon."

"After Charles or Ray?"

"Depends on whether it's a boy or girl."

He laughs and nods.

I love that he gets my architecture references.

"Go straight through," he directs me.

I come out into the kitchen at the back of the house where Peggy is at a counter, chopping beans.

She jolts as she sees us. "Anders!" she scolds. "You should

have gone around the front! This is no way to bring a guest into our home."

He rolls his eyes at her as she grabs a tea towel and dries off her hands. Her white hair is piled up on her head in a chignon.

"I'm going to change my shirt," Anders says, calling over his shoulder to his mother as he walks down the corridor: "Jonas will be here in a minute."

I stand there awkwardly, wishing *I* could change or take a shower.

"Do you need some help?" I ask Peggy.

"No, I'm all done here," she replies, taking off her apron. "I hope you like lamb."

"I do. It smells delicious, but I'm worried you've gone to too much trouble."

She waves off my concern. "I would have cooked for the boys anyway. What would you like to drink? I was thinking about opening a bottle of rosé."

"That sounds great. I'm sorry I'm empty-handed."

"Oh, stop." She goes to the fridge and pulls out a bottle, saying as she cracks open the screw top, "I loved the peach drink, by the way."

"The Bellini?"

"I'd forgotten what it was called, but yes. It was delicious."

"I'll bring you some more puree."

"That wasn't a hint! But I won't say no if you can spare some."

"We can *definitely* spare some," I say with a smile, accepting the glass she passes me and looking around.

The kitchen walls and ceiling are entirely clad with ginger pine, a material that also forms the cabinets and counter.

Together with the orangey-red terra-cotta floor tiles, the overall effect is a tad overbearing.

I notice there's a series of large photo frames hanging on the wall in the hallway and cock my head toward them. "Do you mind if I take a look?"

"Of course, honey, make yourself at home."

The entire downstairs of the house—every room that I can see, at least, including the adjoining living room—features this same ginger pine. It's also tiled throughout, with dark-patterned rugs placed at regular intervals.

What I wouldn't give to get my hands on this place, brighten it up a bit.

I swirl my wine around in my glass out of habit as I study the family photos. The frames are all oval-shaped and vary slightly in size, but each is made of a different material, from dark polished wood to ornate gold-plated metal.

In the kitchen, Peggy is sliding the chopped beans into a pan on the hob, but once she's done, she joins me.

"Who are they?" I nod at a dour-looking couple in a black-and-white photograph. It's very old and shows a man standing to the right of a woman who's sitting in a high-backed armchair.

"That's Patrik's great-great-grandfather Haller and his wife, Sigrid." Peggy's accent is American with a Midwestern lilt, but she pronounces Haller, "Hah-ler," and it sounds Scandinavian.

"Are they the original settlers?" I ask with interest.

"Yes, they are."

Another black-and-white photograph shows a man and a woman in exactly the same pose. I've got to say, it's a little creepy. "They're sitting in the same chair," I realize, peering closer.

"Yes," she replies with a giggle. "That's Henrik, Haller's son, and his wife, Edna." She moves farther along the wall. "And here's Aan and Rose, and Erik with Mary."

They're all photographed in the exact same pose with the exact same chair.

"And here we are," she says cheerfully, pointing at a picture of herself with her husband.

It's a color photograph, as were the last two, and there's no disguising the twinkle in Peggy's eye, even as she keeps a relatively straight face. She looks so young—her late twenties, perhaps. Anders has her green eyes, I realize, and her striking eyebrows.

"We still have that chair." She points into the living room and there, in the corner, is the red high-backed armchair.

"I love it!" I say with delight, going to take a closer look.

The chair's fabric is faded and threadbare, but seeing it here thrills me.

I turn my attention to the rest of the room. Practically every single surface is crammed with ornaments, antiques, and photo frames. And the more I look, the more I want to scrap what I said earlier about getting my hands on this interior. There's over a hundred and seventy years' worth of history inside this house. If it *was* up to me, maybe I'd leave it exactly as it is.

Then again, a lick of white paint would work wonders.

My gaze drifts to a photograph in a silver frame and my heart skips a beat when I realize it's Anders on his wedding day.

"That's Laurie," Peggy says when she sees what's snagged my attention.

And now his wife has a name.

"Anders told me what happened," I say, matching her subdued tone.

I study the photograph. Anders is devastatingly handsome in a fitted black suit, white shirt, and slim black tie. His hair is shorter than it is now and he's looking down at his wife—Laurie—who's laughing up at him. Her blond hair has been scooped into a tousled updo and there are tiny white flowers in it. Her dress is white lace and sleeveless. She's absolutely beautiful.

"One of the worst things ever to happen to our family," Peggy murmurs, her voice strained with grief.

One of?

She must read my mind because suddenly she looks embarrassed.

"How is Patrik?"

"Oh, he's fine," she replies dismissively, making me think that she doesn't place his heart attack up there with whatever other tragedies this family has endured.

Indeed, she seems much more relaxed and at ease than she was in the storm shelter, more in line with Dad's description of her as a "real friendly lady." She must be so relieved to know that her husband is going to be okay.

"I think he's enjoying the rest," she adds conspiratorially about Patrik. "It's the best vacation he's had in years."

"And whose fault is that?" Anders asks loudly as he comes down the stairs.

"Yes, yes, I know. I'm working on him," his mother calls back. She casts her eyes to the ceiling and smiles at me before returning to the kitchen.

Anders has changed into a black T-shirt. His hair is wet and a few very dark blond strands have fallen forward over his green eyes. Teeny-tiny drops of water cling to the ends and I stare at them, startling when he thrusts his hand through those wayward locks and sets them back in place.

"You showered," I whisper accusatorily. "I feel like a right state."

"You're fine," he replies with a frown, nodding toward the kitchen.

He smells of citrus shower gel, or maybe it's shampoo.

A door bangs open and we turn to see Jonas walking into the house from the laundry room.

"Where's my beer?" he demands to know.

"It's coming," Anders replies mock-wearily, going to the fridge. He gets out the rosé first and tops up my glass, followed by his mother's, then pulls out a couple of bottles of beer for Jonas and himself.

"Cheers," Jonas says with a grin, prompting all four of us to raise our drinks and clink them.

We're eating in the dining room at an oval-shaped mahogany table with old-fashioned white doily place settings. Jonas is at one end and Peggy is at the other. Anders and I are in the middle, facing each other.

Steam rises from the tops of the serving dishes that Peggy and Anders have set on the table: a boneless lamb shoulder, glistening with succulent juices, crunchy golden roast potatoes, and buttery peppered beans. Jonas brought over a knife and I figure everyone is waiting for him to carve the joint before serving up the vegetables, but instead of getting on with the job, he puts down the knife and offers his hand to me, palm up. It takes me a second to realize that Peggy is doing the same thing on my left.

Oh shit, they're saying grace!

I've never been at a table where people have said grace before and I feel completely out of my comfort zone. But as I sit there, holding Peggy's soft hand and Jonas's calloused one, and Peggy's gentle American lilt fills the room, saying thanks for our good health, for Patrik's, for my presence at their table, to some people called Ted and Kristie who gifted them Ramsay, as well as Ramsay himself—and I don't even want to think about what *that* means—a strange sort of contentment fills my insides.

I'm not religious, but there is something good and wholesome about this chain of hands that we've formed, this feeling of togetherness.

Peggy finishes speaking and we let go of each other's hands. I lift my head to see Anders looking across the table at me, a small smile on his lips.

And despite everything we said to each other yesterday, I experience a full-body twinge of regret that it wasn't his hand I'd been holding.

19

AFTER DINNER, ANDERS WALKS ME HOME.

"First time saying grace, huh?" His gaze flicks toward me, an amused tilt to his lips.

"Am I that easy to read?"

"Not particularly."

We're both a little tipsy and conversation is relaxed and easy.

"Who are Ted and Kristie?" I ask as we stop to stare at the sky.

It's awash with neon stripes, as though a giant toddler has attacked it with purple, pink, blue, and orange highlighter pens.

"Farming friends of my parents," Anders replies.

"And who, dare I ask, is *Ramsay*?"

"*Was* Ramsay," he corrects, peering down at me. The amber fleck in his eye looks darker in this light, his irises a cloudier green. "I think you know."

"Oh man," I moan, scrubbing my face with my hand as I carry on walking. "I've never eaten food with a name before."

His low laugh makes my skin warm and my insides feel all gooey. I should be embarrassed by the fact that he's turned me into the human equivalent of a roasted marshmallow, but I like this feeling too much.

"It's the best sort," he says, falling into step beside me. "If someone cares enough to name an animal, you'd better believe they cared for them while they were alive too. Ramsay had a good life on the farm before he made it to your plate, which is more than can be said for anything you buy at the supermarket."

"I suppose you're right."

"I know I'm right."

We reach my front door and Anders turns to face me under the porch lights, his gaze drifting to my forehead.

"You've got some dirt." He lifts his hand as if to rub it away and then changes his mind and lets his arm drop, but I still feel the buzz of his *almost*-touch.

"Where?" My fingers land on something gritty almost immediately. "Anders!" I berate him. "Why didn't you tell me earlier? I sat there that whole time next to your mother with muck on my face."

"She wouldn't have noticed. She's a farmer's wife, she doesn't even see dirt anymore."

"Is it gone?" I ask.

He scans my forehead and then searches the rest of my face, causing my blood to hum with electricity as his eyes find mine. He gives me a small nod.

Damn, I fancy him.

He starts suddenly. "I'll see you tomorrow."

"Yes! Thanks again for your help with Bambi today," I say as he backs away.

"Pleasure."

He doesn't meet my eyes again as he turns and jogs down

the steps. Nor does he look back. I know because I watch and wait until he's out of sight.

ANDERS IS STILL very much on my mind the next day as I sit at my new desk in my bedroom, trying to get some work done.

My boss, Graham, has sent over the details of the tender drawings for the primary school extension and, as I study them, I realize that the services engineer must have specified more room around the heat pump in the plant room because my predecessor, Raj, has sacrificed a utility cupboard to make the space bigger.

I was involved in the initial briefing stage when we interviewed the staff to get their input, and the cleaner, Jerry, a forty-something dude with a mullet and bad breath, nattered away for almost an hour. If he doesn't get his broom cupboard, he's going to be pissed.

I work away at reconfiguring the internal design, knowing that if I steal space from the classrooms, the teachers and board members won't be happy either. It's a balancing act, but I solve it by skimming a few inches here and there.

I love my temporary office space. Dad and I went into town this morning and I couldn't believe it when we found this desk in a tiny furniture shop. We tried the place on a whim—we were actually on our way to Walmart—and it's simple but stylish, with moss-green metal hairpin legs and a birch-ply top. It's small enough to fit perfectly in one of the dormer windows, but big enough to hold a desktop lamp, my laptop, and a tray. Luckily, I never travel anywhere without my MacBook Pro, otherwise this remote-working plan wouldn't be unfolding quite so well. And I mention the tray because Sheryl brought one up a moment ago with a coffee and a freshly baked peach, vanilla, and almond muffin and there was just enough room for it to be set down.

I check my emails and find a long, chatty one from Mum and another from Sabrina, a friend who is due to get married in October. She's cc'ed me in with a bunch of mates about her plans for her hen weekend.

Sabrina and her fiancé, Lance, are the only two properly mutual friends that Scott and I have and I've felt a bit in limbo with them since Scott broke off our engagement. But so far, Sabrina seems to be in my corner and Lance is in Scott's.

I don't know how long that can last, though. They won't be able to exclude Nadine forever, if she and Scott remain a couple. And I don't suppose they'll tell Scott that he can't bring her to their wedding. I may be feeling a bit better about our breakup, but I still can't imagine going on my own and seeing them there together.

I click on an email from my colleague Freddie, and discover that he's feeling guilty about taking over Lucinda Beale's extension. He wants to know that I'm okay with it and I assure him that I am. I might have been annoyed initially, but now, as I look across the gently undulating green fields that stretch all the way to the horizon, and the hazy cornflower-blue sky that's dotted with puffy white clouds, I'm scarcely able to believe how lucky I am.

Sometimes, I think as I tuck into the muffin, *life really does give you peaches.*

ANDERS WAS SUPPOSED to be bringing Bambi back today, but as the morning wears on with no word from him, my nerves start to feel a little frayed.

I'm attracted to him. More than I care to admit. And after the way he looked at me last night, I'm not entirely sure that the feeling isn't the tiniest bit mutual after all. So why hasn't he got in touch as he said he would?

I bite the bullet and text him.

Are you still okay to bring Bambi back this afternoon?

He replies within a minute. No. It's ours now.
Thief! I text back, laughing.

Jonas will bring it by in an hour. Pa's home. I'm heading back to Indy shortly.

My stomach bottoms out. Today?
I thought he'd said tomorrow.

Yes

That's all he says, nothing else, no punctuation, nothing.

I fight the urge to ask him when he'll be back—*if* he'll be back.

Drive safely is what I settle on.

He doesn't reply.

IT TAKES ME about a week to stop feeling flat whenever I think of him. At first, I'm furious with myself for developing a crush on someone who even went so far as to *tell* me that he wasn't interested. How on earth I ended up kidding myself that he might have changed his mind is beyond me.

At least I don't revert to thinking about Scott. I spend my days working alone at my desk, my evenings with Dad and Sheryl, or Bailey and Casey, or sometimes a combination of all four, and whenever I have spare time, I crack on with the Airstream renovation.

Eventually my melancholy lifts and I go back to feeling lucky that I'm staying in Indiana for the summer.

IT'S LATE AFTERNOON on Saturday, at the end of the first week of August. In between taking turns to serve customers today, I've been helping Sheryl in the kitchen. Or rather, on this occasion, she's been helping me.

After harvesting a massive crop of rhubarb, and inspired by the Bellinis, I googled cocktail recipes and found one that used rhubarb syrup. Sheryl and I have been sterilizing jars, washing and chopping two-inch lengths of rhubarb, and boiling them up with castor sugar and water, and our efforts have produced several dozen jars of brilliant pink syrup that sparkle under the kitchen-counter lights.

Dad, meanwhile, has been watching the IndyCar street race in Nashville. He called me through earlier because he'd spotted Anders on the TV and was beside himself.

The camera cut away before I got there, but he rewound it for me and, I have to admit, my heart skipped a beat to see him sitting at the timing stand on the pit lane, wearing a black headset and looking all serious.

I thought we'd agreed to be friends, if nothing else. But almost two weeks have gone by without a word.

I remind myself that I haven't texted him either.

I do that, I've realized, make judgments about people, assume they're thinking one thing when I'm often the one who's getting it wrong. Like that misunderstanding Bailey and I had about where to sit at the dining table. She and Casey have come for dinner several times in the last fortnight, and on the first occasion she made a point of seating me next to Dad. I felt a bit silly, actually, as though I'd overreacted and was being a brat. But she was insistent and when I'd got over my initial discomfort, I appreciated that she cared. It helped. I felt more like a part of the family, not once feeling excluded.

"There he is again!" Dad shouts out from the living room. "Wren!"

"I'm coming," I call back.

He's already rewinding and pausing and, on impulse, I get out my phone and take a photo of the TV screen.

I text it to Anders with the message Look! My mate's on the telly!

The race has already finished in real time—Dad had to pause it to see to customers—but from what Anders told us about race days, he's probably still at the track. I doubt I'll get a reply from him anytime soon. I'm not convinced I'll get a reply from him at all.

Bailey is coming over after work, and, when she arrives, I mix us up cocktails—one part rhubarb syrup, one part vanilla vodka, and two parts lemonade—and we take them outside to the veranda. Dad and Sheryl leave us to it. They have a white wooden swing seat and it's my favorite place to sit early in the morning or on cooler evenings, when I can watch the last of the season's fireflies dancing over the soybeans. The plants come up to my waist now and have small green pods growing on them.

Sometimes, Jonas goes by on his tractor or the Gator or

another farm vehicle. Yesterday, I saw him spraying the fields, giant mechanical arms stretching out on either side of his tractor. When, this morning, a crop duster flew over, putting some sort of treatment on the corn, I watched from my bedroom window and pictured him up in the little white plane too. I doubt he was, but it entertained me to think of him buzzing about all over the place, ticking off a bunch of jobs on his list. I can't believe he also works at the garage in town.

I miss Jonas, I realize, and not just his brother. I liked hanging out with them *both* when they helped with Bambi and I'm sad our paths haven't crossed again.

Jonas still hasn't given me an invoice for changing Bambi's tires. I thought about popping in to his work to settle up and ask about replacing the spare tire too, but it occurred to me that he might've wanted to do the job off the books. Maybe I'll go down to the farm tomorrow to sort out payment and see how he's doing.

The oppressive heat broke today. Yesterday it was in the mid-nineties, but today it's only eighty. I've been in Indiana for a month and I've taken to speaking in Fahrenheit.

I glance over at Bailey, who's sipping her drink.

"Shall we go for a walk?" I ask on a whim.

We could wander to the Fredrickson farm now, but I shelve that idea as soon as it comes to me. Bailey hasn't mentioned Jonas since our drunken night out at Dirk's and I've wondered if she's trying to put him out of her mind. If that's the case, I don't want to weaken her resolve.

"Really?" Bailey is unconvinced, but it's a beautiful evening.

"Have you seen the pumpkin patch lately?"

"The pumpkin patch?" She pulls a face. "No."

"Come on," I persist. "The vines started flowering a few days ago."

We head out onto the track and walk past the black barn to the field that butts up against the Fredricksons' cornfield, the one that was struck by hail. The pumpkin patch is sprawled out before us, the blooms looking like yellow starfish in a sea of green.

"This is so good," Bailey enthuses.

Unaffected by the view, she is talking about the cocktail.

I take a sip myself. "Did Casey not want to come out tonight?"

"Nah, he's got Brett over."

"They get on well, don't they?"

"A little too well. I can't get rid of him."

"Do you *want* to get rid of him?" I'm not sure if it was amusement or annoyance I could hear in her dry tone.

"No, he's all right. He hasn't outstayed his welcome yet. He'll know when he has."

She grins, but I wonder if it's bravado. She hasn't been married to Casey for that long, and unlike him, she is new in town.

Is Casey giving his wife enough time and attention? Is he doing enough to ensure that she settles in here?

I don't feel comfortable asking her these questions yet. I have a feeling she'd laugh off my concern.

At least she has Dad and Sheryl nearby, so she's not completely alone.

And she has me too, for now.

A vehicle turns down our road and, with a start, I realize that Jonas is at the wheel. At the sight of us, he slams on his brakes, a cloud of white dust enveloping his black truck, as well as my sister and me. We're laughing and coughing as he winds down the window. It seems fate has intervened and delivered him to us. Whether or not that's a good thing, I don't yet know.

"Ladies," he says with a grin, his eyes moving past me to Bailey.

"Hey!" she exclaims. "How are you?"

"Not bad."

"Where have you been?" I ask.

"Indiana State Fair. What's *that*?" He nods at our pink drinks.

"Try some." Bailey hands him her glass through the window.

He has a sip and grimaces. "Boy, that's sweet." He passes it back.

"Oh! Can you hang on a sec?" I ask. "Your mum would love this cocktail. Will you take her some rhubarb syrup from me?"

"She's already gone. Sorry."

"Where did she go?" I ask with surprise.

"Up to Wisconsin to my dad's sister's place. She and Pa are spending some time up there. They left this morning."

"Oh, cool!"

"Yep, a long overdue vacation." He seems pleased about it. "Anders is heading back here tomorrow, actually. You guys should come over and we can grill out."

"Ooh, okay!" Bailey replies.

I'm assuming "we can grill out" is their term for having a barbecue, but more importantly, *Anders is coming back? For how long?*

I shouldn't care. I *know* I shouldn't care. But fuck it, I do.

"What time?" Bailey asks. "And what should we bring?"

"Four o'clock? And just yourselves."

As soon as he's pulled away, I kick myself because I've forgotten to ask him about the Airstream tires. Never mind, I'll pay him tomorrow.

When I glance at Bailey's face, I see that she's glowing.

Is she happy with Casey?

Is she attracted to Jonas?

I hope that one day soon I'll feel comfortable enough to ask.

TO MY RELIEF, Anders replies to my text later that night. It's only with a laughing emoji, but it's better than nothing. I'm four rhubarb cocktails in—we sat out on the veranda until the stars came out—and maybe if I was sober, I'd leave our exchange at that. But I'm not, and so I tap out a message.

> Saw Jonas earlier. You got your parents to go on holiday?!

I wait a minute, then head to the bathroom to brush my teeth. By the time I return to my room, he's replied.

> Yep. Still can't believe it.

> Jonas invited Bailey and me over for a BBQ tomorrow. Hope that's okay.

> It will be nice to see you.

I manage to stop myself from responding, but that damn text keeps me awake half the night.

20

BAILEY ARRIVES AS I'M FINISHING GETTING READY.
"You look nice," she says, giving me a one-armed hug.
"You too."

She's wearing her denim skirt with a frill-sleeved white lace top.

"This is probably the most summery thing I have with me," I say of my black Reiss playsuit. "I really need to go shopping."

"Where would you go?" she asks.

"Indianapolis? Bloomington?"

"I'll come with you," she replies eagerly. "We could make a weekend of it."

"That would be fun. Can you get the time off?"

At the reminder of her job, her mood takes a nosedive. "Probably not, actually. We've got weddings back-to-back for the rest of August."

"Do you not like organizing weddings?" I ask with concern.

"I do, but every single event I plan takes place at the golf club, so it's all a bit repetitive. My work was much more varied when I was at an agency."

"There are no event-planning agencies in town?"

She gives me a wry grin. "What do you think? The golf club is literally the only place anyone ever does anything major.

Birthday parties, retirement parties, funeral wakes . . . Golf club. The people in this town are seriously lacking in imagination."

"We could go shopping on a weekday?" I revert to our plans. "It doesn't matter when I put the hours in, as long as I do."

"A weekday would be great! How about this Thursday? If we go to Bloomington, I could ask my friend Tyler if we can crash at her place."

"Let's do it!"

It's another hot day, but the humidity is low, so it's not as unbearable as it has been over the last week or so. I've been finding myself longing for a thunderstorm, one that sends lightning spearing across the sky and rain crashing down with a vengeance, but I don't know if that sort of weather would harm the Fredrickson crops, so I haven't wished for it too hard.

"How are you feeling about Scott today?" Bailey asks as we set off down the track toward the farm.

"Better," I reply.

I messaged him last week to let him know I was staying in Indiana.

That's great! he replied, which irritated the hell out of me for some reason. Do you need me to go to the house? Pay any bills? Water the plants?

No, Mum's doing it.

Cool. Let me know if you want me to handle anything else.

I found his enthusiasm patronizing, but when I told Bailey about it last night, she convinced me it wasn't.

"You guys have got history, and it's not like you hated each other before you split up. I bet he misses you. He'd probably love to stay friends."

"Fat chance," I muttered.

We were only two drinks in at the time, but as the night wore on, with Bailey's words running around my head, I started to think about how much he'd enjoy hearing about the Airstream renovation.

When I admitted to Bailey that I was pondering what she said, she encouraged me to send him a picture of Bambi, just to open up a lighter line of communication.

I don't know if we could ever be friends, but could we be friendly?

I'm still thinking on it.

The red barn looms in the distance and then the cornfield on our right ends abruptly, revealing the house set back from the track. Goose bumps break out over my skin at the sight of Anders's BMW parked on the driveway. I hate that I'm affected by seeing him again.

When I fall, I tend to fall hard, and the last thing I need right now is unrequited feelings for a man who's still suffering from the loss of his wife. I give myself an internal pep talk as we walk up the path to the front door and knock.

There's no answer.

I knock louder.

Still no answer.

"Is that music?" Bailey asks as I get out my phone.

I cock my head to one side, listening. It sounds like Sam Fender.

She jogs back down the steps and turns right to walk round

the side of the house. I check my messages as I trail after her, and sure enough, there's one from Anders.

We're at the cabin.

I smile and pocket my phone. We're getting to see the lake house!

The driveway comes to a stop at a scruffy lawn. Over on the right is the storm shelter, half hidden by a strategically placed rose bed. The music grows louder as we cross the grass and reach the wood, our feet crackling through twigs as dappled sunlight spills down through the leafy tree cover overhead. The lake gleams between the tall, slim tree trunks, and as we approach, the smoking smell of a barbecue drifts toward us on a light breeze.

Jonas and Anders are sitting on chairs on a deck overhanging the water, looking very laid-back with bottles of beer in their hands, their long legs stretched out in front of them. Anders looks over his shoulder and spies us, and, as his eyes snag mine, my treacherous heart flips.

"Hi!" Bailey calls.

"Hey!" Jonas calls back, and he and Anders get to their feet.

Jonas lopes over to greet us midway. He seems happy, content, and I don't know if it's the beer or the fact that he has his brother at home with him again, or whether he's simply putting it on for "strangers," as Anders once said he did, but it's so good to see him in an upbeat mood.

He gives Bailey a hug, followed by one for me, then slings his arm around my shoulders as we walk toward Anders.

"Hey," I say to Anders as Jonas releases me. "You managed to get some time off, then?"

"I did," he replies, folding his arms across his chest.

He doesn't make any move to hug us and it strikes me that he's not at all touchy-feely like his brother. I belatedly wonder if he's a bit like Sheryl, protective of his personal space.

Or maybe he's just reminding me that he's not interested.

"Boss agreed to be flexible for the rest of the season," Jonas interjects, clapping his brother on the back.

"That's amazing!" I exclaim, trying to shrug off that disturbing last thought.

"He hasn't taken a vacation in over three years," Jonas says dryly. "I reckon it's the least his team can do."

"You haven't had a holiday in three years?" I ask Anders with alarm, determined not to be put off by the walls he seems to have put up since I last saw him. "Why not?"

He hesitates and then frowns at his brother.

Jonas answers for him: "He's a workaholic."

Anders shrugs at me, the amber fleck in his eye glinting under the sunlight.

"Well, I'm glad you're getting a break now. We brought beer and wine." I offer up the cooler bag, wishing I didn't find this unattainable man so goddamn attractive.

Jonas takes it from me. "What would you like?"

"Wine, please."

He looks at Bailey.

"Same."

He heads off to the cabin.

"Take a seat." Anders nods toward a couple of deck chairs. "I'm just going to check on the ribs."

"Ooh, is that what we're having?" Bailey calls after him.

"Yep. Should be ready soon. Jonas has been smoking them all afternoon."

Jonas comes back outside and sees Anders over at the charcoal grill.

"Yo! Step away!" he hollers. "Take these to the girls."

Anders returns to us, rolling his eyes.

"Your brother is kind of possessive, huh?" I say as he hands me a glass of wine.

"Yeah. I'm lucky he didn't stick me with his meat probe."

"I beg your pardon?"

A laugh bursts out of him, which sets Bailey and me off, and then Jonas comes over, demanding to know what's funny.

The tension is broken by the time we've all calmed down.

"Are you a goth?" Jonas asks me as we tuck into the mouthwatering meal he's prepared.

He's served the smoked barbecue ribs with grilled corn on the cob, homemade coleslaw, and buttery jacket potatoes wrapped in foil.

I pull a face, glancing down at my black playsuit. "You're kidding, right?"

"Emo, then? Or is that the same thing? I've only ever seen you wear black."

"No, it's not the same thing. Emo stands for emotional hard core, which is a type of punk rock music that evolved in the 1990s. Goth is associated with gothic rock, a genre that emerged in the 1970s."

"You've been asked that question before," Anders says with amusement as he picks up his corncob.

I smile, beyond relieved that he's relaxed back into my company. "It's true, I have. And no, I'm not a goth or an emo, I'm an architect and we always wear black."

Anders nearly chokes on his mouthful as he laughs and it scares me how light and jittery my heart suddenly becomes.

The "architects wear black" thing is a massive overgeneralization, but it did apply to more than half of my colleagues at my old London practice.

"No more black after Thursday," Bailey says to me meaningfully.

"I never said I wouldn't buy black," I retort.

"What's happening on Thursday?" Jonas asks us.

"We're going shopping in Bloomington," Bailey tells him.

"*We're* going to Bloomington on Thursday!" Jonas says.

"Really? What for?" I ask.

"Sales stuff. We can drive together, if you like?"

"Are you staying overnight?" Bailey asks hopefully.

"No, there and back in a day."

"Ah, we're hoping to stay with my friend and go out on Thursday night."

"We haven't had a drunken night out there in years." Jonas kicks Anders's foot.

"Did you use to go there a lot?" I ask them.

"Yeah, to see bands at the Bluebird, or to go to the comedy club out the back of Mother Bear's Pizza."

"I love Mother Bear's Pizza!"

"You know it?"

"I went every time I visited Dad and Sheryl. My other favorite place is Nick's English Hut."

"Ah, Nick's is great," Anders enthuses.

Nick's English Hut is on Kirkwood Avenue, a popular street that radiates straight from the campus. Sheryl used to claim IU Bloomington was one of the prettiest campuses in the United States, up there with the Ivy Leagues, but she's a proud Hoosier, so I'm not sure she can be trusted.

It is objectively beautiful, though, with ornate buildings made of local limestone, thick, deep windows, and even the odd turret. It has a bit of an old English feel about it.

Nick's English Hut, however, is about as English as the nearby Irish Lion is Irish. But at least the Lion has leprechaun wings on the menu. No one can accuse them of not getting into the spirit of things.

"Man, Nick's stromboli sandwiches," Jonas moans. "We're going there on Thursday," he tells Anders in no uncertain terms.

"How can you be thinking about your next meal when you're still eating?" Anders asks him.

Jonas shrugs and licks his fingers clean.

"The last time we went to Nick's, Scott reckons he saw John Mellencamp in the loo," I say to Bailey.

She smiles and nods. "I used to see him around Bloomington all the time. He lives the next town over."

"When was this?" Anders asks me.

"A couple of years ago."

"Sorry, who's Scott?" Jonas looks baffled.

"Wren's fiancé," Bailey tells him. "Well, her *ex*-fiancé."

Jonas is taken aback. He glances at his brother, but Anders doesn't react because he already knew I was engaged.

"How long were you together?" Anders asks me evenly.

"Three years."

Jonas looks at Anders again. Then at me. Then at Bailey. She grins at him. He smiles back at her. "So where's *your* husband today?"

"Work."

"What does he do?" Jonas asks, and I'm glad to hear him asking this question so casually, as though it doesn't bother him that Bailey is married.

I hope that means he's not interested in her. I don't like to think of him hitting on a married woman. Obviously, his attachment to Heather is a bit more understandable because of their history, but an affair on any level is deplorable, in my opinion.

"He's a golf tutor," Bailey replies, as I try to focus on the conversation going on around me.

"Golf?" Jonas recoils. "Is he preppy?"

"Not at all," Bailey replies with a laugh.

"He used to have a very quirky, very non-preppy mustache," I chip in.

"Oh, I *miss* his mustache," Bailey laments.

I've seen a bit more of Casey over the last couple of weeks and I really, really like him. I think he and Bailey make an awesome couple. He's amiable and sweet, and she's her usual upbeat self around him. But at the same time, he seems to ground her. I get the feeling he's never angry or mean, and he truly seems to adore her.

And yet . . . Bailey seems unfulfilled.

It might simply be her job—it's hard when one partner couldn't be happier and the other is feeling unsatisfied—but what if it's more than that? What if this town is too small for her big personality?

Bailey and Casey have bought a house here. His entire family is here. He loves his job. He's invested. Even Dad and Sheryl moved here to be closer to them. That's got to feel like a lot of pressure on my sister to be happy.

21

BAILEY HAS "AMERICAN GIRL" BY TOM PETTY AND THE Heartbreakers blaring out of her car speakers and we're singing along to the chorus at the top of our voices, windows down, hot air blowing in and messing up our hair.

Bloomington is about an hour north and we drive through farmland and small towns to get there. We're traveling separately from Jonas and Anders. They're going for business, not pleasure, so we haven't made plans to meet up, but maybe we'll bump into them.

Bailey and I are staying in an apartment right in the city center that belongs to Bailey's friend Tyler. She's actually away right now and was gutted to miss us, but she told Bailey we could grab the key from her neighbor and make ourselves at home.

We spend the afternoon wandering around and going in and out of shops. The third time I make a beeline for darker clothes, Bailey drags me over to a more colorful rail. I am now the hesitant owner of a pair of denim shorts, three T-shirts of varying colors, a blue, white, and yellow ditsy-print dress that cinches me in at the waist, hugs my chest, and floats around my knees, and a black-and-red dress in the same style.

Bailey convinced me to get the dresses because she said I

looked "stunning." I wasn't at all sure, but she was so insistent that I didn't have the energy to argue.

She bought herself a yellow summer dress, a pair of white shorts, and a couple of stripy tops.

In the late afternoon, we find ourselves walking past the quirky, higgledy-piggledy frontage of Nick's English Hut.

"Take a photo and text it to Anders," Bailey urges.

I hesitate, but only briefly.

He replies almost immediately: Are you settling in for the night already?!

Not quite, but it won't be long.

Bailey is looking over my shoulder. "Ask him if they're still in Bloomington!"

Are you still in town?

Yep. Jonas is set on Nick's for a stromboli, actually.

"Ask if we can join them!" Bailey prompts.

"No," I reply, staring at my phone screen. No way am I acting keen.

"Why not?" Bailey asks with a frown.

"Because."

And then another text comes in: See you there?

"That's an invitation!" Bailey hisses, jabbing my phone screen with her finger.

I stare at her contemplatively, and then I finally pluck up the courage to go there.

"Does Casey mind you hanging out with them?"

She shifts on her feet. "I mean, I'm not sure he *loved* it when I told him I was going over there on Sunday, but he didn't cause a fuss. I really like them, especially Jonas. He's so funny."

I hesitate. "You do mean as a friend, right?"

I'm dreading her answer. If Bailey ended up taking after our dad and having an affair, I'm not sure I'd ever forgive her.

She stares at me. "I would *never* cheat on my husband."

"That is *so* good to hear," I say with a rush of relief.

"Oh, Wren." She sighs with disappointment. "I wish you knew me better than that."

Shame washes over me.

"I'm sorry."

She gives me a small smile. "It's okay. There's a lot about you that I've yet to learn too. But we have been getting closer, haven't we?"

I smile at her. "Yes, we have."

"You have nothing to worry about with Jonas and me," she reassures me. "I love Casey. Surely you can see how good we are together?"

I nod. "You guys make a great couple. But are you happy where you've settled, Bailey?" I ask tentatively. "Don't you think Case would consider moving if you weren't? He could always get a job at another golf club."

"No, Wren, I don't want to give up on his hometown yet."

"It's just . . . It's such a small town. There's not much culture. I'm worried you'll be bored there before long."

"I'm kind of bored now, but I need to give it a chance. And making friends will help. Casey might have his doubts about Jonas because of his reputation, but he's much more concerned about me being happy. And Jonas makes me laugh. I like Anders too, but Jonas is such a cutie."

"He is. I like them both too," I confide.

"So?" She nods pointedly at my phone.

Fine. We wanted to go there anyway. I reply to Anders's text: We'll be there in an hour, and then we return to Tyler's to drop off our shopping bags and get ready.

THE INTERIOR OF Nick's is plastered with framed photographs, newspaper clippings, and a ton of Indiana University memorabilia. A bunch of famous people have signed the walls—including Barack Obama, who was here in 2008. I still remember how devastated Dad, Sheryl, and Bailey were that they'd missed him.

We spy Jonas and Anders sitting in a red wooden booth, nursing glasses of beer.

Bailey sneaks up behind Jonas and taps him on the shoulder. His face lights up at the sight of her and he jumps out to give her a big bear hug before doing the same to me.

Anders stays where he is, edging over on the bench seat to make room. I sit down next to him, making no attempt to hug him. I'm getting used to his ways.

It's busy in here but not jam-packed. College doesn't start back until next week—in American terms, summer is over by mid-August. It's a dispiriting thought.

"What have you been up to today?" I ask once the server has come over to take our drinks order.

Jonas smirks at Anders, who laughs under his breath before explaining, "Jonas has been talking to store owners about buying his popcorn."

"I didn't know you grew popcorn."

"Neither does our dad," Anders replies, sliding me a sideways look.

"What?"

"I planted some as an experiment," Jonas interjects, grinning like a naughty schoolboy. "Not much, only thirty acres, but I didn't tell Dad because—" He stops speaking.

"Pa doesn't like change," Anders chips in.

Jonas nods. "Exactly that."

"So Jonas is damn glad our parents have gone away for a while because popcorn only grows to about six feet and it was just a matter of time before Pa drove past that field and noticed that the stalks weren't as high as the others."

"That's so devious," Bailey says with glee.

"Are you hoping to sell it all before you break it to him?" I ask.

"That's the plan," Jonas replies. "I want to bring it to the farmers' markets here too."

I remember the Bloomington farmers' markets well—there are food trucks and live music, and loads of local farmers come to sell everything from fruit and veg to vibrant fresh flowers.

"You should do a drive-in movie night!" Bailey erupts suddenly. "Or maybe not a drive-in—it would be more sociable if people got out of their cars and sat in the barn or under the stars. You could sell tickets."

Jonas laughs and looks at me from across the table. "And we could have your corn maze, Wren, get everyone there from far and wide."

"I still think that's a brilliant idea," I mutter, because I know he's teasing me.

"What's this?" Anders asks.

"The field between our land and theirs," Jonas explains. "When I told Wren we lost it to hail damage, she suggested we cut out a *maize maze*. Get people to pick Wetherill pumpkins before coming to our place for some good ole country fun."

Anders doesn't laugh along with his brother.

Bailey slaps the table. "I *love* that idea!"

"What? No!" Jonas waves her away dismissively.

"Why not?" Anders asks him.

"Are you kidding?" Jonas replies with astonishment. "Can you imagine Pa going for it?"

"Pa's not here," Anders says evenly. "I say it's time you grab that farm by the balls and make what you want of it."

22

THE NEXT MORNING, BAILEY AND I DRIVE SOUTH OUT of the city, park the car, and hike to a disused quarry to go swimming. I'm on edge at the sight of the trespassing warning signs, but there's no stopping my sister the whirlwind.

"I used to hike out to Rooftop Quarry all the time with my friends when I was younger," she murmurs, lying on her back in the water with her eyes closed to the piercing sunlight. "It's been partially filled in now because people used to cliff dive and it was dangerous, but it was beautiful. It provided the stone for the Empire State Building, actually."

"Sounds blissful. Meanwhile, I was walking in the gray drizzle to the Kingfisher Leisure Centre in Sudbury."

I'm treading water, looking all around at the sheer limestone walls that cut straight into the clear emerald-green water. Leafy trees line the edges and a few scraggly bushes cling to the stone.

"Were you sad to leave America?" Bailey asks out of the blue.

I hesitate before replying honestly. "I was sad generally."

"I'm sorry. I used to live in fear of Mom and Dad splitting up."

"They never gave you anything like that to worry about, though, right?"

"Are you kidding?" She kicks her legs down and her head pops out of the water. "They used to argue all the time!"

"Did they?"

"*All the time!*" she repeats, her eyes boggling at me.

"They never used to argue when I was visiting."

"Oh, no, they were on their best behavior then," she replies facetiously. "That was partly why I used to love you coming to stay and dreaded you leaving, because they'd make up for lost time."

"What did they argue about?" I ask, disliking the thought of Bailey suffering.

"Anything and everything. Mom spending too much time at work; Dad making a mess around the house; Mom not being affectionate enough or inviting too many friends to stay; Dad not cooking dinner the way Mom wanted it; Mom being the main breadwinner—"

"I didn't think Dad cared about your mum earning more than him."

"He didn't. *She* did."

"She didn't like him earning less than her?"

"She used to give him crap about it constantly! She didn't respect him for it, hated that he liked his job as a grounds-keeper and was happy with what he earned. She wanted him to strive for more, to be ambitious like her. She pushed him to go for the student services job even though he loved working on the grounds, and when he got it, she still wasn't satisfied. She always looked down on him for not being better educated. I honestly thought it would be the breaking of them, that she'd divorce him and find someone more suited, but she never did.

And somewhere along the line, I guess she made peace with her demons."

I'm stunned. I had no idea about any of this.

"They never would have stayed together if it wasn't for me," Bailey adds.

That's what happened, I realize. Sheryl fell pregnant with Bailey by accident.

Would a woman as proud as Sheryl have admitted that having an affair with a groundskeeper was a mistake from the get-go? Wouldn't she be determined to show everyone that Dad was the love of her life so she could justify breaking up a marriage? I could imagine her putting her mind to making the relationship work, even if, behind closed doors, she wasn't happy.

But they *have* made it work. I genuinely don't get the impression that they're putting on any sort of act. Not now, not for me.

Sheryl is in her mid-sixties now. Retired. And she's so much more chilled out than she used to be. I feel as though she's made her peace with both the life she's left behind and the one that's laid out before her.

I'm glad of it.

Maybe when I was younger, I hoped that their relationship would collapse, that Bailey would be forced to go through what I'd had to go through and that Dad would regret ever leaving Mum and me. I was young and I was hurting. I was resentful and jealous. But I never should have wished what I went through on anyone. In fact, it hurts to think of Bailey having anything less than the truly happy childhood I'd always imagined she was having.

23

T'S MONDAY AFTERNOON AND I'M ON MY WAY INTO town on a mission to buy limes. Bailey and Casey are coming for dinner later and I'm cooking Mexican food, but I belatedly realized we had nowhere near enough juice for margaritas. I could have taken Dad's car to go to the grocery store, but I felt like stretching my legs, so I opted to walk. It was a decision I regretted within about five minutes.

It's a searing hot day with twenty-four-mile-per-hour winds that make it seem as though I'm walking inside a giant hair dryer. Dust is hitting my face, striking my sunglasses and clinging to my lips, and my hair is whipping my cheeks. By the time I reach the grocery store in town, I'm hot, sweaty, dirty, and parched.

Propping my sunglasses on top of my head, I approach the electronic doors, all too ready to welcome the air-conditioning inside. But they open before I get there and a harassed-looking woman emerges, clutching the hand of a curly-haired child who could bring down the sky with the force of his screams.

"Oh, hi!" I say when I realize it's Heather.

Her curly-haired toddler is trying to pull her back into the shop, roaring, "*I WANT IT! I WANT IT!*" with a bright red, tear-stricken face. It's as though his life depends on having whatever it is he's set his sights on.

Heather's expression is murderous, but now she also looks confused.

"Sorry, I'm Wren," I say quickly, having to raise my voice to make myself heard. "My dad and stepmother own Wetherill Farm."

She shakes her head at me impatiently. "And?"

"You were there recently? With your family? Picking peaches? I was just saying hi."

She is staring at me with disbelief that I'd apprehend her under these—or possibly any—circumstances.

"Never mind. I'll let you go," I mumble.

She mutters something under her breath as she drags her child to a car, and I'm blushing as I walk into the grocery store.

The women at the checkout counter are sniggering conspiratorially and I have a feeling they're talking about Heather, but they straighten their faces at the sight of me and one of them calls out a welcome.

"Let us know if you need help with anything!"

"Thanks, I will."

It's a lovely store, selling not only fresh produce, but handmade local gifts like soap, perfume, cards, toys, and jewelry. I find limes quickly, but take my time wandering, sipping from the ice-cold bottle of water I've pulled from a drinks fridge and letting the cool air chill my heated blood as I sniff the scented soaps and sample the perfume.

By the time I've paid and left, my insides have cooled to a more bearable temperature.

Unfortunately, within five minutes of walking, I'm all hot

and bothered again. I'm heading over the bridge when I spy the Gator driving along the grassy verge in the distance. It's almost level with me as I come out onto the road and my face breaks into a grin at the sight of Anders at the wheel.

"You want a lift?" he shouts, pulling to a stop.

"Yes, please!"

I run across the road, elated, and slide onto the cream bench seat beside him. "What are you up to?"

"I was checking on the Johnsongrass under the transmission towers." He nods back at the electricity pylons in the distance, skeletal giants clutching cables with outstretched hands. "We can't get the sprayer under them, so I'll have to do them by hand once this wind dies down."

"Is Johnsongrass a weed?"

"Yep."

Suddenly, he goes rigid, turning to stare at me with wide, disturbed eyes.

"What's wrong?" I ask with trepidation.

"What's that perfume you're wearing?"

"It was in the grocery store in town."

Laurie wore this perfume. I know it instantly. My mouth goes dry.

"I'll get out." I'm about to step out of the open doorway, desperate to take his pain away, when his fingers snag my wrist, stopping me. Almost as quickly, he lets me go.

"It's okay," he says unsteadily, reaching for the keys in the ignition.

I felt that touch all the way to my bones.

We can't arrive back at Wetherill soon enough. The feeling of his hand on my skin lingers as though I've been branded and I don't like it. How much more proof do I need that Anders is not over the death of his wife? The fact that I'm still this af-fected by him makes me feel dirty.

"It reminds you of Laurie, doesn't it?" I say as I get out.

He nods, his expression pained. "My mom used to buy it for her."

"I'm going straight inside to wash it off. Thank you for the lift."

"Wren, wait." He looks mortified.

I hesitate, feeling sick.

"We have that spare tire for you at home. Can I bring it over now?"

"Are you sure you want to? I mean, that would be great, but only if you've got time."

I remembered to pester Jonas about paying him last Sun-day. He resisted, but finally gave me a price for three tires that sounded way too cheap. He point-blank refused to let me pay for the labor.

He nods. "I'll be back in a bit."

"Thank you."

I go inside, drop the limes in the kitchen, and rush upstairs to take a shower.

ANDERS IS ALREADY working on the spare tire by the time I get back outside. He notes my freshly washed hair and winces.

"That was weird. I'm sorry," he mutters.

"You have nothing to apologize for."

I've had time to pull myself together. This is the reality check I need.

"You don't have to wait if you've got somewhere else to be," he says.

"Not at all. But are you really okay to do this? I can't believe you're changing another tire for me. I should know how to do that at my age."

He glances at me. "I'm guessing your dad didn't teach you?"

I shake my head. "Nor my mum. She's even more hopeless at car stuff than I am."

"I can show you, if you like?" he offers.

"Would you? I should stop being so pathetic."

He talks me through what he's doing, and when the new spare tire is secured safely back to the hitch, I head inside to grab Bambi's keys. Anders has asked to see the progress I've made inside.

He's sitting in the front seat of the Gator when I return, one long leg dangling out the door. He's on his phone, but he pockets it when he sees me.

I unlock the outer door of the Airstream and pin back the mesh one, stepping aside.

"The wood was completely rotten," I explain as he surveys the interior. I've gone right down to the metal frame in places. "I still need to take out the wardrobe, kitchen, and bathroom. If you can call it a bathroom." It's only big enough to fit a tiny, grimy toilet. "I don't think I'm going to be able to salvage any of it, unfortunately."

Dad's electric chain saw on the kitchen counter catches his eye.

"What are you doing with *that*?"

"Dad gave me a bunch of tools. I don't know what I'll need yet."

He looks over his shoulder at me, his features riddled with disbelief. "Are you fucking with me right now?"

"It's only an electric one," I reply with a giggle. "It's not like it's a great big petrol-guzzling, limb-chopping chain saw."

"You could do serious damage with that thing!" His voice is raised in alarm. "Your dad gave it to you?"

"Yes."

He shakes his head.

I can't help but be amused at his reaction. "It has a safety switch. He did show me how to use it."

"That was good of him." He presses his lips together, flashing me a contrite look. "I don't mean to be rude."

"It's okay." I shrug him off, smiling.

He peers inside again, his eyes scanning every inch. "An oscillating saw would work better."

"I might not need a saw at all. The cabinets are screwed and bolted."

He turns around and studies me for a beat. "Why don't we take it down to the farm? We've got all the tools you could possibly need and I can help."

"That's really kind, but—"

"Let me help," he cuts me off. "I want to. I'd *like* to. Really."

"Are you really, really sure?" I need a bit more convincing. He's supposed to be here for his brother, not me.

"I'm really, really sure," he insists, and he seems so sincere that I find myself agreeing.

24

SPEND THE NEXT FEW EVENINGS DOWN AT THE FRED-
ricksons' farm, working with Anders on the Airstream renovation. By Friday, we've made great progress and I'm excited
at the clean slate we'll soon have.

Anders has gone to get us a couple of beers and I'm standing and staring at Bambi, my mind working in overdrive.

"I've just thought of something crazy," I say when he returns, after thanking him for the beer.

"What?" he asks.

"It's unethical. It might even be immoral. You'll probably
hate me for it."

"Spill."

"There are so many small villages in England and most
don't have a shop. A few years ago, I came up with this idea of
fitting out a van as a shop and having it drive around villages,
half an hour here, half an hour there, giving people a timetable
so they knew when the shop would arrive. I thought you could
literally call it 'the Village Shop' and have a big sign made for
the van. Anyway, I imagined it having this mechanism at the
rear so the back of the van—like, more than just the doors—
would open up, revealing shelves and magazine racks and

sweets and a bunch of stuff for kids and old people and everyone in between to come and browse."

"I like the idea," he says with a nod. He's been watching me speak this whole time, a small smile fixed on his lips. Then his eyebrows jump up. "Wait, you're not thinking about doing that with *this*, are you?"

"Is that bad?" I ask.

"Cutting up a vintage Airstream? It's depraved!"

I burst out laughing. "You're right."

I'm not proposing we turn Bambi into a village shop. I was thinking more along the lines of opening it up to the elements. The view out the back would be great, and maybe the kitchen could be fitted to the rear so that sometimes, weather permitting, you could cook outside.

Anders stares at the Airstream as I explain my vision, then he walks around to the back, where he stops and stares at it a bit more. I go and join him, taking a sip of my beer.

"You couldn't cut it down the middle because of the window," he says.

"What if the whole back opened up from a single point here?" I suggest, indicating a line of rivets that divide the curved back from the main barrel shape of the body.

"Hinge it at the panel gap," he says thoughtfully before shaking his head. "The weight of the door would pull the whole thing over."

He's right, of course.

"But you *could* have a retractable wheel that comes down to carry some of the weight," he says. "We'd have to check out the frame. It might not be strong enough to support the hinges." He pulls out his phone and types something. I peer over his shoulder and realize he's googled the internal framework of a

1961 Airstream. "Yeah, those aluminum hoops wouldn't be strong enough," he muses. "We'd have to weld a new steel frame to the steel subframe base."

He looks at me.

I beam at him.

He laughs and pockets his phone.

I've been trying very hard since the incident with Laurie's perfume to shift my feelings for him into purely platonic territory. I've pretty much got my head on that side now, but my heart is taking a while to catch up. His laugh still makes me feel as though someone has pumped helium into my chest cavity.

"It would be so wrong, wouldn't it?" I say.

"Yet somehow so right," he replies. "First things first, though. Let's finish stripping her back."

"Him," I correct him.

"*Him*," he agrees, indulging me.

He's been cleaning out the grain bins this week while Jonas has been at work—the two giant silver silos over by the far shed. I had a look inside one of them and it was like the TARDIS—cavernous—with a perforated metal floor and an aeration system that blows hot air up through the grain. Jonas has only just taken the last of the winter wheat to market—they keep it in the bins until they can sell it at a good price. It's hard to believe that soon their two giant Tin Man heads will be full of the soybeans and corn that he and his dad planted back in May.

When Jonas arrives home, Anders calls him over. He listens as Anders tells him what we're thinking about doing with the Airstream.

I'm waiting for the horror to strike his face, but it never

comes. Instead, he nods and says he can order in steel via work, nonchalantly adding, "On one condition."

"What?" I ask.

"We serve popcorn and drinks out of it on movie night."

My face lights up before I can determine if he's mocking me.

"Are you serious?" I dare to ask.

He grins. "I *do* like the idea. But . . ." He shrugs. "I wouldn't know how to go about organizing something like that."

"Bailey would," I tell him without hesitation. "That's what she does: she plans events."

"Yeah, but what about a movie license or whatever else you'd need?"

"She'd have no trouble at all sorting out all of that. She'd welcome the challenge. I know she would."

Bailey has already told me that there's not enough variation in her work—she's bored of organizing weddings and retirement parties at the golf club. She would *love* to get her teeth into something new and exciting. Maybe this is exactly what she needs.

Jonas turns to look at the barn, taking a swig of his beer. Anders and I exchange optimistic glances.

"Don't suppose it can hurt to ask her what she thinks," Jonas says.

"I'm calling her right now." I pull out my phone.

"Invite her over, if she's free. I brought home burgers," he adds. "You're both welcome. Tell her to bring your swimsuits."

"Really?"

"Yep. I'm definitely hitting the lake."

Bailey is keen, so I ask her to pop by Wetherill on her way to grab my bikini.

She's with us within half an hour, clutching her yellow beach bag and wearing a smile just as bright.

The humidity has been high all week and it's been very uncomfortable, so once Jonas has lit the coals, we decide to go for a swim.

The air is hazy with dust and pollen and there are bugs skirting over the glassy water. They scatter when Jonas runs and jumps in from the end of the deck, with Anders hot on his heels. Bailey copies them, shouting over her shoulder, "Come *on*, Wren!" And then she screams when I dive-bomb into the water beside her, which cracks me up because I knew she didn't believe I'd do it.

The temperature is perfect—almost not cold enough—and I swim a little way out and float on my back, looking up at the puffy clouds overhead.

Bailey and Jonas start laughing about something and I raise my head to see where they are, finding them over by the deck, mucking about. But Anders is standing up to his waist nearby, staring across the water to the cornfields beyond the lake.

His skin is smooth and golden brown and my eyes skate over the contours of his shoulders and travel down to the taut ridges of his abdomen.

I glance back up to his face and am flooded with relief that he didn't catch me staring. His forehead is smooth, no tension to be found. This expression of peace on him is rare.

"This place suits you." The words are out of my mouth before I can think better of it.

I don't want to bring him back down to earth with a bump.

"Huh?" He glances at me absentmindedly as I sink to my knees, letting the water come up to my neck.

"You seem content."

He smiles and nods.

"How cool that Jonas is thinking about doing the movie night!" I whisper loudly.

"I know!" he whispers back, looking over at Jonas. "I can't believe the change in him. He's so different from when Ma first called me home."

"Why *was* your mum so concerned?"

"He'd been really withdrawn, and just, sort of, *sad*, I guess. Plus he was drinking more and being reckless around the farm—like he didn't care if he got hurt. But she got really worried when he started cleaning out his cabin. She'd heard it could be a sign of someone trying to put their life in order so they're not a burden after they've gone."

"God," I murmur, horrified.

"Yeah. He's in a better place now, but who knows if he would have spiraled."

"I'm sure it's helped, you being here."

"It's been good for me too."

"Do you think it's helped that your parents *haven't* been here?" I ask carefully as another torrent of laughter tumbles over to us from Bailey and Jonas's direction.

Anders watches them for a moment before nodding, almost resignedly. "Especially Pa. He's always been controlling. When we were kids, he used to drink a lot. Sometimes it made him angry. He wasn't violent, but he could be intimidating. Jonas used to get me out the house and try to take my mind off it. We'd go down to the river or jump on our bikes and hit the motocross trail until we were sure Pa would be passed out on the couch by the time we got home. Eventually, Pa got a handle on his drinking, but he still has a hold over us. We've never been close. You saw how nervous Jonas was about making any changes to the farm."

I nod. "I'm sorry." I blow bubbles into the water as I exhale in a rush, realizing I've barely drawn a breath as he's told me all this.

"I'm just glad that Jonas has had some time here this summer without Pa breathing down his neck." He glances at me. "Do you get along with your dad?"

"Better than we used to. It's helped staying over here for longer."

Dad and I sat out on the veranda together last night, actually. He wanted to know how my work was going and seemed genuinely interested as I filled him in, even though the sound of my own voice almost sent me to sleep.

"When are you going home?" Anders asks.

"I've booked a flight for early October because I have a wedding to go to, but I'll leave sooner if I outstay my welcome. What about you?"

"I have to go back to Indy next weekend, but only for a couple of days."

"For work?"

"I'll drop into the race shop while I'm there, but I'm going for a friend's birthday."

"I'd like to visit Indy again at some point."

"Come, if you like."

"I wasn't trying to invite myself," I protest, even as a thrill goes through me.

"I know you weren't."

"Yo!" Jonas hollers at us. "Get your asses over here before we plan this whole damn movie night without you!"

"Is that what you're talking about?" I call as we wade over.

"That and other things. Bailey wants to turn this place into a wedding venue," Jonas tells Anders. "We might have to pay someone to break Pa's legs so he stays up in Wisconsin for a bit longer."

"Oh, *stop*!" Bailey scolds. "That's awful."

I don't know if Jonas and Anders are taking Bailey seriously or simply indulging her, but we're all smiling as she describes wedding photographs in front of the big red barn and out in the cornfields, floating candles on the lake, a reception inside the barn with festoon lights strung overhead, jars of flowers on every table, a live band, and hay bales for people to sit on.

I'm getting completely caught up in her vision, and then she cries, "You could even do up your cabin and offer it as the honeymoon suite!"

"Where would *I* sleep?" Jonas asks with a scowl.

"In the house, you idiot. Your parents will have left it to you by then."

As they continue talking, I find myself scanning the water's edge on the far side of the lake, where the cornfields climb the hill in the distance. An idea is taking shape inside my mind.

Tomorrow I might go into town and buy a new sketch pad.

25

'M FEELING HOT UNDER THE COLLAR. AND IT'S NOT BE-cause of the outside temperature, nor is it because I'm dressed inappropriately. In fact, I'm wearing my new denim shorts with a white T-shirt, so I probably couldn't be dressed better for summer. No. It's because I'm watching Anders at work with an angle grinder.

He's wearing a visor with in-built ear defenders plus heavy-duty gloves, and sparks are flying out to either side of him with the glow of a hundred sparklers. He's cutting the steel into the sizes we need; later, he'll be welding them together to make the faceted steel frame to which the hinges will be bolted.

"Do all race engineers know how to weld?" I asked him last night.

"Just the ones brought up on farms," he replied with a grin.

The steel had arrived that afternoon, so we'd relocated to the kitchen table to work out the angles we'd need to construct the internal framework.

"Dad's probably got a hundred-year-old set square around here somewhere," he mused, but before he could get up to go and start riffling through drawers in the office, I pulled my own adjustable one out of my backpack.

"I'm an architect, I always carry a set square," I said.

I still get such a kick from making him laugh.

I had a wobble the other day, after hearing that Jonas had ordered the steel. Changing a 1960s Airstream seemed so sacrilegious, but then I considered what architects do to listed buildings all the time. We adapt them to bring them into use, and as long as the adaptations are sensitive and any changes are easy enough to revert back, then it's generally acceptable. With this in mind, and after discussing it with Anders, we decided to bolt rather than weld the steel frame onto the subframe so that it can be easily removed in the future. We're not cutting up any of the Airstream's existing panels, so everything can be put back exactly as it was. I feel better now that we've made that decision.

My phone buzzes and I drag my attention away from Anders to look at a text that's come in.

No way! What's it like inside?

My heart jumps. It's from Scott.

I finally caved and sent him a picture of Bambi earlier, along with the message Can you believe I found this under a tarp at Dad's place?!

There was no good time to hurl it off into the ether. He works with Nadine and for all I know he's living with her too, so there was every chance she'd be there when he received it. I do suspect, however, that she may be the sort of girl who can handle her boyfriend staying friends with his ex. Hopefully, it won't hurt to test that theory.

I tap out a reply. Here's a before shot. I attach a photo I

took before any work began. And here's what we're up to now. I send him one that I snapped this morning.

You've done so much! What will you clad the interior with?

Birch-faced ply, I think.

Nice. Easy to curve.

Exactly.

Please keep sending me updates.

And then another message pops up.

Thanks for getting in touch. It's good to hear from you.

My nerves had settled over the course of our exchange, but they ramp up again now.

You too, I reply.

I stare at the screen for a long moment, but that appears to be the end of our texting session.

As I put my phone away, I try to imagine what it would be like if Scott and I were still together, if he was here helping me with the Airstream renovation and we were planning a trip across America. We got on so well when we went on our road trip last summer.

A memory comes back to me of that holiday. We'd just crossed the border into the national park in the north of Portugal and had decided to walk to a waterfall. The climb down a cliff face to reach it was a little precarious, as was navigating the series of smooth, slippery boulders protruding from the river, but it was worth the effort to reach the glorious white waterfall tumbling down yellow and charcoal stone into a deep emerald-green pool.

Scott dared me to jump straight into the water, which was extremely—though not bitingly—cold, but I intended to take it slowly and let my blood adjust to the temperature. Then I stepped onto a boulder that was just beneath the surface, my feet flew out from under me, and suddenly I was up to my neck and gasping.

Scott found this to be absolutely hilarious, and then the exact same thing happened to him and I nearly died laughing.

The memory makes me smile. We did have fun together. But as I look over at Anders, still hard at work, I can't imagine doing this renovation with anyone but him.

Scott and I had some good times, but we *weren't* a perfect fit.

Another memory from our road trip comes back to me. We were skirting the coastline of northern Spain and I looked out the window to see all these eucalyptus trees stretching along the roadside and planted down the banks. There were so many of them that I thought they must have been an indigenous variety, when I'd always assumed eucalyptus trees came from Australia. Scott assured me they did. He explained that the seeds of eucalyptus trees were brought to Europe from Australia in the late eighteenth century, that the first tree was planted in the greenhouses at Kew in London and the first outdoor tree was planted at a palace in Italy. He said that the Spanish locals were taking out a lot of these trees because they're highly flammable and a bushfire hazard.

He said more than that, listing names of explorers and actual dates, but that's the gist of it.

Was it an interesting story?

Yes.

Was I interested?

Not particularly.

I was at first, but after a while, my mind drifted off and I didn't force myself to concentrate.

And the thing is, I know this was not an isolated event.

There were definitely times that I did not give him the respect that he deserved.

I don't think I belittled him, but might I have done so eventually? Is it possible that I could have ended up being a bit like how Sheryl was to Dad?

It's a difficult thought to process.

I remember how impressed I was when Anders told me that he was a race engineer. I thought being a mechanic for a racing team was cool too, but I was definitely that much more wowed when I heard he was an engineer.

This realization makes me feel a little icky.

But the fact is, I *do* respect Anders. I respect him a lot. And I think he respects me too.

It strikes me, then, that Scott was right. He deserves to be with someone who respects *him*. He was right to choose Nadine over me. He and I weren't meant to be and I can see that now. I overlooked our inherent differences because I wanted to marry a man who was decent and dependable, someone who was on my side, someone I trusted.

And I wasn't wrong to trust him. It wasn't his fault that he fell for Nadine. At least he was honest with me about his feelings for her instead of embarking on a clandestine affair like my dad did.

But his rejection of me still hurts.

And Dad's rejection of me still hurts too.

We might be getting along better than ever, and I know now that maybe there were even times when he regretted his decision to leave Mum and me, but the fact is, he *did* leave. He left *us*. He left *me*.

I wasn't enough for him.

I'm not enough.

Will I ever be enough? Will I ever be someone's perfect match?

Anders could be that person for me, I realize.

But I seem to be a long way away from being that person for him.

Misery engulfs me and tears spring into my eyes at the same moment that the sound of the angle grinder cuts out.

"You shouldn't be sitting in here without ear protection," Anders cautions.

The noise has been deafening, but I haven't been able to drag myself away.

I nod and stand up, grabbing my backpack.

"Wren?" He's noticed my expression.

"Do you mind if I go down to the lake?" My voice sounds husky and my bottom lip is trembling.

"Of course not."

I sling my backpack over my shoulder and walk out of the shed.

Jonas is outside, washing the tractor. Anders told me that he's particular about keeping the farm machinery clean and

I believed him when I saw how shiny the enormous combine harvester is.

Jonas lifts the sprayer as though to get me with it, but then he sees my face and cuts off the water.

"What's wrong?" He looks past me at Anders, who's followed me outside.

"Nothing." I shake my head at him and make to walk past, but he lays a gentle hand on my arm.

"Hey," he says softly.

"I'm a bit sad about my ex, that's all."

I don't elaborate further, but I don't want him thinking this has anything to do with his brother. Even if, in part, it does.

A couple of tears escape and roll down my cheeks. I hastily brush them away and I could be imagining it, but I swear Jonas gives Anders a pointed look.

Anders comes a little closer. "You okay?" he asks. He's not near enough to reach out and touch me.

I nod, taking off my backpack in search of a pack of tissues that I'm almost certain I left on my desk at Wetherill.

Jonas makes a noise of frustration as I continue to search, and I think it's directed at Anders because he gives him a properly dirty look that I definitely did not imagine and then Jonas pulls me into his arms.

The combination of pressure behind my eyes, the lump in my throat, sympathy, and now someone giving me a proper, all-encompassing hug has me crumbling.

I'm up against the wall of Jonas's chest, engulfed in his big arms, and I can't help but cry.

Scott used to hug me all the time and I miss physical affection so much. That was something else I relied on him for. My dad can't even bring himself to hug me more than twice a year.

"Go and get her a fucking tissue," Jonas snaps at Anders.

Jonas mutters into my ear as Anders walks away, "I'm sorry my brother is an emotional dimwit."

"No, he's not." I pull away, defending him. "He's been so supportive of you."

"Yeah, but he should be able to give a friend a hug if they need one. I think he feels he's betraying Laurie by even touching another woman. It's painful to watch."

Wait, *what*? That's why Anders keeps his distance? I'd assumed he was like Sheryl, protective of his personal space.

"I'm going to go and sit down by the lake for a bit." I don't know what else to say. "Please tell Anders not to worry about that tissue."

"Are you sure?"

"I'm sure. Thank you, though."

My eyes are dry by the time I've reached the deck. I sit down on one of the chairs and try to gather my thoughts together. Jonas's revelation has thrown me, although I don't know why: it's obvious Anders is still grieving for Laurie.

I pick up my backpack and pull out my sketch pad, determined to lose myself in my work.

I'm so caught up in what I'm doing that I almost jump out of my skin when, half an hour later, Anders steps onto the deck. I didn't even hear his footsteps coming through the wood.

"Are you going to show me what you're up to?" He nods at my sketch pad.

I've instinctively clutched it to my chest, but it's probably time I overcame my shyness—I've been at this for a couple of days.

"I'm only playing around," I say, already making excuses. "I thought of it when Bailey was talking about a honeymoon suite."

"Can I see?"

He obviously feels that he's left me to my own devices for long enough. I heard the angle grinder restart soon after I got down here.

I hand him the pad as he pulls up a chair beside me.

"Wow," he says the moment he lays eyes on the first image. "I had no idea you could draw like this."

"I used to draw all the time," I tell him as he studies the pencil sketch. "It's been a long time since I've felt inspired, though."

"So these would go around the lake?"

"Over there." I nod at the far edge.

He turns to the next page in the sketchbook and examines it with the same intensity.

I've designed a series of log cabins on stilts that hug the contour of the lake, but the logs would be fixed vertically so each of the buildings could be curved into a different shape. I like the idea of them varying, but still fitting together cohesively. I picture them painted black.

"Like I said, I'm only messing around. But if you guys *did* one day want to use this place as a wedding venue or for other events, I thought there might be reasonable money in being able to offer some accommodations."

"How much might something like this cost?" Anders asks.

"The labor would be the priciest thing, but you and Jonas could probably do most of it. You could use logs from the wood like he and your dad did with the cabin, and install a lake-source heat pump." This would provide cooling in the summer and heating in the winter. "And the windows are all standard sizes," I tell him, because there are a lot of them. "You could buy them off the shelf."

He's surprised because they're assorted sizes, some laid lengthways and others widthways, like a piece of Mondrian artwork. I've devised them to make the most of the views of both the lake and the fields behind them.

"Can we show Jonas?" he asks at last.

"Sure."

"And then we should make a plan for tomorrow."

"Tomorrow?"

"You're coming to Indy with me, right?"

"I am?"

"I thought you wanted to. I'll drive us."

I don't know if he's trying to lift my spirits, but I would love a weekend in the city. And I'm glad he feels comfortable enough in my company to invite me along, even if he *can't* bear the thought of hugging me.

26

Y OU SHOULD GO TO MIDLAND ARTS AND ANTIQUES while you're here. You'll love it. It's in a converted factory—it's massive—and it has loads of mid-century stuff. If you're not intent on spending the whole day at Circle Centre Mall, that is."

"Definitely not—it sounds incredible. Where is it?"

"Within walking distance of my apartment. I'll show you on a map. You might even be able to find some sixties wall lights for the Airstream."

"Are you able to come?" I glance across at Anders in the driver's seat of his BMW.

"I'd better head straight to the race shop once I drop you off."

Most of his team are at a race today, but Anders wants to go to his office to print out some data and play catch-up.

What started as him offering to give me a lift and me researching overnight stays in a motel has turned into him insisting that I use his spare room and join him on a night out with his friends.

I don't know if he's on a mission to cheer me up or if Jonas has guilt-tripped him, but he seems happy enough with the plan.

Indianapolis is a grid city with streets that crisscross out from a central roundabout called Monument Circle. The exceptions to these north–south–east–west roads are four main diagonal streets that begin about a block away from the center and head out of the city. Anders lives on the northeast of these diagonals—Massachusetts Avenue, or Mass Ave., as he calls it— and his loft apartment is inside a converted silk factory. The building is five stories, redbrick, with giant Crittall-style windows. The original factory chimney remains; it starts at ground level and is probably twice the height of the overall apartment block. There's also a round silver water tank on the rooftop that has the word SILK painted across it in red letters.

"This is so cool," I say with awe. "How long have you lived here?"

"Only since February," he replies. "This whole area was covered with about two feet of snow on moving day."

I wonder where he used to live with Laurie.

The corridors to reach the apartment are dull and uninspiring, but inside, the ceilings are high and the window takes up practically the entire end wall of the living room, although this is divided from the main body of the apartment by sliding doors and a sunroom. The kitchen is by the door and it's open-plan, with a breakfast bar.

"The spare room is over there." Anders points across the living room to a door on the left.

His room, I see, is up a few steps, around the corner from the kitchen. Aside from a waist-high dividing wall, it's open to the living room, I assume because it needs to steal light from the giant window—there are none in his room.

The walls are white, the floors are wooden and stripped-back, and the mostly modern furniture has a Scandi vibe, with brown leather chairs and sofas and sleek wooden coffee and side tables.

Hang on. "Is that an Eames chair?" I call over to him with unbridled delight at the sight of the yellow fiberglass rocking chair in the sunroom.

"Yep, got it from the market I was telling you about."

"I am so jealous."

I really, *really* like his style.

Oh, God. Why does he have to be so cool? Why can't he put me off him once and for all by having a collection of freaky little figurines or cuddly toys on his bed?

Who am I kidding? I'd probably still fancy him, even then.

I feel irritably jittery as I go and put my bags in my room. Sunlight is pouring in through the window onto the double bed, which is made up with a crisp white waffle bedspread. It contrasts well with the precast concrete wall behind it. There's an en suite that backs onto Anders's room, so I use the facilities before I head out to the kitchen.

"Do you want me to make you a coffee before I go?" Anders asks.

"No, thanks, I'm fine."

"Let me show you where we are on a map."

He helps me to find my bearings, then gives me a set of keys and promises to try to get back early so we can go to Fountain Square for a look around before his friend's birthday gathering.

I **LOVE MIDLAND** Arts and Antiques as much as Anders thought I would. It's set across two whole floors of a converted warehouse with raw finishes everywhere and I could probably spend the whole day in here alone.

I find a couple of aluminum reading lights with white glass shades that would look amazing fixed to Bambi's wall. The power cords are yellow with age, the switches are a touch loose, and the choice of glass in a moving vehicle is probably a bad idea, but I can't resist them.

Afterward, I wander the streets, passing independent coffee shops, stylish restaurants and wine bars with tables out front, hairdressers and barbershops, delis and boutiques, a gallery, and a museum. There's a historic district called Lockerbie Square right near Anders's apartment where the leafy streets are lined with old weatherboard houses painted in pretty colors—sky blue, mustard yellow, Key lime pie green—and all with picket fences at the front.

I never do make it to Circle Centre Mall. There are so many interesting things to see in this part of town that I hate the thought of catching a taxi to a soulless shopping center.

Eventually, I head back to the silk lofts to get ready, and once more, jitters ramp up in my stomach. I wish I didn't feel so on edge. I could really do with a drink to settle my nerves.

I've taken several six-packs to the Fredrickson farm over the last couple of weeks, so I don't feel too guilty about my decision to help myself to a beer from Anders's fridge. On my way to his kitchen, I glance toward his bedroom and a white photo frame on his bedside table catches my eye, pulling me up short. It contains a color photograph of Laurie and it's hard to miss because the frame must be eight-by-ten inches in size. My curiosity reels me in as far as the steps to his bedroom, which is close enough to make out the detail. She has her long, light blond hair styled up in a ponytail and she's smiling at the camera. Not a full megawatt smile like in her wedding photograph, but her expression is soft, her blue eyes kind. I have this strange feeling that I would have liked her if I'd known her.

It's no surprise Anders is *nowhere close to letting her go*. She's the last thing he sees before he falls asleep at night and the first thing he sees when he wakes up in the morning. He must miss her so much.

At that thought, the restless feeling inside my stomach settles. I don't bother hunting out alcohol, returning instead to my bedroom to finish getting ready.

ANDERS COMES BACK at around six, apologizing that he couldn't make it sooner. He has a quick shower and his dark blond hair is damp when he reappears. He's changed into a charcoal-gray button-down shirt with white snaps, and he's wearing it over a white T-shirt with black jeans and desert boots.

I've opted to revert to my standard, safe black. I'm wearing the fitted, knee-length, sleeveless dress I wore the first time I went to Dirk's, the one with white beading around the V-shaped neckline.

Anders insists he doesn't want to drink much tonight, so I tell him about my day as he drives us south until we hit another diagonal street, this one running southeast away from the city. The farther we get from downtown Indy, the lower and more spaced out the buildings become. They're interspersed with parking lots and are mostly redbrick, some with ornate detailing, decorative cornices, and black metal fire-escape ladders, the sort that you see in films set in New York. There are a few funky graphic murals on the outside walls of shops and apartment blocks and it feels as though we're heading into a younger, cooler district.

"That's the Fountain Square Theatre Building." Anders nods straight ahead. "It's where we're headed."

The building itself is large and a bit drab, but the old-fashioned signage wrapped around the ground floor is bursting with color.

"You're beautiful," Anders says.

What?

I turn to look at him, startled, and see that he's grinning as he points out of the window. I follow the line of his extended finger to some large white lettering, fixed to the side of a building, that reads: YOU ARE BEAUTIFUL.

I laugh. "Well, obviously you weren't talking about me."

"What's obvious about that?" he replies.

"I'm not fishing for a compliment," I assure him. "I know I'm not."

"Are you kidding?" He sounds vaguely incredulous.

"Nope. Bailey's the beautiful one." I change the subject. "What time does the party start?"

His friend Wilson has hired out a duckpin bowling alley, whatever that is. Ten-pin bowling on a smaller scale, I think.

"Eight o'clock, but he's always late. I thought we'd go for a drink at the rooftop bar first."

He drives round the side of the building, past the coolest

vintage neon sign I've ever seen. It projects out from the building and is blue and pill-shaped, with white neon lines wrapping around it horizontally and yellow lettering that reads DUCKPIN BOWLING. Next to it is a FOUNTAIN SQUARE THEATRE sign that's lit with so many bulbs it would fit in well in Vegas.

There are two vintage duckpin bowling alleys in the building and once we've parked, Anders takes me up to the fourth floor to show me the one that we're *not* going to later. It's been restored to its original 1930s design, with a café up here as well as an eight-lane wooden bowling alley. The room is flooded with light thanks to a long line of windows in the whitewashed wall.

We carry on upstairs to the rooftop garden, where the surrounding landscape is completely flat and the view stretches for miles. In one corner there's a billboard that reads FOUNTAIN SQUARE: ANYTHING BUT SQUARE and beneath it hangs a big round clock with the classic red-and-white Coca-Cola sign on its face.

We sit down at a table overlooking the city's skyscrapers in the distance, and a server comes over. I choose a rum-based cocktail and Anders opts for a low-alcohol beer. She walks away, but I can't stop smiling.

"This is one of the most characterful places I've ever been to. I want to move here."

Anders looks amused.

"I'm only half joking," I tell him.

"Do you have an American passport?" he asks with interest.

I nod. Best present Dad ever gave me. "I was born here. In Phoenix."

"How long were you there?"

"Until I was about six. Mum waited until after Bailey was

born before packing up the house and taking us back to the UK. Dad had already moved to Indiana with Sheryl by then. That part of my life feels like a dream when I think about it now."

I tell him about my parents' red-tiled bungalow at the base of Camelback Mountain, about the sandstorms, the cacti, and the cowboy towns, and in the meantime, our server brings over our drinks.

"I'd like to go back to Arizona one day," I say, "to see all these things that I remember, like the Grand Canyon and Lake Powell. I found an old photo album of my dad's recently and the water was so green, with big boulders around the edges. I want to see if these places are as nice as I remember them."

"You could do a road trip in Bambi."

"I'd love that. I'd say you could come too, but there's not exactly space for two bedrooms."

He smiles. "I guess I'll have to get my own Airstream."

"Nah, you can borrow Bambi anytime you like. I really mean that," I say. "He feels as much yours as mine."

"Aw." He seems touched as he picks up his beer.

"Scott and I did talk about traveling across America once," I confide.

Anders nods, his gaze steady on mine. The sun moves out from behind a cloud and strikes his face, lighting up the amber fleck in his eye. He lifts his hand to shield himself as he says, "Laurie and I wanted to do that too."

It's the first time he's willingly brought up his late wife.

"How long were you married?" I ask gently.

He takes his hand down, but squints against the light. "A year and a half, before the accident, but we were together for a couple of years prior to that."

"How did you meet?"

He leans back in his chair. "She worked in PR for the team. She came to most of the races."

"Where did you live before the silk lofts?"

"In Broad Ripple, about half an hour north of here. You'd like it there too, actually."

"I won't ask you to take me."

"I don't mind taking you."

It wouldn't bring back too many bad memories? That's a good sign.

"Are you okay after yesterday?" he asks, his eyebrows pulling together.

"Yeah, sorry, that was embarrassing." I wriggle in my seat and my leg knocks against his.

"Not at all." He sits forward again and rests his elbows on top of the table. "Your ex upset you somehow?"

"No, it wasn't anything he said. I sent him some pictures of Bambi because I thought he'd like to see what we'd done and we had a nice text exchange, but I guess I'm still coming to terms with some stuff."

His eyes narrow with concern. "Did he have an affair?"

"No, but he fell for his co-worker and realized that she was the one. And I was *not* the one."

"He's an idiot."

I laugh, but he barely cracks a smile.

"What does he do?" he asks as I brace myself against the intensity in his expression.

He makes me feel like I'm plugged into an electrical socket when he looks at me like that.

"He's a landscape gardener. He runs his own business."

He nods, his gaze still holding mine.

"Nadine, his new girlfriend, works with him. She's not a bad person. When she realized she'd developed feelings for him, she tried to hand in her notice and walk away. I think I happened to see the moment Scott finally accepted that he'd fallen for her and couldn't let her go."

His bottle hitches against his lips and he brings it down, giving me a quizzical look.

I tell him about that day in the park. "Scott had this expression of longing on his face when he stared at her. It's hard to explain. But when she met his eyes and neither of them broke the contact, I sensed there was an attraction between them. I felt sick," I remember with a shudder.

"I'm sorry," Anders murmurs.

"It's okay. Really, it's okay. I can see now that we weren't right for each other. I think Scott—or maybe Nadine—did us both a favor." I smile at him. "So tell me about Wilson. Is he one of your teammates?"

"No, actually." He snaps out of his reverie. "I met him at a live blues bar called the Slippery Noodle. He's a musician."

I perk up with delight. "Really?"

"Yep. That's another place you'd love. It's Indiana's oldest bar—they say it's haunted," he adds, smiling. "It's only a five-minute drive from my apartment now, but I used to go there all the time when I was younger. Wilson and I would often get talking at the bar—we've been friends for years."

"I can't wait to meet him."

We have one more drink up on the roof before heading downstairs to the basement. The space down here is furnished with authentic 1950s and '60s paraphernalia, with red-and-white-checkered floor tiles in the dining section and red vinyl chairs and barstools. Neon signs hang on the walls as well as vintage posters, and there are glass-block partition walls dividing up the areas.

Loads of Anders's friends are here already and it's such an interesting, eclectic crowd. He introduces me to artists, musicians, and even an architect with kind eyes and a hipster beard. There's one woman who's wearing a 1950s red-and-white-polka-dot dress and she carries it off so well, right down to her red hair styled in a retro side sweep, that I ask Anders if she dresses like that every day. He tells me that she does.

By the time Wilson arrives to much fanfare, I'm three drinks in and well on my way to drunk. Wilson is about six feet tall and slim, dressed all in black except for a silver-studded belt around his narrow hips. He has chunky black locs that come to well past his shoulder blades.

"Who's this?" he asks Anders, his brown eyes gleaming.

"This is my friend Wren," Anders replies.

That's how he's introduced me to everyone, his "friend Wren."

"Happy birthday," I chirp.

"Wren's an architect," Anders tells him, a smile playing about his lips.

"Have you met Dean?" He nods at the bearded hipster.

"Only briefly."

"Where are you from?"

"England."

"I hear that. Where in England?"

"A place called Bury St. Edmunds."

"I have never been to Bury St. Edmunds, Wren. Tell me about it."

I describe the fairy-tale ruins and the historic architecture, going into detail about a tiny little pub called the Nutshell, which is one of the smallest pubs in Britain and is crammed full of a bunch of weird stuff, including a mummified cat.

Anders seems as fascinated as Wilson to hear about my hometown, but he lets his friend do the talking. And I think that this must be something Wilson is good at, asking lots of questions and putting people at ease. But the more he asks me, the more I realize that this is him. He's interested—in people, in things. And in turn, I find myself asking him questions about his music, the instruments he plays—which seems to be all of them, but he loves the electric guitar the most.

Anders stays with us for a while before going off to get more drinks, and then he leaves us to it, mingling with his friends. It belatedly occurs to me that he gave Wilson a hug when he arrived, and he threw his arm fondly around Dean's shoulders when he introduced us, but he's not tactile with any of the women. He still seems intent on making it clear that he's unavailable, even though it's been almost four and a half years since he lost his wife.

I guess everyone handles grief differently, but it's desperately sad to think of him keeping up his barriers for so long.

After a while, the red-haired girl in the fifties-style dress comes over and Wilson introduces us properly. Her name is Susan and she's a photographer, but she also works at a record store up the road from here. She insists I come and visit her sometime so she can play me this vinyl record by an obscure band that she recently discovered in an antiques market.

Dean joins us and I lose more time talking to him about architecture. He's recently been working on a coffee shop that's housed in a mid-century former bank building and has just finished designing a low-lying modernist house with an over-hanging roof and giant sliding glass doors. They sound like the sort of projects I would kill to work on.

And maybe it's the alcohol rush, or maybe it's the-grass-is-always-greener syndrome, but I feel as though I'm in the middle of one of my favorite nights out ever.

I haven't really found my tribe yet in Bury St. Edmunds. My only good friend is Sabrina, but she and her fiancé, Lance, feel intrinsically linked to Scott because we met them while we were together. All my other pals from work and uni are in London or spread across the country. I'd love to have a big group of local friends like this. Anders is lucky.

Wilson insists I team up with him and one of his bandmates, Davis, for our first game of duckpin bowling. The lanes are shorter than ten-pin bowling alleys and the balls are smaller, but it's essentially the same concept: hit the things at the end.

Of course, I can't hit them for the life of me. I'm far too drunk.

"What am I doing wrong?" I ask Anders.

"I can't tell you, you're not on my team," he replies with a smirk.

Susan, one of *his* teammates, knocks down all but one of her pins on her third go and he throws up his arms and cheers for her.

"Who cares if we win or lose? It's playing the game that counts!" Wilson exclaims, putting on an English accent and projecting his voice like some lofty Shakespearean actor. "But you *are* twisting your arm at the elbow," he mutters in my ear.

"What do you mean? Like this?"

"No, like this." He grabs my arm and holds it straighter.

I try to correct my throw, fling the ball down the wooden

alley, and take out every single one of those damn pins. I'm so astonished, and then so elated, that I jump up and down on the spot and cry, "YES!"

Wilson high-fives me, then Davis does too, and I look at Anders with such glee, only to find him already laughing, his face full of affection. I am so full of *like* for him in that moment, and when he doesn't break eye contact, neither do I.

His head tilts to one side and his eyes seem to darken as his grin fades to a small smile. I feel as though I'm a fly trapped in honey—no, a mosquito caught in amber; unable to unstick myself from his steady gaze.

His attention moves to my lips, and my heart spikes with adrenaline as his eyes snap back up to my face. I catch the blazing heat in them before he winces and looks away.

He jumps to his feet and picks up a bowling ball. It takes me a moment to realize he's simply taking his turn.

"Time to *whoop* your ass," he says in a light, playful tone.

I force a laugh, but what the hell? Did I just imagine that connection between us? He seems to have completely reverted to normal, while I can barely draw air into my lungs. My pulse is sky-high, slamming under my skin, and he appears completely unaffected.

I do my best to follow his lead, but it's hard.

We stay for a couple more hours after we finish the game, laughing, drinking, chatting, and eating, until eventually we call it a night and Anders takes us home.

"Want a nightcap?" he asks as he unlocks his door.

"I'm so sorry you couldn't drink," I lament.

"I didn't mind. I was happy."

"Were you?" I ask. "Happy?"

"Very," he replies with a smile.

Man, he is so sober.

"Please can you get very drunk now?" I ask, wobbling my way to his leather sofa and falling onto it.

"I'll do my best. What do you want?"

"Something soft."

He brings me a fizzy water and a whiskey on ice for himself, and then sits down on the armchair to my right.

"I had such a good night," I say. "I really like your friends."

"I'm glad. They like you too."

"They're all so interesting."

"*You're* interesting."

"*You* are," I bat back, drunkenly.

He laughs and shakes his head, bringing his glass to his lips. He pauses, then lowers his glass again.

"That thing you said earlier, about Bailey being the beautiful one. Didn't your dad ever tell you that you were when you were growing up?"

"Nope," I reply bluntly.

"But he said it to Bailey?"

"I assume so. I mean, look at her. We're nothing alike."

He frowns. "I disagree."

"Come on, even Jonas commented on how different we are."

"He's wrong. You have the same eyes," he says. "Not color, yours are prettier, but they're both almond-shaped."

Prettier? I shake my head, even as my heart lifts and swells. "My eyes aren't anything like hers. Hers are big and boo-like."

He's understandably confused at this description. "I don't know what that means, but I do think you both have big eyes. And you both have perfectly straight noses."

I grin at him, tickled by the fact that he's obviously taken some time to consider this.

"Have you two always got along well?" he asks.

"No, not really, not when we were younger. We didn't *not* get on, but we weren't close before this trip."

"Why not?"

"Partly because of the age gap, partly because we haven't spent much time together, and also, we're just *different*. She's much more outgoing than I am. I've always felt a little small in comparison. We've bonded this summer, but ultimately this is *her* family I'm staying with. I'll always feel like my dad is more hers than mine."

His eyebrows pull together. "I'm sorry you feel that way. It seemed clear to me when I came inside that time that your dad really dotes on you."

I blow out a breath. "My dad can't even *hug* me. I mean, he hugged me when I came here and he'll hug me when I leave, but this side of my family doesn't really do physical affection. Not with me, at least. I think the only time Sheryl has ever hugged me properly was a couple of weeks ago when she was apologizing for something she did when I was younger."

He has me anchored with his attention, compelling me to explain in more detail.

"She hid that photo album I was telling you about. Bailey used to like looking at it and Sheryl took it away from her. I think she felt threatened by me, by my mum, by my dad's history with us. She never let me get too close to her, used to make me feel like I was a nuisance. I remember once when I was about eight or nine, she got a perm and her hair was so curly and shiny. I was dying to see what it felt like, but when I tried to finger one of her curls, she batted me away. She wasn't that nice to me when I was growing up."

"Do you think that might be partly why you're insecure?"

"Am I insecure?"

"For someone as clever and talented as you are, I think you're quite insecure."

I stare at him, my insides fluttering as I try to make sense of his words.

"I don't suppose it helps that my dad deserted me. And then Scott did too," I add with a flippant shrug.

It's yet another thing I've tried to make light of that he doesn't find funny. His gaze is pressing and intense. Heat shimmers over my skin.

"I think I should probably head to bed. I'm too drunk for this conversation," I decide suddenly.

He nods, slowly leaning forward and resting his elbows on his knees, his glass cradled in his hands. He watches me as I stand up.

I am hyper-aware of his attention as I go and refill my water from the bottle in the fridge. I head back across the living room to the bedroom, hesitating before turning around to say good night. He's still looking at me, and for some reason, I can't speak. I stand there, motionless, waiting, though for what, I'm not sure.

"You *are* beautiful, Wren."

He says it so quietly, so sincerely, that I open my mouth and close it again.

His eyes hold mine for so long that my thoughts scatter like bowling pins. I try to untangle our gazes, but I'm wading through honey again, locked in amber. Something inside me begins to unravel, unfurling toward him. I feel myself being pulled in his direction, but when I take a single step, his eyes drop to his drink.

"Good night," he says.

He knocks back the contents of his glass and I spin on my heels, shutting myself in my room and trying to wrestle my hammering heart under control.

IN THE MIDDLE of the night, I get up to use the bathroom and I swear I can hear the sound of a woman laughing on the other side of the wall.

But in the morning, when I wake up, I wonder if I dreamed it.

27

ANDERS IS STILL ASLEEP WHEN I VENTURE OUT OF my room, in urgent need of drugs to cure my headache. I sneak past his bedroom, eyes firmly averted, and snatch up my handbag from where I dropped it by the door last night. If I wasn't suffering so badly, I wouldn't dare risk waking him up. Quietly filling a glass of water from the tap, I return to my bedroom and climb into bed.

My mind is racing through everything that happened last night, but it keeps jumping back to *You* are *beautiful, Wren,* and that look on his face.

I didn't think he was attracted to me, but now I'm not so sure.

I feel too edgy to fall asleep again, so eventually I get up and take a shower. By the time I reemerge, Anders is moving around the kitchen.

"Hi!" I exclaim, going to see him.

"Hey," he replies gruffly, not quite meeting my eyes.

My stomach dips. *Please don't let things be weird between us . . .* I rally myself, determined not to let us take a backward step.

"Coffee?" he asks as I sit down at the breakfast bar.

"Please. Last night was so much fun." I inject warmth into my tone, keeping it light and friendly. "I was so wasted, though. I hope I didn't make too much of a tit out of myself. I had to hunt out Tylenol earlier. How are you feeling?"

"Okay." He nods and scratches the back of his neck, his body twisted toward the coffee machine.

He's wearing a rumpled gray T-shirt. I think he might've slept in it.

You are *beautiful, Wren.*

I steel myself against memories that make my heart flip.

"Did you sleep okay? You look tired," I say.

"I am a bit. Cream? Sugar?"

"Yes, please. Two."

I'd take three because I'm hungover, but I resist.

"How about we go out for breakfast?" I suggest. "I could do with a nice greasy fry-up. Do you have to work this morning?"

"No. I wouldn't mind heading back to the farm sooner rather than later, though."

"Had enough of the big city already?" I ask with a grin.

Perhaps he's had enough of *me.* Oh.

He shrugs and gives me a small smile.

Was he just being kind last night? Was that the sort of thing he'd say to any female friend to make them feel better? I'm scared I've been reading too much into the looks we've shared.

"We can go whenever you're ready," I say. "I can come back another time."

"Let's go out for breakfast," he decides suddenly. "There's a place on the corner that I think you'll like."

I like that he knows what I'll like.

I squeeze the thought shut as soon as it occurs. I need to work harder at fortifying my mind.

WE GO TO an independent coffee shop that has giant windows on the two walls adjacent to the streets. Inside, it's painted dark gray and has a mishmash of threadbare armchairs and sofas to get really comfy in. Old books and tattered board games are piled up on shelves by the bar and I get the feeling people can lose hours in here.

As we sit down, I point out an armchair that is the same old-fashioned style as the one his family has at home. He laughs with me at the thought of his mum trying to keep a straight face when she was mimicking his ancestors.

"Do you reckon Jonas will be up on that wall with his wife one day?" I ask.

"I don't know where he's going to find one," he replies wryly. "I think he's exhausted all the available women in town."

"Maybe he needs to come and spend some time here, find himself a nice city girl to convert."

He smiles. "We could do a life swap."

"You do love it at the farm, don't you." It's not a question. I'm thinking of how peaceful he looked when we went swimming last weekend.

"Yeah, I do." He stares thoughtfully out the window at the cars passing by. "Jonas put so much pressure on me to come home. I told my boss that my family needed me. My *brother* needed me. But now I'm wondering if Jonas got me to the farm for my sake more than his. I think he knew I needed some time away from it all."

"Sounds like he's acting like your big brother again;

taking care of you, rather than the other way around. That's how it was when you were younger, right?"

He nods, tapping his teaspoon gently against his oversized coffee cup. "I wish I could stick around for harvest. Jonas has been looking at hiring a farmhand."

My heart sinks at the thought of him leaving.

"Maybe I'll still get a chance to help out a bit."

"If you do, can I have a ride in your tractor with you?" I ask with a grin.

Light and airy, light and airy.

"Of course," he replies with a smile.

ANDERS CONTINUES TO warm up, and by the time we're pulling up outside Wetherill, we seem to be back to normal. I'm relieved.

"Go and give them a hug," he orders me as I climb out of the car. "I dare you."

"I'll see." I turn around and duck my head so I can look at him through the open doorway. "Thanks again. I had such a nice time."

"Me too."

I straighten up and shut the door before things can get weird again.

We've spent the last part of the journey talking about my family and he's convinced me that Dad—and maybe even Sheryl—have likely wanted to hug me on countless occasions, but they've held back because they haven't wanted to overstep. The fact is, and Anders agrees with this too, they simply don't know me that well. They're unaware that I've kept them at bay because I've been worried about getting hurt. If I want to change the narrative, I can—it's within my control. But I probably need to make the first move.

I look over my shoulder as I reach the front door, knowing already that Anders is long gone.

Sheryl is in the kitchen, at work with a fruit peeler.

"I should have known I'd find you here," I tease. "Ooh, pears?"

"First of the season!" she sings.

"Just in time. I was getting a bit bored of peaches."

"Apples are coming in now too," she tells me.

She has batter splattered across her apron and in her hair.

"Where's Dad?"

"Out in the barn. How was your weekend? I didn't think we'd see you before dinnertime."

"Have I come back too early? I hope you don't mind."

"Of course not. We missed you," she says to my delight. "Did you have fun?"

"So much fun." My eyes dart up to the cake mixture flecking her gray bob. "You have a little . . ." I point north of her right temple.

"Where?" She dips her head toward me.

"There."

"Can you get it out?" She's a little exasperated.

"Of course, yes, sorry. I didn't think you liked people touching your hair, or, you know, invading your personal space."

"I *don't* like people invading my personal space," she replies, her brown eyes meeting mine. "But you're not *people*, you're *family*."

I reach up and, to my surprise, my nose starts to prickle as

I concentrate on gently removing the cake mix. I feel Sheryl's gaze on me the entire time.

"This is one of those things, isn't it?" she asks gravely. "A mistake I made when you were younger."

A lump forms in my throat and I nod.

"Can I have a hug?" I ask impulsively, thinking of Anders.

"Of *course* you can, honey!" she replies, her voice jumping up an octave as she opens her arms to me.

"What's going on here?" Dad interrupts. He's just come in through the front door and his eyes are wide with surprise. "Where's *my* hug?"

I laugh and go to break away from Sheryl, but she clings to my waist, opening up her other arm to widen the circle.

And I don't think it's because she wants to keep control or doesn't like being excluded. I kind of get the feeling it's because she's not quite ready to let go of me yet.

28

"RIGHT, THAT'S IT," JONAS SAYS TO BAILEY AS SHE pockets the black ball. "I think you should divorce that Casey dude and marry me instead."

"As if, you big oaf." She shoves his arm.

He laughs and racks up the balls for a second game and I smile at their camaraderie, convinced now that their friendship is purely platonic.

It's Sunday night, a week after our trip to Indianapolis, and the four of us have gone to Dirk's to play a few rounds of pool.

Anders and I have spent every evening of the last week working on Bambi, plus all of yesterday and today, and that's on top of the work he and Jonas have been doing to get the farm ready for harvest.

I'm used to arriving at their place and finding them hot, sweaty, and smeared with grease and dirt. They've been refueling farm vehicles; changing engine oil, air filters, and tires; and doing software updates. They use different headers—big pieces of machinery that go on the front of the combine—to harvest different crops and they all have numerous moving parts, any of which could malfunction and put a stop to the harvest, so they've been rigorous about checking everything over.

But earlier, when I went over to theirs, they were tearing

around the motocross trail behind the sheds, whooping like little kids as they went over the jumps. My heart felt full as I watched them.

The corn is beginning to turn now—it's going golden from the bottom up—and the green leaves on the earliest planted soybeans are dappled with yellow spots. Even our pumpkins have ballooned. I can't believe it'll be September in a few days.

Anders and I are *this* close to finishing Bambi. This afternoon we reassembled the end panels and fixed a rubber seal to the new rear-door opening to keep out rainwater. We're going to do a proper test tomorrow with the pressure washer and after that, once we know there are no leaks, we'll fix birch-faced ply to the interior walls and lay lino on the floor.

We're both so happy with how it's coming along and have been working hard, but tonight we wanted to kick back and relax. Bailey and Jonas did too. Earlier, they finalized an advert for movie night and sent it off to the local paper to run later this week. Bailey is excited, but Jonas seems nervous. He still hasn't told his parents what he has planned.

Peggy and Patrik have decided to stay up in Wisconsin for a few more weeks, and I think Jonas hopes that the first outdoor movie event to be held not just at the Fredrickson farm, but anywhere in town, will somehow escape their notice.

But it's only a matter of time, according to Anders—probably mere days—before one of their friends mentions it to them.

Anders hopes it won't cause his parents to come back early.

After his initial teasing, Jonas is now on board with my maze idea, although he says he'll call it a "maize maze" over his dead body. He said I can design it if I like, so I've been doodling in my sketch pad, planning it so that it begins and ends by the pumpkin patch on our property.

Dad and Sheryl have agreed to us ticketing the maze from the barn, which will not only save Jonas and Anders having to be on hand to welcome customers, but also means that people might stop at Wetherill to pick produce. It's a win-win situation. Dad is getting a banner made for the sign on the other side of the bridge.

I realized after our discussion that I should have told Dad and Sheryl that Patrik and Peggy are unaware of all these plans, but then I thought at least they can claim ignorance if it turns out to be a problem. I really hope they don't put a spanner in the works.

IT'S MY TURN and luckily, Jonas has left a ball by a pocket for me. I hit it, but somehow manage to bounce it off the cushion instead of putting it in.

I curse and pull an apologetic face at Anders.

He grins at me and cups the back of my neck, bringing me closer. "Who cares if we win or lose? It's playing the game that counts."

It's a brilliantly dry impression of Wilson from last weekend, but I'm so shocked by the physical contact that I don't even laugh.

He lets me go, leaving a searing heat behind.

I force myself to giggle and then go and retrieve my drink from a nearby table.

How can a small touch between friends leave me feeling so shaken?

I watch furtively as he takes his next shot, noticing how the muscles in his arm lengthen as he leans across the table, the way his green eyes narrow with concentration. His black-and-white-checked shirt is hanging open and the gray T-shirt he's wearing beneath is riding up, revealing a flash of tanned skin above his belt buckle. I imagine sliding my hands over his flat stomach, feeling his muscles tighten beneath my fingers, and a hot flush comes over me.

No. Stop it.

I quickly look away to the bar and do a double take when I realize Heather is standing there.

I glance at Jonas, but I don't think he's noticed her. She's with a couple of friends.

I widen my eyes at Anders across the other side of the table. "What?" he mouths.

I jerk my head toward the bar.

His expression darkens when he sees her.

Jonas has his arm slung around Bailey's shoulders and he seems very chilled. Anders goes and quietly says something in his ear.

The change in Jonas's body language is dramatic. He stiffens and two seconds later, he releases Bailey and turns to face the bar.

Heather has already seen him. She's gone still, the hand that's carrying her drink frozen halfway to her lips. And then she recovers and takes a sip, lifting her other hand to wave at him.

Jonas gives her a long, significant nod and then turns his back on her, draining his glass in one mouthful.

Whoa. He is definitely still affected by her, judging by that reaction. The tension between them is palpable.

"Casey!" Bailey shouts suddenly, waving like a lunatic across the bar.

"Hey!" Casey waves back, weaving through the tables to get to her.

She throws her arms around him. "What are you doing here? I thought you were seeing Brett tonight!"

"Canceled on him. Figured it was time I came and hung out with my wife and her friends instead. Hey, Wren," he says warmly, giving me a hug.

I hug him back happily, delighted to see him here.

Anders comes over to be introduced, and then Bailey pulls Casey toward Jonas.

"Hey," Jonas says, shaking Casey's hand. He's friendly, but preoccupied.

Unfortunately, I think it's going to come down to the rest of us to make Casey feel welcome.

"How's *Fortnite*?" I ask him with a grin. "Kill any kids lately?"

I laugh at his sheepish expression and tell Anders that Bailey got mad at him the other night because he was halfway through a game and dinner was ready.

"I told him to get his ass here right now," Bailey chips in.

"And Casey said—what did you say, Casey?" I prompt.

"I said, if I come now, everyone will see my avatar standing there and will know my wife's called me for dinner."

"And *I* said," Bailey interjects, "everyone will see your avatar standing there and think your mommy has told you to go to bed."

"Have you ever played *Fortnite*?" Casey asks Anders as he laughs.

Anders shakes his head.

"Come over sometime."

"No, don't," I say. "I might never see you again."

Suddenly, I realize that Jonas is no longer with us. Bailey notices too.

"Where's Jonas?" she asks.

Heather's friends are at the bar, but she's missing.

"I don't know," I reply with a frown. "His ex came in. Maybe he's gone to have a word with her."

Casey buys a round of drinks, then, after waiting another ten minutes, Anders invites him to take his brother's turn at the pool table.

I think we're both distracted by what's happened to Jonas. God only knows where he's gone or what he's doing. But I think we have a pretty good idea of who he's with.

29

M AYBE I SHOULD GO LOOK FOR HIM," ANDERS
says after we've said goodbye to Casey and Bailey
and we're heading toward the bridge.

We only stayed another hour or so after Jonas disappeared.

"I'll come with you, if you like?"

He reels sideways. "You'll willingly get on the back of my bike?"

"Yep. I trust you."

"We *have* come a long way," he teases.

"I might change my mind by the time I've sobered up."

But then I picture myself wrapping my arms around his waist from behind and I don't think I will.

Urgh, what is *wrong* with me? One touch and I'm weak at the knees.

"I can't believe we'll probably finish Bambi this week," I say.

"I know!"

"And then I'll no longer have an excuse to come over and hang out with you every evening."

"You don't need an excuse."

It's getting worse. The struggle to overcome these feelings is growing harder and harder.

We walk on in silence for a minute, the sound of the river rushing beneath us as we cross the bridge. On the other side, we come out to the fields falling away before us and a sky full of stars rolling back over our heads.

"I hope Jonas is okay," I say. "Heather really gets to him, doesn't she?"

"Like no one I've ever known."

"What does he see in her?" I'm mystified.

"I have no idea," he replies. "Treat 'em mean, keep 'em keen. She's always had some sort of hold over him."

"He seemed on edge even before she turned up."

"He's stressing about Pa and the farm."

"What do you think your dad will do when he finds out what you're up to?"

He shrugs. "Who knows? He's always been unpredictable. Hopefully, Ma will talk some sense into him. She seems to be the only person who can."

"Will your mum be supportive, do you think?"

"Oh, she'll be all for it. Anything to make Jonas happy. It was her idea to go away. She wanted to give him some time without Pa around, allow him a chance to imagine a future on the farm and being in charge." He releases a long breath before saying, "When Pa came home from the hospital, she actually brought up the idea of selling."

"What? The *farm*?" I ask with surprise. I thought they never would.

"She said enough was enough, our family had broken their backs over it for too long and there was no shame in letting someone else take it over."

"What did your dad say?"

"He one hundred percent disagreed with her."

We smile at each other.

"But I don't know, I think the fact that Ma even considered letting the farm go freed something up in Jonas. I think it somehow took some pressure off. He's been so upbeat these last couple of weeks. You and Bailey—"

"Mostly Bailey."

"There you go again," he mutters. "He adores you, Wren. And he loved your vision for the cabins around the lake. He keeps looking at your sketches on his phone."

Jonas asked if he could take photos after Anders went and showed them to him.

"You and Bailey have both been godsends."

"Aw." I lean in and affectionately bump his arm. I feel him stiffen and I'm momentarily disheartened because I'd give anything for us to be more tactile with each other. But then he closes the gap between us, his arm brushing against mine as we walk. It's almost frightening how blissful it feels to be this close to him.

"How old is your dad?" I ask, trying to keep our casual conversation going so he doesn't feel the need to distance himself from me again.

"Eighty-two in December."

"And your mum?"

"Seventy-six."

"So she was almost forty when she had Jonas?"

"They'd been trying for a family for years. Jonas and I actually had an older brother, Lars. He died when he was a baby."

"Oh, that's so sad!" Could this be the family tragedy Peggy had referred to?

"It was a crib death, nothing anyone could have done. But it took my mom a long time to get pregnant with Lars and then again with Jonas. Ma said they were surprised when I came along only two years after him."

"Do you have any photos of Lars?"

"There's one in the living room at the farmhouse, and Ma has others. She still visits his grave often. He's buried in the graveyard, beyond the lake."

"You have a family graveyard?"

"Yes, behind the bushes, over on the left."

"Are all your ancestors there?"

"Only the ones who lived and died on the farm."

"That must make it even harder to let the farm go."

The thought of the bones of his ancestors lying deep under the earth on their land—they tie him and his family to their place forever.

Then again, that would be the case whether or not they own the farm. They will always have history there. The Fredrickson farm will always be their family legacy.

We reach Wetherill and Anders nods up at the house. "Which is your room?"

"The one with the two dormers at the end." I point at the upper level.

It's funny, it really *does* feel like my room. The guest room at Bloomington never did. It hosted a gazillion other guests and visiting university lecturers and was so sterile compared to Bailey's room, which was kept exactly as she left it, complete with her childhood toys, including a doll's house that I coveted.

No one else has ever stayed in my room here aside from me. I know that won't always be the case—it is a guest room, after all—but I suspect I'll always feel at home here.

"Sometimes I see you and Jonas when you're out in the

fields," I tell Anders. "It distracts me from work, which is a good thing."

"I'm sorry you're not enjoying your job much at the moment."

"It's okay." I'm touched by the concern in his voice. "At least I got to stay in America for longer. And I've been feeling more inspired lately, so that's good." I nod ahead at the track, to prompt him to keep walking. "I said I'd come with you."

"You haven't sobered up, then?" He looks down at me with a small smile.

We're still standing side by side and I'm soaking up the warmth of his body heat, the feeling of his soft shirt pressed against my bare arm.

"I'm fine, actually." I smile back up at him. *God, he's lovely.* "I'm not ready to call it a night yet. It's too nice out here."

The stars are pinpricks of light in black velvet and the air is cooler than it's been, the humidity sliding away as we come into autumn. The weather forecast said we'd have rain this week, but right now there's not a single cloud to be found in the sky.

"Do you sketch much for work?" Anders asks me, his boots scuffing the dirt on the track as we walk. We're no longer touching, but I still feel close to him.

"No, everything's done on a computer. I used to do sketch perspectives at my old practice, though."

I was quite in demand for them, actually. Sometimes clients struggled to visualize the final design, so I'd sketch it out in 3D and color it up, but I did it freehand, so it looked more like a piece of artwork than a standard computer visualization. Clients loved them, which, in turn, made my boss, Marie, happy.

"You have a flair for this," I remember her saying.

She's French and had lived in the UK for something like

thirty years, but her accent was still thick. "No one else can do them like you."

I liked working with Marie. She was in her late sixties, but showed no signs of wanting to retire.

An idea comes to me and I wonder . . . If she's still running a practice, would she be interested in my perspective sketches on a freelance basis? All I'd need is photographs of the existing buildings and plans.

I decide to drop her a line tomorrow and ask. It was the part of my job I enjoyed the most—that and actually designing.

As we arrive at the farm, a car starts up the drive, its headlights nearly blinding us.

"Who's that?" Anders asks, perplexed, as the car crawls forward.

He puts his arm out to hold me back and the heat of him seeps straight through the cotton of my shirt and into my skin.

"It's Heather," Anders says with shock as she passes, and I see her, her long dark hair tied up in a high ponytail and her face etched into a scowl.

"What the fuck are you doing, Jonas?" Anders murmurs with disappointment as we watch Heather drive up the track toward town.

It's a question he repeats much more angrily after storming down to the cabin.

Jonas is sitting on a deck chair by the water.

"She's *married*, for Christ's sake!" Anders yells at him. "She's got *three kids*!"

"She wanted to talk," Jonas snaps. "Nothing happened."

"Yeah, *yet*," Anders says pointedly. "She's sinking her claws into you like last time. She's not good for you! When the hell are you going to accept it?"

"I think it's a bit rich of *you* to tell me what's good for *me*."

"Don't start," Anders warns, and his voice sounds strange, uneasy.

"What are *you* doing?" Jonas asks, not with anger, but with exasperation. "It's been nearly four and a half years. When are you going to start living again?"

"I *am* living."

"Barely! Look at what you've got in front of you. You can't even fucking see it. You won't let yourself see it."

"Don't do this." Anders glances over his shoulder at me before returning his eyes to his brother, who still has his arm outstretched in my direction.

My heart is a bass drum pounding in my ears.

"I can't," Anders says, shaking his head. "You know I can't."

"Yes, you can," Jonas replies vehemently.

He drops his arm and stares at his brother.

And then Anders says, in a voice so low I can barely hear him, "I fucking can't and you know it."

The next thing I know he's stalking away from his brother, in my direction.

"I'm sorry, Wren," he mutters, not meeting my eyes as he passes.

He doesn't give me any indication that he wants me to follow him so I stay where I am and watch him walk back toward the house, my heart hammering so hard it's shaking my foundation.

"Wren."

I turn around at the sound of Jonas's voice.

"Come and sit with me a minute."

I walk unsteadily toward him.

It's clear Jonas has something to say.

30

Y OU WANT A BEER?" JONAS ASKS.

I shake my head.

"You sure? Let's go inside," he suggests when he sees me wavering.

I follow him into his cabin and take a seat at his small wooden table. The edges are rough and unfinished and I have a feeling he made it himself.

He cracks open a couple of cans and passes one to me before pulling out a chair and sitting down heavily.

I raise my can to my lips as he glugs from his, then I almost choke on my mouthful when he says, "He likes you."

I shake my head at him, coughing. "Not true. Not like that."

"He likes you, Wren. Exactly like that."

"You're wrong."

"And I think you might like him too."

"It doesn't matter if I like him," I reply, fervently shaking my head even as my stomach begins to somersault at the thought of this being true. "He's still in love with Laurie. He told me that he's nowhere close to letting her go. He said that, Jonas. He made it very clear."

"Do you want to know how I know he likes you?" he asks me.

I stare at him, my nerves stuttering. "How?"

"Because every night over the last week, after you've left, he's gone inside to watch videos of Laurie on his phone."

Is that who I heard laughing through the walls of his apartment?

"How does that mean anything? He misses her."

"You know what? I don't think he does. He feels guilty," he says. "It's guilt that binds him to her, not longing or love or anything else."

"Why would he feel guilty? It wasn't his fault, was it? *Was* it? The accident?"

Jonas shakes his head. "No, not at all. He wasn't even there."

"I don't understand what happened. He said it was a go-karting accident, but I don't get it." Go-karts are small—how could they kill a person?

"Her scarf got caught in the wheel axle," Jonas explains, swallowing heavily. "She shouldn't have been wearing one, and that go-karting place has since been shut down for negligence. But it was cold and she was at her friend's birthday party and she thought if she tucked it into her jacket along with her long hair, then it wouldn't matter. But at some point her hair must have irritated her, so she let it out and brought the scarf with it. It unraveled and got caught in the wheel axle, which kept turning, cutting off her oxygen supply."

I cover my mouth with my hand. She *suffocated*?

"It was an accident, a *tragic* accident," he continues gruffly. "I thought Anders was making progress. He moved into a new place earlier this year and finally took off his wedding ring, and I thought that was it, that was the sign. And it's been help-ing, him spending some time here, getting away from the city and the life they used to share together. But he came back from Indy so happy after the time you spent there with him. He's falling for you, Wren. I'm sure of it."

Anders has made it so clear that he doesn't want anything more than friendship from me, so my mind has been cast into doubt every time I've thought I've felt a spark between us. But now, with Jonas's words, that spark has burst into flame.

He's still talking. "But he keeps watching those goddamn videos. I'd delete every last one of them if I could, but I know he'd get them again from somewhere. It's as though he can't stop himself from trying to keep her memory alive. But she is *gone*," he says. "And he needs to *live*."

"He wants the same thing for you," I realize out loud. "You need to let *Heather* go, and *you* need to live."

He shakes his head and smiles sadly, his eyes on the table. "I know I do," he mumbles, dragging his hand over his face and exhaling with defeat.

"What do you see in her?" I ask, trying to focus on Jonas for a minute. This is important. *He's* important.

He brings his hand down and shrugs. "I don't even know anymore."

"Because if you don't mind me saying . . ."

He lifts his eyes to look at me.

". . . I think she's a bit of a bitch."

His eyes widen—I've massively overstepped—and then he throws back his head and laughs at the ceiling.

I laugh too, remembering her coming into the barn and being so rude to me, even as she held her sleepy toddler. And then I look across the table at Jonas, at his shaggy milk-chocolate hair, and my heart skips a beat.

"Her little boy. His hair."

"He's not mine, if that's what you're thinking."

"How do you know?"

"We haven't slept together in over five years."

"So, her oldest son? Her daughter?"

He shakes his head. "Trust me. The timing doesn't stack up. I used to wish that wasn't the case. I used to wish those kids were mine, so bad."

"Have you met them?" I ask, and it wasn't intended as a quip, but now I can't keep a straight face.

"Maybe I did have a lucky escape," he replies with a chuckle.

"I think you definitely did. And I'm not talking about her kids now. Jonas," I say imploringly, reaching across the table to cover his hand with mine, "you can do so much better. So, *so* much better. But you've got to open up your heart to other women, give someone else a chance. In the meantime, let Heather sleep in the bed she's made for herself."

He clears his throat. "I'll think about it." Then he gives me a meaningful look. "Now go and talk some sense into my brother."

THE FLAME IN my stomach flickers as I walk up to the house. I am so nervous. The side door is unlocked, but I call Anders's name before venturing inside. The kitchen light is on, as is the living room light, but he's nowhere to be seen. Then I hear footsteps upstairs.

"Hello?" I call out.

The movement stops momentarily, then it starts up again.

I walk to the bottom of the stairs. "Anders?"

He appears at the top of the stairs, looking very harassed, and then I notice the bag slung over his shoulder.

"What are you doing?" I ask breathlessly.

"I've got to head back to Indy," he replies with regret, dropping the bag at his feet. He doesn't come down the stairs.

"Why?"

"We've got races on the West Coast, this weekend and next. My boss wants me there."

"You're *leaving*?" I ask as he scratches his head. "*Tonight*? For how long?"

"I don't know."

The fire in my belly is doused with icy water. "Can we talk about this?"

He shakes his head. "There's nothing to talk about. I've got to pack the rest of my stuff."

"When did your boss ask you to go back to work?"

"He always hoped I'd do the last two races of the season."

"But why are you leaving so suddenly? I thought we were going to finish Bambi this week." It's the only normal thing I can think of to say.

"I'm sorry." His voice is strained.

"What about movie night? Will you be here for that?" It's at the end of September.

Pain flits across his features and he appears conflicted as he stares down at me. He gives me a single slow nod, before asking, "Will you?"

"I think so."

His shoulders drop a little.

"I don't understand what's happening," I say quietly.

"Nothing is happening," he replies, and he sounds so tortured that I hear the double meaning in those words.

Nothing *is* happening—*can* happen—between *us*.

"I've got to get on," he says, and he feels so far away, so unreachable. He's at the top of the stairs and I'm at the bottom, his uninvited guest, and the staircase between us feels like a boundary I can't cross.

My heart fractures right there in front of him. It's fully broken by the time I reach Wetherill.

31

'M OUT ON THE VERANDA, SITTING IN THE SWING CHAIR, my music playing in my ears as I stare across the fields. The corn is golden now from top to bottom. Jonas says harvest is imminent. He's hired a young farmhand called Zack to help him. There's still no sign of his dad returning, nor any word from Anders.

It's been ten days since he left and I've been so sad. I'd barely even acknowledged the depth of my feelings for him, but now I feel almost as though I've gone through another breakup.

Jonas came to see me the Monday after he went. He was worried he'd pushed Anders too hard, too soon. I didn't know what to say. For all I know, he could be wrong about his brother's feelings. But the seed he planted during our heart-to-heart in his cabin has taken root in me and shot up into something that I can't ignore.

I've been listening to unrequited-love songs, which is a little melodramatic of me, but Kate Nash's "Nicest Thing" has come on now and the lyrics speak to me.

"Hey, Little Bird!" Dad exclaims with dismay as he comes out of the front door. "What's wrong?"

I shake my head at him, but he sits down beside me and opens up his arm. I put my feet down and lean against the soft flannel of his shirt, breathing in the soap-and-laundry-detergent smell of him as tears roll down my cheeks.

"I'll help you finish the Airstream," he murmurs.

"That's not why I'm sad," I reply.

"I know," he says. "But I'm going to help you anyway."

THE NEXT DAY, I wander down to the Fredrickson farm to ask if Jonas will tow Bambi back up to ours.

"Weren't you going to do some sort of water test first?" he asks. "Come on, let's do it now," he adds before I can answer.

"Have you heard from Anders?" I ask as we walk into the shed.

"I called him Thursday," he replies. "He's staying out on the West Coast for the next race."

It's this weekend at Laguna Seca, near Monterey—the last race of the season. The weekend before that he was in Portland, Oregon. I know because Dad did his usual thing of calling me through when Anders was on-screen. I think he realized his mistake when he saw my face. My dad has put two and two together, it seems.

"How about your parents?" I ask. "Any news of when they're coming back?"

"Just in time for movie night," he replies wryly. "Pa knows about it now."

I gasp. "What has he said?"

"I haven't spoken to him, but no doubt he's his usual skeptical self. Ma heard about it from a friend in town who was excited about coming. She says she wouldn't miss it for the world."

"They won't try and pull the rug out?"

"Nope, it's happening. Will this baby be good to go for popcorn and drinks?" He pats Bambi's side.

"That's the plan. Will the popcorn be ready in time?"

"I'll harvest it early next week if the weather's right." His smile drops. "I wish Anders could be here."

"When shall we carve out the maze? Pumpkins should also be ready starting next week." We're more than a week into September and they're finally turning from green to orange.

"You finished designing it?" He accepts my change of subject.

"Yep."

"I'll probably screw it up," he warns.

"How about I sit in the tractor with you and give you directions?"

"That sounds perfect. Oh man," he says suddenly. "Please don't give up on him."

My mood deflates. "What can I do, Jonas?"

"I wish I knew."

OVER THE COURSE of the next week, Dad and I fix geometric monochrome gray vinyl to the Airstream's floor and birch-faced ply to its interior, and although my heart aches every time I think about Anders, there is a lot of joy to be found in working side by side with my dad.

When I ask Jonas if he can recommend an electrician, he comes over himself to fit the lights and sort out the wiring.

Afterward, we head into the cornfield to cut the maze and it is way more fun than I'd anticipated.

I direct him. "Five meters forward, then left. No, *left! LEFT, JONAS, LEFT!*"

For a man of so many talents, it is hilarious how often he gets his left and right mixed up. Add in the fact that I keep using the metric system instead of feet and yards and we have so many missteps, we have no idea if the maze will actually work.

Bailey and Casey come over the evening after we've cut it, and it's great to see how much friendlier Jonas is with Casey now that Heather isn't stealing his attention. Bailey, Sheryl, and I get quite tipsy on the last of the rhubarb-syrup cocktails, while Dad, Casey, and Jonas have a few too many beers. The six of us laugh so much as we try to find our way through the maze, and even though I designed the damn thing and Jonas cut it, Bailey and Casey are the first to reach the middle. Jonas and I have laid out a bunch of hay bales around a central, really quite rubbish, scarecrow.

"Your scarecrow needs some work!" Bailey hollers across the cornfield.

"You sort it out then!" I shout back.

"I'm too busy planning movie nights and weddings! Mom! *MOM!* You've got to do something about this scarecrow!"

Jonas has agreed to host a wedding at the farm next month. Bailey said it would be the perfect trial as the couple who are getting married have such low expectations.

Her words, not mine, but it did make Jonas and me laugh.

The bride is three months pregnant and she wants to get hitched before her bump is too noticeable so that she can wear her grandmother's wedding dress.

Bailey knew she was flying close to the sun by offering up

the barn instead of pushing the couple into using the golf club as a venue, but the couple would have struggled to afford the wedding package she normally sells. She's really been enjoying pulling together a last-minute wedding on a budget and it's heartwarming to see her so happy.

I wish I could stick around to see the fruits of her labor, but I have to go to Sabrina and Lance's wedding in October. I missed Sabrina's hen weekend a couple of weeks ago at the end of August—there's no way I can miss her wedding too, even if I don't welcome the thought of going alone. I may not have hard feelings toward Scott anymore, but it won't be easy seeing him with his new girlfriend at our mutual friends' nuptials.

JONAS AND I eventually make it to the middle of the maze and we cheer, high-fiving each other before sitting down on a hay bale.

I didn't realize, but the big red barn is full of hay bales from the wheat harvest back in June. Normally, Jonas would hang on to them for a while before selling them as animal bedding when the market isn't flooded with hay, but he's planning to clear them early because the proceeds from the movie night and wedding are more than covering the costs of any lost profits. He'll keep some back for makeshift seating.

"I wish Anders was here," he says to me as we sit side by side.

I suspect it won't be the last time I hear this sentence coming from his mouth.

"Me too," I admit morosely.

"Give him a call," he implores.

I sigh. "His friend Dean got in touch with me earlier."

Jonas casts me a sideways look, his brows drawing together. "And? I know Dean. He's an architect, right?"

I nod. "We met at Wilson's birthday party. He followed me on Instagram afterward and now he's messaged me."

I'm almost ready to submit the tender drawings and then I'll need to crack on with the construction package, which is even more detailed. But a few days ago, I emailed my old boss, Marie, and she replied straightaway to say that she would absolutely be interested in commissioning me for some projects she has coming up. It inspired me to update my Instagram feed with some of my old perspective sketches. They obviously caught Dean's attention.

"And?" Jonas says again.

"A position is coming up at his practice. Dean asked if I might be interested."

Jonas turns to look at me properly.

"It's maternity cover, so it's not permanent, but . . . I don't know. I'm considering it."

"You're thinking about staying in America?" His face breaks into the biggest grin, and when I nod, he picks me up and swings me around, causing my feet to hit the scarecrow and knock it over.

"Jonas, stop it!" I'm squealing with laughter. "Look at the damage you're doing!"

"Oh man, I would *love* you to stay in America!" he exclaims when he finally puts me down, and it makes me think back to what Anders said about his brother before he left: *He adores you, Wren.*

I wonder how different this summer would have been if Jonas and I had felt anything other than platonic affection for each other.

I'm glad we haven't. I adore him too. And I'm so happy he's my friend. I sense he always will be. I'll miss him if I do end up going home for good, but I hope that we'll catch up whenever I come to visit.

"I've got to go back to the UK in about three weeks for a wedding, but I might return sooner rather than later. Dean has asked me to go into his practice later this week to have a chat."

"Text Anders," he begs me. "Text him right now and ask him to meet you for a coffee."

Maybe it's because I'm tipsy and I don't have the head-space to think about protecting my heart, but that's exactly what I do.

Anders replies as we're finding our way out of the maze. We've given up on the puzzle and are cutting a beeline straight through the corn because I'm desperate for a wee. Luckily, each stalk is planted far enough apart so that cheating humans such as myself can quit when we want to.

I'm at work on Thursday, Anders says, and my heart sinks until I read on. Could do dinner? You're welcome to use the spare room if you want to stay.

And at that, my stupid heart soars.

32

*'VE LEFT A KEY FOR YOU WITH MY NEIGHBOR AT #12.
I'll be back at around 6.*

I close the door of Anders's apartment behind me. It looks the same—it's stylish, clean, and tidy—but everything feels different.

As I put my overnight bag in the spare bedroom, I glance toward Anders's room and jolt at the realization that Laurie's photo is not on the bedside table. I didn't know I was looking for it until its absence was the first thing I noticed.

Where has it gone? What does this mean? Anything? Nothing? *Everything?*

I've been feeling edgy all day, even though the day itself has been great. Dean walked me through some of the projects he's been working on and he even took me to see the amazing Visitors Pavilion at the Indianapolis Museum of Art. I feel so inspired. I would love to work with him, but there's a lot to consider. He told me I could take my time to think about it because his employee isn't going off on maternity leave until the end of the year. I don't imagine he'll have any trouble filling the position.

Anders comes home just after six. I've relocated to the

breakfast bar and am tucking into the bottle of white wine I went out and bought from the deli up the street. At this rate, I'll be an alcoholic by the end of the month. My nerves are shredded.

"Hi," Anders says, and his expression is as soft as his greeting.

He looks tired, and maybe even a little sad, but he's still heartrendingly gorgeous.

"Hi," I reply.

"How was your day?" he asks.

"Good." I straighten my shoulders and offer up the bottle. "Do you want a drink?"

"Sure." He gets another glass out of his cupboard and comes over to sit beside me at the bar.

He doesn't hug me, nor did I expect him to, but his nearness alone has every nerve ending in my body pulling toward him. It's an effort to act like nothing has happened, but technically, nothing has. He has no idea how heartbroken his departure left me. It's a small mercy.

I pour wine into his glass and slide it toward him along the countertop.

"I saw your driver came second in the championship," I say, wondering if I can force things back to the way they were, if moving forward is not an option. "Congratulations." I clink his glass as he picks it up.

"Thanks," he replies with a small smile.

"Bet he would have won if you hadn't taken the time off," I joke.

"Don't." His quiet laugh warms my blood. "Ernie keeps saying the same thing."

That's the name of his driver.

"Do you get on with him?" I ask, trying to appear unaffected, as though my whole body is *not* aching with longing.

"Yeah, he's all right. He's got a bit of growing up to do, but he's quick. He'll get there. Did you make it to Circle Centre Mall?"

I shake my head. "I didn't come here to go shopping. I was catching up with Dean."

"Dean?" He's perplexed. "My friend Dean?"

"I thought he might have mentioned it to you. He has a position coming up at his practice. He wondered if I might be interested."

"His practice? Here? In Indy?"

I nod.

I don't know what to make of the look on his face. His eyes flare wide and he turns away from me, staring across his kitchen at the wall.

"You would consider moving to America?" he asks in a detached monotone, his jaw tensing.

"Why not?"

Why does he seem so unnerved?

"Actually, I'm going to go take a shower." He slides off his stool and leaves his glass where it is. "Are you hungry?" he calls over his shoulder, and I sense he's making an effort to sound normal.

"I am a bit."

"I'll be quick. Leave in ten?"

"Sounds good."

We walk to the restaurant, a German place called the Rathskeller, which is in the basement of an ornate nineteenth-century theater building only a few minutes away from

Anders's apartment. Anders tells me it's the city's oldest restaurant still in operation today and it's like nowhere I've ever been. There's a quaint formal dining room that has the feel of an old Bavarian inn about it, and outside is a biergarten where they often have live music.

We sit in the lively Kellerbar, where multiple moose heads look down at us from the walls and old-fashioned medieval castle banners hang from the high wooden ceiling. Our server leads us to a cozy table for two that's set against a rough stone-clad wall.

"Another great place you've taken me to," I say warmly.

"There's a server here named Wayne who has the most incredible memory. A buddy of mine who went to live abroad came back after eight years and Wayne brought over the German beer he used to like drinking, as well as the loaded fries he loved, without him even asking."

"That's amazing!" I look around the bar. "Is he here tonight?"

"No, must be his night off." He peers down at his menu, so I do the same.

"I should probably go for a German sausage or something, but I've got to say I really fancy the sound of those loaded fries."

"They are great," he replies. "You should have what you feel like."

"Is the pretzel nice?"

"Yeah, let's get one to start with. You'll love it."

From the moment he came out of his bathroom, wearing the same outfit he wore on the day of the storm—a black-and-white-and-gray–checked shirt over a white T-shirt and black jeans—I've found it hard to pull my eyes away from him.

He, on the other hand, seems to be struggling to meet my eyes at all.

What I wouldn't give to know what's going through that head of his.

We place our order and our server takes away the menus.

"I finished Bambi," I say, trying to sound casual.

"You did?"

I nod. "Dad helped. And Jonas too. He came and did the electrics."

"How's he looking?"

"Jonas or Bambi?"

He snorts. "I was talking about Bambi." His brow pinches and those two furrows appear. "But is Jonas okay?"

He didn't want to part from his brother so abruptly. So why did he?

"Jonas is fine," I reply.

I tell him about the farm and what's been happening since he left, how the preparations for movie night are coming along. He's entertained when I describe us trying to cut the maze, but at the same time, he seems sad that he missed it.

"Why don't you come back to the farm for the weekend?" I ask. "The maze is opening on Saturday, families will be picking pumpkins, it will be good ole country fun," I add with a grin, mimicking Jonas. "And you should see the scarecrow Sheryl has made for the middle of the maze. It's one scary motherfucker."

He throws his head back and laughs and when he looks at me again, his eyes are dancing, lit from within.

"You left so suddenly." I can't hold the words in.

He sobers up and casts his gaze downward.

"Why, Anders?" I press him gently.

He doesn't answer at first and I'm not sure he's going to at all, but then his eyes meet mine and the intensity in them knocks the breath out of me. The air between us feels charged. But then he sighs quietly and his expression changes into something I've seen somewhere before.

It comes to me in a wave of déjà vu: this is how Scott looked at Nadine when he realized he was in love with her.

"Anders," I whisper, sliding my hand across the table toward him.

He freezes, staring at it. And then he gives me a tortured look. My stomach bottoms out, but as I begin to withdraw, he breathes the words, "Fuck, no," and catches my hand with his.

Goose bumps spring up along my entire arm, racing all the way to my neck and down the other side. And they're not butterflies inside my stomach, they're fireflies, and they've lit up my insides with a warm glow, swooping and whirling.

I'm overwhelmed by the unguarded emotion I see in his eyes, the raw need and unadulterated longing. And I'm engulfed with love—and also relief, because I'm *not* alone. He *does* care for me too.

But then he glances past me and his expression morphs into one of pure horror. I watch, confused, as he slowly straightens, sitting back in his chair and slipping his hand from my reach, leaving me wanting.

I look up as a woman arrives at our table. She's in her mid-to-late fifties, blond, attractive, and well-dressed, with light blue eyes. Her lips are pressed into a thin line, her facial features taut with distress.

"Is this why you haven't visited as much lately?" she asks Anders, jerking her chin at me.

"Kelly—" he starts to say, shaking his head.

"In sickness and in health!" she hisses, and he visibly recoils. "You swore it, Anders!" She stares down at me, and I balk at the ferocity in her blue eyes. "And you're okay with it, are you?"

"Please, Kelly," Anders begs. "She doesn't know."

"Know what?" I ask.

"That he's married!" Kelly cries with disbelief. "He's *married*! To my daughter, *Laurie!*"

A cold sweat breaks out over my skin. Anders has gone gray.

"I thought Laurie died in a go-karting accident." My voice doesn't sound like my own.

"No. My daughter, his *wife*," Kelly says, nodding pointedly at the man opposite me, "is very much alive." She shakes her head at him damningly, and then her blue eyes begin to water.

"I will call you tomorrow," Anders promises her quietly as he pushes his chair out from the table and stands up. He lays his hand on her arm, but she shakes him off and his jaw ticks as he gets out his wallet and places some notes on the table. "Wren, we should go," he prompts.

I push my own chair out and stand up, my legs feeling unsteady.

What the fuck is going on?

"I am so disappointed in you," Kelly says to Anders as he passes.

He flinches as he guides me out through the bar.

33

"W HAT JUST HAPPENED?" I ASK AS SOON AS WE'RE
outside.

"Let's talk when we're back at my apartment."

"Anders? Is Laurie still alive? Are you married?"

"Please, Wren, I'll explain at home."

"Is she in a coma or something? *Anders?*"

"Please," he begs, casting me such a devastated look that
my mouth abruptly closes.

It's the longest five-minute journey of my life. Thoughts
and questions are attacking the walls of my brain, desperate to
be heard. I'm shivering even though it's balmy, and beside me,
Anders is pale and silent, his shoulders hunched and his hands
shoved deep into the pockets of his jeans.

He unlocks his apartment and nods, stoically, toward the
living room. I feel nauseous as I make my way to his sofa and
sit down.

Anders pushes his coffee table out of the way and swings a
chair into its place, sitting down directly in front of me. He
leans forward, his elbows on his knees and his hands clasped
between them as he stares at me directly.

"Laurie is alive," he tells me unwaveringly, and I think I die a little myself, right then and there in front of him.

"And you're still married to her?"

"Yes."

"You lied to me," I whisper with horror as pain lances my heart.

He shakes his head fervently.

"You said you were married for a year and a half!"

"*Before* the accident."

"But you spoke about her in the past tense!"

"Only when it was called for, not to mislead you," he replies.

"*You didn't tell me!* That's lying by omission!"

He bows his head and nods once, accepting blame.

"Does Jonas know?" My voice has risen. "Of course he does," I say bitterly. His parents too.

"I don't like to talk about it, but it's not a secret," he replies. "There are people in town who know too, but it's no one's business but my own—and Laurie's family's, of course, but they live here in Indianapolis."

"Is she in a coma?" I ask breathlessly, unable to shake this feeling of betrayal. I've fallen for a liar.

"No. She's unaware and unresponsive."

"I don't know what that means."

"She's in a permanent vegetative state."

"What does that *mean*?"

"She's awake, but she doesn't know what's going on."

"She's *awake*?" I *really* feel as though I'm going to throw up now. "Where is she?"

"At home with her parents." He swallows, and then his eyes fill with tears. "Laurie might be alive, but she's *gone*, Wren. My wife is gone. Her mom still holds out hope that she may regain consciousness, but it's extremely unlikely."

"Could it happen, though? Could she come back to you?" This is a living nightmare.

"It's not impossible. There's a case of a woman who regained consciousness after almost three decades, but for most, the possibility of recovery is nonexistent."

"What is she *like*?" I mean now.

He draws in a long breath before launching into an explanation. "She blinks if you make a loud noise and takes her hand away if you squeeze it too hard. She has basic reflexes like coughing and swallowing, but no meaningful responses. She's not listening when you speak to her, her eyes don't follow you when you walk across the room, and she shows no sign of experiencing emotion. She doesn't know who you are or what you might mean to her."

"How are you so sure?"

"The doctors are certain. It's heartbreaking, but it's a fact." The tears that have been swimming in his eyes break free and spill down his cheeks, and I watch them as though I'm dreaming.

"She wouldn't want to live like this," Anders says. "But when the doctors initially talked about withdrawing life support, Kelly went a little mad. The final decision was mine, as Laurie's spouse, and I considered it, not just for Laurie's sake, but for her parents' too. We were all in limbo, unable to properly grieve or move on, but I didn't have it in me to make the call. Kelly wouldn't have allowed it, in any case. She would have fought me to hell and back, taken me to court, I know she would have. She was nowhere near ready to let Laurie go, and I wasn't either, so when Kelly said she wanted to take Laurie home and care for her, I went along with it." He takes another long, shaky breath before continuing. "But I think I might have made the most terrible mistake."

"How?"

"Kelly gave up her job and put her whole life on hold to look after Laurie, and that's what she does every single day. She feeds her, bathes her, brushes her teeth, empties her catheter. She does everything. *Everything.* Going to the Rathskeller would have been a very rare night out for her, and her husband, Brian, Laurie's dad, must have been at home because Kelly would never leave Laurie on her own. Brian goes along with what Kelly wants, but it's putting a massive strain on their marriage. He's angry and bitter every time I go to visit. Laurie wouldn't survive without Kelly caring for her, but she could live for years in that state. Decades, even."

"And you think Laurie wouldn't want that?"

"I know she wouldn't."

"Could you . . . Is there something . . . Could you still do anything about it?"

He says he wants the best thing for Laurie, for her family, but I hate myself for asking.

Anders stares at me and I'm half expecting his expression to transform into one of revulsion and disgust, but his face remains full of regret.

"I will never be able to set her free if I fall in love with someone else."

And then this darkness, this cold wave of misery and despair, washes over me.

It's an impossible situation. To show his wife compassion would be to destroy her mother, but he might have been willing to make that excruciating choice at some point in the future if he truly believed in his heart that it was in everyone's best interests.

But if he falls in love with another woman, if he lets himself love me as I suspect he wants to, he will never be able to withdraw life support from his wife. It would be considered a selfish, despicable, murderous act.

Everyone would say he'd killed her to be with me.

He drags his hand over his face and shudders, and I can't help but sit there in shock and stare at him.

34

TOSS AND TURN ALL NIGHT LONG. IN THE END, I HAD TO leave Anders alone in the living room, too shaken to talk anymore. He accepted it and, I think, welcomed it. It was a lot to take in, for both of us.

Laurie might be alive, but she's gone, *Wren. My wife is gone.*

That's how Jonas described Laurie too. He said she was gone. Not *dead. Gone.*

Even *I* phrased it, *Casey said you lost your wife . . .*

To use the word *died* would have sounded crass, but what if I *had* put it differently? What if I had said, *Casey said your wife died in a car accident a few years ago?* Would he have corrected me in the same way that he corrected the timing and the circumstances?

How will I ever know? How will I know when or if he would have told me about her? Did he think I'd return to England none the wiser? Forget all about him? Is that what he wanted?

When I think about the look on his face when he heard I might move to America and take the job with Dean, I think that maybe it was.

He's so much worse than Scott. At least Scott was honest

with me. Scott never lied, he never took the easy path. He made difficult choices, but he believed them to be right.

I feel a sudden rush of respect for him, which somehow makes this situation feel worse.

I thought Anders was honorable. He would have been willing to quit his job—a job he *loves*—to do the right thing by his family, his brother.

He *is* a man of honor.

My head hurts. My heart aches. I don't know what I'm still doing here, but the thought of getting up and leaving, of leaving *him* . . . I don't think I can do it, not yet.

I AWAKE WITH a start, disoriented. I must have fallen back asleep. Someone is knocking on the apartment door, but then it stops, and what happened last night comes rushing back to me in a flood.

Where's Anders? I wonder as the knocking sounds again.

This time there's no end to it, so I jump out of bed and venture out of my room in my black silk pajamas.

There's a note on the coffee table with my name on it and I snatch it up, glancing toward Anders's room to see that his bed is made and empty.

Had to go into work, his note says. *Please call me when you wake up.*

I hurry across the room, thinking that maybe he's forgotten his key, and I suddenly want to see him, so badly.

But then I open the door and find Kelly standing there and I almost have a heart attack.

"Anders is at work," I tell her.

"I know," she replies. "I just saw him leaving. It's you I want to speak to."

"What do you want?" I ask, and I don't mean it to come out sounding as rude as it does. "Come in," I add hastily, trying to make up for my manners.

"No," she replies. "I'd like *you* to come with *me*."

"Pardon?"

"I'd like you to come and meet Laurie."

A chill runs down my spine.

"Why?"

"Because I want you to meet my daughter. I want you to meet Anders's wife. I think it's the right thing for you to do. And I think it's the very least you *can* do, under the circumstances."

I swallow and shake my head.

"Call Anders," she commands me. "Call him if you must. But I know he'll agree to it."

I stare at her in disbelief.

"Call him," she orders. "I'll wait here."

My heart lurches as I push the door to, leaving it slightly ajar. I return to the spare room and pick up my phone, staring down at it for a moment before dialing his number.

"Wren," he answers.

"Kelly is here," I tell him.

"*What?*" He sounds perturbed.

"She wants me to go with her to meet Laurie."

He doesn't say anything, but I can hear background noise. It sounds as though he's in his car and I'm on speakerphone.

"Anders?" I prompt.

"What do you want to do?" he asks me quietly.

"What do you mean, what do I want to do?"

"Would it help?" he asks. "To meet her, to understand?"

"Are you serious?"

"Please do whatever you feel is right." He sounds both pained and resigned. "I am fine with whatever you decide."

Cursing, I end the call.

Can I do this? Might it help to see Laurie? Might it help me to walk away? Do I *want* to walk away?

I don't know the answer to any of those questions, but suddenly I'm stripping off my pj's and pulling on my clothes.

I follow Kelly in Dad's car, keen to have an escape route if it all becomes too much. She drives north through a leafy suburb where houses of all sizes and colors line the streets.

How many times does Anders make this journey? Every month? Every week? Every day?

I see a sign for Broad Ripple and wonder how close he and Laurie used to live to her parents.

It feels as though time is moving in slow-motion, but we've only been driving for about fifteen minutes when Kelly turns into a driveway outside a medium-sized white house with black window surrounds, a gray slate roof, and Doric columns running along the front of a small veranda.

My nerves are like snakes in my gut, writhing and coiling and twisting my insides into knots. I can't actually believe I'm doing this and I'm still not exactly sure *why* I'm doing it, but somehow I'm reaching for the handle, climbing out, and shutting the car door behind me.

What is beyond the glossy black door of this pretty house? What am I about to see that I will never be able to forget? I sense that this moment will stay with me forever, whether Anders is in my life or not.

Kelly unlocks the door and ushers me into the hallway, her

lips thin with dislike and determination. But then a change comes over her and she brightens her expression and calls out, "I'm home, Laurie, honey!"

I hear movement from the room adjoining the hallway and my heart skips a beat, but then an older man appears, looking frazzled. He sees me and his bushy eyebrows almost hit his receding hairline.

"She came," he says out loud, gawping at me.

"Brian, this is—Wren, is it?" Kelly asks me flatly.

I nod, recalling that she overheard Anders say my name last night.

"This is my husband, Brian, Laurie's father," she continues her introductions. "And this," she says in a forced, happy manner as she walks into the next room, "is Laurie! Hello, honey," I hear her say warmly.

My heart is pounding so loudly I wouldn't be surprised if Brian could hear it.

He stares at me, his face etched with misery, and nods toward the next room.

I put one foot in front of the other and walk through the arched doorway into a living room. It's spacious and well lit, with shiny wooden floors, white walls, and an array of leafy plants. But that's all I can take in. My attention has zeroed in on the blonde in the wheelchair.

She's facing away from me, her head dipping slightly to the right. The long, luscious locks that I saw in photographs have been cut to jaw-length and lie limply against her slim neck. The ends of her hair are uneven, a little ragged, as though someone has done their best to feather them without much success. She's wearing a pale blue T-shirt with lace cap sleeves.

Kelly goes around to the other side of the wheelchair and

pulls out a slim wooden dining chair from under the table. "How are you, my darling?" She's talking to Laurie as though I'm not even there.

I can't seem to take one step farther into the room. I stand and stare as Kelly picks up some hand cream from the table and squeezes some out before lifting Laurie's right hand.

"This is your favorite hand lotion, isn't it?" she asks her daughter as she massages it in, before looking up at me and letting the smile slip from her lips. "And we listen to your favorite songs and watch your favorite TV shows, don't we?" She pulls her gaze away from me to smile brightly at her daughter. "You're in there, aren't you, Laurie? You're going to come back to us, I know you are," she murmurs with torment before looking up at me again. "Don't just stand there, come and meet my girl."

I swallow, more on edge than I have ever been in my life.

This is Anders's wife. He married her almost six years ago, promised to love her in sickness and in health.

Until death would they part.

I strengthen myself, because I owe Laurie this. I've fallen for her husband and I am so very sorry.

But I didn't know, I tell her silently. *I would never have tried to take him from you if I'd known you were alive. I never would have fallen in love with him in the first place.*

Do I love him?

I'm not sure, standing here in Laurie's parents' house, in enemy territory with a woman who hates the very sight of me, that I do.

How could I?

How could I ever forgive him for this?

I never want to go through anything like this ever again.

I just need to get through the next few minutes and then I can leave.

As I force myself to walk around the chair, Laurie's legs, half hidden by a sunflower-yellow skirt, come into view. Kelly continues to massage her daughter's hands, all the while talking to her lovingly, a devoted mother. The smell of Laurie's perfume mingles with the hand cream and I recognize it as the scent I sampled in the grocery store in town. No wonder Anders reacted so strongly to smelling it on me—Kelly probably applies it to her daughter's wrists daily.

I force my eyes downward from the top of Laurie's head to her face, to the woman I saw in a wedding photograph smiling up at the man I'd put on a pedestal. I prepare myself to see her beautiful face, the face I've seen in pictures, a face lit with love and joy.

But that's not what I find when my eyes finally reach their target.

Her cheeks are gaunt and washed out, drooping slightly where her head has dipped to the side. Her blue eyes are dull and lifeless, staring unseeingly at her mother's lap. Her lips are thin and pale and turned down at the corners.

I'm awash with shock and horror. Because she does not look like the woman I've seen in photographs. She barely resembles a person at all. There is a human body sitting before me, flesh, blood, and bone. But the soul who existed inside it seems to be long gone.

I understand now why Anders can't stop watching videos of her. He wants to remember her like that, as the woman he married, the laughing, happy girl of his dreams. The person he thought he would spend the rest of his life with, have children with, grow old with.

And I wonder, as ice floods my veins, how he can bring himself to come here. How he can see his beloved wife like this, day after day, week after week, month after month, year after year. How he can bear to know that there may be many more years of this existence laid out before him. And I understand how he must have felt so much more content when he was at the farm. How desperately he needed to get away from the city and the crushing pressure he must feel to visit. I bet he comes here every single day that he can. Because that's Anders. He *is* a man of honor, of duty.

He would have come, feeling guilty that his mother-in-law had put her own life on hold to care for her daughter. He would have come, knowing that his father-in-law was angry, maybe even at him because he hadn't taken on the responsibility of caring for his wife himself. He came when he must have felt weighed down with the burden, with heartbreak, with despair. He came and he never would have stopped coming.

He never *will* stop coming.

He will never abandon her.

As I watch Kelly treating her daughter with so much love and gentle care, my heart shatters into a million pieces.

And it shatters for her, this poor woman, Laurie's mother. I feel so desperately sorry for her. It is the most appalling, tragic situation, because Anders is right. Laurie is *gone*. They have *lost* her. And I don't believe that she is ever coming back. Yet they will live like this—all of them—until Laurie's body gives up of its own accord and she slips away for good.

But right now, she is Anders's wife and he is bound to her.

35

'M CRYING SO MUCH THAT I HAVE TO PULL OVER: FULL-
body-racking, animalistic-sounding, heart-wrenching sobs.
It's a while before I'm able to navigate back to Anders's
apartment without being a danger to myself or others.

Anders has been calling me, but I've been in too much of a
state to answer. I wonder if he's spoken to Kelly or Brian, if he
knows I've seen Laurie.

My head is telling me to return to his place, pack up my
things, and go. To leave him be. It's about time I remove myself
from his life so he doesn't have to go to the trouble of trying to
eject me again. But I can't walk away until I tell him that I understand. He deserves that, my understanding. And I do understand now.

I no longer blame him for not telling me about Laurie. He
has every right to not want to talk about her. It isn't his fault
that I developed feelings for him. He tried for a long time to
not give me any reason to think that he might care for me too.

The thought of him endeavoring to keep his wife's memory
alive as he struggled to keep up his walls destroys me. He must
have felt so torn.

I let myself back into his apartment and pack up my things before unpacking them all again to take a shower and brush my teeth. I can hardly think straight. Once I'm ready, I repack my things and go to the sofa to lie down, feeling utterly drained and desperately sad.

I must fall asleep because a featherlight brush along my arm rouses me. When I open my eyes, Anders is standing there.

"Are you okay?" he asks in a low voice.

His eyes are creased with pain. He's suffering—deeply—and it hurts to see him in such agony.

I sit up, my arm still tingling from his touch.

"I'm sorry," he murmurs, backing up a couple of paces as I get to my feet.

He's wearing slim-fitting black trousers and a short-sleeved black polo shirt with his racing team's logo printed on the breast pocket.

"No," I say as he searches my face. "You don't need to apologize to me."

I step toward him and slip my arms around his waist, and his breath hitches as I lay my face against his chest. A moment later, his hands seek out my hips.

To go from only our hands touching yesterday to our full bodies today is almost too much. But I tighten my grip on him, and, in turn, he gathers me closer.

We're flush to each other—our chests, stomachs, hips, and thighs are aligned—and my heart has inflated with so much compassion and sorrow that I think I might burst. I want to wrap him up in my love, try to take away some of his pain.

"I'm so sorry for what you've been through," I whisper.

He shakes his head and begins to withdraw.

"What you've done for Laurie and her parents, for your brother and your parents. You're a good man," I say. "You tried to keep me at a distance and you haven't done anything wrong."

He's stopped trying to pull away from me, but we're not pressed as closely together as we were.

"You're right about Laurie," I say. "She's gone. And I am so very sorry you lost her."

His chest expands as he shakily inhales.

"I'm so sorry," I repeat as tears fill my eyes. "It's not your fault that I couldn't help falling for you."

The breath he draws in this time is sharp and raw.

"I'm going to leave now, though, let you be. I don't want to be another problem for you to have to worry about."

As I go to step away, he gasps and clutches on to me, and it's a desperate, anguished act. And then his body starts to heave, and it's the most distressing thing I have ever heard, the sound of him sobbing.

I'm lost after that. I hold him as tightly as I can, but I don't have the strength to stop myself from joining him.

To see this strong man who has held it together time and again for so long, for his family, for Laurie's family, for me, to see him finally let himself go . . . It wrecks me.

Eventually, he stops crying, but his chest continues to jerk with great shuddering breaths. His arms loosen around my waist, so I take the hint and slide my hands down to his slim hips before taking a final step backward. He stares past me at the sofa, his eyes bloodshot, his nose swollen, his cheeks damp, and his dark blond hair in disarray.

"I'll take that fucking tissue now, please," I tell him, and he lets out a short laugh and meets my eyes momentarily, remembering Jonas getting cross with him because he couldn't bring himself to comfort me that time.

That feels like a lifetime ago. Life seemed so much smaller than it does now.

He turns and walks up the steps to his bedroom, then opens the door to his bathroom. I hear him blow his nose before he reappears with a handful of tissues. I sort myself out and return to the sofa.

He comes and sits beside me.

And maybe I shouldn't, but I edge closer, drawing my knees up so they're lying sideways against his lap. He doesn't tense up, so I think it's okay.

"Will you show me a video of her?" I ask.

He shoots me a look, taken aback.

"I'd like to see what she was like, when she was alive."

It wasn't a slip of the tongue. She may not be dead, but she's not really living, either.

"Are you sure?" he asks warily.

"Yes."

He unhurriedly gets his phone out of his pocket and brings up his photo collection. From my position beside him I see an album entitled "Laurie," but I don't realize I'm holding my breath until he's pressing play and passing me his phone.

The screen comes to life, showing Laurie and Peggy in the living room at the farmhouse. There are multicolored balloons attached to the ginger-pine walls and both Laurie and Peggy are clutching champagne glasses. The background noise is of people talking.

"Happy birthday, Ma," I hear Anders say fondly from off-screen.

"Thank you, darling," Peggy replies happily, raising her glass to him.

Laurie smiles up past the camera, at her husband, her blue eyes merry. Then suddenly she nods past him as a chorus of "Happy Birthday" begins.

Anders jerks the camera away to Jonas, who's carrying a cake blazing with dozens of candles in from the kitchen. The room is full of people and I have a feeling this is a significant birthday—Peggy's seventieth, perhaps, six years ago. Everyone falls silent as Peggy readies herself to blow out the candles, and then Laurie appears again at the edge of the frame and Anders adjusts his angle so she's sharing the screen space with his mother. Peggy only manages to blow out a third of the candles on her first go, and I watch Laurie's face as she, in turn, watches her mother-in-law, giggling as Peggy blows and blows and blows.

"Oh, you do it, Laurie," she snaps good-naturedly, giving up on her fourth attempt.

"Are you sure?" Laurie asks her laughingly.

"Only if you don't steal my wish," Peggy teases.

"It's all yours," Laurie replies warmly, stepping forward and blowing out the last few remaining candles.

Everyone in the room cheers, but Jonas's cheer is the loudest. He's still holding the cake at the side of the shot, but Anders's attention is focused on his wife.

She looks at him and the film ends, freeze-framed on her laughing face.

I stare at the screen.

"She's so beautiful, Anders."

He releases a quiet sigh and takes his phone from me.

"I think I would have liked her."

He nods. "She would have liked you too."

She certainly wouldn't like me if she knew how I feel about her husband. I understand entirely why Kelly is so furious— she's defending her daughter because her poor daughter can't defend herself.

My heart contracts as my resolve stiffens. I need to do the right thing. I've already caused so much pain to Laurie's family—and to Anders too, which is the very last thing I wanted to do. I'm not so selfish that I'd choose to make their lives even more complicated and upsetting.

"Oh," Anders says suddenly, abruptly getting up from the sofa and leaving me feeling cold without his body heat. "I wasn't sure if you'd eaten since yesterday?" He looks over his shoulder at me and I shake my head.

"I dropped by the Rathskeller on my way home. Got you those loaded fries and pretzels."

I sit there in a daze as I hear him opening and closing the microwave, setting it, the clinking of plates and glasses and cutlery. And I want to stay, but my entire body feels racked with pain because I've just fallen in love with him a little bit more and if I don't go now, I'm not sure I'll ever find the strength.

I force myself from the sofa. I force myself to walk into the bedroom. I force myself to pick up my belongings. And I force myself to make my way through the living room to the kitchen, where he has his back to me, upending the fries into a bowl on the far counter. And this is so much harder than it was to walk into Laurie's house and face her mother, her father, *her*. *This* is the single most difficult thing I've ever had to do.

"Anders," I say quietly.

He turns around, sees me standing there with my bag, and looks utterly crestfallen.

"Please don't go."

"I have to," I reply.

Fresh tears shine in his eyes. Maybe he thinks that I'm walking away because it's too hard for *me*, because I'm so insecure that I feel threatened by his beautiful wife or that I simply can't handle his terrible circumstances. He probably has no idea that I'm leaving because I don't want to be yet another burden to him.

It doesn't really matter what he thinks. The important thing is that I go.

Tears begin to spill from his eyes and he shakes his head imploringly. I mean to step away, but he steps toward me before I can make my feet move, sliding my bag off my shoulder to the floor. He cups my face with his hands and stares into my eyes, anguished, silently asking me not to leave.

I slowly reach up and brush my thumb across his cheekbone and down the side of his face. His skin is warm and his stubble is rough, and I find myself smiling as I stare into his grief-stricken eyes, my vision going blurry.

"It's okay," I whisper, blinking to free my tears. "We'll always be friends, right? If you'll still have me?"

He swallows. And then he nods, letting me go and lowering his head.

I step away, pick up my bag, and walk out the door.

36

L AST NIGHT I DREAMED THAT I WAS AT ANDERS'S APART-
ment. I was sitting on his Eames chair in the sunroom,
warmth and light spilling onto my face from the giant
Crittall windows. I could hear Anders in the kitchen, making
dinner, and it occurred to me with a surge of joy that I lived
there, that it was *our* apartment, that he and I were together.
Then I looked down at my stomach and saw a bump and felt
such a flood of love for the baby we were having together.

I woke up with a start and stared into the darkness for a
long time afterward, my heart galloping wildly as I tried to shut
out that perfect vision of an impossible future.

But is it impossible? I wonder as I lie awake now. *How long
would I be willing to wait for him?*

I feel an intense rush of longing for the child in my dream.
I was ready to start a family with Scott. How many years could
theoretically go by, with me putting my life on hold? Would I
be too old to have a baby? How much would I be willing to
sacrifice, to *risk* sacrificing, to be with Anders? Wouldn't it be
better for me to move on, to get over him, and hope that the
real love of my life is just around the corner?

I feel heartsick at the thought of that person being anyone
but him.

It doesn't help, being here. I know I can't possibly take the job Dean offered me, not now. When I fly back to England next weekend, it will be to stay. The thought brings with it a fresh wave of pain, not because I'm finally going home, but because I'm leaving. I fled the UK to put some distance between Scott and me and now I'm fleeing America to escape Anders.

One foot in front of the other, one day at a time. The most pressing thing right now is getting through movie night tonight.

The last week and a half has been a whirlwind of activity. The maze opened last weekend and I've been helping Dad and Sheryl welcome customers, in between doing my own work, of course. The sound of children laughing as they've tried to find their way to the middle and out again has been one of the few things to put a smile on my face.

Jonas has been in the fields with Zack, the farmhand he hired to help him with harvest. It's been raining on and off, but the breaks due to the weather have given him time to finish getting the barn ready. He's shifted all but forty of the hay bales and we're hoping the weather will hold because, ideally, we'd like to have the screening outside. The hay bales will work as makeshift chairs for people who forget to bring their own—we plan to set them up in a semicircle this afternoon, facing the screen that the mobile cinema company is bringing.

Bailey has been such a star, pulling everything together. I'm so proud of her. She and I will be serving popcorn and drinks out of Bambi tonight—she's hired machines for the purpose. The Airstream is not fitted out with furniture or cabinets yet, so we'll use freestanding shelves and tables. It'll be a bit crowded inside, but I'm excited to use Bambi at last.

Jonas sold a large quantity of the popcorn he'd harvested to a popcorn company, taking the rest to a factory where they packaged it up, ready for sale. He's fulfilled his orders from the stores in Bloomington and others farther afield and he plans to sell what we don't use tonight at farmers' markets.

Yesterday evening, Peggy and Patrik arrived home while Bailey and I were at the farm. We've been helping Jonas sweep out the barn and string up lights, inside and out.

At the sight of his dad, I'm pretty sure Jonas drew a breath that he's probably still holding, but Peggy was so happy to see her son, giving him the longest hug. Patrik was more reserved and a little dour, but he wasn't unpleasant. Bailey and I left them to it, but we'll see them today, of course.

I spoke to Jonas after I returned from Indianapolis. I wasn't ready to talk, but he came calling for me, so I dragged myself out of the house and we went for a walk down to the river.

He wanted to know what had happened, and when I explained I'd met Laurie, his face fell off a cliff.

"I wish one of you had told me." I tried not to let bitterness creep into my tone.

He apologized, but said he hadn't felt it was his place.

"They may still be married, but they're not really," he said.

"How can you say that?" I asked with incredulity. "They *are* married, that's the end of it."

"What if he divorced her?" he asked, turning to look at me.

I blanched. "He will never do that and you know it."

"But what if he did?" His eyes scanned my face.

"Stop it, Jonas," I snapped angrily. "Despite what you said, he *does* still love her, and he'd never hurt her parents like that."

We walked in silence for a while, and then he asked, "What does she look like these days?"

"Why, when was the last time you saw her?" I replied out of interest.

"Not since she was in the hospital. Ma visited a lot at first, but she hasn't been in a couple of years."

"Why not?" I didn't expect that of his mother, nor of him.

"When her eyes opened and it became clear that the lights were out and nobody was at home, I didn't see the point."

"That seems a bit callous," I muttered, immediately regretting it when he got angry and defensive.

"She's dead, Wren! Or as good as dead, anyway," he added, his voice flattening. "But whatever, what the fuck, it's not your problem."

I walked away from him then, shouting over my shoulder that I didn't want him to follow me.

We haven't spoken of Laurie or Anders since.

BAILEY IS ALREADY at the farm and I'm heading there shortly. The movie won't kick off until sunset, which is around seven thirty, but we're welcoming people from five thirty and it's three thirty now.

Jonas is planning to barbecue burgers, and Bailey's friend Tyler has arranged for a mobile bar to come from Bloomington. She works at an events company, which is where she and Bailey met when my sister was just an intern. When Bailey rang her, panicking that the permit to sell alcohol had not been granted in time, Tyler pulled some strings. She's coming along tonight. It will be nice to finally meet her.

There's a good chance Anders will come too, but I'm trying not to think about that. I'll be too crushed if he doesn't.

DAD IS FINISHING up telling a family of four where to find the maze and the pumpkin patch when I pop into the barn to say that I'm on my way.

I smile at the family as they exit.

"Have fun!"

"Thank you," they all cutely call back in unison.

At least most of the people around here have good manners.

"I'm heading down to the farm," I say to Dad. "See you there later."

"Look at you!" he exclaims, emerging from behind the counter and opening his arms.

I'm wearing the red-and-black ditsy-print dress Bailey convinced me to buy when we went shopping in Bloomington, the one that hugs me in all the right places, flaring softly at my knees. She had to persuade me to wear it tonight too. She knows that the two dresses I bought still haven't made an appearance, but the nights are drawing in and I'm running out of opportunities to wear them before next summer.

"Do I look all right?" I ask uncertainly.

"You look beautiful," Dad replies.

It's not that I desperately want to be told that I'm pretty, or beautiful, or that I even particularly care that much what I look like. I'm fine as I am, I really am. But *oh*, it's the way that he said it, my *dad*, as though he's told me all my life. The casualness of it makes my eyes water.

Because it doesn't matter what the rest of the world thinks, every child should be told that they're beautiful by their parents.

"We won't be late," Dad promises as he gives me a hug. "We can't wait!"

We let each other go and I begin to turn away, before pausing and turning back to pluck a tiny twig from his hair.

He laughs when I show it to him, and I'm still smiling as I walk out of the barn.

I'M TRYING TO prepare myself for not seeing Anders's car on the driveway, but I'm so on edge as I come past the cornfield that I almost don't register the sound of his laughter. And then I spy him up ahead, walking side by side with a striking redhead toward the barn.

I can't see her face, but her wavy hair cascades down her back and her legs go on for miles, and when Jonas appears, the delight on his face is visible from here. Who *is* she?

Whoever she is, I bet she's beside herself to be flanked by these two brothers. How could she not be?

My jealousy is irrational and I know it, of course, but it does cause me to wonder how many advances Anders has had to fight off. He must be so over it.

One foot in front of the other, Wren. It's my new mantra.

Jonas catches sight of me and lifts his hand. The redhead turns around to see who he's waving at, but my attention is focused on Anders.

He's seen me.

And his smile has faded.

I feel as though my rib cage has closed around my heart, squeezing it in a vise. I hate that it hurts him to look at me.

"Wren!" Bailey yells, distracting me. She jogs toward me, her eyes all big and boo-like as she slows her footsteps a few feet away. "You are *killing* it in that dress!" She comes forward to give me a hug. "You okay?" she asks in my ear.

I nod against her shoulder. She knows all about what happened with Anders, and chewed Casey's ear off for him not being more clued up about Laurie, as if the poor guy could help what he did and didn't know.

She releases me and smiles sympathetically. "Come and meet Tyler," she urges, hooking her arm through mine.

"Is she the redhead?"

"Yep. Have you seen Jonas's face? He can't stop drooling."

I laugh. "Is she single?"

"Yep. I bet she'll be interested too."

"How could she not be?"

Bailey grins at me. "You weren't."

"Yeah, but *Anders*," I reply with a shrug.

"I wasn't either."

"Yeah, but *Casey*," I say with another shrug, because the more I see them together, the more convinced I am that they're perfect for each other.

Bailey smiles. "He's growing back his mustache, you know," she tells me casually.

"Is he?"

"Yep. So all is right with the world now."

I giggle, even as my heart continues to thud as we walk across the dusty farmyard toward the others.

I think she's happy, but I know Bailey, at least I do *now*, after this summer. She's not the sort of person to let life happen to her. She'll grab life by the horns and make it work for *her*, and if it doesn't go well here, if she and Jonas don't carry on running events that she enjoys organizing, if she continues to be bored by life at the golf club, then she'll do something else.

I know she will. Whether it's here in town, over in Blooming-ton, or farther afield, and Casey will move mountains to be with her. He won't be happy unless she is, that's a fact. So they will be okay. Of that, I'm certain.

"Tyler, this is my sister!" Bailey calls as we approach.

"Oh, hey!" Tyler exclaims, meeting me halfway to give me a hug. "I've heard so much about you!"

She's stunning, with sparkling blue eyes, a face full of freckles, and a smile that could light up a room.

"You too. It's so good to finally meet you. Thanks so much for letting us stay at your place last month."

"You'll have to come back so we can have a night out to-gether," she replies.

"I'd love that."

Jonas comes over and sweeps me up in a hug, growling a greeting in my ear and putting me down right next to his brother.

Subtle, Jonas, subtle.

I look at Anders, my heart flipping and flipping and flip-ping.

"Hey," he says quietly, a small smile on his lips, two creases between his perfect brows, his startlingly flawed eyes resting on mine.

"Hi," I reply, wanting more than anything to reach out and smooth those creases away, once and for all.

Stay strong, the voice inside my head reminds me. *You have to be strong for him.*

But then Anders steps forward and takes me in his arms. I breathe in sharply, barely even registering the clean citrus scent of him or his hard chest pressing against mine before he lets me go.

My stomach dips, my smile wavering at the realization that he just hugged me and I was so tense, I didn't even hug him back.

"Right, come on, Wren," Bailey chirps, and I know she's attempting to rescue me because I don't think it could be any more awkward. "Can you get the Airstream out of the shed, Jonas? We need to set up."

"I'll do it," Anders offers.

"Bailey, can you tell me where you want the mobile bar?" Tyler asks her.

"Crap," Bailey mutters, stopping and turning around. "You all right?" she asks me.

"Fine."

Anders and I walk alone, toward the shed. So much for escaping the awkwardness of the situation.

"How have you been?" he asks.

"Okay," I reply, nodding. "How about you?"

"Fine." His reply is clearly far from the truth. "Sorry that was weird back there," he says after a moment of painful silence. "I was trying to be . . ." He shakes his head. *"Friendly."* His tone is wry, self-deprecating.

I bite my lip and look at him again and this time he meets my eyes and smiles. His gaze drops to my lips before flicking away.

"Right, where's the Airstream, then? Let's see what you've done to her."

"Him."

"Him," he obliges me.

He spends a few minutes checking Bambi over, smiling as he traces his fingers over the birch-faced ply Dad and I curved around the inside walls.

"It looks great," he says, turning on the 1960s lights that I bought at the antiques warehouse. "The retractable wheel works okay?"

"Yes, really well."

"Got to always remember to put it away before you tow this thing anywhere," he cautions.

I nod. He's already warned me how important this is.

"So, when are you going to do your trip across America?" he asks as he checks over the back door seal.

"I don't know," I reply with a shrug. "Maybe next summer."

"You won't go sooner?"

"I doubt I'll be able to get over here again before then."

He freezes. "Where are you going?"

"Back to the UK."

He stares at me. "You're leaving?"

I nod. "A week from today."

"For good?"

"I think I need to."

I catch his look of devastation as he averts his gaze. "Will you close her up? *Him!*" he corrects himself as he walks away. "I'll back up the tractor."

I DON'T GET a chance to speak to Anders again as we get everything ready, at least, not more than a few words here and there.

Peggy comes over to say hello when Bailey and I are in the process of getting the drinks and popcorn machines up and running, and she seems thrilled by the *Fredrickson Family Farm* logo Jonas had designed for the popcorn packaging.

Bailey has to duck off when the mobile cinema company arrives, but Peggy stays to chat with me for a while, telling me all about Wisconsin and what a perfectly relaxing time they had there. It wouldn't surprise me if it's a place they'd consider retiring to.

As it's such a lovely evening weather-wise, I've opened the rear door and put serving tables on the ground outside. Anders helped Jonas bring his charcoal grill up from the lake and barbecue smells infuse the air. A local five-piece bluegrass band, friends of Casey's brother, Brett, arrive and set themselves up. Bailey told me about them—they didn't expect to be paid; they just thought it would be a fun night and good exposure. Even their warm-up music adds to the overall ambience.

When Bailey turns on the festoon lights, I step out of the Airstream to have a look at how the lights glint off the silver exterior while the inside glows warmly. I can't help but smile as I drink it all in.

Bailey has to keep ducking off to organize various things, so I'm left on my own for a while, and as customers start to arrive, a queue forms outside Bambi.

"Want some help?" Anders asks, popping his head through the doorway.

"Please," I reply without thinking. I'm run off my feet.

We work side by side, serving popcorn, drinks, and candy.

"Your mum is in her element," I say to him once we're on top of things.

He looks across at her. She's stationed herself beside Jonas, who's flipping burgers while she takes payments and offers condiments.

"She's happiest when she's in the kitchen."

"Maybe she'll open a diner in Wisconsin."

"I can picture it," Anders says with a sideways smile at me.

He takes my breath away every time.

"Where's your dad?" I ask, steeling myself.

"Here he is now," he replies with a frown, nodding across the yard.

His dad is heading straight for Jonas. He still has a slight limp, but his injury doesn't slow him down. Anders is tense beside me.

"You should go on, son," we hear Patrik urge him gruffly. "You should be welcoming people as they come. I can take over here."

Jonas stares at him, speechless.

"He's right," Peggy interjects, giving Jonas a nudge. "You're the host. We can manage here."

Patrik holds out his hand for the big silver spatula Jonas is clutching.

Jonas looks dazedly at Patrik's hand, then at the spatula, before slowly surrendering it.

Patrik claps him on his back as he walks off.

"No way," Anders murmurs with astonishment.

"The fact that your dad offered to help or the fact that Jonas stepped away from the barbecue?"

"Both," he replies with a grin.

We have a big flurry of orders before the movie begins and then Bailey comes over to ask Anders if he can relocate some of the hay bales so that families can sit together. She sticks around to help me and when Dad and Sheryl reach the front of the line, the four of us look at each other and giggle.

"Can you take a photo?" I ask Dad, handing over my phone.

Bailey and I throw our arms around each other and beam

at the camera. Dad clicks off a shot and I let Bailey go, but she turns and kisses me on the cheek.

"Love you, sis."

"I love you too," I reply warmly.

"You girls," Sheryl says, tears filling her eyes as she smiles at us. "Look at our girls," she says to Dad.

"They are something," he replies with awe, shaking his head.

"There are other customers waiting, you know," Bailey snaps, surreptitiously swiping at her own eyes. "Get all emotional on us later."

Sheryl smiles at her knowingly before leading Dad away. I lean over and press a kiss on my sister's cheek.

AS THE SKY'S colors fade into darkness, the festoon lights are turned off, and the movie begins, I sit down and soak up the atmosphere. There must be upward of two hundred people sitting out here, under the stars, and most have brought their own chairs and blankets. The air smells of hay, popcorn, and fresh evening dew, and despite my underlying melancholy, it's impossible not to feel sparks of happiness at how well the evening has gone.

Peggy and Patrik are sitting with Dad and Sheryl at the back. Bailey and Casey are cozying up nearby. Jonas and Tyler are still standing by the mobile bar, paying way more attention to each other than to the film, from the looks of it. And I'm sticking close to Bambi so I'm ready to open up again at intermission.

I'm not sure where Anders is and I can't help but be preoccupied looking for him. I'm guessing he's somewhere near his brother, but I'll rest easier once I know.

I completely forgot to bring a chair or blanket of my own, so I'm perched on a hay bale, shivering a little. The mobile cinema company supplied headsets, so the film audio is playing directly into people's ears rather than blaring out of loudspeakers.

I jolt when a blanket is draped around my shoulders. I look up to see Anders. He comes to sit on the hay bale beside me.

I didn't know it was possible to love so fully and hurt so deeply at exactly the same time.

"Thank you," I whisper.

He nods, staring ahead. His face is lit by the light of the big screen and I notice he doesn't have earbuds in.

"Where's your headset?" I ask as I remove one of mine.

"I think they ran out," he replies with a shrug. "It's okay. I've seen this film loads of times."

"Me too, but *Ferris Bueller's Day Off* never gets old." I pass him my right earbud.

He glances at me. "Are you sure?"

"Of course."

He takes it from me and we sit side by side, sharing the audio.

I long to snuggle up to him, like Bailey is doing with Casey, like Sheryl is doing with Dad.

A wave of loneliness crashes over me and I feel sick with sadness and confusion. As the film gets into full swing, I barely crack a smile, let alone laugh.

Anders shifts to make himself more comfortable, resting his hand just behind my back, and I feel a straight line of warmth from where his arm is stretched out, barely touching me. I can't help myself: I lean against him. A moment later, he slips his hand around my waist and pulls me to his side. My heart contracts as I rest my cheek against his shoulder, intensely aware of every inch of skin where we're connected.

This is as close as we're ever going to get.

It's true what I said to Dad all those weeks ago when he collected me from the airport: *You can't help who you fall in love with.*

Dad couldn't help falling in love with Sheryl.

Scott couldn't help falling in love with Nadine.

I couldn't help falling in love with Anders.

But I *can* help what I do about it.

Intermission comes around and I feel the ghost of a kiss being pressed to the top of my head. As the festoon lights come on and people start to get up, I hastily take out my earbud and hand Anders the headset.

"Thanks for the blanket."

I leave it on the hay bale.

"Do you want some help?"

"No, it's okay."

As I walk away from him in the direction of Bambi, I can't help but think of all the times he walked away from *me* without so much as a backward glance. I want to be that strong, that determined, but curiosity gets the better of me and I cast a look over my shoulder.

He's sitting where I left him, with his elbows on his knees, staring after me and looking utterly wrecked.

I feel a full-body shock as our eyes connect. But by the time I reach the Airstream and glance over again, he's gone.

And then it occurs to me to wonder: Did he just kiss me goodbye?

My hands begin to shake violently.

Suddenly, I see Jonas striding toward me, parting the crowd.

"This is bullshit," he says angrily as he reaches me, staring me down.

"What's wrong?"

"Bailey?" he snaps over his shoulder. "Can you take over for Wren? I need to talk to her."

He frog-marches me around the back of the barn.

37

"J ONAS? WHAT IS IT?"

"Like I said, bullshit."

"What are you going on about?"

"You *love* him!" he yells at me, letting me go and rounding on me.

I recoil.

"And he loves you!"

I realize that he's not angry, he's upset. These Fredrickson brothers are hard to read sometimes.

"So what if I do?" I raise my voice in turn. "What good is that to anyone?"

"If you didn't love him, I could understand you wanting nothing to do with him. His life is complicated. But you *do* love him. I just saw it written all over your face."

"But his life *is* complicated, Jonas!"

"And that's too much trouble for you, is it?" he demands to know, and I can see that he's disappointed in me.

"It's not too much trouble for *me*! I care about *him*! About Laurie's *parents*! About how much it will hurt *them*!"

He hesitates. "Is that true?" he asks. "You're walking away because you care too much, not because you care too little?"

"Yes!" I cry.

He shakes his head at me despairingly. "You've got this all fucking wrong. You need to fight *for* him, not walk away."

"What's the *point*? That will only hurt him more! He'll be torn between Laurie and me, between Laurie's parents and me!"

"Laurie is *GONE*! Don't tell me you don't know that! Anders is *alive* and *here* and you've got to convince him that he's worth fighting for. I'm not saying it's going to be easy. But someone needs to go to battle for him, to get him away from Laurie's parents. He's fucking *drowning*, Wren. They're pulling him under. This is not the time to walk away, this is the time to *fight*. You're the only one who can do it. God knows, I've tried. My mom has tried. We've all tried to convince him to divorce Laurie and live his life, and if not divorce her, then at least live the way he wants to. He's made enough sacrifices for her and her parents over the years. Last year, he was headhunted by Ferrari, for Christ's sake, and he said no! He gave up the chance to work in Formula 1 and travel the world because he felt too guilty. But he needs to stop feeling beholden to Kelly and Brian. He has no control over what they do—their choices are their own. At this rate, he'll be stuck in this half-life until Laurie can be laid to rest, and I don't even want to think about how wrung out he'll be when that day finally comes." He steps forward and places his hands on my shoulders. "But you can help him, Wren. You can give him something to fight for. *You* are worth fighting for. Show him that you're willing to fight for him too."

MY HEAD IS reeling when Jonas leaves me standing behind the barn. Is he right? About all of it? I thought I was being self-sacrificing by removing myself from the situation, but I realize all I've done is make Anders feel even more alone. I've deserted him, abandoned him when he needed me the most. I thought *I* was lonely. How must *he* feel?

The thing is, if it was anyone else, Anders would fight for them. He simply won't fight for himself.

Jonas is right. I have to get in his corner.

The idea of being the other woman, the person Laurie's parents will hate with a vengeance, makes me shudder. But maybe, by adopting that role, I can take some of the heat off their son-in-law.

I'll think about that later. The most important thing now is finding Anders.

And Anders is nowhere to be seen.

The second half of the movie begins to play and he doesn't return to our hay bale. There's no way I can sit still and wait for him, so I get out my phone and text him.

Where have you gone?

He doesn't reply, and after twenty minutes, I make a snap decision to check the farmhouse. I sneak off and try the side door, expecting to find it locked, because what sort of family leaves their home open when there are a couple hundred people wandering about?

The trusting sort, as it turns out. The door is unlocked, so I venture inside, calling out Anders's name. I check the kitchen, the living room, the dining room, and the office, and when there's no sign of him, I tentatively climb the stairs to the first floor. I call out his name again as I walk along the corridor, but can hear no movement behind any of the doors. I don't dare open them—I already feel bad enough about trespassing.

Afterward, I search the entire farmyard, from Jonas's cabin to every single row of cars parked behind the barn. As the film finishes and people start to pack up their things and walk or drive back to town, I stand on the track and look out across the dark fields. The dry, crispy cornstalks sway in the breeze, whispering.

He could be anywhere.

Jonas comes over to me. "There's always tomorrow."

"What if he returns to Indianapolis?"

"He won't. He promised to shell corn with me."

"Shell corn?"

"We're harvesting the fields, Wren," he says facetiously, as though he's told me a hundred times before. "That's what we say: we cut beans and shell corn."

"Cut beans, shell corn. Got it."

He grins at me. "We'll make a farmer's wife out of you yet."

"Not if Tyler beats me to it," I bat back.

His eyebrows jump up and he barks out a laugh.

"You did seem very cozy over by the bar."

"She's a nice girl," he replies with a shrug.

I smile and glance at the dark fields again, sobering as I turn back to him. "Can you hide his car keys, just to be on the safe side?"

"I'll sleep with them under my pillow," he replies.

"I'm not joking."

"Neither am I."

Jonas sends Bailey and me packing with the rest of our family, saying he'll tackle the cleanup in the morning. He can't start "shelling corn" until the afternoon, when the sun is out and the dew has evaporated—the moisture levels have to be exactly right or the crop could be ruined.

I lock up Bambi and take one last look around for Anders, but wherever he is, he doesn't want to be found.

AS I'M FALLING asleep, a message comes in, jolting me awake.

> Sorry, I needed some fresh air and then got talking to my mom.

Fresh air? We were sitting outside! I tap out with a smile, so relieved that he's replied.

> Ironic, isn't it?

Hope you're okay. When he doesn't answer, I add, Jonas says you're helping with harvest tomorrow. Can I come for that ride in your tractor with you?!

I wait and wait for his answer.

> Okay.

I wonder if sleep will ever come easily again.

38

WEAR THE OTHER DRESS I BOUGHT IN BLOOMINGTON,
the blue, yellow, and white ditsy-print with buttons all the
way down the front. It's a gloriously warm day so it's the right
weather for it.

It's also a perfect day for "shelling corn." After spending
almost three months watching the stalks turn from green to
golden, I'm excited to see what harvesting entails. I can hardly
believe I'm going to be sitting next to Anders for hours on end
in the confined space of a tractor. I can't wait.

I'm bringing my rucksack with some snacks, water, and a
jumper in case it's cooler later. When Jonas is out harvesting
the fields, sometimes he runs well into the night, and I'm in it
for the long run.

I mean that in every sense.

Honestly, I feel racked with anxiety at the thought of putting myself out there today and being rejected. If Jonas hadn't
spoken so plainly, so passionately, I'm not sure I'd have the
courage to fight. Anders is right, I am insecure. But it's time to
put on my big girl's pants.

I FIND ANDERS with his mum and brother, over by the first big shed. All three of them turn to watch me as I approach and I could not feel more self-conscious.

"Well, aren't you as pretty as a picture!" Peggy calls, beaming.

I think I must blush from head to toe. I can't even look at *Jonas*, let alone Anders.

"You ready?" Anders asks me.

"Mm-hmm." I glance at him to see that he's smiling, but my eyes dart away again.

"There's a picnic in the fridge, under your seat," Peggy tells me.

"Wow, thank you. Wait, you have a fridge in the tractor?"

"We're not going in the tractor, we're going in the combine," Anders says. "I thought it might be more fun."

Jonas punches his arm, grinning.

As Anders turns away, I catch Jonas's eye. I expect him to find my discomfort amusing, but his expression is serious.

I nod at him. He nods back, and we follow Anders into the shed.

The combine is gigantic, ivy green with bright yellow hubcaps on wheels that are taller than me. The corn header has been attached to the front—a wide green contraption lined with what looks like a row of green rockets.

Anders climbs up several wide rungs of a ladder to the door, opens it wide, goes inside, and then turns back toward me.

"Be careful," he warns, taking me by my forearm as I slowly reach the top.

He pulls the door closed and moves over to the driver's seat while I sit down, my skin burning from his touch.

There are windows on all four sides of the cab and they're huge—it's like a glass box on wheels.

I once made the mistake early in my career of designing wall-to-wall and floor-to-ceiling windows in a south-facing London studio apartment. When I later bumped into the owners, they moaned that it was like living in a greenhouse.

But as the combine rumbles into life, air-conditioning kicks in. Phew.

Peggy and Jonas move out of the way and Anders turns around to look out of the enormous rear window, holding on to the back of my seat for support as he reverses the giant machine out of the shed.

I can't help but study him as he concentrates on the maneuver. He's wearing a moss-green T-shirt that brings out the color of his eyes and the twisting of his body has caused it to stretch at the collar, revealing smooth, tanned skin and the contour of his collarbone. I can feel the heat from his arm on my shoulders as my eyes travel along his lean muscles. I don't even try to stop myself from looking because I'm laying my heart on the line today. I've got nothing and everything to lose—and I plan to give it my all.

Anders meets my eyes before he drives forward.

"What are you thinking?" he murmurs.

"I'll tell you when we don't have company," I reply.

He tugs his eyes away from mine to look past me at his mother and brother.

"I'll take you to the farthest field I can find."

At his low tone, butterflies swarm into my stomach.

We drive along the dusty track and turn right onto the sun-bleached road, the hazy blue sky stretching overhead and golden fields all around. After a while, Anders pulls off the road onto the grassy verge and then we're staring down at acre upon acre of dried-out corn swaying in the breeze, like waves on the ocean.

He presses some buttons on a digital display and we advance slowly on the cornfield, the green rocket teeth drawing in the stalks. He turns round to look out of the rear window, so I do the same, and to my amazement, corn kernels, fully shelled and free of chaff, are pouring into the combine behind us.

"You going to tell me what you were thinking?"

"I'm warming up to it," I reply.

He raises one eyebrow and faces forward again, returning his attention to the digital display. "Well, with the way this yield is looking, we've only got about twelve minutes before Jonas will be coming with the grain cart."

"*Twelve minutes?* That soon?"

"Yep."

"What's the grain cart?"

"It's a trailer towed by the tractor. I'll unload this lot into it and he'll take it back to the farm to empty it into the grain bin."

It's not as noisy in here as I expected it to be, just a low hum of the engine as we move at an unhurried pace, gathering up cornstalks and leaving behind a flattened field of crispy, shredded chaff.

"This is kind of addictive," I say as I peer over my shoulder again.

"I bet you wouldn't still feel that way if you were out here at two in the morning," he teases.

"Is that how long you're sometimes at it?"

"When the conditions are right, we can go all night. But obviously, you can head home whenever you want to."

"No way. If you're staying, I'm staying. Don't you have work tomorrow, though?"

"I can go in late."

I turn toward him and lean my shoulder against the seat back, crossing my legs. He glances down at my knees, at the white trainers on my feet, and then he swivels to look out the back again.

"Sometimes I think I spend more of my time looking backward than forward," he says.

"In more ways than one?"

He meets my eyes. It's a moment before he replies. "I guess you could say that."

I am so jittery as I stare back at him. I have so much to say and no idea where to start. It's just as well we're going to be out here all day.

"Have you warmed up yet?" he asks me.

I shake my head.

He narrows his eyes at me, puzzled.

"How were your parents after last night?" I ask.

He smiles and faces forward again. "They were good. I was up late last night, talking to Ma and Jonas. We had another long chat this morning with Pa too."

"What about?"

"Ma and Pa are going to step down."

I gasp with delight and he smiles at my reaction.

"They've agreed it's time to hand over the reins to Jonas. Pa told him he was proud of him, that he wished he'd had the guts to try something different himself."

"Wow! That's incredible."

"Even Ma was surprised." He stares ahead for a while and then he sighs quietly. "Last night, she told Jonas and me something we didn't know, that Pa has suffered with depression all his life. She said that before we were born, there was a time when she was seriously worried about him. When she saw Jonas withdrawing and drinking more, and then realized he'd been clearing out his cabin, she panicked because they were all things Pa did too. Luckily, she had a therapist friend all those years ago who had some knowledge about depression. Ma doesn't know what she would have done without her." He exhales heavily and I reach over and squeeze his knee. He looks down at my hand for a moment before continuing. "Pa's carried a lot of weight on his shoulders over the years, trying to protect Ma, Jonas, and me without ever really going about it the right way. But hearing all this from our mom cast a different light on everything. Jonas and I felt so sorry for him."

I let him go as he reaches for a CB radio on a curly black wire, bringing it to his lips. "Can you come now?"

"*On my way*," Jonas replies, his voice crackling over the air.

"We're almost full," he tells me.

"Already?"

"Yep."

"What did you think of Tyler?" Anders asks, leaving the darkness of his parents' pasts behind.

"I thought she was really nice. Jonas seemed to like her."

"He took her number."

"Did he? Awesome! I was half expecting Heather to turn up and steal away his attention."

"She tried to buy a ticket, just one for herself, but Jonas told her he thought it would be best if she stayed away."

"No way! Really?"

He nods.

"Yes!" I punch the air and he chuckles.

"I don't think Jonas is going down that road again."

"I hope not."

JONAS ARRIVES WITH the grain cart before long, riding beside us while a big arm extends from the combine and unloads the corn into his trailer. He aligns himself perfectly and Anders doesn't slow. They even turn the corner at the end of the field without spilling any kernels.

"That was so smooth," I say with amazement as Jonas drives off back to the farm.

"You going to tell me what's on your mind in the next twelve minutes?" he asks with a playful smile that suddenly transforms into a frown. "Something's wrong," he says as he studies the digital display. We slow to a stop and he cuts the engine. "Excuse me." He squeezes out past me, his legs knocking against my knees as he swings the door open and climbs down the ladder with the ease of someone who has been doing it his whole life.

I lean out of the door and watch with concern as he opens up a dusty panel on the side of the combine.

"Don't you fall," he calls up to me.

"I'm holding on tight," I reply, liking that he cares enough to keep reminding me. "Can you see what the problem is?"

"The drive belt to the threshing drum has snapped," he replies distractedly, climbing back up to the cab and reaching for the CB radio to fill Jonas in.

"*Okay, hang tight,*" Jonas replies resignedly. "*I'll check if we have a spare when I've finished dumping this load, but I think I'll have to order one. Could be a couple of hours. You want me to send Ma over on the Gator to get you?*"

Anders looks at me, silently requesting a response. I shake my head.

"No, we're fine here," he says into the receiver, his eyes still on mine.

"*Good*," Jonas replies, falling silent.

Anders frowns at the CB radio as he docks it. "Good?" he mutters before shrugging and looking at me again. "Picnic down by the river?"

My stomach awakens with a flurry of nerves.

I climb down from the combine and stand in the warm sunshine, waiting for Anders to get the food and a couple of cans of soft drinks out of the fridge. He chucks me a picnic blanket and I sling it over my shoulder.

The river is at the bottom of the hill, lined with leafy trees that are beginning to turn. In a few weeks they'll be awash with reds, oranges, and yellows—I wish I could be here to see them.

We walk over the section of the field that has already been harvested, kicking up chaff and the occasional chunk of dry yellow corn that has evaded the combine.

When we reach the river, Anders lays down the blanket in the shade of a tree and waves his hand, inviting me to sit. He joins me once I'm settled, passing me a can and cracking one open for himself. He takes a sip before pulling sandwiches out of a bag.

"We've got chicken or ham and cheese. Take your pick."

"You choose first. I'm not that hungry."

"No?"

"I'm too nervous to eat," I admit.

He stops what he's doing and looks at me. "Why are you nervous? *Wren*?" he demands when he sees that my hands are shaking.

322 • PAIGE TOON

"Sorry. I'm a bit of a wreck."

"Why?"

"Because I have something to say and I'm scared to say it."

"Go on," he urges gently.

I take a deep breath and then force myself to stare at him. "When I left you at your apartment, it was because I thought I'd be hurting you and Laurie's parents by staying. I could see how torn and guilty you felt. Kelly and Brian would hate you to move on from Laurie, but I do think, in time, they might understand."

He shakes his head in adamant disagreement and stares at the river.

How will I ever get through to him?

"I know that you don't want to hurt Laurie's parents, but you didn't marry them, Anders. You didn't make promises to *them*. Their daughter is gone and it is a terrible tragedy, but you can't give up your own life to make them happy. Because you never *will* make them happy, no matter what you do. They will live with grief for the rest of their lives, *no matter what*. And that is not your fault. Nor is it your responsibility. Nothing you do will ease their pain. You do realize that, don't you? Anders?"

I wait until he looks at me, his eyes damp and those two damn creases back between his brows. I edge closer, kneeling directly in front of him, my heartbeat reverberating through my body.

"You can still love Laurie in sickness and in health for the rest of your life," I say earnestly. "But love the *memory* of her," I implore, a lump swelling in my throat.

I've been researching vegetative states this morning, so I understand a little more about Laurie's condition.

"Her body doesn't feel anything. No pain, no suffering. There is nothing you can do that will help or hurt her."

I feel as though I'm spinning, a kite caught in a tornado. I think he can see how lost I am because suddenly he's reaching for my hand. My skin thrums under his touch, but the contact tethers me enough to go on.

"I don't want to walk away from you," I whisper, tears filling my eyes. "Laurie is gone, but I'm here, and I'm asking you to let yourself love me."

Tears spill down my cheeks and the next thing I know he's brushing them away with rough fingertips as they fall.

"I *do* love you, Wren," he says in a low, insistent voice, cupping my face with both hands. "I've been trying so hard, for so long, *not* to fall in love with you. But it's impossible."

My stomach was a tightly coiled Slinky, but now it begins to flip over and over down an imaginary staircase.

He's not finished.

"But I can't leave her. I won't divorce her."

His words are like bullets, piercing my gut. I remind myself that I expected this.

I nod at him. "I'm not asking you to. But please . . . Will you just allow yourself to picture what it could be like? Between us? If I returned to America after my friends' wedding and took the job with Dean? If I was the person you came home to? Not that I'm expecting to move in with you," I mumble. "At least, not straightaway." I cover my face with my hand. "This is so embarrassing."

I know I'm asking a lot. He's been trapped inside this life for so long that I don't think he can conceive what it would be like if he didn't have to live this way.

His fingers circle my wrist and he gently pulls my hand down from my face.

"I *have* imagined that life," he says, his eyes shining. "I wish—*so much*—that things were different."

An idea comes to me, a last-ditch attempt.

"Give me today," I ask him. "Be free, just for one day. You've given Laurie and her parents years. I'm asking for one day. I'm asking you, no, I'm *begging* you, to not think about them today. Cast aside your guilt and your responsibilities for a single day and be here, with me, *completely*. I'm going back to England on Saturday. You never have to see me again after that if you don't want to. But please, Anders, let me have today. You owe me that much."

I absolutely detest myself for resorting to emotional black-mail. He owes me nothing, but making this poor man feel as though he also has some sort of duty to *me* might be the only way to persuade him.

It's for his own good, I remind myself as Jonas's words come back to haunt me: *He's fucking drowning, Wren.*

Anders studies me, his jaw twitching, and hope begins to fill my heart because it's clear that he's thinking about it.

I've pushed him so hard, which is very out of character for me. But I don't want to leave knowing I could have fought harder. I'd rather live with embarrassment than regret.

"Today," I repeat. "Just you and me. Here and now. No guilt, no remorse. Just openness and honesty between us. Please."

He's still staring at me, and on impulse, I reach out and run my thumb over the creases between his eyebrows.

"What are you doing?" he asks with a half laugh, mildly amused despite the intensity of the situation.

"I really want to get rid of your worry lines."

He catches my hand and presses his lips to my wrist and my stomach contracts, my breath hitching, my eyes widening all at once.

"Today," he whispers with intent.

My heart leaps.

"Today."

39

"WHAT DID YOU THINK, THE FIRST TIME YOU SAW me?"

We're lying on our backs, our hands intertwined blissfully between us as we stare up at the trees. The air around us is filled with the sound of birds chirping and water tumbling over rocks in the nearby river.

I'm tingling all over, my blood zinging in my veins, but my heart still hasn't recovered from the stress of the last half hour. I'm not sure when I'll get over it, if ever, but I've put my discomfort into a box along with Anders's guilt. I'll deal with it later. As will he. It will be much worse for him, of course.

"I thought, 'Who is that hot goth emo chick dancing to Stevie Nicks at the bar?'"

I turn my head and laugh at him. "You did not."

"I did," he insists, grinning at me. "Well, apart from the 'goth emo' bit."

I roll over onto my side, not letting go of his hand.

I can't believe I'm holding his hand . . .

"Why, what did you think of me?" he asks.

"I saw you out of the corner of my eye as you came into the bar. I could tell there was something different about you. You and Jonas both stood out, and I kept trying to catch a glimpse of your faces. Eventually, I saw Jonas when you were both over at the pool table, but you remained elusive. Until you went to take a shot and your eyes met mine and I felt as though the whole world stood still."

He grins at me and I blush.

"Sorry, that was corny."

About as corny as the contents of his combine harvester.

He turns onto his side, letting go of my hand so that his is free to prop up his head.

"And then we met and you thought I was such a dick," he teases, reaching across to tuck a lock of my hair behind my ear. My skin buzzes in the wake of his fingertips.

"You *were* a bit of a dick," I agree with a laugh. "But I was drunk and annoying, so I think we're even."

"You were pretty wasted," he concedes with a smile. "But I liked you."

We're in some sort of parallel universe right now. He's spent the whole summer looking away from me and now I can finally stare into his flawed green eyes uninterrupted. It's indescribable how thrilling it feels. I'll never get used to it. No amount of time will ever be long enough. I wish I could tell Jonas to never come with that replacement part for the combine.

A rush of panic reminds me that we *don't* have all the time in the world. Or at least, we *won't* if I can't break through to him once and for all.

"I can't pinpoint when I fell for you, though," I say.

His eyes soften. "I know when *I* realized I was a goner."

"I think I saw the moment on your face," I admit.

He raises an eyebrow at me inquisitively.

"Was it at the Rathskeller?"

"No, it was at the bowling alley. When you scored a strike. You were so happy, and then you glanced over at me—"

His smile fades and I frown at him.

"But you winced and looked away as though you were in pain."

He nods. "It hurt to love you."

I reach over and smooth those creases away. "Not today," I murmur. "Don't let it hurt you today."

We stare at each other for a long moment and then he slips his hand around my waist and slowly draws me to him. The gap between us closes to mere inches and everything seems to go very still—*I* go very still; even my heart holds in my chest for a beat.

His gaze lingers on my mouth and all of my senses sharpen, the air around us beginning to crackle. When his lips finally meet mine, I jolt with electricity from head to toe.

The world speeds up again and I'm lost in sensation, shivers rippling down my body in waves as he pulls me flush to his hips. Our kiss intensifies and deepens, our tongues locking and colliding, and my heart is beating frantically, all reason erased from my mind.

Then he's lifting me on top of him and sitting us both up, his hands sliding along the backs of my bare legs to settle my knees on either side of his hips. My fingers skate along his broad shoulders and I lean in to press my lips to the hollow at the base of his neck. He bucks beneath me as my teeth graze his skin, holding me in place. The friction between us is unbearable. I want him like I've never wanted anyone or anything, and I can feel him and there's no denying he wants me too.

Our kisses grow hungry and desperate and he clutches me to him, letting out a low growl that vibrates through my body.

It's the single sexiest thing I've ever heard. But then he slides his mouth away and pants against the side of my neck. My shivers are out of control.

"Wren. I'm losing it."

"Me too. Please. I need you."

I don't know if any of that was intelligible, but suddenly we're both in a frenzy. My fingers are on his hips, his belt. His hands are beneath the hem of my dress, skirting up to the tops of my thighs. He doesn't stop me as I unbuckle him, nor do I stop him as he tugs at the flimsy fabric separating us. I stand up quickly to rid myself of the obstruction and then I'm slowly sinking down, and, oh, it's completely overwhelming.

I swear, I will have bruises on my hips from where his fingers are digging into me, and I'll want to get them tattooed there so I remember this moment for the rest of my life.

Not that I'll ever forget it.

We begin to move together and I feel so much, so intensely. The fireflies in my stomach have multiplied and I am so full of light and love that I think I'll explode. I can't imagine what it's like for him—it's been four and a half years.

"Don't wait for me," I say against his lips.

"Come with me," he replies.

And heat spreads up my body, bringing with it intense waves of pleasure, and as I detonate, he holds me still and stares into my eyes before falling with me.

I'M PRETTY SURE that as soon as Jonas sees us, he guesses what's happened. It takes him a long time to wipe the smile from his face, and that only happens when he and Anders are in full mechanic concentration mode, taking out the broken part and replacing it with a new drive belt. It looks complicated from where I'm standing.

It's early evening by the time we get going again. The sun's low rays are casting the most beautiful light across the fields, making them appear even more golden.

Anders reaches across and links his hand with mine, and as the sun sets and the stars appear, and Jonas comes and goes, emptying the combine into his grain cart, I fall deeper and deeper in love.

We talk about everything and nothing, listen to music, and sit in companionable silence. And I so desperately *want* this life. A life with him. The thought of him not wanting it too absolutely terrifies me. But I keep tamping down these moments of dread, living for the moment, as I've asked him to.

When, at three o'clock in the morning, Jonas finally tells us he's calling it a night, Anders returns to the farm and parks the combine in the shed.

"I'll give you a lift back in the Gator," he says.

"Not on your motorbike?" I reply with a smile.

"It's too noisy. It'll wake your dad and stepmom."

"Is that why you wheeled it home that time?"

He nods.

"Aw." I did wonder. "Actually, can we walk?"

"Anything you want."

We take it slowly, arm in arm, and when we reach Wetherill, he kisses me deeply and unhurriedly under the stars on the doorstep.

"I don't want this night to end," I whisper against his lips.

He looks past me to the swing seat and cocks his head.

My heart lifts.

We sit there, cuddling, until the sky begins to brighten and the stars dim.

"Will you come and stay in Indy with me on Friday night?" he asks, smoothing his hand over my hair. "I'll take you to the airport on Saturday morning?"

"I would love that," I reply, my insides flooding with warmth and joy as I realize what this means, that this is not the end, it's the beginning. I feel so full of happiness and hope for the future.

As he walks away against the backdrop of a sky awash with pinks and purples, I stand on the steps and wait. Sure enough, he looks over his shoulder and waves at me before disappearing from sight.

The smile is still on my face as I fall into bed and slip off into a deep, dreamless sleep.

THE NEXT DAY, I awake to a text that he must have sent on his way home.

See you Friday x

Can't wait, I text back. I miss you already.

He doesn't reply.

I give it a day before asking: Are you okay?

No response.

I try calling.

He doesn't answer.

And I grow scared, really scared, scared that he's fallen back into that life, the life that was drowning him, scared that

Laurie's parents are pulling him back under, scared that he's all alone with no one to fight for him. I feel as though I'm in water, trying to scramble out onto a slippery bank, but I keep falling back in. I'm no longer on solid ground.

I keep calling as I pack up my things. Calling when Bailey, Casey, and Jonas come over for a farewell dinner on Thursday night and Jonas tells me he hasn't heard from him either.

And I'm panicking and I don't know what to do, but I will see him tomorrow and hopefully he'll tell me that he just needed a few days to clear his head.

But then a text comes in from him.

What time are you coming?

Five, if that's okay?

Yes, I'll come home from work early.

Are you okay? Where have you been? I've been worried.

Two more hours pass before he replies.

I'll see you tomorrow.

Dad drives me to Indianapolis, chatting with me the whole way, but I can't escape this hideous feeling of something being terribly wrong. I couldn't even say goodbye to Sheryl and thank her for everything she's done for me without feeling like I was going to be sick. She made me promise to come back soon and I told her I'd try, but so much depends on what happens when I see Anders.

Is he bringing me to his apartment just so he can tell me to my face that it's over?

As soon as this thought strikes me, I sense that it's true.

My heart is racing as Dad pulls up outside the silk lofts. I force myself to stay in the moment with him as he gets my bags out of the boot.

"I'll take it from here, Dad," I say with a bright smile, trying to hold it together and pretend that nothing's wrong.

And while we have made real progress this summer, he still doesn't know me well enough to read when I'm acting.

He takes me in his arms and tears prick my eyes as I hold him, my dad.

"I love you," I say in his ear.

"I love you too, Little Bird. Fly back to us as soon as you can."

When his car has turned out of the car park, I get out my phone and call Anders.

He doesn't answer.

I text him. I'm outside your apartment.

I'll buzz you in.

No. Answer your phone.

I call him again. This time he picks up.

"Wren?" he asks with confusion.

"Is it over?" I demand to know. "You and me. Is it over?"

"Wren, come inside," he says quietly.

"No, Anders. Tell me now," I order him. "I want to know if it's over."

"Please come inside," he implores.

"You can't do it, can you? You can't be with me while you're still married to her. And you won't leave her, you won't divorce her, you won't cause any pain to her parents, even though this life is tearing you apart."

There's silence at the other end of the line.

I hear him breathe in and I know that I've lost him.

"I can't," he says. "Please come inside so we can talk."

"No," I reply morosely. "No. There is nothing more to say."

I end the call and drag my suitcase out to the road, looking left and right for a taxi. Instinct has kicked in and I know exactly what I need to do. I'll go straight to the airport, see if I can catch an earlier flight, and if not, I'll stay at the terminal until the morning.

But I don't want to see his face, not one more time, never, ever again.

A taxi pulls up and the driver winds down the window.

"Airport, please."

He climbs out of the car, puts my suitcase into the boot, and I sit in the back and buckle up.

I stare at Anders's apartment, wondering if he's on his way out here, wondering if he's changed his mind and will try to stop me.

Who am I kidding? I know he won't. And right now, I don't even want him to.

I am *done*.

The cab pulls away from the curb.

40

T'S SABRINA AND LANCE'S WEDDING DAY. I'VE SPENT the last week on autopilot, going through the motions without feeling a thing. I can't even cry.

Yesterday, I met Mum for lunch. She knew something was deeply wrong, but all I could say was that I'd fallen for the wrong man. I promised to explain more at some point, but I still can't even wrap my own head around it. I must be in shock.

Mum wanted to know who was coming with me to the wedding today. I said no one. She asked if Scott was bringing Nadine. I said I presumed so, but I hadn't spoken to him and I didn't want to bother Sabrina by asking. I can't even find it in me to care.

I don't care what I look like either, but I make an effort for the bride and groom because no one wants to see a washed-out wraith at their wedding.

Black is calling to me, but I opt for navy lace. My dress is sleeveless, lands just above my knees, and clings to my curves. I wear it with navy high heels and leave my hair down. It comes almost to my shoulders now, and is lightened by the sun.

I sit alone in the church on Sabrina's side. Scott is two rows in front of me on Lance's. Nadine is not with him and I neither know nor care what it means. I'm numb.

The only time I break is when Sabrina and Lance say their vows to each other up at the altar. My friend looks so beautiful with her dark hair braided across her crown. She's wearing a long, slimline white gown and Lance is handsome in a charcoal suit.

I am in the moment with them, but I cannot hear "In sickness and in health, till death do you part," without thinking of Anders.

He stood up at an altar and listened to a vicar saying those words to him and his bride, asking for a promise, a lifelong commitment.

And I can imagine his face as he said, "I do." He would have looked at Laurie with so much love, and I bet he didn't even smile. I bet he was serious, feeling the gravity of the situation. And maybe she smiled at him as he said it, maybe it brought tears to her eyes.

But whatever. I don't fucking care anymore. My insides are cold steel.

I don't even know if he's tried calling me because I blocked his number on my way to the airport, then switched off my phone as an extra precaution. Maybe one day I'll allow myself to think about that day on the farm, when the bruises have faded—and I don't mean the ones on my skin.

But right now I want to wipe anything Anders-related from my memory.

SCOTT COMES TO find me after dinner, when I've had a few drinks and have warmed up enough to do small talk with Sabrina's friends from university. They're a lovely bunch and I'm having a nice time. I'd really be enjoying myself if it weren't for that bastard back in Indianapolis.

Oh God, he's not a bastard. I don't mean that. I asked for a day; he gave me a day. He never gave less than he promised.

These thoughts are dangerous so I try to stop thinking them.

"Hey," Scott says, his hand on my shoulder.

I look up at him, at his open, smiling face, and I think, what a lovely, uncomplicated man you are.

"Hey," I reply, my voice softening as I get up to give him a hug.

His embrace is oddly familiar, yet utterly alien.

The girl who was sitting next to me heads to the bar with her friend, so Scott takes her seat.

"How are you?" he asks, his brown eyes searching mine.

"I'm fine, how are you?"

"I'm good." He nods.

"I see you've had a haircut." His dark brown curls are closer to his scalp than they used to be. They're barely curls at all.

I used to trim his hair for him occasionally. I remember once describing it as the rich, dark color of peat, to which he jokily replied, *Are you calling me a bog monster?*

Got to say, I preferred it longer.

"Had to find myself another hairdresser," he replies with an awkward half laugh.

"Ha. Serves you right." How I've got the strength to tease him, I do not know.

"You look nice," he says.

I shrug. "This old thing? You too."

He's wearing a navy suit with a white shirt, unbuttoned

at the top. He was wearing a tie earlier—that was navy too. Unwittingly, we match.

"Are you here with anyone?" he asks.

"Nope."

I don't ask him if he is. I can see that he's not.

"How was America?"

"Good."

"Did you finish the Airstream?"

"I did."

"I hoped you might send me some more pictures."

"Sorry, I meant to." I really did. "Do you want to see some now?" I offer.

"I'd love to."

I get out my phone.

I DON'T KNOW how it happens, but two hours later, we are laughing and talking like old friends. And I'm kind of enjoying myself, which surprises me. I still don't know if he's with Nadine or if they've split up, but it doesn't matter. I no longer love him, he no longer loves me, and I feel at peace with his decision to end our engagement. I want him to be happy, and hopefully, one day, I'll find happiness with the right person too.

"Where's Nadine tonight?" I ask to distract myself from the memory of Anders.

Curiosity has finally got the better of me.

"She's staying with her parents in Norfolk."

"Oh, right. Everything going well, then?"

He nods, and okay, my heart does squeeze a little. I'm only human.

"Why didn't she come tonight?"

"I thought it might be better if I came alone."

"Not because of me, I hope," I say sharply. I don't want his pity. Is that what this is?

"No, not really. I mean, I thought it might be nice to see you, without her. For old times' sake. Being here with Sabrina and Lance . . . I don't know," he mumbles uncomfortably.

That was actually really decent of him. But I already knew he was a good man. Nadine is lucky.

"I am glad we got to catch up," I say.

He smiles at me, meets my gaze for a long moment, then his smile slips away.

"I'm really sorry about everything."

"It's okay. Scott, honestly, it's okay." I reach out and touch his forearm as his dark eyes glimmer under the low-level lighting. "You were right. About me, about everything. I've done a lot of soul-searching in America, and I didn't give you the respect you deserved. *I'm* sorry."

I've stunned him. He hunches forward and drags his hand over his mouth.

"And I'm also sorry if I looked down on you. I didn't mean to."

He recovers, shaking his head. "You didn't outwardly. But there's nothing wrong with knowing what you want in a partner and striving for it. Life's too short. You've got to be honest with yourself about the sort of life you want, the sort of person you'd like to spend it with. As long as you're kind to the people around you, which you are, you should be true to yourself."

I was wrong. I do still love Scott, even if in a different way than how I did before. A tiny part of me always will.

"Thank you," I murmur, reaching across and slipping my arm around his neck.

We rest our foreheads on each other's shoulders for a brief, tender moment, before releasing each other.

"I'm going to head home," I tell him, blinking back tears.

"Are you okay?" he asks me with concern.

I nod. "I will be. Don't worry, this is not about you. Wipe that look of guilt off your face, please. I can't stand it."

He laughs at me, I smile at him, then I gather my things and go say goodbye to Sabrina and Lance.

My mind is racing as I walk home, and all of the feelings I've been suppressing over the last week are welling back up, threatening to consume me. I welcomed the numbness, that yawning, horrible, hollow feeling. I'm genuinely terrified of the pain I can feel building now. I step up my pace, desperate to get home before it engulfs me.

He never promised more than he gave. He is an honorable man.

And I am still overwhelmingly, devastatingly, earth-shatteringly in love with him.

I should call him. I should tell him that I forgive him. Not that it was his fault, what happened. I pushed him too hard. Yes, I was doing what I thought was best for him, but he'll be blaming himself for how it turned out.

What was it like for him to return to Indianapolis after what we had done? The guilt must have been unbearable. Did he go straight to see Laurie? Did he confess to her parents? I imagine her mother losing it at him, weighing him down with shame. He must have felt so full of self-loathing and regret.

Oh, Anders. How could I ever think that one good day with me could unravel four and a half years of suppression? Of *course* he was going to need more time. I should have been more patient.

Is it over? Really and truly over? Could I go back to being

his friend, at least? Someone to support him and love him, no matter what?

If I'm honest with myself, I don't know that I can. I don't think I have the strength. The realization makes me crumble.

I need to get home before I lose it right here on the pavement.

I wonder if he's in as much pain as I am. It terrifies me that he might be in even more.

41

One week earlier

ANDERS

PULL INTO KELLY AND BRIAN'S DRIVE AND SIT AWHILE before reaching forward and cutting the engine. The heaviness in my chest feels so much worse than usual.

I don't know if I can do this.

That thought runs through my head.

But I told them that I'd come today, so I'm here.

I stare ahead at the house, the house my wife grew up in, wondering how her parents can stand it.

Memories of Laurie are imprinted on every inch of this place. She told me her childhood was lonely at times with no siblings, but her parents doted on her.

How often did she sit in that living room as a little girl, doing a jigsaw puzzle with her mom or making her dad watch one of her puppet shows? How many after-school snacks have been made in that kitchen, how many ball games played in that backyard?

Her parents must have walked past her bedroom a hundred times when she was a teenager to see her on the phone to her best friend, Katy, lying on her belly on her bed with her legs kicked up behind her. Actually, she probably would have closed the door, but they would have heard her voice, the sound of her laughing.

I feel so sad for them that all their memories are no longer pure and untainted. Because how can they remember her as she was when they live with her as she is now?

I get out of the car before I spiral.

When Kelly opens the door, the weight inside me densifies. I used to look at her and see parts of Laurie and I liked imagining the sort of woman my wife might grow into. It used to make me feel optimistic.

Now the sight of her fills me with dread.

"Hello," she says with a barely there smile, giving me a quick hug. "How are you?"

Her eyes dart away from me almost as soon as she's asked this question. Lately, she hasn't wanted to know the answer, hasn't wanted to see my face as I've lied and said that I'm fine.

I cannot bring myself to tell her that I'm fine today.

Not after this week, when every minute has felt like a waking nightmare.

Not after yesterday, when Wren got into a taxi outside my apartment and took herself off to the airport because she couldn't stand to see me.

And definitely not today, now I know that she's gone.

The thought of her pain cripples me.

EVERYTHING FELT SO intense when I drove away on Monday morning. I didn't tell Wren I was heading straight back to Indy because I knew she'd worry about me getting behind a wheel when I'd been awake all night, but I wasn't tired.

I've seen films where people say, "I feel so alive," and I've been like, yeah, whatever. But that morning I got it. I was so aware of every single thing.

I could see the sun glinting off Wren's bedroom windows, sparkling like gems, and I pictured her inside, imagined her falling asleep as soon as her head hit her pillow, and I felt so much love for her.

I could see spiderwebs caught up in the grass on the roadside, millions of crisscrossing silver threads, glistening with dew.

And I pulled over to look back at the barn across fields yet to be harvested, glowing vibrant red in the sunrise. I gave myself a minute to let myself feel it, all of it. I felt happy. I hadn't felt happy in so long.

I sent Wren a text—See you Friday, with a kiss—already wondering how I was going to get through the week. I hated to leave her. I wanted to turn back.

But I didn't. And the farther away from her I got, the heavier I felt.

I planned to go to my apartment for a shower before heading into work, but I began to feel weird and shaky. I thought maybe it was the lack of sleep or food, but when I got inside and saw the empty space next to my bed where Laurie's photograph should have been, this panic started rising up inside me. I went to the drawer and got it out, and then I needed to sit down because the sight of my wife's smiling face made me feel weak.

How had I put her away, managed to forget for a while that she even existed, how had I *enjoyed* doing that?

I felt like the sky was crashing down on me, so I got in my car and drove straight over to see her.

Brian had already left for work and, like a coward, I was

relieved to have escaped him, but Kelly suspected the moment she laid eyes on my guilty face that I'd crossed a line.

"What have you done?" she asked me.

"I'm sorry," I whispered.

And then she knew that the line I'd crossed was reprehensible.

"How *could* you?"

I'll never forget that look on her face as long as I live.

"I don't want you here," she said. "*Laurie* doesn't want you here. Go home and get yourself cleaned up. You disgust me."

"I need to see her," I said. "Please," I begged.

"Goodbye, Anders."

She closed the door in my face.

And fuck if I lost it.

I've never felt such rage, such fury. I wasn't angry at *her*, I was angry at myself, but I damn near broke that door down. One of the neighbors came outside to holler at me and others must have wondered what the hell was going on, but I didn't give a crap.

Kelly let me in eventually, if only to shut me up. She yelled at me to pull myself together and her face was red and riddled with repulsion.

Brian had already carried Laurie to her wheelchair, so I fell to my knees in front of her and sobbed. And she stared past me, unseeing, unfeeling, while I felt it all.

Kelly came into the room in the end and tried to pull me to my feet, tried to get me to sit in a chair, but she gave up after a minute and sat on it herself.

As she rubbed my back, I thought that maybe she'd forgive me, but I knew I'd never forgive myself.

I've been back every night this week, with the exception of

last night, trying to make amends, trying to reconcile what I did. Every time Wren has come to mind, I've thrown her out. Every time she's called or texted, I've felt like I could be sick.

As the days have passed, I've grown more and more detached from her. I want to forget all about what we did, erase it, get some distance from her. Sunday feels unreal.

Yesterday morning, I considered calling her to tell her not to come, but it seemed gutless, saying it on the phone. I thought it would be better to tell her in person, but that was a mistake. I don't know what I was thinking.

I'll never forgive myself for what I've done to her either. But I throw that thought out too, because I'm here with Laurie. And I shouldn't be thinking about Wren. Not now, not ever.

"Anders," Brian says as he comes down the stairs, hard-faced, grim, his usual greeting.

"Hi." I force myself to meet his eyes, but can't help looking away first.

I saw him on Wednesday, briefly, but he stayed in the kitchen for most of my visit. Kelly had no doubt told him what I'd done. I've disgusted him too.

"Can I get you a coffee?" Kelly asks me, and her tone is softer than I'm used to.

"Yes, please," I reply.

Everything feels so strained, but I'm trying to force myself back into our routine.

I walk through to the living room and sit down in front of Laurie.

"Hey." I pick up her hand, detesting how hollow my voice sounds. "You're so cold."

She's always cold. I think of Wren, of how warm she was, and snap that trapdoor shut.

I squeeze Laurie's hand, trying to warm her up, and then I feel this horrible compulsion to squeeze her hand so hard that she'll pull it away from me, just so I can get some sort of human response from her.

I don't do it, of course. I feel cruel for even thinking that I might. But sometimes I wish she'd work harder at showing me that she's still with us.

"Laurie," I whisper, entwining my fingers with hers.

Cold.

I flash back to lying on the blanket with Wren, hands linked between us, and the pain is so acute I stop breathing.

Laurie coughs, startling me.

"Are you okay, my darling?" Kelly asks Laurie, coming through with two coffees, one for me and one for herself. She rubs Laurie's back and I watch Laurie's mouth as she coughs again.

My eyes travel up to hers, but they're vacant, dull, and I have to look away again.

I remember Wren staring into my eyes as I held her on top of me, the look on her face as we moved together. Goose bumps race down my neck before I can block out the memory. I feel alive again, just for a few seconds, and I'm still trying to stamp out the thought, but I can't stop seeing her face. So I force myself to look at Laurie, at my *wife*, and I want her to fucking look at me too, to see what I've done.

She's on her way back to England. I've hurt her so bad. I'm so incredibly sorry.

Look at me, dammit!

I duck my head, feeling like I'm losing it because I'm trying to get into Laurie's line of sight, to try to get her to meet my eyes.

"What are you doing, Anders?" Kelly asks, all snippy.

"I don't know," I mutter, sitting back and scrubbing my face with my hand.

"Has she gone, then?"

She means Wren.

I nod and look away at the wall. "Yeah. She left today."

"Good."

And I can't help it. I turn to stare at her, at Laurie's mother, and I feel such intense loathing for her that it scares the living daylights out of me.

She's oblivious, taking a sip of her coffee, but before I can tear my gaze away, she meets my eyes and visibly recoils.

I look down at my hands as shame washes over me, over-powering dread and guilt for a while to become the most dom-inant emotion.

"Did you see her yesterday?" Kelly asks, and I wish that she'd drop it, because honestly, I don't know how much more I'm going to be able to take.

"No. She didn't want to see me."

"You told her over the phone that it was over between you?" She sounds disapproving, and I almost can't believe that she can hate Wren and yet feel defensive of her at the same time.

No one should hate Wren.

It hits me, with the force of a truck, that I've pushed her away for good this time and she is never coming back.

At that thought, grief swallows me whole.

Brian rushes through. "What the hell is going on?"

"Anders!" Kelly cries. "Anders!" She shakes my arm.

"What the hell did you say to him?" Brian demands to know.

"I didn't say anything!"

"Anders! Come on, son. It's okay."

I'm aware of them only distantly.

And all the while, Laurie sits there, motionless, and stares past me at the floor.

I'M ON THEIR couch, curled up on my side, and I can't stop crying. They're in the kitchen, arguing, and I want to feel sorry about it, sorry that I've caused them pain, but I'm too sad.

"Here, it's okay," Brian says, coming through to me.

He says it so gently—more gently than I've heard him speak in probably two years—but it's embarrassing and it makes the pain worse.

"I'm sorry," I mumble.

"Don't worry about it," Brian replies, patting my back like I'm a little kid.

"Is Kelly okay?"

"She's fine."

From the way he said it, I don't think she is.

"I'm sorry I've upset her."

"She's fine," he repeats, but I know I need to sort myself out, go home, get out of their space.

I sit up, feeling as though concrete has set in my veins. Laurie is in her chair with her back to me.

"Here." Brian hands me a tissue.

I'll take that fucking tissue now, please.

The memory of Wren is like another punch to the gut.

"Come on, son," Brian says as I hunch over. "Come on, son." He doesn't know what else to say, so he keeps saying the same thing over and over as I cry like a baby on his couch.

I must apologize twenty times or more before I'm able to get into my car and drive home. And I want to call Wren, so badly. I want to see if she's all right, if she made it home okay, but I realize she's probably still in the air.

It occurs to me that I could call and hear her voice on her voicemail greeting, but knowing Wren, she wouldn't have recorded one. I dial her number anyway and I'm right: it's a standard recorded message.

Fighting against the rational part of my brain that's telling me to leave her the hell alone, I pull over and type out a text message.

I am so sorry. I hope you get home safely.

It's lame, but I press send anyway. The Message not delivered response tells me that she's still in transit. Which means that she sat in the airport all night, waiting for her plane.

The thought brings on a fresh wave of misery.

It's either that or she's blocked me.

I don't know which is worse.

KELLY CALLS ME on Monday evening, but I divert her call, texting to say that I'll see her tomorrow after work. But on Tuesday, I can't bring myself to go anywhere but home to bed. By Wednesday, she's chasing me.

I'll come tonight, I text her.

We'd like to talk to you, she replies. Please come over.

My dread multiplies.

It's been taking all of my strength just to go into the race shop each day, but at least work is a distraction. I've spent most of my time in my office, working on the design for next year's car and trying to keep human interactions to a bare minimum.

I tried texting Wren again, but got another Message not delivered response. I'm pretty sure she has blocked me and I don't blame her, but the thought of it makes me feel as though I'm standing at the edge of a chasm, only a thin thread keeping me from falling in. I think I'm going slightly mad.

This feeling intensifies on the drive to Kelly and Brian's on Wednesday night. My skin is crawling, my gut roiling.

Kelly answers the door, wearing sympathy on her face that I neither want nor deserve. At least she doesn't ask me how I am.

"Hello, Anders," Brian says in a tone that surprises me.

It's rare for him to greet me with kindness.

He waves his hand toward the living room and I follow Kelly in, but come up short when I don't see Laurie in her wheelchair.

"Where's Laurie?"

"It's okay, she's upstairs," Brian reassures me, but not before fear has gripped my chest.

"Is she all right?" I ask as he ushers me to the couch.

"Yes, we just decided to put her to bed early."

I glance at Kelly as she sits down, but she seems to be avoiding my gaze. Brian looks at her, then at me.

"We wanted to talk to you about Wren," he says.

"No, please." I shake my head. "I can't talk about her." Not to you. Not to anyone.

"It's okay." He reaches out and squeezes my shoulder.

Kelly looks at me then, her lips pressed together.

I shake my head at her, silently begging her not to start.

"We think you should divorce Laurie," she says.

I freeze and stare at her in shock. Her eyes fill with tears and my insides are shredded.

"I'm so sorry." I can barely hear myself speaking. "Please. I will never be unfaithful to her ever again. I swear."

"Anders, stop," Brian says abruptly. "That's not what this is about."

It's only when he holds me still that I realize I've been rocking.

"We don't want to see you wasting your life," he says. "You're a good man. You've stuck by our daughter through thick and thin. We know what you've sacrificed for her. But we've lost sight of how much it's hurting you. We want you to go out there and live now. We want you to let Laurie go."

I hunch over and begin to shake. The couch depresses beside me as Kelly moves to sit closer.

"You're like a son to us, Anders," she says. "We care about you. Laurie has already lost so much. We don't want to see you lose everything too."

"I don't want to divorce her," I manage to choke out.

"It's the right thing to do," Kelly replies in a husky voice. "It's better that you have a fresh start."

She squeezes my hand hard and I think she's trying to compensate for the fact that she's shaking too, but grief is racking her entire body.

"And while you're still married to Laurie," she adds waveringly, "you have the final say over her care." She inhales raggedly. "And I want my baby back."

"I will *never* take her away from you," I swear as she begins to sob.

"Come now." Brian reaches past me to rub his wife's back. "We have a lot of talking to do," he tells me meaningfully.

"I'm not putting her into a hospice!" Kelly wails at him.

"Okay, okay," he soothes.

But I sense their discussion isn't over.

I wish they *would* put Laurie into a hospice, get some sort of life back. Then I picture Kelly standing alone in this house, looking around at the empty space, wondering what it is she's forgotten to do, and I don't think she ever will.

She will not let her daughter leave this house until she is ready to leave in a coffin.

And I begin to cry so hard that I feel as though my chest is caving in. The thought of Kelly and how much pain she's in and how she still manages to speak to Laurie in the same way that she always has . . . How she still holds out hope that Laurie will come back to us . . . It kills me to witness it.

Sometimes, I imagine Ma in Kelly's position and I wonder if she would continue to hope too, even when everyone else has given up, and the thought of her suffering has kept me awake at night.

"You need to go after Wren," Brian says.

"I can't," I sob. "She's gone."

"Then you need to get her back."

"I can't."

"You can," Kelly says firmly, barely controlling the quiver in her voice. "I was so angry and disappointed in you both at first, but I've had time to think about it. Wren came here when she didn't have to and that must have been very hard for her. She's a good person. I can see that. Despite everything, I liked her. And Laurie would have liked her too. Laurie would want you to go after her."

"Laurie would want you to be happy," Brian interjects hoarsely.

He reaches for an envelope on the side table and passes it to me.

"We thought this was the least we could do. We want you to know how much we mean what we're saying."

I open the envelope with trembling fingers and pull out a piece of paper. I stare at it. It's a plane ticket for Friday night. *This* Friday night.

"Go and get her back," Brian urges.

I sniff and shake my head, stunned. "She'll never forgive me."

"Yes, she will," Kelly says with absolute certainty. "But first you need to say goodbye to Laurie."

This is why they put her to bed early, I realize in a daze as I climb the stairs. They wanted to talk to me without her sitting there.

And now they want me to have some privacy while I say goodbye.

I stand outside my wife's childhood bedroom for a minute, trying to compose myself, before walking in and closing the door behind me.

She's lying in her double bed, under the yellow polka-dot comforter she had when she was a teenager, sleeping on her back and snoring lightly. Her room still looks pretty much as it did back then. Her parents never had any need to redecorate and Laurie liked coming over to see it like this, with all the memories it held.

So her books are still on her bookshelves, her fairy lights are still around her headboard, her photographs are still on her wall in a giant collage, with her face smiling out from so many of them.

I'm breathing shallowly, unable to draw enough air into my lungs as I go and sit on her bed. The motion of the mattress moving changes her position slightly and she stops snoring. I pick up her hand and look down at her face, and I'm glad that she's asleep because it's better than seeing that empty look in her eyes.

Without thinking, I lie down beside her, resting my head on the edge of her pillow, still holding her hand in mine. I interlink our fingers and watch as her chest rises and falls, her heart continuing to beat even as it no longer feels pain, or love.

"I love you," I whisper.

And still her heart beats on.

IT TAKES ME almost two full days to pull myself together, but by Friday afternoon I feel as though a lot of the weight has lifted. I called in sick yesterday, and last night, Ma turned up at my apartment. Kelly had filled her in and she arrived when I was at my lowest point, when I felt as though I'd been transported back in time to when the doctors first diagnosed Laurie. It was as if I'd lost her all over again.

Ma sat down with me and told me that my grief was good, that it would allow me to heal. I didn't believe her—my feelings were too overwhelming—but she was right. I think I needed to acknowledge the pain, really let myself feel it, and then give myself permission to shed it.

I didn't realize how much power Kelly and Brian have held over me these last few years, how much I needed them to be the ones to set me free. They were the only people who could, apart from Laurie, and she doesn't have any choice in the matter.

I didn't say goodbye to her. I will see her again, and her parents too.. They will always be a part of my life. But somehow, I think I'm finding it in me to let Laurie go.

And now I'm going after Wren.

I've tried calling her, felt I should warn her that I'm coming, but my calls go straight through to voicemail. Texts come back with that same Message not delivered sign, so I'm ninety-nine percent certain she's blocked me.

When I call Jonas to ask for his help in getting a message to her, he says that I should just "get on the fucking plane and tell her how you feel to her face."

"That didn't work very well last time."

"This is the only way that you'll convince her you mean it," he insists.

"But I need her address."

"I will get it for you. Bailey is seriously pissed at you, though, so I don't know how. I'll work it out. Just . . . get to the airport. Go get her. And good luck."

I hit another stumbling block when my flight is delayed due to a technical failure. The plane is overbooked and the terminal is full of disgruntled passengers, but I'll miss my international connection if I don't get to Chicago on time, so I decide to rent a car and drive. The trip gives me time to think.

Time to think about how I will persuade her to give me another chance.

Time to think about how I will prove to her that I love her— *so much*.

Time to think about how I will convince her that I will never push her away again, that I'm in this, with her, for life.

And I think about Wren, about that first time I saw her dancing at the bar, about the way I later caught her eye and found it hard to tear my gaze away, let alone resist sneaking looks at her again and again.

I think about the first time we spoke, how her English accent made me feel strangely edgy, and how funny she was when she was drunk, claiming to have a good sense of direction because she was an architect.

I think of her squealing with delight when she scored a strike at duckpin bowling. I think of the small, secretive smile on her face as she watched me weld the pieces of Bambi's frame together, and her look of concentration in the days before that as we sat at the kitchen table and worked out the angles we'd need.

I picture her in the lake at the farm with the sun sparkling off the water and lighting up her big, hazel-colored eyes. And I let myself remember that perfect day almost two weeks ago that feels like another lifetime.

That day gives me hope for the future, hope for a future that I will not give up striving for.

I've just got to make her see it, believe it, feel it too.

I drive straight to Chicago and make it in under three hours, dropping off the rental car and running to the check-in desk. I cannot believe it when they reveal that this flight is also delayed due to a technical failure, and when the airline finally makes the decision to cancel the flight, I bury my head in my hands and try to tell myself that these obstacles are not a sign; they're simply one more hurdle to jump over on my way to get to Wren.

I manage to get myself onto an early-morning Saturday flight and, in the meantime, Jonas comes through with an address. He reminds me—and I can't believe I forgot it, but my head is a mess—that Wren is at a wedding today.

By the time I reach Heathrow, pick up my rental car and drive to Bury St. Edmunds, it's almost eleven o'clock at night.

I've been to the UK a couple of times before—once on vacation and once for work—and I love how different it is here from back home. I stare out the window at grand Georgian manor houses with ivy growing up the front and quirky medieval buildings with crooked walls and exposed beams, and eventually I turn into a street lined with two-story Victorian row houses.

Wren lives in the only house with a white facade in a sea of gray brick. It has a small bay window and a dark green door with a hanging basket out the front filled with flowers. It's sweet, but not really what I would have imagined for her. I don't know how she ended up living here, or if she loves it as much as I want her to love where she comes home to at night, but I'm looking forward to finding out. I'm looking forward to getting to know her—properly—on every level. I want to stay up talking through the night with her again, hold her hand as the sun sets and the stars shine brightly, and still be with her when the world turns and the sun comes up again. And as I sit down on her doorstep and wait for her to come home from her friends' wedding, I no longer feel scared.

Because I know that this is right. *We* are right. And she's too smart to think any differently.

I hope she lets me hold her. I hope she lets me make up for hurting her. I hope—

And then I see her, walking along the pavement in sky-high heels with her head down and her arms crossed over her chest and her hips swaying, and my heart swells, even as the rest of me goes still.

I shakily force myself to my feet, not wanting to startle her.

She's at her gate before she looks toward the door, and my stomach lurches at the look of devastation on her face a split second before she almost jumps out of her skin in fright.

"I'm so sorry," I blurt, stretching my hand out toward her. I'm apologizing for scaring her, not for everything else I've done. That's going to take a hell of a lot more doing.

She stares at me, several emotions crossing her face, one after the other—vulnerability, disbelief, hurt—and then her expression settles into something I recognize: love.

I walk forward and wrap her in my arms, tucking her supple, warm body against mine, and I hold her. She clutches me back just as fiercely. She's stronger than she looks.

And I realize: I haven't broken her. I haven't broken us. This is Wren. Wren doesn't give up. She doesn't quit.

And neither will I. Not on her. Never again.

EPILOGUE

THE LOOK ON HIS FACE . . . I WANT TO KISS HIM, BUT I can't tear my eyes away. He's so beautiful, and his pupils are dilated, here in the shadows under these trees. The black almost swallows up the amber fleck in his eye.

This is so intense. It reminds me of the first time we made love, right here, under these very trees, by this same river. New leaves, new water, no threat of guilt or regret.

Not everything is the same.

He clutches me to him and I sense that he's close. So I nod to let him know that I'm with him and he locks my eyes so intently, seeing me, all of me, as we fall together.

AFTERWARD, HE COLLAPSES onto his back, holding me on top of him as his fingertips run lazily over the thin fabric of my dress.

It's the middle of June and we've been "helping" Jonas to harvest the first of the winter wheat this afternoon. I wore this dress especially—as soon as I knew we were coming to this field. It's the red-and-black-ditsy-print one—the same as the blue, white, and yellow one from the September before last, but different.

He obviously had the same intentions because he brought the same picnic blanket.

He laughs lightly, so I lift my head to look at him.

"I should have told Jonas the drive belt had snapped again. That would have bought us more time. No, stay," he murmurs as I start to get up.

He pulls me back down, catching my mouth in a kiss. His hands come up to clasp my face as he deepens the contact, slow and sure.

"Don't you start again," I warn against his lips with a smile, and it takes a real effort to draw myself away. "He'll be here in a minute, checking up on us, wondering why we've stopped."

"I think he'll probably guess that we don't want his company right now." He presses a tender kiss to my shoulder.

"I'm not risking it."

"We'll hear the tractor," he protests as I reluctantly get to my feet.

"Still." I begin to fasten the tiny buttons up the front of my dress.

He undid them this time, down to the bottom of my rib cage. Damn near devoured me.

A shiver goes through my body and I smile at the memory, even though it's fresh.

"Where are you going?" he calls after me as I walk down to the river.

"Taking a bath," I reply with a grin.

"With your dress on?" he asks with surprise.

"I'll hold it up and go in to my waist. I'm not taking it off if Jonas is about to arrive."

"No, come on, let's go for a swim," he urges. "I'll tell him to leave us to it."

I look over my shoulder to see Anders simultaneously tugging his T-shirt over his head and texting.

I laugh at him as he walks, buck naked, toward me.

"Off," he commands, jerking his chin at my dress.

"I've only just done it up!" I reply with pretend indignation.

And then his lips are on my neck and his fingers are getting busy with my buttons and my knees are so wobbly that it's all I can do to keep myself standing upright.

Thankfully, it's absolutely sweltering today, because I'm not sure I'd want to swim in this river in the fall.

Ha, I mean *autumn*. I've only been living here for a year and a half, but sometimes it feels longer. Other times, my recollections are so vivid it's as though they happened yesterday.

Today is bringing back memories, both good and bad. As much as possible, I try to let the good soak in and the bad wash away, and even Anders seems to be here, with me, in the moment.

But that's not always the case. When those creases appear on his brow, there will be times when I'll want to climb onto his lap and smooth them away, but I also know that sometimes he needs to feel the pain. And he always comes through the other side stronger, more at peace with himself and the world.

"WE SHOULD GET on," I murmur after our second time.

I sound sleepy, intoxicated.

"Are you okay?" he checks, the heat from his body seeping into my back, his warm arms encircling me from behind as we stand in the shallows, the sun pouring down on us from high overhead, making the nearby rocks sparkle.

"I'm fine. Better than fine. I love you."

"I love you too. *Oh no you don't*," he erupts darkly, his body tensing and his ears pricking up, and I hear it—the tractor.

I scramble after him, squealing with laughter as he shouts a string of swear words at his brother and helps me to pull on my clothes before seeing to his own.

"Can't you save that sort of shit for your honeymoon?" Jonas shouts at us as we emerge from the shadows of the trees.

He's leaning against his tractor's wheel, tapping his foot, waiting for us.

Anders shakes his head at him, unimpressed.

Jonas laughs. "I get it if you don't want to work today, but can you please tell me so I can call Zack in? I don't want to miss a whole day of harvest ahead of the weekend."

"Don't get your panties in a wad, we've got it under control," Anders replies dryly, holding his hand out to me and flashing me one of his heart-stopping grins as I hurry to catch him up.

I laugh as we walk back to the combine together.

It is a little crazy, what we're doing. Any other bride-to-be would probably be running around stressed right now, but that girl doesn't have Bailey the whirlwind organizing her wedding.

WE WOKE THIS morning to sunlight pouring into the cabin. It's where we stay when we come to visit, now that Jonas is up at the house. Anders asked if we could make a few changes to the place and Jonas didn't mind—he's not sentimental—so we widened the openings in the wall to create a giant picture window that looks out at the lake from the bedroom and put in a couple of smaller, high-level ones with views up to the trees.

Then we went shopping for mid-century modern furniture at Midland Arts and Antiques. We had so much fun that day.

Jonas is still interested in building the cabins on stilts around the lake, but he's been kind of preoccupied lately. I imagine he'll crack on with them in a year or two and hopefully I'll be able to help.

We come down here pretty much every weekend that Anders is not at a race. I've been to the occasional race with him—Dad too—but usually I chill at home in Indy or come here for some family time. Dad and Sheryl still refer to the guest room as my room. They have another, smaller one they use if old friends come to stay.

I love that I still have a place with them, that I still feel so welcome. I'll be staying there later, once we've finished with these two fields.

Anyway, this morning, after waking up to such a lovely day, we went to the farmhouse to have breakfast with Jonas and Tyler, and as soon as Jonas mentioned that he wanted to get started on the harvest today, Anders looked at me and raised an eyebrow.

"We'll help," I offered quickly.

Jonas, Tyler, and even little Astrid looked at me as though I'd gone mad, but I'm probably imagining Astrid's expression because she's only eight months old.

So cute, though. Like cutest-baby-you've-ever-seen cute.

I'd worried Anders and I might be rushing into things when we moved in together after I left the UK, but at around the same time, Jonas was getting Tyler pregnant.

Anders later told me that his brother called her the morning after movie night and asked her to go on a date with him. She agreed and they've never looked back.

Both Anders *and* Bailey used to fill me in on how speedily things were developing between them—Bailey would hear it from Tyler as well as from Jonas, and she was as delighted as I was to hear that they had fallen hook, line, and sinker for each other.

If the pregnancy was an accident, it was a happy one. Jonas proposed and Bailey organized her second shotgun wedding.

She appreciated that Anders and I gave her a bit more time to pull things together.

WHEN I CAME home that night from Sabrina and Lance's wedding to find Anders waiting on my doorstep, I could hardly believe my eyes. I had been wrestling with so many emotions during the walk, but I had just determined to unblock his number from my phone and give him a call.

I knew he would have tried to contact me, knew he'd be worried, and I wanted to put his mind at ease. I wanted to tell him that I understood, that it was all too much too soon, and if he'd asked for my forgiveness, I would have granted it. God knows, he didn't need another block of guilt to weigh him down.

But I wanted to ask for his forgiveness too. I shouldn't have pushed him so hard, and I shouldn't have abandoned him.

I thought that maybe I could still be someone he'd allow himself to depend on, someone to take the weight off if he needed to talk. I knew it wouldn't be easy, but I wanted to do it. My last thought as I approached my house was that maybe I *did* have it in me to wait for him.

So when I found him on my doorstep . . .

I didn't know what was happening, why he was there, whether he'd come for me or was visiting for work. But when he

366 · PAIGE TOON

gathered me close and whispered that he loved me, when he asked me to please forgive him, when he swore he would endeavor never to hurt me again as long as he lived, I sensed something seismic had happened.

We went inside and he told me all about Kelly and Brian, how they'd bought his plane ticket and sent him to me with their blessing. And the relief was so immense; the lightness I felt at seeing the expression of peace on his face was like no rush I'd ever known.

We talked and cuddled into the early hours of Sunday morning, then I took him to my favorite café, No. 5 Angel Hill, for breakfast. We sat in my usual place by the window, on a tan leather bench seat that once belonged in a vintage car, and as he looked with wonder at the towering, ornate Abbey Gate across the road, I looked at *him* and felt pure, unbridled joy.

For the first time in more than six months, I was able to wander around Bury St. Edmunds without any pain. We explored the ruins in the Abbey Gardens and ended up at the tiny Nutshell pub that I told him and Wilson about all that time ago at the duckpin bowling alley. Anders was tickled by the pub's small size and all the quirky curiosities contained within, and he confessed over a pint of beer that he'd love to spend some time in the UK. I sensed he was trying to tell me then, that early, that we could make it work no matter what, that if I wanted to stay in England or move to America, or if I changed my mind at any point, then we had options.

I do think we will go back to the UK one day. Anders could take a job in Formula 1, although it wouldn't be with Ferrari, the team that once headhunted him. That team is based in Italy, but then, what's to say we couldn't go and spend some time there too? I've been doing freelance sketch perspectives on top of my full-time employment, so I could probably work from anywhere.

I feel so optimistic about the future—and even more importantly to me, so does Anders.

But back when we were deciding where to live, I asked if he still liked Indy and enjoyed working with his current team—he did—and if he would be happy for me to take the job with Dean—he was.

So that's what we decided to do.

We knew it would be close to Christmas by the time I'd finished the work on the primary school and handed in my notice to Graham, not to mention packed up and vacated the house, so we decided to delay our move until the New Year so we could also spend some time with Mum and her boyfriend, Keith.

Anders flew back over—he had also come for Thanksgiving at the end of November, when his whole team had time off—and it was perfect, watching him bond with Mum and then the two of us getting to experience a British Christmas together before we left to put roots down in another country.

Walking into Anders's apartment in Indy with him was one of the happiest moments of my life. It has been so much fun getting to know the city and all his favorite haunts, becoming friends with his friends, and making some of my own. And I adore what I do now. Yes, there are still downsides, as there are with any job, but I feel so much more inspired going into work each day, and Dean is the coolest boss. More of a friend, really. I was walking on air when he made my position permanent.

Scott was sad to hear that I was moving away. We've stayed in touch, albeit sporadically. He and Nadine sent us a wedding card, wishing us all the best. I doubt they'll be far behind us. They're still going strong, still living in Bury St. Edmunds. They're friends with Sabrina and Lance now and it doesn't hurt, not like I'd initially imagined it would. I'm glad they're happy.

I do miss Bury and its crooked old buildings, fairy-tale ruins, and quaint little pubs and cafés, but we're going back at Thanksgiving, when I'll be taking Anders to the Christmas market, and I know we'll never stay away for too long. Mum's been to see us a couple of times too, and she and Keith are here right now, of course.

WE STAY OUT in the field until dusk, when the fireflies come out, and then we go for a motorbike ride back to the place where we first met, lying on the grass and watching as the sun sinks toward the horizon and the green lights bobbing over the fields grow brighter.

Eventually, reluctantly, Anders takes me back to Wetherill and kisses me good night on the doorstep.

Dad and Sheryl have invited Mum and Keith and Bailey and Casey over for dinner. They did say Mum and Keith could stay in the guest room—I sense Sheryl wanted to smooth things over there too—but Mum opted to stay at a hotel in town. Only we can know our personal limits, what we're able to endure, and for Mum, staying with Dad and Sheryl would have been too much.

It was the same for Kelly and Brian, I imagine, when they declined our invitation to come to the wedding. Kelly called me direct to say that she appreciated the invitation and sincerely hoped it would be the happiest of days, but she felt that it wouldn't be appropriate for them to join us. She and Brian couldn't leave Laurie, for a start, but she also worried that their being there might take some of the shine off Anders's day. I was relieved they said no, to be honest, but grateful Kelly called me to talk it through.

Anders still goes to see them and Laurie every month or so, but it doesn't weigh him down like it used to. I've been with him on a few occasions when Kelly and Brian have encouraged him to bring me. It's never easy, but they're kind to me and I know it helps Anders to feel more at peace with the situation.

He was worried at first that I'd be bitter about the fact that it had taken his in-laws to convince him to divorce Laurie, but I understood. He needed them to release him from his obligations. A man as honorable as Anders can't break free of his chains on his own.

ON SATURDAY MORNING, Bailey comes over bright and early to get ready with me. She looks so beautiful in her burnished-gold, matte-satin dress, her chestnut hair piled up into a tousled bun.

As for my outfit, it's a constructed design formed of alternating juxtaposing fabrics: silk and matte satin. It's architectural and I love it. I didn't think I'd ever wear white—or in this case, cream—but then I saw this dress and couldn't imagine myself in anything else.

Although a few old friends have been lovely enough to fly over for the wedding, Bailey is my only bridesmaid. I remember when I used to refer to her as my half sister—I can't even think when I stopped, when she simply became my sister—but now she's also my friend. My *best* friend. There's no one I would rather have standing at my side today.

Apart from Anders, of course.

Jonas will be there for him.

Fredrickson brothers and Elmont sisters.

Bailey and Casey are happy, still making a go of things here in town, and Bailey is still employed at the golf club, albeit part-time now. The rest of the time, she works with Tyler to arrange events at the farm. The two of them have been talking about setting up their own company, but Tyler wants Astrid to grow up a bit first. I love that she and Jonas gave their daughter a Swedish name.

Jonas wonders if one day she'll want to take over the farm herself.

"Who says it has to be the oldest brother?" he asked aloud a few weeks ago, when he'd had a few beers.

Whatever happens, I know that he'll be okay. He loves what he does, but if farming is not the path his children would choose for themselves, he won't force the issue.

Patrik and Peggy are coming tonight, traveling down from Wisconsin, which is where they retired to. I think it's been good for them, getting some distance. I'm not sure Patrik would ever have put his feet up if he'd lived locally.

They're doing well. Patrik is actually going to be driving the tractor that will be bringing the wedding party to the farm in a covered trailer that we've hired specially. Jonas suggested it, more as a joke than anything, but I loved the idea. He offered to drive us himself, but I thought he should be with Anders today. Anders told me that his dad was looking forward to getting behind the wheel again.

IT'S TIME. I'M nervous and I don't know why—I have never felt more certain about anything in my life. I think it's because so many people will be here and I've never enjoyed being the center of attention.

I sit between Mum and Dad on the way to the farm, holding their hands as the hot wind slams against the plastic cover of the trailer. The weather is brutal, but it could be worse. At least it's not a tornado.

My palms are sweaty. I'm glad we're getting married inside the barn. The high ceiling means it never gets too hot in there.

Everyone is quiet on the journey—even Bailey. She smiles at me, smiles at her mum. I look across at Sheryl and smile at her too. We had a nice time last night—even Mum seemed relatively relaxed. Sheryl took her outside to show her the orchards and I think they made some sort of truce.

Patrik pulls up outside the barn and a few stragglers turn to look. I wonder where Anders is—up at the altar already, I imagine.

Dad helps me down from the trailer and we walk together to the barn, but then he lets me go.

"See you in a while, Little Bird," he says, giving me a kiss on my cheek and smiling at Mum.

I turn and take her arm.

I couldn't walk down this aisle without her, not after everything she's done for me. She practically raised me single-handedly. But I didn't want to walk down the aisle without Dad either, so he's taking Bailey to the halfway point and then he'll wait to accompany me the rest of the way. It's unconventional, but it feels appropriate.

The band starts playing a gentle acoustic number, guitars and other strings. The lead singer sounds like Sufjan Stevens. Wilson put us in touch with them, but he and his blues band are playing later.

Everyone files inside, leaving Bailey and Dad and Mum and me alone.

Bailey looks at me. "Love you, sis."

"I love you too."

"I'd wish you luck, but you don't need it. Just have fun."

I nod at her, fighting to control my emotions.

She hooks her arm through Dad's and walks through the big double doors.

Then it's just Mum and me.

"Thank you for doing this," I say to her, my eyes pricking with tears.

"Thank you for asking me to. I'm so proud of you, Wren."

"Don't, you'll ruin my makeup."

She laughs. "You ready?"

"Absolutely."

I'm aware of it, the heads turning toward me, but the only person I see is Anders. My love. Up there at the altar in his slim-fitting black suit. Waiting for me.

There's so much light and love and hope and happiness in his expression. I know he'll see the same emotions reflected in mine.

I smile at him and he smiles softly back at me, and I let go of Mum, take hold of Dad, and go to him.

We don't say the usual vows. There's no mention of death or parting. We simply promise to love and honor each other and to always be there, as long as we're needed. That's how we put it. And I know that Anders will have thought of Laurie as he said those words to me, that I'll never have his whole heart, not while hers is still beating. She will always be a part of our relationship, our marriage, until the day that she's not.

But I'm okay with that. I love Anders and all that comes with him. I want to hold his hand over every bridge he has to cross and I hope he never feels alone again.

WE'RE IN PHOENIX, eight days later, when we receive the news. In the foothills of Camelback Mountain, staring out of the wide-open door of Bambi at the desert landscape, Anders accepts a call from Brian. And I know as soon as he answers that Laurie is gone.

"Will you wait for us?" Anders asks hoarsely.

After he ends the call, I hold him as he sobs. It is finally over.

Laurie died of organ failure, that's what Brian said. Was there a tiny, fear-filled part of me that wondered if she'd died of a broken heart? I'd be lying if I said that there wasn't. But deep down, I believe Laurie was ready to go, to be set free. And now, hopefully, her parents will be able to get some semblance of a life back.

Kelly never did allow Laurie to go into a hospice. She loved and cared for her until Laurie took her very last breath. I hope this gives her some peace now, that she can live the rest of her life without regret, knowing that she did everything she could for her baby.

We cut our honeymoon short to drive home for the funeral, but there are many moments of love and joy to be found in these days. Anders is upset, but not broken, and I sense he also feels a great deal of relief.

I stand by his side at the funeral, holding his hand as he says goodbye to Laurie for the very last time, and then we go home.

We go home to our apartment, to see the sun shining in through the giant windows, and we sit on our sofa together, our limbs intertwined until Anders gets hungry and heads into the kitchen to prepare us something to eat.

I stand up and walk into the sunroom.

"Do you want a beer?" Anders calls out to me.

"No, better not."

He gives me a quizzical look—I wouldn't normally turn down a drink at this hour on a Friday night, and especially not after the day we've had—but now is not the time to explain.

He can wait until tomorrow to find out that our lives are about to change forever. For now, it will remain my little secret.

I sit down on the Eames chair, place my hand over my belly, and turn my face up to the sun.

ACKNOWLEDGMENTS

I've never opened my acknowledgments without first mentioning my readers, and that feels even more important now than ever. My regular readers have had to hold off an extra year for this one, so I really hope it was worth the wait! I absolutely loved writing this story—even if it did make me cry on every single re-read during editing. Anders, Wren, Jonas, and Bailey will live in my heart for a long time. I hope they've found a place in yours too, whether you're new to my books or have been with me for years.

If you *are* new to my writing, please feel free to say hi on Instagram / Facebook / Twitter / TikTok @PaigeToonAuthor. You can also sign up to receive my newsletter TheHiddenPaige via www.paigetoon.com—sometimes I send out free short stories and exclusive content.

By the way, IndyCar fans might wonder who on earth Luis Castro is, the racing driver who gets a mention in Chapter 17. You're not going mad; this is a reference to a character who appeared in my third book, *Chasing Daisy*. I do sometimes include little crossover links in my novels, so you may even hear from Wren, Anders, Bailey, and Jonas one day in the future.

I am indebted to the whole team at Century / Cornerstone / Penguin Random House for showering *Only Love Can Hurt Like This* (and me!) with so much love, care, and attention from the get-go, but special thanks to Venetia Butterfield for putting your faith in me in the summer of 2021 and for all your words of encouragement since, and my outstanding editor Emily Griffin—I adore working with you! Also (in alphabetical order because you're all awesome): Charlotte Bush, Claire Bush, Briana Bywater, Monique Corless, Amelia Evans, Emma Grey Gelder, Rebecca Ikin, Laurie Ip Fung Chun, Rachel Kennedy, Roisin O'Shea, Richard Rowlands, Claire Simmonds, Selina Walker, and Becca Wright. Thanks also to my copy editor Caroline Johnson.

A huge thank-you to my incredible editor Tara Singh Carlson at G. P. Putnam's Sons / Penguin Random House, and also Ashley Di Dio, Emily Mileham, Maija Baldauf, Claire Winecoff, Tiffany Estreicher, Hannah Dragone, Monica Cordova, Anthony Ramondo, Chandra Wohleber, Ashley McClay, Alexis Welby, Ashley Hewlett, Brennin Cummings, Samantha Bryant, Jazmin Miller, and everyone else on my US team—I feel very privileged to be able to include you in the acknowledgments for this book and I'm so excited to be working with you on the next!

I'd like to say thank you to all of my foreign publishers, but especially the crew at S. Fischer Verlag, who brought my debut novel, *Lucy in the Sky*, to German readers and have been with me ever since. Thanks especially to my lovely editor Lexa Rost.

Thank you to every single Bookstagrammer, BookToker, blogger, and reader who has ever taken the time to write a review or mention any of my novels in your social media posts. It honestly makes me smile so much to see them and I can't thank you enough for the support you've shown.

For help with my farming research, I am very grateful to Sam Clear and his father, James, for taking me behind the scenes on their farm, and extra thanks to Sam for allowing me to pester him with endless questions afterward. Thanks also to Regan Herr from the Indiana State Department of Agriculture and Dennis Carnahan, who both really helped bring Indiana farming to life for me.

For all things racing, thank you to Phil Zielinski, and also my dad, Vern Schuppan, who not only raced in IndyCar and the Indy 500 in the '70s and '80s, but also later ran a team out of Indianapolis. Much of this book is inspired by the time I spent in both Phoenix and Indianapolis with my family, so thanks to my mum, Jen, and my brother, Kerrin too, for those memories.

Massive thanks to Susan and Dean Rains—especially Susan for reading and helping to edit an early draft of this book—but also because you guys introduced me to so many of the cool places I've written about! Greg and I have such good memories of our time there with you. Thanks also to Wendy Davis, Sequoia Davis, Chelsea Davis, and Paul Ehrstein for your help with my Bloomington research.

Thank you very much to Katherine Reid for her proofreading skills, and all my other friends who have helped or listened to me prattling on about this book at some stage or another, especially Lucy, Jane, Katherine S., Kim, Bex, Femke, Sarah, Chen, Mark, Georgie, Colette, Ali Harris, Dani Atkins, and Zoë Folbigg. Thanks also to my lovely parents-in-law, Ian and Helga Toon.

Thank you to my husband, Greg, who has been with me during every single step of my writing career and has helped me in countless ways, but never more so than in the last year. I honestly don't know what I'd do—or where I'd be—without you. I feel very lucky to have you in my life. Also, cheers for all your help with my architecture research! Handy, with you being one and all . . .

Last but not least, thank you to my children, Indy and Idha. Thanks for putting up with me when I'm on a deadline, and for making me smile every single day. I love you xxx.

ONLY LOVE CAN HURT LIKE THIS

Paige Toon

A Conversation with Paige Toon

Discussion Guide

BOOK
ENDS

PUTNAM
— EST. 1838 —

A CONVERSATION
WITH PAIGE TOON

What inspired you to write *Only Love Can Hurt Like This*?

I live in a small village that is surrounded by farmers' fields and I'm always out walking, listening to music, and coming up with story ideas. The scene where Wren meets Anders for the first time—in the fields, out under the stars, walking home after a few too many drinks at a bar—has been playing in my mind ever since I went for a night walk myself one time during the pandemic. But the story line featuring Anders is what really compelled me to write this novel, and everything else fell into place around it. It's inspired by real events that I first heard about when I was living in Indianapolis during my twenties. More recently, I learned about this same thing happening to someone else, and I almost couldn't imagine a worse hell for the people affected. The research that I consequently did broke my heart, and I knew that I would be in for a world of pain once I put myself into my characters' shoes and began to write. I work in an almost Method-acting kind of way, but I love getting completely lost in a story and really feeling it *all*. If I'm connected, then I've found that my readers are connected, and it brings me a lot of joy to know that we're all ultimately on the same journey together.

Were Anders or Wren inspired by real people?

My characters are rarely inspired by real people, although there are always elements of myself in them: things I've thought, conversations I've had—often only inside my mind, when my imagination is playing out a random scenario. Usually, the idea for the plot comes first and the characters are formed around it, depending on their circumstances and what has brought them to the point that I'm telling their story. So Wren is feeling quite fragile when we meet her, but she's trying to be brave, and Anders has a strong sense of loyalty and duty that initially distances him from Wren. I'm often inspired by emotions that I want to capture, and in this case there's an awful lot of longing and heartache going on, but for reasons I hope readers will understand and empathize with.

Only Love Can Hurt Like This is a love story that has a strong sense of place. Do you have a connection to Indiana?

Yes, I love to write about places I've lived and visited—it makes the stories feel so much more real to me—so it was a joy to write about Indiana, where I spent time both as a child when my dad was racing in IndyCar and also in my twenties when my dad ran an Indy Lights team there. (Google Vern Schuppan if you're interested.) My parents actually lived in the Real Silk Lofts—the apartment block where Anders lives—and I've also included other real places in the book that I used to enjoy going to. I have so many fond memories of my time in that city—it was partly what inspired my husband and me to name our son Indy!

Why did you choose to set the novel primarily on a farm?

I've wanted to write a book set on a farm for years, ever since moving out of London to rural Cambridgeshire. The farm near me is owned by a family who have passed it down from generation to generation for over two hundred years. It got me thinking about the responsibility that the younger generation must feel to not let their family farm fail. I already knew that depression is alarmingly common among farmers, but the more research I did on this subject, the more the story around a family of farmers and two brothers took shape inside my mind.

Only Love Can Hurt Like This is not only a romance, but a story about complicated family bonds and expectations. Why was this an important aspect to include in the novel? How do you think it adds to Wren and Anders's love story and their individual journeys?

My novels—especially the ones I've written in more recent years—are multilayered because that's what keeps me interested as a writer. I think I'd be bored penning a straightforward love story about straightforward characters. Weaving in other elements—like family, friendships, and careers—adds depth and makes the characters feel more well-rounded and realistic. Wren and Anders feel incredibly real to me, because I know not only them, but their families too. I know where they've come from and can empathize with the journey they're going on. I'm emotionally invested in them and their families, and ultimately, hopefully, that comes across in my writing so my readers will care about them too.

Bailey and Wren's sisterhood evolves so much throughout the novel, and Jonas and Anders's brotherhood feels relatable. What do you feel is special about sibling relationships? What do you think lies at the core of each of these dynamics in *Only Love Can Hurt Like This*?

I think with siblings, you let them see you, warts and all. You let down your guard with them, much more than you do with friends, because there's a certain elasticity that keeps you bonded together. It would take a lot more to cut loose from family than it would with friends. But you also can never wipe the slate clean, not like you can when you start college or a new job, where nobody has preconceptions of you. What interested me about Wren's dynamic was that she really didn't know her family that well—and vice versa. She believes that she knows what they think about her, but she often gets it wrong. I loved developing her relationship with Bailey, helping them to move from a surface-level relationship to something much deeper. And Jonas and Anders . . . Don't get me started on those two. I *adored* writing about their brotherly love, about the role reversal of older brother and younger brother and how Anders steps into a more protective role when Jonas is struggling. The bond they have is so strong. It gives Wren something to aspire to with Bailey.

It was so fun to see Wren's creative side come out when she was renovating the Airstream. Do you have a connection to Airstreams, or architecture? Why did you choose architecture as Wren's profession?

My husband is an architect and we've been together since university—I've learned so much about the profession over the years that I thought it was about time I wrote about it!

As for Airstreams . . . I don't have one, but now I really, *really* want one. I do have an old camper van which broke down so many times that it's now been retired to the bottom of the garden. I wrote the entirety of *Only Love Can Hurt Like This* from the coziness of its interior, which is complete with fairy lights, fluffy blankets, and heating. You'll find pictures on Instagram of when I traipsed down there in winter at the crack of dawn while frost still covered the ground. It's a lovely place to write from.

If you could pick two celebrities to play Wren and Anders in a movie adaptation of *Only Love Can Hurt Like This*, who would they be?

I can't answer this question for any of my books! My characters don't look like anyone inside my head. They feel so real to me that to try to pluck an actress or actor out of thin air feels impossible. I have so much admiration for casting directors! My characters do have certain elements that remind me of real people, but none of them would be right for the role. I remember watching *Dexter: New Blood* and thinking that Wren has facial features a little like Deb's, with her slightly narrow face and big eyes. River Phoenix came to mind when I pictured Anders's sharp eyebrows. And Jonas, hilariously, is loosely inspired by a guy who appeared on *Love Island Australia*. He brought the phrase "caveman crossed with a model" to mind, though now, apart from his general size and body shape, Jonas doesn't resemble that man inside my mind at all.

In your opinion, what do you think is the most important romantic quality a partner can have? What lesson, if any,

would you give to readers falling in love or trying to find their person?

It's so hard to name just one romantic quality. There's a combination of things that are important in relationships and everyone's combination requirement is different. For me, kindness is right up there. If someone is kind, it follows that they'll be inherently decent and those are the qualities I'd like in a friend—I wouldn't want to spend my life with anyone who wasn't also my friend. Attraction is important, as is mutual respect and being able to laugh together. I'm lucky enough to have all these things with my husband, but there are plenty of times when we don't gel. Frankly, I think life would be a bit dull if we always got on. I don't believe in soul mates or The One. I think there are loads of people out there who fit together really well, but there will always be ways in which you don't fit. And that's okay. A wise person once told me: you can be married or you can be right. Nobody is perfect, and that includes you, so look for someone with qualities that you admire, but do consider cutting them some slack if they don't tick every box.

Without giving anything away, did you always know how the story would end?

More or less, but I wasn't sure how neatly things would be tied up—I wanted to let the characters live and breathe and find their own way to the end of the novel. The narrator switch wasn't planned—I reached that point in the story and realized I wanted to see what was happening from another perspective, and I'm so glad I got to step into that character's shoes. Those pages were some of the most emotional I've ever written.

What's next for you?

I'm currently creating a writing course which will be live via Domestika by the time *Only Love Can Hurt Like This* hits the shelves. I'm often being asked by readers how to go about writing a novel, so I thought I'd put fifteen years of experience down on film and hope that it might be helpful to some people. And then I'll be getting stuck into writing my next book . . . It's another impossible love story, but it's told over a longer period of time, so readers will really get a sense of the characters and the journeys they go on. I did a Zoom call recently to talk the idea through with my US and UK editors, Tara and Emily, and they were both in tears by the end. I was too, actually, so I absolutely can't wait to get started! I guess it's a little strange that I enjoy inflicting so much emotional trauma on myself, but I'll certainly never be bored, doing the job that I do. I get to spend several months a year imagining little movies playing out inside my head, feeling all the emotions under the sun, and I'll never take for granted how lucky I am to be making a living out of it. I'm already so invested in these characters, so I know that their story is going to completely sweep me away.

DISCUSSION GUIDE

1. If you were Wren, how would you have responded if you saw your fiancé fall in love with another woman? Do you think Wren handled that situation well? Why or why not?

2. How do you think Wren's parents' divorce shaped Wren's outlook on life? If her parents hadn't divorced, do you think Wren's life would have gone down a different path? If so, how?

3. Before Wren goes to visit her family in Indiana, she has many preconceived notions about how they feel about her. Have you ever believed something to be true about a friend or family member that you later discovered was different? If so, what happened and how did you feel (or what did you do) after finding out the truth?

4. What was your favorite scene in the novel, and why?

5. Why do you think Anders and Wren are drawn to each other? What do you think each does for the other that makes their relationship special?

6. *Only Love Can Hurt Like This* is not just a story of love, but of sibling bonds. What do you think is the most

important quality in a sibling? Do you think Wren, Bailey, Jonas, or Anders possess this quality? Do you have a sibling, and if so, what do you think is their best quality they bring to your relationship with them?

7. In Chapter 36 Wren says, "I didn't know it was possible to love so fully and hurt so deeply at exactly the same time." Have you ever experienced this feeling? If so, what happened and how did you cope with those emotions?

8. If you could move to one place for the summer, where would it be, and who would you take with you?

9. Do you think Wren did the right thing after finding out the truth about Anders? Conversely, do you think Anders did the right thing keeping his secret from Wren? What would you have done if you were in his shoes, or in hers?

10. Did the ending surprise you?

ABOUT THE AUTHOR

Paige Toon grew up between England, Australia, and America and has been writing emotional love stories since 2007. She has published fifteen novels, a three-part spin-off series for young adults, and a collection of short stories. Her novels have sold over 1.5 million copies worldwide. *Only Love Can Hurt Like This* is her first novel published in the United States.

VISIT PAIGE TOON ONLINE

PaigeToon.com

@PaigeToonAuthor

@PaigeToonAuthor

@PaigeToonAuthor